PRAISE]
SALINEE GOLDENBERG

"*Rich with Thai culture, Buddhism, and martial arts,* The Last Phi Hunter *is a seamlessly woven fantasy debut that examines one's race, personal identity, and of course, love. This is for readers who want a dark Asian fantasy infused with Thai culture and mythology! If you've been craving a different blend of SFF, you'll get a kick out of this one.*"
R.R. Virdi, USA Today Bestselling author

"*This well-crafted story offers a thrilling adventure with a heart.*"
Gabriela Houston, author of *The Second Bell* and *The Bone Roots*

"*The Last Phi Hunter is an intoxicating and addictive read that simply cannot be put down. It is filled with rich Thai-folklore, unforgettable characters, and a world that you can't help but love! It is a journey you must take with them that will leave you wanting more!*"
Silvia Desiree, @bookishdesiree 🎵

"*An engaging Asian-inspired dark fantasy with mythic imprint, This is a humorous and fun debut.*"
Elena, @elena.luo 📷

"*With the perfect balance between high stakes and humor,* The Last Phi Hunter *is a vivid journey through a compelling and layered world. Goldenberg has brought to life a set of morally-grey characters that you can't help but root for.*"
Amber, @seekingdystopia 🎵 📷

Salinee Goldenberg

THE LAST
PHI HUNTER

**ANGRY
ROBOT**

ANGRY ROBOT
An imprint of Watkins Media Ltd

Unit 11, Shepperton House
89 Shepperton Road
London N1 3DF
UK

angryrobotbooks.com
twitter.com/angryrobotbooks
Monsters & Men

An Angry Robot paperback original, 2024

Cover by Ilya Nazarov and Alice Coleman
Edited by Gemma Creffield and Desola Coker
Map by Salinee Goldenberg
Set in Meridien

ISBN 978 1 91599 814 9
Ebook ISBN 978 1 91599 815 6

Printed and bound in the United Kingdom by TJ Books Ltd.

9 8 7 6 5 4 3 2 1

MIX
Paper from
responsible sources
FSC® C013056

For Dad, who gave me my love for stories.
For Mom, who inspired this one.

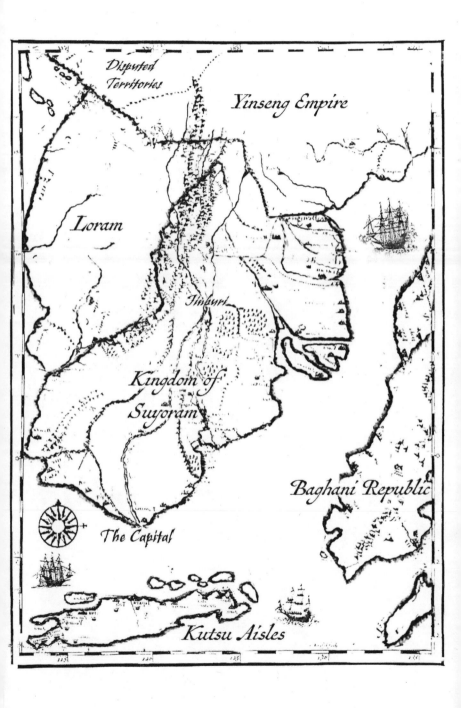

Chapter One

The Hunter

No two phi were ever alike, but every Hungry Ghost and demon in old Suyoram shared one thing in common – they had all been human once. And that made them more dangerous than any other creature, dead or alive.

Perched on a high branch of a chamchuri tree, Ex watched the kongkoi and prayed to the devas it would take the bait. The young phi hunter scarcely breathed, every muscle tensed, dark eyes steady beneath his fearsome khon mask, his body as still as the tree itself.

The Hungry Ghost took two tentative hops forward on his one foot, cat-ears flicking, owl-neck head twisting every which way. The pale grey-green flesh of its skin coiled and unwound around its throat in tandem with its nervous twitches.

Patience. Ex could almost hear his masters now. *Patience is one of our greatest weapons.*

But the second the phi entered Ex's range, it took every ounce of patience he had not to drop down and stab it with a real weapon. He'd been after this bastard for three days and nights, with no food or sleep, and about half of that time was spent here, in the Everpresent – the realm of spirits and magic that simmered between the threads of the physical world and the deva's.

For hunters, it was second nature to walk in the Everpresent. In there, colors were bright enough to taste – reds spicy, blues soothing, yellows sweet as sunbeams. Scents were read in history and motion – a trail one can follow, the age of spilled blood. Sounds were sharper. Ex could hear the sticky smack of spit in the phi's mouth, and the low, distorted hum of dark energy from his hiding spot.

Still, dipping in and out of the Everpresent like a starved koi fish took a toll on Ex's nerves. He ached for a hot meal and a warm bed, but most of all, he needed the coin to pay his dues. He'd be back to the guild soon and feared the wrath of the masters if he came up short. Again.

His fist tightened on the hilt of his chainblade as the kongkoi neared a pile of meat that had once been the fattest macaque in the forest. The phi bent down, its tubular snout twitching. Its tongue snaked out and flicked over the carcass. Sniffing again, the creature then jerked up, neck spinning all the way backward for whatever had alerted it. Ex rolled his eyes with a soft exhale and grit his teeth.

A moment later, the phi returned to the corpse, clearly deciding that whatever it heard wasn't worth giving up a fresh meal. The hairs on its ears relaxed, and with a satisfied grumble, it tore in, teeth first. This was the hunter's chance.

Ex leaned forward, bracing his feet against the branch.

A rustle in the canopy, then a quick movement caught the corner of Ex's eye. A troupe of monkeys were warily approaching, led by one as fat as the dead one below it. They stared at the slurping kongkoi, muttering amongst themselves. Then, the biggest, burliest female stared at the hunter, anger glinting in her dark eyes. Ex shook his head ever so slightly in a lame attempt to communicate that no, he was not the man who murdered her husband, but he was very sorry for her loss–

She screeched a high-pitched monkey scream, and they all scattered in a flurry of fur and squealing. The kongkoi's head snapped up. Mortal animals were of no threat to a Hungry Ghost, but then its gleaming yellow eyes locked onto the hunter's.

The phi screamed its namesake out loud. "Koi!" And Ex pounced.

Half a second late.

He missed the head but flattened the body. The pair wrestled together as the kongkoi's pathetic, twig-like arms slapped at him. Its arms were withered and useless, but the fact it had them at all meant there might be more things inside its body. Valuable things. A second skull? A parasite full of eyes and claws? A heart encased in ice?

As the kongkoi's hypothetical value increased, so did Ex's intrusive thoughts of shrimp bami noodles, spicy chili-basil fried fish, fermented quail eggs and rice, huanglai curry...

The phi gnashed its jaws, spewing chunks of its own disgusting meal on Ex's full-face mask. Its teeth caught the armored part of his forearm, near his elbow. One of the fastenings cracked, which excited the phi. It excited Ex, too. Those teeth were decently sized, and phi teeth were always in demand.

Sensing blood, the kongkoi giggled and tried to rip the rest of the hunter's arm off. But Ex raised his other arm, the one holding his blade, and stabbed.

The sickly greying flesh of its thigh split open. It screeched in dismay, pressing its face against Ex's mask. But then it reared back as if it had been burned when it recognized the design, one that showed this human wasn't the average woodsman.

Hunter! The kongkoi's voiceless words surged through the Everpresent, fear crashing in icy waves. *Wait! This dead thing was not my doing–*

You know why I'm here, Ex returned.

Ex shoved his forearm further into the phi's mouth and against the ground, pressing all his weight down.

Hunter, it wasn't me! You are making a mistake! I will bring you to the real killer, let me go!

First rule of phi hunting – never make deals with a phi. They always lie.

Ex leaned in, snapping its jaw in half. The phi twitched once, then laid still.

Watching the glow leave its eyes, the second rule came to mind – Phi are deadliest after they die, make sure they bleed.

Most only died once, and some didn't bleed at all, but it was best practice to be patient. Hunters often waited hours, or even days during their hunts, so what was a few more minutes?

Ex figured it was less of a rule and more of a mantra, to remind them that these ghosts were once humans whose life choices led them into this karmic fate. It was okay to be brutal.

A yawn interrupted Ex's thoughts. Well, it had its chance to revive, and must have decided getting murdered over and over by a pissed off, ravenous phi hunter wasn't how it wanted to spend the rest of its miserable existence.

After a quick appraisal of its body parts, Ex concluded the real money resided in its foot, specifically the gnarled, yellow toenails that flaked when he tapped them. The village elder's reward for killing the ghost was fine too, but half of that would go to the guild. Any money he made from selling body parts went straight into his pockets.

"Koi!"

The sneaky phi kicked Ex with his over-sized foot and sent him flying. He smashed against a tree and flopped to the ground, covered in splintered bark. Delayed revival tactic. Not a bad move. Then it took off running like a one-footed jackrabbit.

Seeing that his blade was still sunk into its thigh, Ex rolled over in time to snatch the attached chain. The kongkoi zipped into the brush with an awkward gliding hop, dragging Ex along with it. Thick bushes with spindly branches whipped at him, and rocks scraped against his body. But the hunter held on, bouncing over muddy, mossy roots, scattering any nocturnal animals in their way.

Wrapping the chain around his hand, Ex pulled and inched himself towards the phi, cursing it with every pull.

Accept your fate, asshole.

Its head turned backward to stare at Ex in disbelief, broken jaw lopping around like a rooster's neck.

Please, hunter! The fear rose to terror, now piercing sharp like an icy breeze. *I vow I will never kill again! Spare me and I promise, I'll–*

Everyone's gotta eat.

They burst out of the thicket, and the kongkoi collided face-first into the iron-hard bark of a great teak tree, the corded trunk at least ten arm spans around. The momentum whipped Ex forward and he smashed into both tree and ghost.

If blades wouldn't kill it, magic would have to do.

The kongkoi squirmed like a trapped worm and gnawed at him, but it was pointless to bite with a broken jaw. Ex swiftly backhanded it, then pinned its leg to the ground.

Uttering in the voiceless tongue, words imperceptible to human or phi ears alike, he called upon the Smoking Palm of Anewan.

The edges of his fingers lit up like embers. With a blaze of dark red light, molten magic dripped down the kongkoi's leg and seared canyons into flesh and bone. The kongkoi wailed as Ex squeezed the spell, raising the intensity. The phi's kneecap melted and its leg severed into two, both pieces thrashing. Bright white blood poured out in one long rush that finally ended with a trickle, like an emptied bladder.

After catching his breath, Ex returned to the ordinary plane of awareness and the vivid Everpresent dissipated, leaving him in the dark. He cringed at the sudden roar of insects, and the tasteless air. It was always a bitter shock, returning to the ceaseless, mortal world, or what some hunters called the World of Men, the Long Day, the Veil, or his favorite, the Blinds.

After a quick chant of gratitude to the First Hunter for a bountiful harvest, Ex hummed as he went about his work, popping each of the kongkoi's eyes into a sack, coiling up the tongue into a jar, yanking each tooth from the gums, then shearing away skin and muscle in search of anything else of value.

Sadly, nothing much. He set aside the kongkoi's major organs and tossed the rest of the remains into a pile for the Hound – Ex's occasional hunting companion. He would appreciate the flayed skin, spindly bones, and noodles of sinew once he followed his nose to the kill.

Ex saved the kongkoi's bulging stomach for last, his good cheer withering. With a slow breath, his carving knife sunk into the swollen gut, carefully gliding around the edges. He peeled back the skin. And met the half-digested face of its last victim.

A small boy. Small enough for the kongkoi to swallow most of his head whole.

Gooey gut fluid pasted the boy's short hair to his pale forehead, his eyelids remaining closed in what could be mistaken as peace. The rest of the missing villagers stewed together in a confused jumble of splintered bones, mottled flesh, and twisted hair. Loose fingers grasped for nothing, teeth glittered like gems amidst the viscera. They were hardly recognizable as human, though he found bits of jewelry that might be used to identify some of them. Ex knew their loved ones would appreciate the closure.

As he parsed these small tokens from the mess, his chest boiled over with anger. How terrified that little boy must have felt when this monster cornered and chased him into the dark. All the residual terror of the victims soured the coagulated blood with the stench of fear, cold and heavy under his palms.

The third rule of phi hunting – exploit their fear. Hunters and phi are closer to one another than they are to the rest of the living world. These moments reminded him why, despite their monstrous habits, the phi did have fears. Most of all, they feared people like him.

Ex placed the child's head into a separate sack, then tossed the rest of the villagers' unrecognizable remains into the discard pile.

Maybe phi hunters mirrored their prey with their powers and spirit magic, but Ex had to believe he was still human in every other way. Even if others vehemently disagreed.

Chapter Two

The Escort

Even though Ex was behind schedule, there was one post-hunt ritual he had yet to break.

After dumping the head of the kongkoi at the village elder's house, he received a fraction of the coin he'd expected, the old man citing a poor harvest. To "make up for it," he threw in a voucher for a free meal at the public house and a promise to set Ex up on a "date" with the blacksmith's daughter. Ex had to admit, it'd been a long ride, and the offer for company was tempting, but he didn't have time for that. He declined the girl, but took the food.

Grumbling, he headed to the communal eating and watering hole in the village square – a wide, open-walled structure with a steepled roof for the rain, and raw teakwood floors you could spit on without feeling guilty. The place was full of unwashed farmers, grunting and guffawing over steaming bowls of pork stew and bottles of rice wine. Great stubs of men, with big healthy guts, sour armpits under arms the size of his head. Past-due serving girls picked amongst them, snipping at grabby hands, or openly flirting. The younger ones let their half-tied chest sarongs speak for them.

If you've seen one provincial village off the Long Road,

you've seen them all, and very little set this one apart. Ex leaned against the bar where an older uncle set down the chef's choice for the night. He shot him a side eye but not a word.

Pork was his least favorite meat, but after three days of fasting and magic, he'd eat the inside of a pig's asshole. After dumping copious amounts of chili flakes and fish sauce onto the thick, fluffy noodles, the hungry hunter hardly tasted anything before it hit his stomach. He slurped up any remains and plopped the empty bowl down with a suppressed belch.

Then came the wine. He needed a lot of it to feel better about getting ripped off again. The parts he'd pulled off the kongkoi would have to bridge the deficit if, of course, he could manage to sell them. The annual Hunters Meet was only a week away, and showing up to the guild without his dues would be completely humiliating.

A ragged musician played hesitant notes on a wood flute while his buddy sat next to him, slurring the words of a politically charged ballad that didn't even play at subtlety.

It's a blessed life for the lord of the swine,
Swimming in your money and your woman's sweet wine.
Drunk on the dregs of his own brother's blood,
He won't check the weather if it shows him a flood.
His squealing spawn might look like a swan,
But on a throne of shit.
Pig is king, pig is king, pig is kiiiiiiiing.

In the northern Nahkon province, it was popular to openly resent the government. The great capital city was far, far to the south, nestled between three rivers and the sea. Despite the obvious dislike for the crown, this village still stood, and its people still lived. They still wore the sak lek tattoos that indicated their service to the king, so they couldn't have sided with the Uprising of the Relentless Rains.

As his head hummed with a pleasant buzz, Ex smiled to himself. He had one last phi to hunt before returning to the

Capital, and if he succeeded, he'd never have to worry about respect or dues ever again.

"You were here a few days ago, right?" said the old uncle after he brought Ex his second bottle of wine. The loose, dark skin of his arm wiggled as he dragged a rag across the counter, mopping up all evidence of the meal.

"I was." Meeting with the elder, who'd promised him a far better reward. But Ex kept that detail to himself.

"Thought you were passing through. Why'd you come back? A girl?"

"You could say that."

"Ah. The blacksmith's daughter, was it? She's quite healthy, hair as dark and smooth as midnight silk, *and* in desperate need of a husband."

"I'll get my blade sharpened the next time around," Ex said. The man chortled, seeming in good humor as he worked. "But I have a date with the witch on the lake."

Uncle paused, hand tightening around his rag, and a dribble of brown water escaped his knuckles. "You shouldn't go through the forest, stranger. There's a kongkoi in that wood."

"Not anymore." Ex grinned and proudly pulled his half-cloak aside to reveal the emblem embroidered on the breast pocket of his coat. Everyone knew the symbol, used ever since man began to encroach into wild lands. When a troublesome phi was about, the locals carved or painted two diagonally intersecting lines on the trees surrounding the area. Often, they'd place offerings underneath it, in an attempt to appease the violent ones. Then, after a hunter cleared the ghosts and demons from the haunted ground, they would return to the warning and slash a line across it to complete the symbol.

The Phi Hunter Order.

Right then, the musician finished his ballad, and a rare spot of silence hovered over the public house, during which the uncle responded, "A phi hunter? Here?!" He jerked back as if Ex had spit in his mouth. Spoons stopped scraping bowls, conversation died, and he didn't need a neck like the kongkoi to know everyone was sizing him up.

Shit. That's what he got for trying to show off. The elder called on the guild for action, instead of sending for the hopeful prayers of the Sangha. That was respect, wasn't it? Ex had assumed the locals shared their leader's faith in the phi hunters.

Then again, he did get ripped off afterward. He'd mistaken practicality for respect.

Ex finished the rest of his wine in one gulp and dropped a coin on the table. "Thanks for the soup, uncle."

As he headed out, a full-bearded, girthy man stepped in his path, flanked by two equally girthy men with much patchier facial hair. Their triangular-necked cotton shirts displayed ample amounts of chest hair, skin damp from working long hours in the sun. Ex was more of an olive-skinned young man in dire need of a tan, due to his mostly nocturnal profession. The thought reminded him that he'd promised the witch he'd be there by sunrise, and dark, territorial spirits still stalked these woods.

"Rushing off in the middle of the night?" The biggest one's lip curled as he showed a few teeth in his tangled forest of a beard.

"Walking, actually."

"Huh. I know your type," he screwed up his nose, as if Ex were the one that stank. "And we don't like *whispers* on our lands."

"Well, that's a relief." Ex tried to appear nonplussed. "Whispers" wasn't a heavy slur towards low magic users, but it wasn't polite, either. He didn't practice that type of magic, but most laypeople made little distinction between the magic practiced by a grave-digging necromancer versus a high society sorcerer. And Ex doubted they'd know the difference to the "grey" magic practiced by hunters. "I was just leaving." He took a hopeful step forward and prayed that they'd get out of his way.

They didn't. Girthy's beady eyes slid downward to Ex's waist, where he surveyed his tool belt, focusing on the hunting dagger, chainblade, and carving knife. Ex wouldn't usually wear all his weapons in public, but he was in a rush to get drunk and fed.

"What are you up to with all that?" He pointed to the belt. "Digging up the dead?"

"For starters, getting rid of the kongkoi that killed how many?" Ex pretended to ponder. "Oh, yes. *Four* of your people this month. Including a..." The words hung on his lips, his mind jumping back to the delivery. He'd seen the dead boy's mother go into the elder's house as he was leaving, despite the sleepless hollows under her eyes, she couldn't have been much older than him. But the despairing wail that drifted from the house was something deep and eternal, as if all grieving mothers could draw upon the same resonance–

"Liar." The man jabbed a finger in his face. "Our elder respects the Sangha. He called upon a priest! We don't like whispers in our–"

"I heard you the first time." Ex flicked the finger away, growing impatient. This man was obviously itching for a fight, and he doubted he could be convinced to scratch somewhere else. "Let's just get this over with." Without ceremony, he unfastened his cloak and tossed it onto the nearest table. His belt followed, landing on top with a clunk. Ex considered taking off his coat, but he looked far more impressive with it on, the padded shoulders especially. He cracked his knuckles and his neck, then assumed a basic muay-boran boxing stance.

The rest of the public house gathered around, as if the two men were about to start a match. It was probably the best entertainment they'd get all month, stranger versus local bully.

The man scratched a mole on his neck and glanced at his two companions with a frown.

"No? We're behaving as adults? Great." Ex relaxed and gathered his things. "I'm glad we could find peace. I'd share a drink with you, but I've had my fill of pig shit for the night. Could you step aside, please, sir? Your rather girthy frame is blocking the–"

He slugged him in the face.

Ex hit the ground with an *oof.* The house erupted into cheers of encouragement. So... maybe it was a little more than two bottles of wine.

Girthy yanked Ex back to his feet by the collar. "Smartass, stuck-up highlander scum!" he growled, shaking him. "I'm gonna mop the floor with you."

Highlander scum? Stuck-up? The mountain province villages where he grew up made this town look like a metropolis.

Ex slapped him with an open palm, practically a pat on the cheek. Far more of an insult than injury. Girthy's expression read confused, then much angrier at the young man's lack of effort. He hauled Ex to his feet and smashed his fist into his face again.

Ex stumbled into one of Girthy's friends, who rabbit punched him with perfect timing. Someone grabbed his arms from behind and held him there.

"Smart-ass hunter," Girthy said as he peeled off his shirt, perhaps not to dirty it with the smart-ass hunter's blood.

Ex spat some blood anyway. "Get that repressed self-loathing out of your system?"

The guy hit him in the gut, and the crowd roared in joyful approval. His captor released him, more amused to let him stumble around, eating punch after punch. Ex's head swam in dizzy circles, but otherwise, he felt no pain. If he saw an opening, he slapped him, which only infuriated the big man more and more. Throughout the beating, Ex wracked his brain for a spell to use that, one, wouldn't kill the man, and two, wouldn't burn the whole place down.

The list was short. And if they didn't like how he looked now, they would hate how he looked while in the Everpresent. The best move was to give them a show, wait until they grew tired and bored, then crawl miserably out to the mud and heal himself. Maybe uncle at the bar would buy him another bottle for the entertainment.

"Let him go."

A woman's voice cut through the herd of unsavory men like the proud screech of an eagle in a valley of ragged dogs. The confidence in her tone gave Ex an involuntary shiver. Girthy froze mid punch, then stepped back with a baffled sneer. The crowd parted before the woman who spoke, revealing a statuesque form. They cringed as if the sun were behind her.

Ex's vision was spinning after one particularly nasty crack to the jaw, and he could only make out a couple of strands of raven black hair hanging from underneath her hood. Tall and a little lumpy, her arms were well muscled, and she sported a pot belly, almost as large as Girthy.

Was this the aforementioned blacksmith's daughter? No, this woman didn't fit in here. She smelled like jasmine and silk, her riding shoes weren't broken in, and a sabai blouse coupled with chong kraben – wrapped trousers – were not in any way proper for a countrywoman. Ex was surprised he hadn't spotted her when he first walked in, but he'd been on a straight line from the saddle to the bar.

"Says who? You, wench?" Girthy spat at her feet.

"Pick on someone your own size," she said.

"Hey," Ex protested, coughed, then spat out a tooth. "I'm not that small." But even if he was only slightly above the average size, compared to this guy he looked like a starved shrimp.

"You don't belong here either, redskin." Girthy took a step towards her.

His mistake.

With one smooth movement, she hopped a long stride forward then front kicked him in the balls. She kneed him in the face on his way to the ground. Perfect muay-boran form, with so much effortless style the devas would cry, something you'd see in the rings over in the floating city.

The man dropped, completely unconscious. Silence followed.

"Anyone else?" she said. The guy behind Ex released his arms and went to help drag Girthy away with as much dignity as possible, which was precious little.

Uncle yelled for everyone to get back to what they were doing, so the musician piped up again. The cheery atmosphere attempted to return but had gone sour. Disapproving glares stabbed at the clear loser from all sides, raising the hairs on Ex's neck. He could imagine their thoughts – *what a sorry excuse for a hunter! Saved by woman?!*

The worrisome thought that the musician was already composing a demeaning song about the whole incident made him inwardly sigh.

Time to go. The witch was waiting for him, after all.

"Thanks, stranger," Ex said to his savior, unsteady on his feet as he grabbed his things. "You didn't have to do that, though. I had it all under control."

"Clearly."

Before he could respond, a rumble in his guts made him gag. "Need air," he blurted and ran down the stairs. He stumbled across the muddy village road and vomited into the horse trough. The bottom barrel rice wine tasted decent enough going down, but like vinegar coming back up. He spat a few times and wiped his watering eyes before trying to stand.

"Hunter. I heard you were heading out of town."

The woman stood behind him patiently, only the lower half of her face showing. Her chin was heart-shaped, her lips unpainted and set in a frown. Ex noticed the dagger at her hip made of Suyoram steel, but the design was decorative, not something any old thug would carry around.

"Uh." He tilted his head, attempting to peer under her hood. "What was your name?"

"Arinya," she said.

"Arinya." A musical name, mid-country or southern, rolled off the tongue nicely. "I'm very grateful for your help in there." He glanced around for Ramble but didn't see him where he should have been, next to the two donkeys. Brownie remained, and the dutiful old lady cast him a disapproving side eye.

"You're welcome," Arinya said. "And you are?"

"Ex. I'm a–"

"Phi hunter, I heard." She smiled with oddly straight teeth. "It's hard not to notice."

He wasn't sure how to take that, so he shrugged and turned away to run a hand over his face and dip into the Everpresent. Just long enough to utter a voiceless chant, bringing in the ambient magic that flowed so freely in the high north.

The Kiss of Shivah cascaded across his skin, tingling in all his wounds. The bruises healed, the cuts mended, the missing tooth started to regrow. The tooth would take a bit longer.

When he peered back at the woman, she hadn't moved. She was staring at him with intense interest, lips parted in wonder.

"Well. I should be going." Healed now, Ex took a step backward, edging towards Brownie. "I promised the witch I'd be there by sunrise, and if you know the Witch of the Bent Lake, you know you don't keep the old gal waiting."

"I know of the witch, and I need to see her as well. I thought perhaps you might escort me."

"I'm going tonight, through the woods," Ex said, expecting her to shirk away at the thought. Her expression didn't waver. Maybe another approach. "By the way you handled Girthy in there, you don't need an escort. But spirits? No, you should wait until sunrise and stick to the roads."

"My horse died, and I've been stuck in this town for days.

Everyone's scared of the witch and refuses to help me. And because of my... condition, I can't walk quickly enough. Otherwise, I would."

"What condition is that?"

"You don't see?"

At his silence, she sighed, pulled back her hood, and opened her cloak. Her eyes stunned him – the richest brown he'd ever seen, deep like burnt gold richer than he could ever afford. Bright like glistening chestnuts found in the forest after the rain. More than that, there was a steely glint behind her challenging stare, a confidence he could only aspire to.

"Devas, you're beaut-uhhh..." He bit his tongue just in time to avoid saying something drunk and stupid. Though the Kiss of Shivah had healed his wounds, it didn't account for intoxication. "...A brunette."

True, her dark hair was stick-straight, tied back with a red ribbon. Some loose strands hung around her face, which remained steadfast. She arched a delicately plucked brow, then set her hands on her hips. "Try again."

Then she stuck out her substantial belly, back arched, hips forward. It felt rude to stare anywhere but her eyes, but after she nodded downward, the issue dawned on the young man.

"That's a baby." He pointed to the proper place. "There's a baby in there."

"You're about as quick as your defenses."

"Hey." He lifted his finger so fast he swayed on his feet. "If I wanted to, I could have tied that bastard in a knot. But I don't want to give us phi hunters a bad name. People distrust us enough already."

"Hmm, if you say so. Now, will you help me or not?"

"You want to go see the witch?" Ex chewed on his lip, considering all the possible ways that could go wrong. "Should you really be on horseback in your, ah, condition?"

"Look, I didn't ask for your advice," she said. "I have money.

If you won't let me travel with you, will you sell me your horse instead?"

Ex glanced over to Brownie in alarm, and sputtered, "Never! I would never, I swear." Ramble, however... If only he didn't have so many supplies to haul around. "Sorry, cousin, none of the horses are for sale."

"Do you think I can't handle myself?"

"No, no, of course you can," Ex said, though it should have been obvious that a drunken farmer was a clawless kitten compared to even the weakest phi. "But you're pregnant."

"Why does that matter?"

"The scent of the unborn. It's a delicacy for Hungry Ghosts."

Arinya drew a slow breath, as if fighting the urge to slap him. She reached into her cloak to remove a small purse and tossed it over. It plopped into Ex's hand with a satisfying clunk. Just by the weight, he could tell it would help plug the hole the kongkoi left in his pockets.

"...Hop on, then."

"Excellent," she said in a measured tone, as if he'd passed a test.

Ex busied himself with Brownie and made room, which mustered all his concentration. Even though he was no longer drunk, his dexterity hadn't quite returned. He helped Arinya up, worried that her swollen belly might tip her sideways. She moved with impressive balance and didn't seem to need his assistance at all, only accepting his hand out of courtesy.

While he adjusted her pack with the saddlebags to make sure the weight was evenly distributed, she said, "Are those your donkeys?"

"What? No! I have another horse."

"Oh. Where is it?"

"He's... around." Hopefully. Ex walked towards the trees, whistled once, and waited. Whistled twice and waited again. Brownie clopped over, the loyal mare that she was, although her approach felt somewhat condescending.

"Just give him a second," he assured Arinya, thankful for the dark so she couldn't see his flushed cheeks. She smirked but mercifully didn't comment.

The bushes crashed as the Hound bounded onto the path, skidding to a stop. Arinya squealed in fear, as any sane person would do. The Hound was mostly wolf, but also half spirit. He was a big boy, half the height of a horse and almost the same weight.

He snarfed and shook leaves off his head, fluffing his thick, majestic blue-black mane. He glared at her with his blood-red eyes, a trait he shared with Ex when the hunter was on his magic.

The Hound sat and tilted his head.

"Hey," Ex said. "Have you seen Ramble? Can you go get him?"

The Hound tilted his head to the other side, then scoffed and pretended to yawn. Fetching was far beneath him.

"*Alright, look,*" Ex muttered without moving his lips, subvocal but easily heard by the Hound's sharp ears. "*Go get him and I'll give you that buckwraith giblet–*"

Before Ex finished, the Hound bounded off, disappearing into the woods.

"Was that your dog?" Arinya's hands were clasped protectively over her belly. "I've never heard of anyone taming a greatwolf. Is he–"

"Please don't say that. Especially not in front of him. The Hound isn't my dog, he isn't a greatwolf, and he's a hundred percent untamed."

"The Hound? That's his name?"

"That's just what I call him. He prefers to remain unnamed."

"If he isn't your dog, why is he with you?"

"The Hound is wild, he does as he pleases. We only travel together when he wants. He has an insatiable thirst for phi blood." He let his gaze drift toward the forest, settling into the darkness. "And I kill phi, so it's useful to me. It works out.

Honestly, I find him much more reliable than any human I've ever worked with."

The trees crashed again, and this time Ex had to jump out of the way to avoid Ramble's big black body. Pissed that the Hound was snapping at his hooves, Ramble sputtered and spat as he thrashed around. With a huff, he then pretended to just notice his hunter, and snorted again as he sidled up.

"Thank you," Ex told the Hound, who didn't give him a second glance before slinking back into the woods. Ex gave Ramble a sarcastic pat before climbing on. Ramble did the infuriating thing where he'd take a half step back just as Ex threw his leg over the saddle. It made him fumble at best, and at worst, banged the saddle into his testicles.

"Stop showing off," Ex growled. "I will turn you into glue, I swear on my grave." Ramble blinked lazily, smug, knowing he wouldn't. Perhaps he'd never forgiven the man for gelding him. To be fair, Ex would have been pissed too.

"Wow," Arinya said, sounding like she was impressed, or that she thought he was an idiot. Probably both.

With things in order, Ex gazed into the woods, then back to her, searching her face for any semblance of doubt. She met his eyes with none, but he had to ask her one more time.

"Are you sure you want to come with me?"

She smiled. "Sure as the rain."

"In dry season. Right." He laughed and shook his head with a shrug. "Alright then, miss." He kicked Ramble a little harder than necessary and the animal obeyed, for once, starting into a trot. "We got a witch to see."

Chapter Three

The Guardian

Though it was the dry season, the Emerald Forest of northern Suyoram remained just that – evergreen. Not as thirsty as other woods in the midlands, or as dense as the monsoonal swamps. Ex and Arinya rode under its towering pines and ancient hardwoods with webs of scarlet ivy lacing through the foliage. Pale, fluffy ropes of swaymoss hung from the branches where hissing lemurs bounced amongst the canopies.

Ex was not sure what he was thinking, escorting a pregnant woman through these woods, but it was a lot of money, and the last few months hadn't been fruitful. Phi were territorial, but they weren't stupid. There were traces of the kongkoi's blood still fresh on his boots, and he'd hoped that would be enough discouragement for lesser Hungry Ghosts.

He had killed the kongkoi because it was eating the villagers, not because it existed. Trying to hunt down every phi would be like trying to destroy an anthill by picking at them with chopsticks.

That being said, it was a mistake to think that phi hunters had any sort of empathy towards the creatures. Many of the older hunters considered them pure evil, and their eradication a noble cause. Others thought of them as pests, as useless as termites or mosquitoes. Regardless of their personal opinions, all hunters considered them harvest, body part price tags, a way to make a living. It was a trade just as much as it was a tradition.

Ex had rinsed his mouth and chewed on ginger mint sticks, yet a film of sour wine still coated his teeth. He ate a handful more, then offered some to Arinya.

"What is this?" She turned the candy about in her hand as if it might bite her.

"You've never seen mint kingmung? Where are you from?"

She hesitated, then flashed him a pleasant smile. "I'm from the outskirts of Sapphrachorn."

Anyone could tell a mile away that she was from the south, judging by the fine cloth of her cloak. A rundown river town like Sapphrachorn leaves a trace of mudfish in your clothes, no matter how many times you wash them. Beneath the musk of travel, her skin still hinted at jasmine. It was a wonder she managed to travel this far north without getting robbed.

Even so, he returned her wry smile. "You're far from home."

She raised an eyebrow. "What about you? I've never heard the name Ex before."

"I took it after one of the First Hunters, Master Exaran."

"It's not your real name?"

It was his turn to pause. "It *is* my real name. It's not the name I was born with, if that's what you're asking. We receive our hunter names when we join the guild."

"I see. Where are you from, then?"

"I grew up in the Capital, at the guildhall in the old city."

"You were born there too?"

"Well, no, but–"

"Where were you born?"

"A mountain province near the border."

"Oh. Which province?"

Ex knew small talk was what normal people did, but it was starting to make him squirm.

"I was really young when I left," he said, tone short.

"Sorry to pry," she said. Maybe she sensed his discomfort. "I just hate silence."

Silence? Ex often forgot that laypeople never heard the murmurings of spirits or felt the tenor of ambient magic that buzzed everywhere up in the high country, between the layers of sensation.

"It doesn't matter to me where someone is from, only where they're going." Arinya took a tentative bite of the kingmung, chewing slowly. "Aren't you going to ask me why I've come to see the witch?"

"I wasn't going to ask. It's none of my business." He had his suspicions, though. "I'm not thinking about that. Not at all."

"If you're wondering, I know who the father is." She pointedly patted her belly.

Ex was going to protest, but she had a playful glint in her eye, so he shrugged and concentrated on the road ahead.

They rode for a while in silence, which had grown far more uncomfortable now that she'd pointed it out. He tried to think of something to say, but anything that crossed his mind was either dumb or a question he wouldn't want to answer himself.

She broke first, to his relief. "Why are *you* going to see the witch?"

"Every three months I make my rounds through here, before the full moon. Mali's been a customer since I've been on this route. She actually pays. Unlike most people these days." He frowned, thinking back to the elder, the meal token, and the attempted pimping.

"Most people?"

"It's getting worse every year. Once the problem's solved, and they know I won't do anything to them, it's all excuses and swindling. You'd think they'd be more appreciative, especially up here."

"Strange. I would have guessed only a few, if they knew of your abilities." She said "abilities" funny, like it was a disease, turning up her nose.

"Why are you making that face?"

"I'm not making a face."

"Yes, you are. I can see in the dark, you know."

She huffed, then turned away, hiding her expression behind her hood.

"Honestly, you're not what I expected. I thought you'd be a ghost-pale, grumpy, grizzled old man with scars all over you. And glowing red eyes."

"Well, I'm the youngest hunter in the guild," Ex countered. "It'll take me a while to get grizzled. The grey skinned, red-eyed thing, that's only when we're on magic. And did you see my scar? It's pretty deep."

"Where I come from, boys your age usually join the monastery. Or the army. How did you become what you are?"

"What I am? I studied and trained just like any other trade."

"It doesn't sound like any trade I've ever heard of," Arinya said. "I've heard things about phi hunters."

"Oh, here we go," Ex said, preparing for the slew of misinformation sure to follow. "Let's hear it."

"That you don't sleep…"

"That's a myth. We do, just less often when on the hunt, and usually during the day."

"That you only eat spirit blood."

Ex laughed at that. "My favorite dish is shrimp bami noodles. Have you ever tasted spirit blood? Hell, any magic? If you're really from Sapphrachorn, you must have had a low magic tonic at least once in your life. Magic tastes like shit."

"…That you never get hot or cold or feel pain…"

"Define 'never.'"

"Hmm, okay…what about your face?"

"What about my face?"

"They say your faces grow into a khon-mask when you hunt phi."

"What? No, we wear actual masks when we're in the Hunter's Trance." Ex considered getting his out to show her, but realized it was in Brownie's pack.

"You can speak to one another without speaking."

"Well, that's just magic. Most people can't hear voiceless words."

"That you can burn down a house with a single spell..."

"We swear oaths to never hurt people."

"What about burning houses?" She raised an eyebrow, and Ex couldn't tell if she was playing with him or not. "Are houses protected by your oath?"

"Well, sometimes it's necessary in order to kill certain types of phi. Look, girl–"

"Don't call me 'girl.'"

"Look, lady, if you're worried about any of these things, why would you ask me to escort you?"

"I'm not worried," she said with a scoff. "But the reason I asked you is because I didn't have much of a choice."

Ex chewed on that while he brought Ramble to a stop in front of a particular ring of swaymoss trees that marked the hidden path towards the lake. The main road would eventually lead there too, but would add at least a day to wind around the treacherous lands too thick for man to cut through. Then you'd have to walk along the riverbank for two hours. Going through the wilds was much faster.

"Here we are," he said. Arinya peered into the blackness of the forest, and finally her steely front wavered. Ex fished around in his tincture pack for an ointment, and once he found it, tossed it to her. "Dab this on your wrists and belly."

"What is it?" She popped the cap and gagged. "Oi, that's strong. Is this some kind of honey?"

"Demons hate sweet things."

"I see." Then she laughed, nerves audibly sharp underneath. "Are you calling me sweet?"

Ex's mouth opened to shoot back a flirty response, but nothing clever enough came to mind. Before the silence grew too awkward, she threw the bottle back.

"We really have to go through there, hmm." Her voice was so low he wasn't sure if she was talking to him or herself.

"Don't worry," he said. "It won't be long."

Ex led them off, following a small vein of a crimson root that danced above and below the ground. The steadily uphill way twisted around thorny thickets and treacherous sinkholes. Every so often, glowing eyes blinked in the distance, reminders that they were trespassers here. The slinking coils of a far-off python gave Ramble a shiver, but, from the sound of bones cracking, it had already captured its dinner.

In the abyss of dark, a flash of red between the trees let him know the Hound wasn't far away. Funny, Ex wouldn't have expected him to make an appearance, but perhaps his sometimes-partner was feeling a bit protective.

If Arinya had been on her own horse, chances were high it would have been long gone, thrashing off into the night at the first mysterious growl. But Brownie was accustomed to the wilds. Ex was more worried that something would spook the human. He glanced back to make sure something hadn't silently snatched her out of the dark. She flinched and her head swiveled at every tiny noise, but her composure was steadier than expected.

The tiny roots of the Guardian tree grew larger and larger, eventually rising to snake above ground. It burrowed straight through rocks, fearlessly claiming the land for itself. Out of pure respect, other trees grew sparser around it, leaving only emerald moss and small white flowers as company.

Glowflies circled above, and after they walked through a trench split apart by the tree, Arinya straightened up and gasped.

From all directions, thick pale roots wove across the forest floor and rose to connect to a great web – the sinewy trunk of an immense bodhi tree. Massive in presence, it was the idol in the center of its own temple. Its branches reached far into the canopy, beyond sight, which begged the question – was it part of the forest, or was the forest part of it?

Amongst the twisted cords where the trunk touched the ground, laid small bones, wilted flowers, fruit seeds, and shiny rocks. The creatures of the forests knew to pay their tributes.

Small pools of water collected in roots that had curled around into reservoirs. They reflected the light of the stars, and brightened the clearing, even though the sky wasn't visible through the heavy canopy.

"I've never seen anything like this before," Arinya whispered, as if speaking too loudly would disturb the slumber of the trees. "It's beautiful."

"You should see it in the Everpresent." Ex slid off of Ramble. "Wait here a minute."

As he walked forward and steadied his breath, he eased his awareness into the Everpresent. A layer of splendid texture rushed over all his senses, every scent and sound swelled, magnified. The sweet aroma of a freshly peeled banana, the bubbling rustle of water as a young nightcrow bathed, the rapid patter of ants crawling across the rubber tree nearby as they carried rotting leaves to their queen.

The Blinds were so drab and grey compared to the brilliance seen in this state. Each shade reached deep beyond his eyes, and if he let his gaze soften, the colors vibrated at an audible frequency, all senses bloomed and a harmony resonated in an indescribable comfort – this was reality at its purest form, a reality severed when one walked away from nature.

It wasn't usually so serene. When a hunter entered this state, they were most often casting a quick spell, tracking a phi, or communing with spirits. There was no time to admire the soft hues of the flowers when rotting teeth gnashed in their faces, or when they needed a few moments to piece together a shredded liver before bleeding out.

The Everpresent was always beautiful, but the Guardian's sanctuary was even more special. Every wild place had a living heart. And like a heart, they required attention and care.

Kneeling in front of the tree, Ex removed a vial from his pack filled with his own blood and poured it next to the other offerings. He drew a symbol of homage. *For disturbing your slumber.* He pressed his palms together in a wai, then lifted his hands to his forehead.

The symbol lit up with a soft glow and sunk into the moss, which quickly grew over. It was silent, the Guardian judging the small offering. Then a deep rumble coursed from the tree, vibrating the entire clearing. Water rippled in the small reservoirs between the roots. The swirling glowflies stood still, hovering in place as they watched their god approach.

The knots and gnarls on the bodhi tree shifted, its bark flexing into cords of muscle. A jawline formed and pushed forward, swirling to create the fierce, curling mouth of a lion. Immense, unblinking eyes grew above his snout, which sprouted fangs. Tiny pinprick pupils blinked to life and focused on the very essence of the insignificant human before him.

The Guardian of the Emerald Forest.

Hunter. You return with a gift.

When he spoke, all went silent.

A small tribute, ancient one. Ex kept his hands in a wai, but lowered them to heart-level and peered up at the forest god. *I have come for passage through your lands.*

To where?

To the Witch on the Bent Lake.

As the Guardian drew breath, the entire sanctuary pulled inward, and as he exhaled, expanded. The smell of his immense powers completely overwhelmed all other senses, and his presence overwhelmed all other beings. All others were but helpless, soft creatures laying mercifully in his jaws.

Why should I grant you this?

Because I've slain the kongkoi plaguing your lands, ancient one.

The tree strained as the Guardian stretched towards Ex, his wide nostrils flaring. A breeze ruffled through his hair as he sniffed him.

The stench of demon blood. His pupils dilated, and his jaws widened in a terrifying grin. *So you have, hunter.*

Ex bowed his head.

I accept your tribute. With a groan, the Guardian's roots shifted and the ground quavered as they rearranged beneath the earth. Sprouting at the edge of the clearing, long tendrils of roots rose and pushed aside trees as if they were curtains, creating a path. Ex smiled, impressed at himself with how smoothly it went.

Then the Guardian's pupils focused beyond the hunter.

Your gift still breathes.

Behind Ex, Arinya clutched Brownie's reins with white-knuckled fists. She stared at him in shock. Beyond the tiny dips for spells here and there, when hunters submerged fully into the Everpresent, they appeared very different to those in the Blinds. His skin appeared pale grey, as did his hair, eyes glowing red, bright enough to scare someone who'd never seen it before.

And from the Everpresent, she appeared equally grey to him, with just a spot of red light where her heart beat. And another lower, in her abdomen, much smaller but brighter.

You mistake my intention. Ex's own heart pounded as several of the Guardian's roots rose, reaching towards her from behind, just out of her sight. *She's my passenger, and that's her passenger. She is not the tribute.*

Why else would you bring a blinded human here? Her kind cut down my children and tear away my skin. If the phi did not poison my lands, I would welcome its violent acts towards their scourge.

Ex stood then and took a step forward. With as much menace as he could, without being blatantly disrespectful, he met the Guardian's giant eyes.

No other hunters walk this path. If you want me to continue my service, oh great one, then do not harm them.

The Guardian's frown deepened, his eyebrows lowered as he cast his eyes back onto the hunter. A low growl emanated from his being as he decided whether or not to wring the human's puny neck for his belligerence. This was a pure spirit, practically divine, and they were on no common law other than the perception of the Everpresent.

Then the great being sighed in obvious disappointment, and the forest floor deflated. With a swirl of bark, his face melted back into the bodhi tree.

Beware, hunter. That one is marked.

Before Ex could ask what that meant, the Guardian snapped him out of the Everpresent without ceremony – a root popped out of the ground and flung him across the moss as if flicking a booger. Ex bounced and thudded flat on his face at the edge of the sanctuary, right at Arinya's feet.

She jumped, hands clasped over her mouth. From the nearby trees, Ex caught the whining pant of the Hound's laughter.

"Ex! What was that… that… that face?"

He sat up, glaring at the Guardian for the unnecessary indignity. The tree was probably laughing at him too.

"Kind of an asshole," he muttered, and brushed the dirt off. He climbed back onto Ramble, who was also snorting in amusement. Brownie was the only one who cast him a sympathetic eye. "Let's go."

They rode through the passage the Guardian had gifted, following the lane of red roots. The path was wide enough to ride side by side.

"I never knew such magic existed," Arinya said, staring back over her shoulder as the trees maneuvered back to close off the sanctuary. "What was that thing?"

"The Guardian of the Emerald Forest. That one always gives me a hard time."

"Was that place *always* there?"

"There? Not in the literal sense. The heart of the forest lives everywhere, if you know where to look." The truth was, if he wasn't so late, and if she weren't so pregnant, he would never ask the Guardian for passage. Those favors were precious. And with the god spirits, you never knew what they might want in return.

"Incredible," she said, and then grunted. Ex glanced over in alarm, where she clutched her stomach, concern lacing her features.

"Are you okay?"

She nodded with a grimace, and wiped her brow. He started to sweat too and then peered at her belly. "Is it... are you, uhh..."

"Is it much further?"

"Not much," he said, and urged Ramble faster. As Arinya made more suppressed groans, the Guardian's cryptic words returned. She was marked, or was it the child? Ex doubted Arinya would know, or would tell him if she did.

It was then that he realized these were no ordinary passengers.

Chapter Four

The Midwife

By the blessing of the Guardian and his granted passage, it wasn't very long until the trees rustled and stretched apart like the yawning mouth of a cave, bringing forth a symphony of crickets and toads. The dark waters of the Bent Lake stretched before the travelers, the rocky outcrops of its shores at odd angles, true to its name. Tiny ripples in the water reflected the full moon, big and bright as a golden coin hovering amidst the stars. Soon the Rom Laithong would occur, a kingdom-wide, weeklong festival that heralded the rainy season, and the waters would rise another meter.

By then, Ex would be back at the Phi Hunters' Guildhall, bearing a successful hunt to celebrate the new season with the others as they gathered for the festival. With hunters walking their own separate routes, it was rare they saw each other after finishing their training.

If all went well, Ex would bring the bounty of the true demon he'd been hunting for two years. And he would finally get the recognition he deserved.

After they hurried around a large, fallen tree, partially submerged in the waters, they arrived at a simple, circular cottage standing on stilts above the water, with a narrow bridge connecting it to the shore. Candlelight ebbed from the window. Ex's nose stung from the garden, filled with all types of herbs and some especially strong aromatics. Next to it was a chicken coop and a tiny barn, where some animals were asleep. He left the horses near their friends and helped Arinya down.

"Thank the Enlightened Lord," she moaned, holding her belly. "I think she knows we're here."

"How do you know it's a she?"

"I just do." She smiled. Then she grimaced again and doubled over, enough for him to have to grab her arm to steady her.

As they carefully crossed the bridge, Ex blurted, "Can I ask you something?"

Her posture stiffened. "What is it?"

"Are you gonna..." He chewed on his words, unsure how to phrase a deeply personal question. She straightened up, pulling away from him to walk on her own.

"You said it was none of your business, and I tend to agree."

"Right, sorry." He shook the thought off. It really was not his concern. He'd held up his end of the bargain, and that was enough. "Alright, can't keep the woman waiting. Last time I did that she hit me with a curse. I pissed fire for three days." He hoped Arinya might laugh at that, but she only sighed.

Ex knocked. No one answered. He knocked again. Would Mali be out this late? No, she wouldn't miss a delivery. He always made his stop around this time.

"Are you sure she's home?"

He pressed his ear to the door. There was murmuring... no, singing. Arinya started to huff, and he pounded the door again, this time with a fist.

"Mali!" he yelled. "It's Ex. I'm here!"

The singing stopped, and footsteps pattered before the door swung open. Mali burst out with a guffaw as her five-foot two-inch frame leapt forward like a pouncing tiger. Her arms wrapped him in a death grip, and she planted a huge, slobbery kiss on his eye.

"Ex, my boy!" she exclaimed. "What are you doing here so late, child?"

"What do you mean? I'm on time," Ex said, disturbed at her scandalously half-tied sarong. An eye-watering stench expelled from her. "Holy hell, Grandmother. You're drunk as a drowned hog."

"Naaah," she pushed him away and brushed her long, silver hair back from her face. Her eyes twinkled with drunken merriment, a few wrinkles the only indicator of her true age. She waved her hand and stumbled inside. "Come on, come on in. Have you eaten yet?"

The cottage was much larger inside than it appeared from the outside, the work of an illusion ward that also hid her location from locals who dared wander her way. Dried herbs and small animal limbs hung along the walls on color-coded strings. Unlabeled jars crowded the shelves with an assortment of powders and viscous liquids. Ex recognized a few. Thankfully, the lids were on, or the air would have been suffocating.

Despite the larger space, it was still cramped. Her whole life was crowded into this one room. All two hundred years of it. Reflexively, Ex and Arinya both slipped off their shoes before entering.

A thick aroma of cinnamon and sandalwood bubbled from the stove. Arinya's muffled groans grew more desperate, so Ex took her arm and helped her to sit on a daybed.

"Mali, there's a problem, she's–"

"I thought…" Misery temporarily forgotten, Arinya gaped at Mali's svelte frame. "I was told you were two centuries old. You don't look a day over fifty."

Mali whirled around, her eyes narrowed to slits. "Where'd you come from?" She glared at Arinya, then Ex. "Who is this and why is she here?"

"This is Arinya, and she needs your help." He eased Arinya down onto a quilt-covered daybed. "Why are you so drunk, Granny? I've never seen you drink before."

"Must there be a reason?" She walked over to a shelf, throwing aside parchments and tins and tools. A bag of assorted bird bones rattled onto the carpeted floor. She grunted, growing increasingly frustrated, then went to the kitchenette, pots and pans banging around. "Where are my glasses, dammit! Did you steal them, Maroo?"

Her owl, camouflaged in the clutter, spun his head all the way around, prompting Ex to jump. Huge, unblinking yellow eyes bore straight through him, triggering an eerie reminder of the kongkoi.

Mali cooed and strode past him, arms outstretched to cuddle the creature.

"Mali." Ex gently tugged her sleeve. "Can you please see to my passenger... er, to her? I think she's in labor."

"Oh, *really*? You think so?" Mali snorted and pushed him away. She snatched something off the counter, then stumbled on the carpet before kneeling by Arinya. "Open up, dear girl. This will help the pain."

Arinya opened her mouth, and Mali shook out some blue powder that dissolved on her tongue. "What did you come to me for, girl? I'm no midwife, and you look too far along to want to abort."

"Somatra told me you could help."

"You spoke to that old curmudgeon? Does he still have that awful mustache? How do you know him, anyway?"

"He told me you could make a birth gem."

"Birth gem?" Mali scrunched her brows. "You don't want the baby now? You want the baby *later*?"

"Please." Arinya gritted her teeth and clutched her belly. "I can't have her now. But I don't want to lose her."

"What the hell is going on?" Ex demanded. He had no idea what to do with himself, so he sat down at the kitchen table and started fidgeting with a fork.

"Ah, my poor child," Mali said, her eyes softening. "I'm in no condition for that spell."

Arinya's mouth hung open, her tongue still blue from the powder. "But… Grandmother, I have no other choice."

"What's the problem? Are you scared of the birth? You seem healthy enough," Mali squinted harder at her. "Something else, is it?"

"I…" Arinya hesitated, and the desperation in her eyes made Ex so uncomfortable he had to look away. "Please, I can… I can pay. And I have more if it's not enough."

An uncomfortable silence followed. Ex spun the fork around a few times, then peered over. Mali stood stock still, staring deeply into Arinya's eyes. She placed a hand on Arinya's forehead, and he detected a soft twinge of magic. The vibration was so low, however, he couldn't tell what exactly it was. But then Mali's attention snapped to settle on him.

"You have to do it, Ex."

"What? Do what?" A pit of dread grew in his gut. "I don't know how to, uh, deliver babies."

"No, not that!" She lowered her head menacingly, prompting him to scoot back in his chair.

"I have no clue what you're going on about."

"Pah! You've done this before, boy, you must have. For spirits whose essence you need to preserve and transfer into another vessel."

"You mean a soul-capture? I've done it on phi, not an unborn child." He shook his head profusely. "No, I'd rather not do that. It's probably forbidden."

"No choice!" Mali smiled, sounding too giddy for his liking. She clasped her hands and twiddled her fingers as she thought. "At its core, this is a very simple thing. Do you have a gemstone, dear?"

Arinya reached into the pouch on her belt and pulled out a pendant with a sapphire jewel set in a golden clasp. Mali took the pendant and turned it about. It must have been hellishly expensive… and was oddly familiar. Ex felt like he'd seen it before, and that sensation of familiarity bordered on sinister.

Everything about the situation made him uncomfortable, and his eyes darted to the door.

"I think I'll wait outside."

"What are you sitting there for, boy?! Can't you see the woman's in labor? Do something useful!"

"Um, like what?"

"Boil some water. Find some rags. No, find my glasses first. No, find them second. Boil some water first. And then grab those pillows, bring that red vial over, the one on the wall next to the, the... next to Maroo. Quickly!"

With Arinya's increasingly intense groans and Mali berating him as background, Ex busied himself trying to do all those things, growing more and more panicked by the second as he realized they both expected him to perform the spell.

Beyond general training, every phi hunter had their specialties, and not all spells were created equal. A soul-capture was considered a ritual, rather than a spell. His skill level for rituals was, well, very low, aside from descending into the Hunter's Trance.

This wasn't one he could mess up and shrug off with a bashful laugh. If he wasn't careful, he could end up trapping everyone's souls in that necklace, including Maroo. Despite the disturbingly intimate visual of the three to five of them swirling about as an ethereal mix of beings, he had no desire to spend eternity trapped in that unrelenting awareness as a shiny rock on the floor of a witch's hut.

Ex placed the requested objects nearby, averting his eyes as Mali stripped Arinya's trousers. Arinya seemed to be in a trance herself, her cheeks flushed and brow covered in sweat. Not knowing what else to do, Ex dabbed her face gently with a clean towel. Maybe the woman in labor noticed how terrified her new assistant midwife was because she gave him a weak smile.

"It's okay, Ex," she said. It seemed backwards that she was the one comforting him.

"Can't you do this?" Ex asked Mali, his voice pathetic and weak. The old witch fixed him with a heady, authoritative gaze.

"Low magic is too unreliable for this process."

"Really? That's what you're going with?"

"Ha! Listen, Ex. I'm drunk as an excommunicated monk. We're quite fortunate that you two ran into each other." She smacked his arm. "Where are my glasses?"

"I couldn't find them."

"Useless child," she muttered, then handed him the pendant. "This is the empty vessel. The soul goes in here. Collect it before the body comes out and draws breath. It's about to come out. Are you ready?"

"N-no," Ex stammered. "Nonono, I'm not ready."

Mali glared at him, but her tone remained cheerful for Arinya's sake. "Here we go, my dear! No, don't push! We must capture the soul before the head crowns."

Shit. He imagined running out of the hut, jumping onto Ramble and riding straight back into the woods. Could he live with the shame? Shaking his head, he knelt on the other side of Arinya, who met his eyes with the same steadiness she had when they first met. He tried to return the look, but it shook him. They were complete strangers. The fact that she trusted him at all – not only as an escort, but now with the life of her and her child – maybe should have been flattering, but instead he was stunned.

Terrified.

Can't fuck this up.

He closed his eyes and slowly crept into the Everpresent, holding back his full awareness and leading with his senses. Soul-capture was a delicate ritual. The chant and rhythm had to flow correctly through the mind.

First, he drowned out Mali's mutterings and focused on Arinya's labored breathing, then moved beyond to settle in with her heartbeat. The grain in the wood of the hut deepened into canyons, filled with echoes...

Rapid thudding of blood vessels through heart chambers, signals spitting down the spine in crackling nerve endings. Two beings in one, then one becoming its own, and flowing into the vessel… Each breath timed perfectly – inhale, exhale, cycle. Let everything else go.

Once he felt the pattern, he followed the trail of it, focused on each form of every silent syllable, and most importantly, the spaces in between.

The breath. The presence of it. The breath was everything.

The pendant in his hand grew warm, then burned. The strength of the ritual built upwards, outwards, everywhere. It wove a spiraling tension focused around the gem.

The passage began to open.

Mali yanked his hand from Arinya's belly and shoved it lower. He almost fell out of the ritual. By the thread of a syllable, he clung desperately to the rhythm of the spell. The structure beneath was solid. It was working!

Arinya started to yowl, a blood curdling scream that raised the hair on his neck. Mali muttered curses to the devas. Ex ignored everything except the words, and then there it was.

A tiny heartbeat in the sea of grey.

It was a baby girl, but only for a heartbeat. Before breaching into the world, the crown of her head touched his fingers. Her little body shifted, fluttered, and became ethereal. Ex gasped as her essence danced around his hand, almost inquisitively. And with the last voiceless chant, she was sucked into the waiting vessel with an astounding force.

The vessel slammed shut and flung him across the room. He smashed into the cabinet by Maroo, who screeched, his feathers flapping in Ex's face before a shelf of books buried him. His whole arm smoked, and some of the books started to burn. He swatted at the flames before Mali emptied an entire bucket of water on his head and a thick cloud of steam hissed into the air.

"Ex!" Mali kicked the charred books away, ashes fluttering up as he sputtered and wiped water from his eyes.

"Where is it? Where'd it go? Do you have it?"

He opened his palm and the gem was still there, though it had changed from sapphire to dark violet. Mali grabbed it, but jerked back, hissing in pain.

"It's still hot," she said, eying him. "How much fire is in you, boy? Can't you pull it back?"

Ex grunted, unamused, but Mali guffawed and ruffled his hair.

"You'll get it under control someday. See, wasn't so hard, was it?"

Arinya moaned from the armchair. She'd curled onto her side, her hair plastered to her face, cheeks completely flushed. Ex thought there would be blood, and thanked all the devas there was not.

"Did it work?" she whispered.

He held up the pendant triumphantly. "One baby soul, captured, er, sleeping in here. Until you want it. I guess."

"Oh." She flopped back, relieved. "May I see it?"

It felt considerably heavier than it had been before, but also much more fragile, even if it wasn't. It felt... precious.

Ex brought the gem over to the mother and placed it in her cupped hands, just as reverently as if he were handing over a tiny, squealing human.

"Beautiful," Arinya whispered, tears drifting down her cheeks. "How I wish I could have seen you now." She gazed at it, and then kissed it softly. She pushed herself up by her elbows and struggled with the clasp of the necklace.

"Here," Ex offered. She lifted her hair aside and he fastened the pendant around her neck. Her fingers caressed the gem in awe.

"She's in there," Arinya said, then laughed, a sound as light as butterflies. The pure love in her eyes mesmerized him, made his chest hurt. He couldn't look away. "Can you believe it, hunter? You delivered a child."

Ex wasn't sure if he'd call it that, but when she gazed up at him with eyes so soft it felt as if the world had faded away, he could only shake his head in disbelief. No words could describe the churning, bright feelings he had. He wasn't even sure what they were. With a smile, she settled back on the cushions with a content sigh.

Mali said something or other, but Ex couldn't focus on her words. He wondered what the masters would say when he returned home. Maybe there was a badge for this.

But the laugh died on his lips. He could never tell them. A soul-capture ritual was not something to be performed lightly, and everything had happened so fast. He hadn't had time to think about the implications of what he'd just done. There was a being in there now, at the complete mercy of the beholder. He had no idea what type of awareness it had, if any, or if it would grow, or how it could be born later.

Could it even be born later?

It wasn't his concern, he told himself. He had a job to do.

Chapter Five

Narissa Awakens

Racahoo! Rachoo! Just as they did for the past ten thousand, nine-hundred and forty-seven sunrises, the roosters announced the start of the day.

And every sunrise, Narissa was already awake, the orange gleam of the rising sun haloing her tall, stately figure as she walked along the worn, grassy footpath next to the Namleng River. Wrapped in a modest brown and red sarong, she carried a basket in hand, heavy with the spoils from her foraging. Fishermen stood knee deep in the shallows, their fishing poles stationed along the banks as they checked their nets. Soon, their wives would arrive to wash their clothes and their children.

After walking an hour back from the wild arboretum, she passed the outskirts and reached the entrance of Jinburi, where the trading town had finally stirred awake.

At the crossroads of two rivers, the midland city market burst with color. Fruits of every shape and size arrived from all over northern and eastern Suyoram, as well as the neighboring countries. Stalls lined the streets, surrounded by colorful people with battling languages. The merchants arrived in their canoes, and buyers crowded the docks to make their deals, exchanging money and goods back and forth by baskets attached to long poles.

Narissa hadn't been sleeping well lately. Her eyes ached with the remnants of constant nightmares – glimpses of a desperate escape through the dark forest from a three-eyed horror that did not know death. Were they visions, or long distorted memories? It was odd to dream at all. Perhaps her recent anxieties were due to the approach of her thirtieth year. Each year felt heavier and hungrier than the last.

The raucous smell of fresh fish and human sweat quickened Narissa's step. When she passed the butchers row, her stomach turned and she averted her gaze from garlands of smiling pig heads and fatty duck corpses. She was used to the overwhelming stench of humanity, and had learned to endure it. She focused on the blooming jasmines, and the waft of sandalwood incense from one of the many spirit houses. She was almost out of the market when a male voice cut above the racket.

"Excuse me! Miss!"

The middle-aged man walked around her, then pressed his hands together in a wai, bowing his head.

"I believe you dropped this." He reached into a pouch at his side and pulled out a small comb, the handle inlaid with pearls. It was beautiful, but it wasn't hers. Her expression must have said as much, because he laughed, and said, "I'm joking. It's a gift. I sell them, and I thought a pretty lady like yourself might fancy one."

She would have excused herself politely and gone on, not one to make small talk with strange men, but something about him made her hesitate. He looked familiar, yet she was sure she'd never seen him before. Admittedly she was bad with faces, but judging by the green and yellow zigzag pattern woven into his blouse, he was a visitor from the land to the east. He certainly smelled like a stranger, without the trace amounts of Frangipani blossoms that all those local to Jinburi carried, thanks to the efforts of the provincial governor's gardens.

A gift was a gift, however. It would be rude not to accept. Narissa smiled and her fingers brushed his as she took it.

"Do you live here with your family?" he asked.

"No," she said. "I live alone."

The veins in his neck pulsed. His heartbeat must have quickened.

"An independent woman." His voice dropped, breathier, "Do you run a business? From your home?"

"Yes," she said.

His smile grew.

"Well, surely it's a boring walk all alone! Might I carry your basket?"

Her gaze dropped from him to her basket, the lid clasped shut. Then she dipped her head in a nod and handed it to him. With a grin, the merchant took it, but immediately wavered under its weight.

"My, this is much heavier than it looks," he laughed, then hoisted it to rest under his arm. "You must be a very strong girl."

Narissa said nothing, but smiled politely and continued down the road, passing stilt houses with sharply gabled roofs, townspeople leading their working animals to or from the fields. The young man hurried to her side. He seemed content to walk in silence, and Narissa made no effort to make conversation. They turned off the main street and walked further into the quiet neighborhoods.

They arrived at the last house on the road, a good distance farther than the others. For a three-room home with enough land for her animals, it had been very cheap, due to being the closest to the swamp. Two black-tipped white cats lay on her low stone fence, bright blue eyes blinking languidly in the sun.

Narissa paused at the entrance, then peered at him expectantly. "Have you come for my services?"

He licked his lips and nodded quickly. Narissa opened the gate and led him through her sparse yard, grass crunchy in the dry season, then up the steps to her house. He stumbled as he avoided a few chickens, then craned his neck to gape at the flowers tied up to dry along the railing.

Inside, the sour-sweet scent of mushed limegrass and aloe lingered in the air from her work that morning. The unfinished salve lay on her apothecary table, somewhere in a mess of unlabeled jars full of colorful powders and viscous liquids, bowls of dried herbs and insect parts. Aside from her workspace, her home was tidy and alive, a garden of house plants bringing the dark wooden interior to life.

"Have a seat, please. I'll put on some tea." She gestured to the wicker couch. She'd invested in blue silk cushions, as it was important to make her customers feel comfortable during consultations. Most had minor ailments and complaints – burns and scars, a lingering cough, an achy joint from an old injury, businessmen in search of luck tokens. But many also confessed their deepest fears – to turn a spouse's straying eyes, impotent men in search of respite, women desperate for love. These days, she had fewer and fewer customers, and none as young as this man. People were beginning to abandon the old ways of home remedy and low magic.

As Narissa watched the water boil, she heard the man approach her, his breath hot as he panted in the heat. Slowly, his hands circled her waist, and he pulled her body against his.

At first, Narissa was too shocked to react. No, it hadn't been the first time in the last twenty-nine years a man had made advances on her. But she'd always been able to smell their intent a mile away and avoid their touch. Why had she let this one get so close? Was it because he reminded her of Kiet?

He pressed his hips against her buttocks, his erection an inquisitive rod.

"I'm willing to pay whatever your price is," he murmured, his lips brushing her neck. Her heart began to pound, veins pulsing with an aching need. He fumbled for the tie to her sarong as he laid sloppy kisses on her shoulder.

Her body responded as a woman would. She arched her back, letting her spine extend. His hands grew hurried, and he groaned in frustration. He clumsily yanked the hem of her dress over her waist. Then he laid his sweaty forehead against her shoulder blade and busied himself with undoing the wrap to his chong kraben.

He poked at her womanly entrance, failing to find it. She reached back with her hand to assist, and his knees buckled. He gasped, drooling as he mushed his face into her back and left it there, letting out a long, strained groan.

Narissa's eyes lit up with a sickly green glow, and she grinned a crocodile smile, each tooth a jagged point.

Canines slid from her gums, growing a full inch longer. She licked her darkening lips and her neck elongated ever upward. On and on it went, like a cord of putty, levitating almost to the ceiling. The skin stretched, tendons slid away, and the vertebrae in her spine detached with a tiny click, just below her skull.

Her entrails followed her head, tickling as they squeezed through the hole in her throat.

Despite being detached from her body, Narissa still felt the young man's fingers digging into her waist, sharp as fishhooks, his sweaty face flush to her back, completely oblivious.

Like a rising ribbon, her head curled around, and the last of her intestines slopped out. She hovered behind the man involved in his act, her jaws stretching wide as a cobra intending to strike. Her thin, forked tongue slid forth from her teeth and flickered across his neck, tasting his blind lust. He shuddered, but remained oblivious to his certain demise.

Her stomach had been far too empty for far too long.

Mraaawwwww!

With a thump, one of her cats jumped onto her kitchen table, scattering a bowl of crushed peppercorns. For a brief second, she watched the creature and his judgmental stare... and then saw the reflection of her act in his big blue eyes.

Not this, not again. She was so close to breaking the curse.

Saliva oozed from her mouth as she hovered above him, her tongue twitching, yearning for the sweet taste of human blood. Just this one time, and she would have to go another twenty years without.

A drop of saliva fell from her mouth and splattered on the top of the man's head. He startled, then finally opened his eyes. First, half-lidded confusion, then hysteria.

His scream sent the cat running.

Slack-jawed with horror, the man staggered away from the headless woman's body, only to fall on his backside to stare at her dripping organs dangling above. All the blood drained from his face.

"Y-y-you're a krasue!"

Wait, this isn't what it looks like, she tried to say, but it came out as a spitting hiss.

Still screaming, the man jumped to his feet and dashed for the door. Unfortunately for him, he ran straight into the couch, flipped over, and smashed his face on the ground. Out cold.

Narissa slid back into her body like a snail into its shell, organs resettling inside her skin. Hands shaking, she fixed her sarong. Her breath came in panicked gasps as she hastily removed a spoonful of dark brown powder from one of the many jars on the counter, then smeared a wet cloth into the mixture until it was coated. Then she crouched by the man and dabbed the cloth into his slack-jawed mouth, making sure the drug dissolved on his tongue. He wouldn't remember a thing when he woke up, aside from following someone home he'd assumed was a prostitute.

Best to let him think that.

Narissa dragged the young man's body into the road and left an empty bottle at his side. She touched the side of the unconscious man's neck, checking his pulse one last time. With a pang of heartache, she realized that her beloved Kiet had that same exact mole on his cheek.

How I miss you, Kiet. The phantom memories of his morning kisses sent shivers along her neck. And then with disgust for herself and everything that she was, her mouth watered, remembering how his blood tasted that night.

After she locked her gate, she walked to the back of her house and pulled aside a dirty straw mat, revealing a dark burrow. This was a bad place. But it served as a reminder. Obviously, she needed one.

Pulling it aside, she descended into the tunnel. Fine wine-red dust clouded the ground, each step staining the hem of her dress. If she were in her true form, she would be able to see in the darkness, but now she carried a candle.

A curtain obscured the end of the tunnel, but she stopped before it.

For years, she'd been sleeping in a human bed, on a soft mattress with cotton sheets. But was it hopeless? Was this where she really belonged?

A deep voice boomed from behind her, a voice too deep and resonant to be heard by human ears.

"You test your vows."

The figure in the threshold of the tunnel was not from this plane. With wide shoulders and a thick, ox-like body, he wore the jeweled armor of a celestial warrior. His shoulder pads and boots ended in curled points, his heavy gauntlets were tipped with iron claws and made of the Crocodile King's skin.

He wore a green-skinned khon mask, fierce features highlighted with blue and gold lines, a bulging glare above a snarling, curled mouth with two tusks jutting up from his lower jaw. A single-tiered golden crown stood on his head, denoting him as a descendant of Ravaya.

"Indrajit," Narissa murmured. The deva's name conjured an air of somber ceremony. She closed her eyes, fighting tears. "I don't know what came over me."

"I did not grant you amnesty only for you to return to your sinful ways. You have abstained for twenty-nine years. A mere fraction of time, and seconds more would grant you your humanity."

Narissa brushed her tears aside and faced the deva lord. Though imposing here, he must have appeared far more impressive in his own realm. It would be a great many births and rebirths until she might be able to witness his true form.

"Why did you appear?" she said, her hand tightening around the candle so hard the wax wilted. "Only to scold me?"

Indrajit crossed his great arms across his great chest. "Mere curiosity. You're the only phi who has come this close to breaking their curse."

Shame flushed her cheeks.

"I've been having dreams."

"Don't tell me a dream was enough to tempt you."

"A nightmare." Narissa's gaze drifted back to her nest. "Is it because I'm so close to becoming human?"

"Perhaps," Indrajit said, though his tone was softer. "Or perhaps it was a cry for help from your neighbor in the swamp."

Narissa startled at Indrajit's mention of the elder phi in the swamp. It was an ancient being, a legend, one whose name was known and feared throughout the countryside. "What happened?"

"There are some things more dangerous than the phi themselves." The deva's mask did not change, but she heard the challenging smile in his voice. "Beware, Narissa."

Chapter Six

And the Pret

While Mali made tea, Ex brought in her requests, along with a pile of other things he'd collected over the last few months, including the kongkoi's toenails, still fresh. The old hedgewitch had finally found her glasses, and after wiping them off, slid them onto her nose.

"Ah, Ex, my boy." She blinked a few times, the lenses making her pupils three times their size. She grinned. "Thank the devas you're still just as handsome as I remembered. But you should really do something about that scar."

"I like it. It makes the other hunters take me more seriously." He shrugged out of his coat and hung it on the back of a taxidermied badger near the daybed, where Arinya lay slumbering peacefully. Creepy thing to sleep next to. Hopefully she wouldn't get a fright when she woke up. Just in case, he moved his coat to cover its face.

"Hmph. As if those ruffians could take anything more seriously... Now, tell me, how did you meet that lovely girl?"

Embarrassed to be caught gawking at the new mother, Ex quickly walked over to the table and plopped down across from Mali, where his tea was still warm. With a smirk, the old witch picked through his wares, cross referencing some old dusty tome that had managed to escape the fire.

"We met in that hovel village by the Long Road," Ex said. "She fought a bunch of goons who were beating me up."

"Ex!" Mali stopped her inspections to reach across the table and box his ears. "What did I tell you about starting fights?"

"I didn't start it!" He tried to block her spindly arms, but she was fast. "I'm going to cut you out of my route, you old hag. You're wildly abusive."

To his dismay, he noticed the kongkoi toenails in her discard pile. "Hey, what about those? Those are fresh."

Mali clucked her tongue with a shake of her head. "They're beautiful, but too rich for my blood."

With a sigh, he sank back into the chair, deflated. He contemplated skipping the huntersmeet to avoid the shame of complete failure. Mali's smirk twisted into a grin.

"So... are you the father?"

"What? No! I told you, I only met her a few hours ago. That village has really gone to shit, by the way. The elder ripped me off and tried to pimp out a girl. You don't actually deal with those people, do you?"

"Don't change the subject, boy. How old are you now? There's not a chance you could resist a pretty young thing like that. By the devas, look at her. Beautiful! That couldn't have been the first time you touched that–"

"Grandmother!" Ex glared at the cackling old perv. "Trust me, I think I'd remember." He had no idea why Mali developed the impression he was some kind of rake, sleeping with strangers as if he were collecting cards, but she sure decided to run with it. He wasn't thrilled with her line of teasing, especially in front of Arinya, even if she was asleep.

Mali chortled, shaking her head. "No sense of humor, you hunters."

Ex idly stirred his tea, staring at the swirl of leaves. Nothing like this had ever happened to him before. He'd met people on the road, sure, and sometimes they'd share a campfire together, maybe a drink. But it wasn't often. There were some places in the old country where hunters were still revered, but those routes were reserved for the veterans.

Down here, tradition was being inched back further and further in exchange for "progress." The king wanted more roads, more towns, more temples, more taxes... and as the spirits receded, so did the respect from the populace.

"Where are you bringing her?" Mali said as she held a severed icebat wing up to the candlelight. Tiny crystals sparkled on its skin.

At first, Ex didn't comprehend the question. At his dumbfounded silence, Mali jabbed a thumb towards Arinya.

"I'm not bringing her anywhere. She paid me to get her here, that's it. I'm on my way to Jinburi Swamp after this."

"And why are you going there?" Mali cast him a cruel eye, and to his chagrin, placed the bat wing back in its cloth, folded it, and moved it to her rejection pile. He'd been confident she would have gone for that one. She went onto the next package, which was a cold bag of firelight gecko skins. She picked through the hot hides with chopsticks.

"Shar-Ala." Ex waited for her to be impressed, but she wasn't. "He's there, I know it."

"You're still chasing after that one phi, hmph."

"It's not just any phi!" He sat up in his seat. "Shar-Ala is a legend."

"You speak as if I wouldn't know of him. Boy, I've been around long enough to remember when no one would sleep without boarding up their windows in fear of his serpent arms creeping in. Not that it could stop him. But he hasn't been heard of for decades. Longer than you've been alive."

"I know, old lady. You tell me that every damn time," Ex muttered. "Everyone tells me that."

Mali moved on from the gecko scales to a stack of various spirit organs wrapped in wax paper. "Why do you want to kill him?"

"He's a true demon. If I bring him back to the guild, I'll get my true demon slayer badge." Ex tapped the empty space on his forearm where the sak yant tattoo would go.

"That's it?" Mali snorted. "There are hundreds of phi running amok, causing grief." She pointed at the badges on his other arm for effect. "Meanwhile, this demon has made not a sound in decades, yet you want to slay it as a trophy?"

He wasn't sure how to respond to that, so he shrugged and took a long sip of tea. "So what? Shouldn't I prove myself to the guild?"

"You shouldn't have to. You're doing just fine, see?" Mali picked up one of the phi gizzards. "Perfectly butchered. Not a single tendril of flesh wasted."

"Maybe so, but if you haven't noticed, the pay is shit. I don't even have enough for my dues this month." He rested his head in his hands. "Besides, I don't want to be just a butcher of minor ghosts, peddling organs to ornery witches, getting paid with pork stew. A true demon slayer is sought after. Paid premium!"

She still didn't seem impressed.

"Did you know that there's only three living true demon slayers in the guild? When I kill Shar-Ala, I'll be the fourth, and the youngest. Ever."

"If that brings you happiness..." Mali said. "But I suspect there's more to it than that, isn't there?" Taking Ex's glum silence as confirmation, she smiled gently and placed the gizzard into the discard pile.

Ex had hoped that Mali would finish her purchases so he could go, but she kept nodding off, then startling herself awake with a snore. She demanded that he stay until morning, fixing him with the elder stare that could guilt anyone younger than a hundred into giving in. It was only a few hours until sunrise, so he supposed it couldn't hurt that much.

Mali staggered into a little nest of cushions near Maroo, and Ex walked out to bathe in the lake, mulling over her words.

Spirits twisted around the depths, creatures never seen by human eyes. Mali lived here for a reason. She was a user of old, low magic and thus deeply connected to the earth. But low magic users couldn't enter the Everpresent and speak to these beings as hunters could. Although, spirits weren't worth bothering for idle chatter, and he sensed they didn't want to be disturbed.

Both hedgewitches and hunters shared a similar disdain for new magic, a practice regulated and watered down, an invention of the king's reformations. Publicly, the king had come to some supposed enlightenment, but many believed it was only a cover for his real motive – pressure from the outside world, powers that were becoming more and more interested in getting a foothold into Suyoram for trade and influence.

Regardless of the politics, the king's decrees banned more and more rituals, calling them "barbaric and ignorant." Shrines were torn down to put up temples with what they called "enlightened" architecture. Following the course of the kings before him, he continued to expand the roadworks, tearing deeper into the forests, logging the trees, burning the swamps, and running the spirits further into the wild north.

Most provinces complied, but those villages of the Relentless Rains refused to cut through the most sacred of their woods, where they still paid reverence to the spirits. That defiance led to withheld taxes and open rebellion. Though they fought fiercely, in the end, they were no match for the might of the crown.

Ex floated on his back and stared up at the stars, wondering what the world had been like before. The other hunters talked about how the kingdom once held them in the highest regard, when commissions from the crown kept their belts loose and their feats were sung about in the streets. That was all changing, they said. Some muttered that the trade itself wouldn't last much longer.

Some even said Ex might be the last of them. The last phi hunter.

He let himself sink underwater for a while, until the moon distorted into a wavering light.

One thing the guild often spoke about were true demons – especially ones they had all aspired to slay, yet never found. Shar-Ala was one such phi, but so old and elusive that they assumed he'd gone far away from Suyoram. The tales of his dark deeds mesmerized Ex more than any of the other demons. Centuries ago, Shar-Ala had once been the ruler of a long-destroyed kingdom in the north. He was a villainous, cruel man who tortured his subjects when they dared disobey him. The stories went that he ordered dissidents to be captured during the night, only to be returned to their families disfigured or blinded, if alive at all.

The stories diverged, however, on how he died. Some said he was drugged and drowned by one of his wives. Others, that he went mad and burned himself in his own court. Regardless, after many incarnations spent as a hungry phi, he never regained his merit, and he embraced darkness, descending further into a waking hell until finally becoming legend.

During their first hunt into the swamp, Ex and the Hound caught a glimpse of Shar-Ala's shadow and followed him into a deep cavern. As a hunter, it would be unseemly to be afraid of the dark, but being underground was another thing entirely. Ex hated it. Despised it. Hated hunting any phi that made their homes in holes. But this was Shar-Ala, so exceptions were made.

Unfortunately, it turned out to be the lair of a taul, and that was where he received the scar across his forehead. A taul was a worthless phi, being half man but twisted into a monster from failed attempts at necromancy. He had no useful parts, not even spirit blood.

However, his lair had a few things he must have collected, things stolen from the nearby town, and most notably, bones of their missing townspeople. Those returns were always appreciated.

But in one of the taul's journals, before he went mad, Ex found very valuable information. The taul had summoned Shar-Ala and attempted to bind him to the land. Apparently, he thought the demon would make a good guard dog. Of course, that backfired.

To the taul's credit, part of the spell had succeeded. Even though Shar-Ala was a roamer and could appear anywhere, the ritual had partially bound him to the swamp. But only on those three nights in which the ritual had been performed.

So, the true demon returned for three days, every three months. And for the last year, Ex had been there each time to find him.

All the hunters, including Master Seua, had told him this was a pointless mission. A complete waste of time when he should be earning his keep. Ex left the water and dried off, then sat on the rocky shoreline and meditated on the idea of letting it go.

As the sky grew a muted blue, dawn threatening, Ex lingered by the slumbering horses and, checking his gear again, counted his coinpurse and sighed. The other hunters managed to make their dues. He didn't know what he was doing wrong. Maybe it was the route itself, composed of a bunch of cheapskate villagers and broke hedgewitches. It'd been over a year, so he supposed he could ask for a reroute, but that wouldn't bring him to the swamp when he needed to be there.

He reached into his tracking bag and pulled out his mask. He ran his finger over the carved details of the solid, lacquered wood, a thin sheet of steel between two sides, no eyeholes. The mask was a sacred rite, awarded only after a hunter killed their first phi, alone. Before then, they wore featureless ones, with only the guild symbol. Master Seua said it was for the phi to know the odds were in their favor.

Funny how the hunters made every trial in the guild as lethal as possible yet wondered why membership enrollment had fallen so far down.

It was custom made by a very specific artisan, a retired hunter and master of his craft. Ex was told he stayed in the Trance when carving and painting them, sometimes for days, with no food, water, or rest until the souls of the First Hunters moved him. Once he finally envisioned how the phi would learn to know the new hunter, he went to work.

When he created Master Seua's mask, he'd had a vision of a blue tiger standing on top of a mountain, and so his mask and hunter name reflected that.

Ex didn't know if he was messing with him or not, but Master Seua told him that when the artisan created his mask, he saw a vision of Exaram, one of the First Hunters, a female Venara who served King Maaba.

The Venara hunters didn't wear masks, but in the vision, Exaram had worn a red and black one with white eyes, the face of a snarling wolf. As a result, he'd received not only her mask, but her name.

"They will know this face and fear you," Master Seua told Ex. "As they did her."

Shar-Ala would know. And after he was slain and his soul returned to the hellish realm of Hungry Ghosts, he would tell them all that name.

All of them would fear him.

"There you are."

In the early morning, Ex swayed lazily in his hammock, which he'd fastened between two mango trees. He tilted his head back to see the old hedgewitch walking over, ghost-like in the soft mist. She carried a tray with a small plate of rice and cut up fruits and vegetables, along with a little bowl of dark red liquid.

"Morning, Mali," he yawned. "Brought me breakfast in bed?"

She grumbled and proceeded to the Spirit House on the edge of her yard. Found all over Suyoram, Spirit Houses looked like tiny pagodas on pedestals, with a platform to leave your offerings. Those could be tributes to ancestors or devas, or to placate and ward away destructive spirits, or ask for favor from the Enlightened Lord himself.

Mali had grown her altar to fuse with a fig tree, the bark itself forming the steepled roof and platform. After placing the bowl of rice, blood, and fruit down, she lit an incense stick and made a wai to her forehead as she murmured a prayer.

"Have you paid your tributes today?" She cast him a disapproving eye.

"I think my tribute at the Guardian tree still holds up."

Finally, Mali smiled, impressed. "You saw the Guardian? My, you are quite a special boy, Ex. Other hunters don't have the same reverence for the ancient ways."

"That hardly makes me special. It only makes me a backwoods mountain tribal, in their eyes." And in the eyes of the kingdom, worse.

"Again, with their eyes," Mali sighed, then began to walk back inside. He rolled out of his hammock to walk with her.

"Have you picked out what you want yet, Grandma?"

"No! Aren't you going to ask about your lady? She's still recovering."

"Recovering from what? The baby didn't even come out the... *traditional* way."

"You daft boy. Carrying a child takes a toll on the body, a toll that burrows much deeper than the physical self. You are creating a soul at its most pure. Summoning it into being as it takes its first breath."

"But... it didn't *take* its first breath," Ex said, a little lost now that he was thinking about it. "If the soul only comes at its first breath, then what did we capture in the gem?"

It had to be something. He'd felt its weight and presence, but not quite a consciousness. His limited experience with soul-captures always involved already living, breathing beings.

"It is nothing yet. A waiting vessel inside of another." Seeing his baffled expression, Mali sighed. "That doesn't mean a mother wouldn't care for it, or feel pain, in body and mind. I don't expect you to understand."

"Is she okay?" He asked, glancing nervously towards the cottage.

Mali shoved a bag at him. "Make yourself useful and fetch me some lily milkcap mushrooms. There's a pond in the woods a mile east, I've marked the way. Look for the blue swanfeather flowers."

"Maybe I should say good morning, first–"

"Not until you return with those. Don't worry. The sweet thing will still be here when you get back."

"I'm not worried," Ex grabbed the bag with a scoff.

Mali smiled. "Of course you aren't. Now, hop to."

Ex wasn't sure what a lily milkcap mushroom was, but with magic and magical creatures, most things were named literally, especially by low magic users. The sorcerers in the cities were the ones who gave spells bombastic names that sounded far fancier than they were. It was all about appearances for them. As for hunters, theirs were based on history. Their powers were poetic. Master Rei had told him it was taken from the devas. They had substance beyond.

The coos of partridges and cheerful chirps of sunbirds sprinkled about the woods. Along with the rhythmic calls of insects, the whole forest seemed to yawn and stretch, basking in the sun. Various tree rodents rustled through the branches, and a few gibbons chattered from their territory high above. A family of deer scattered as he tromped through.

Mali's signal flowers began to appear on the trees, dark blue blossoms with curled, tapered petals. True to their name, they resembled swan necks, and their skinny stems curled up the darker hardwoods. Their faces pointed in the direction of the pond, while all others looked east, hungry for the morning sun.

Ex considered going into the Everpresent, just to see if any daytime spirits were about. They were rare and almost always simple beasts, like their mortal cousins. He didn't *need* the Everpresent to see them – any person could, magic user or not. But he'd need it if he wanted to see past the restraints of time and space to find their tracks, or commune with them. But he decided it was better to save his energy, as it took a toll after a while, and he'd had a rough few weeks.

He started to daydream again, wondering where Arinya really came from and why she didn't want to have her child, at least right then. Maybe it was an affair? Or was she running from someone? He felt more than a little uncomfortable about soul-trapping a human and had never heard of anyone choosing to do such a thing.

Mali mentioned something the Sangha preached – at the first breath, the soul entered. Anything before was only energy building, like growing an organ. If there were any higher thoughts, they were contained in a plane above the mortal realm, and much would be forgotten once the soul was reborn.

Honestly, Ex didn't know what to believe. In the rural highlands, they had casual respect for the Enlightened Lord, but his village respected the devas above all else. It was a culture shock when he first went to the Capital – well, was taken to the Capital, moreso. All the gilded temples, and lacquered idols, and grand displays of wealth and power acquired from conquered lands…

A heavy crash jarred him out of his reverie. He immediately ducked into a crouch, taking cover behind a bush. It sounded as if something fell, like a tree, or a boulder. The next one came much closer, so close the ground vibrated a little, and a flock of birds took flight.

Ex peered around, searching for the source. Between the clustered trunks, a tall, grey figure moved in the middle distance. He couldn't make it out. There was the pond, though, a serene spot of lily pads and mossy rocks, the sun's reflection bright.

Another thump and frogs splashed into the water. An elephant, maybe? A twenty-foot-tall elephant?

Then the trees parted, bent completely aside by two long, skeletal hands.

Not an elephant. A phi. The towering, skinny ghost stepped through the trees, its legs and arms nearly as thick as a goat. For such a large creature, its mouth was but a hole the size of a pinky finger. A skull-shaped, human head blinked round, all-black eyes craning to and fro, checking for… hell, men like Ex.

But it had nothing to fear, and Ex took his hand off his blade. This was a pret, a type of miserable Hungry Ghost that was cursed with an insatiable hunger, yet unable to eat or drink anything due to its tiny mouth. That didn't stop it from trying, though.

It knelt by the pond with another resounding thump. With two hands steadying its weird, awkward body, it lowered his head to the pond and made pathetic slurping noises.

A sad sight. Ex wanted to help it somehow, but it would be pointless. These creatures were cursed with karmic punishment. No amount of carving out a larger mouth would do anything. Thanks to a previous life of gluttony, greed, and selfishness, they eternally starved. At least long enough to atone for their sins before a higher deva decided it had suffered enough.

How long would it take until it gave up? Once, while hunting with Master Seua, Ex watched a pret try to stuff the carcass of a deer down its mouth for two hours. It was excruciating, and he fell asleep three times, each time smacked awake by his mentor.

This is important, he'd said. *Understand that we mustn't hate our prey, that phi may sometimes be pitied.*

Great Elder Nokai liked to prattle on about karmic justice and the wheel of reincarnation. But the truth was that it seemed like no one really knew. It was a mystery how the devas doled out their judgment. Most other hunters only cared what the phi did in their current state. It was hard to pity a monster when a mother recounted the loss of her child, or when a demon's belly bulged with human bones.

But the pret, Ex could feel bad for them. Who would say no to a life of hedonistic delights, if you could afford it? Well, *he* would say no, or at least liked to think he would.

He waited for a few minutes before a deep sigh deflated him. This was going to take forever, and he wanted to get back to make sure Arinya was alright. And Mali had his pay, of course.

With soft steps, he padded into the clearing. The pret was so focused on its futile efforts that it didn't notice. As Ex peered at some of the rocks, searching for the milkcaps, a deep, mournful groan startled him. He tried to catch his balance but slipped on a rock and tumbled into the pond with a splash.

His feet failed to reach the bottom as he bobbed underwater. With a gag, he resurfaced, and when he shook the water from his face, the deep, tear-soaked eyes of the phi bore into his. They regarded one another, man treading water, phi sucking at it. But in order for it to hear him, Ex had to enter the Everpresent.

The pond brightened, saturated into glowing hues of azure and jade. Ex quickly spotted the mushrooms, small and pulsing with energy before taking in the markings on the pret. They were similar to sak yant tattoos, but with constantly scrolling letters. These were its misdeeds, branded into its sallow flesh in the undecipherable language of the devas.

Hello, Ex said.

Hunter. It didn't seem alarmed, only curious, mildly annoyed. *Why have you come before me?*

I don't mean to disturb your meal. Ex treaded towards the rock with the most mushrooms on it. *Carry on.*

The pret grunted. *And now you mock me. My endless misery. Are all hunters so cruel?*

Seemed it was a whiny one. *Depends on who you ask. Most people say we're doing the world a favor, ridding your cousins of their cursed existences.*

Does butchering my kind bring you joy? Do you think you are immune to karmic reckoning? What will be your curse, I wonder?

I expect a parade. Ex smirked, scraping the mushrooms into a bag. *The devas will thank us for our service, as they did the First Hunters.*

The pret grunted again, then sat back and folded its elbows on its knees. *Let me tell you how I earned this curse, hunter.*

Whiny *and* talkative. Ex opened his mouth to protest, but the ghost went on anyway.

In my life, I was indeed a man of voracious appetites – an unquenchable thirst for wine and women and all manner of base desires. But these were not born out of nothing. Pain and loneliness drove me to such ends. And in my later years, when my health ailed me from continuing, I sought refuge in a monastery. It was there that I learned self-control.

Fascinating, but I really must go–

I emerged a new man, set on making amends for those I'd hurt. But another appetite began to consume me, one that could not be measured in the physical realm.

Done with his collection, Ex pulled himself out of the pond, and sat on the bank. He pulled off his shirt and wrung it out. *Okay, I'll humor you. What was it?*

Pride, it said. *Pride and glory. The laurels and attention I received for my good deeds brought me to a place of desire once again. Even after I settled my debts, I sought even more honors, not for the act itself, but for my own satisfaction.*

Ex chewed on his lip, frowning. *What's so bad about that?*

My intentions came from an impure place, and soon my methods took a dark turn. Desire is endless. Desire is poison. Desire will only cause suffering.

With a groan, the pret's head drooped down like a tree weighted with snow and it sat in silence. Surely there was a lesson to gain, but Ex willfully let it sail right over his head. He hopped to his feet and tipped his head to the ghost.

Thank you for the interesting story, spirit. I wish you better merit on your next life.

Hunter, wait.

Ex was halfway to the trees, but something in the phi's voice stopped him. Something desperate. He turned back with a guarded expression, eyes darting around for some kind of trap.

Would you end my life? The pret bowed its head, long, winding hands steepled into a wai. *Despite your childish insolence, it would be an act of deep mercy.*

Why would I give you that? I need a good reason to kill even the most despicable demons. Though it would be mercy, how much good would that do for its next life? It would likely be reborn as another Hungry Ghost. Maybe even something worse for negging on its first punishment. Besides, it was common knowledge not to gamble with devas. They didn't have rules to follow or break.

It is a selfish ask, I know. I persist even in this despicable form. But I can offer you something in exchange, something that will aid you. You hunt Shar-Ala, do you not?

How do you know that?

It made an awful choking noise, which Ex supposed was a laugh. *I am attuned to selfish desires, and I can sense it in your aura–*

It's not a selfish desire, Ex snapped. *Shar-Ala has done horrible things.*

It matters not to me, hunter. But if you grant me this mercy, I will grant you a boon that will help you in your endeavor.

First rule of phi hunting – never make deals with the phi. It wasn't only inadvisable, it was stupid. They were liars. But pret weren't quite demons, were they? They didn't murder people or destroy crops. And for an entire year, Shar-Ala had evaded him. To the other hunters, a year was nothing. If Master Seua actually approved of his goal, he'd have told him that patience was the key. But for some inexplicable reason, Ex felt like he was running out of time. It felt as if the guild itself was running out of time.

What was the harm in taking this gift? Besides that, a pret's tongue fetched a fair price.

"I guess it's your lucky day," Ex said, and drew his knife.

Grateful tears coursed down its cheeks. The pret couldn't smile with its wretched mouth, but bowed its head as the hunter approached.

Chapter Seven

The Fighter

In a grand mood, Ex made his way back to the lake, humming the "pig is king" ballad as he walked. He felt like his fortune had finally started to turn. Not only did he earn a good-sized payment from Arinya, but with this gift from the pret, his hunt for Shar-Ala had an even better chance of success. Maybe Mali was right. A little extra tribute might keep his luck going, so he plucked a few berries to place upon her Spirit House.

Right before he reached the edge of her property, a man's voice murmured in the distance. It stopped him short. No other hunter made this route, and Mali terrified the villagers. Perhaps it was another brave traveler like Arinya, in search of some charm or another?

He peeked out of the woods from behind the big fig tree that separated her land from the forest.

Near the cottage, behind a large, washed-up log, five men huddled together. They were all wearing dark red shirts covered by armored chest guards, eyes dark and bright under bucket helmets. Soldiers from the Suyoram Crown, judging by the two fighting elephant emblems on their chest pieces. Why the hell were they here?

"The heathen is a dangerous witch. Leave her to me."

Ex's attention snapped to the one who seemed to be in charge. In contrast to the others, he wore no armor, and only silk robes, covered from head to toe in swirling fire and floral patterns. Rather than a helmet, he wore a hood clasped into a half-cape, with a veil around his face.

Sorcerer.

Unlike hunters, they didn't enter the Everpresent, drawing their magic instead from energy in the Blinds. Most of their spells were curses, hex rituals, blessings, or alchemy. But unlike witches, they didn't give back to the spirits. There was no exchange, as they thought themselves higher beings. Furthermore, they maintained strict diets, for what reason Ex couldn't fathom, but it sounded like the most miserable part of it all.

"Should we wait for the others?" one man said, the captain of the guard, by the look of the extra emblem on his collar and slightly fancier helmet. He clutched a sword in hand while two others carried arquebuses, fingers on the triggers. The last soldier held a weighted net and kept staring at the cottage nervously before shifting his focus back to the sorcerer.

"No," the sorcerer said, anticipation heavy in his voice. "We can handle a couple of women, can't we? The prince grows impatient."

What was happening? Did the king finally outlaw *all* low magic? Ex's coat and weapons were still hanging in his hammock. He had his chainblade, but it was made for killing and capturing, not battle. What did he think he was going to do, anyway? A bar brawl in a provincial shit hole was one thing, but he couldn't assault an officer of the crown.

The door to the cottage opened and Mali walked out with a bucket, her long white hair pulled up in a large bun, stark against her dark skin. Dressed in robes and skirts stitched out of patterned fabrics and animal skins, she whistled as she walked to the garden and busied herself with the agberry bush, completely unaware.

Agberries worked well for pain, which meant that Arinya might be worse off than he'd thought. Ex had no idea what these bastards wanted with them, but they obviously hadn't brought gifts. He started to panic, adrenaline firing up his nerves. He couldn't just sit by and watch, but these were soldiers, with real weapons. Surely, they knew how to use them...

The sorcerer signaled to the men, who readied themselves. He then lifted his hand with drama, much higher than necessary, and spoke the words of new magic. Ex heard them as clear as day. That was another difference between hunters and sorcerers. Sorcerers commanded magic through their own, self-entitled, mortal tongue. Hunters harnessed it.

Some brand of stunning spell laced along his hands. The captain nodded to his men, who emerged from behind the tree and rushed towards Mali.

It had to be now.

Right before the sorcerer stepped out, Ex burst from the trees. He grabbed his chainblade knife-side, then whipped the handle. It snapped and coiled around the sorcerer's extended arm. He whirled around, eyes wild, sputtering in dismay.

Ex yanked and the man tumbled. Just as if he were a phi, Ex dashed and crashed into him with his knees to his chest. For a split-second, Ex sat there, in control, blade in hand, readied at the man's throat. This was where he'd normally make the kill, if it were a phi. This was a human.

This would be murder.

The sorcerer recognized Ex's hesitation and grabbed his wrist. A shock wave zapped through him and knocked him on his side, joints twitching. Ex clenched his jaw to keep his teeth from chattering and held his numb arm.

A blast sounded and a bullet splintered the log behind him, an inch from taking off half his head. Ex ducked another one. The two riflemen repositioned themselves, reloading. The others were still rushing at Mali, but Ex had to worry about the sorcerer whose hands had curled into claws as he built up another spell.

Desperate, Ex tackled him and followed with an elbow to the temple. The man blocked and kneed him in the side. When Ex doubled over, he grabbed his shoulders and went for another. Ex stepped on his foot, then hooked his leg, falling backward for leverage at a nasty angle.

A sickening crack followed, and the man collapsed on the ground, screaming.

Despite the broken leg, the sorcerer snatched something off his belt, and Ex wrestled his wrist to the ground. The object cracked open, and a blaring white light blinded him. If he didn't believe it before, Ex was certain now that this asshole was going to kill him.

Frantic, he dropped into the Everpresent, where he saw the sorcerer's grey form pulsing with dark purple energy. A cloud collected in his throat as he prepared another attack.

The Hand of Khun Phaen – yes, that would do it. Ex uttered the voiceless words, and his hand dissolved into an ethereal phantom weapon. He sank his fingers past the man's skin and into his throat, where the spell burned hot and heavy. With a quick squeeze, he extinguished it. The rapid thud of the man's heart caught his eye.

It would be nothing to crush it from here.

"Insolents!" Mali screamed from her garden, and a soldier answered with a cry of pain. Another called for magic support, panic causing his voice to crack. The sorcerer's eyes widened and he tried to speak, but clutched his throat. He was disarmed and immobile, clawing at Ex's face in desperation.

Fingernails tore at the flesh of Ex's head, yanking out some hair along with it. He quickly jumped away and ran semi-blindly towards Mali and her assailants.

A squishy thing caught his foot, and he staggered forward, directly on to the captain. The soldier's blade pierced the skin on Ex's arm and a tingle of warning let him know it wasn't too bad – not good in any sense, but pain worked differently for phi hunters.

Ex had red blood and could bleed out like any other human, but like the demons he fought, he could still hold a polite conversation throughout.

The captain must have expected a reaction and didn't guard against the oncoming strike. Ex punched the handle of his chainblade into the captain's nose, mashing it wide open. Blood burst from his face, onto Ex's own. With a disgusted sneer, he tossed him away with extra vigor. Ex didn't know why there was that much blood, maybe he had some kind of condition? Then again, he'd never busted a human's face open like that.

The shouts faded as the last two attackers retreated towards the trail, dragging the sorcerer hastily by the arms, who bounced along with them while his painful screams were hardly more than a hiss. He wouldn't be walking for a few days, never mind casting spells.

Mali sucked her teeth and spat, hands on her hips as she glared at the remaining two as if they were naughty children caught digging in her garden. The captain still rolled on the ground, hand pressed to his face. The witch took a running start and kicked him in the guts.

"Get out of here!" she screamed. He scrambled to his feet and staggered after his friends.

The other one – who was actually the squishy spot Ex tripped over – resembled a pile of cooked beef. Only his head and half his torso remained, where the rest of his body had been struck by the decay spell Mali cast, a spell that witches often used to make compost for their gardens. His twitching hand still clutched his net as his lips sagged in horror.

"Ugh, what the shit!" Ex stammered and pointed to him. "... can you help him?"

"Help?" Mali turned up a lip. "Why the fuck would I do that?"

"It's the proper thing to do!"

"He just tried to kill me! And you. And likely your lady."

Ex opened his mouth to protest, but Mali cut him off. "What? Do you want me to grow him a new set of legs? Pah. I have a limit of words left on this world, but if you want to waste yours on him, don't let me hold you back."

Healing himself in the Everpresent was one thing, but Ex had no propensity for that type of magic – after all, when would a hunter need to heal their prey? When he looked back at the man, the rest of the rot had consumed him. He was gone. A pile of fertilizer Mali would likely use for her flowers.

The witch wasn't wrong. These people attacked them. Yet Ex still felt sick, as if he were at fault for it all. Then he noticed the blood coursing down his arm in a torrent, dripping onto the mud. With a sneer of disgust, he descended into the Everpresent, pulling strings of magic into his wound.

"What's going on? Ex?"

Mid-heal, his head snapped up at Arinya's voice, and he waved, flinging blood through the air. Her mouth screwed up in shock and her eyes widened as she looked from the pile of meat before her to Mali casually finishing her gardening, and Ex, covered in blood like he'd been dancing at a black magic orgy.

"Hey," he smiled. "Are you feeling better?" She didn't move, gawking, and Ex remembered where he was. He left the Everpresent, and let the spell run its course.

"Are you okay?" She walked cautiously across the bridge and took a wide berth around the soldier's body before she approached. "You're hurt."

"I'll be fine," he said, turning away self-consciously. Indeed, his damaged muscles and nerves were already snapping back to place. Once he was decent enough, he glanced over.

He hadn't seen her yet in broad daylight. Arinya had freshened up and changed, filling out her clothes nicely. She had a gracefulness to her, a refined manner in the way she carried herself that hinted at an aristocratic upbringing.

"What happened?" she asked, eyes still wide in concern. "I heard screaming."

"That happens when men are foolish enough to come around causing trouble," Mali said from her garden, yanking agberries off a bush.

"One of them said there were more on the way. And they mentioned the prince." Ex peered at the witch. "Is the crown after you, old lady?"

"Hah!" Mali held one of the small blue berries up, popped it in her mouth, and offered some to Arinya. "If they wanted to kill me, why would they bring a net, and a sorcerer? You felt that new magic, didn't you, boy?"

"Sure did."

She nodded, distant anger in her eyes.

"Go get cleaned up now," Mali said to Ex, then guided Arinya to sit down on a garden bench with her.

No longer bleeding, Ex flexed his fingers. With everything back in place, he kicked off his boots and walked down to the water. Being bloody was one of the things he hated most in the world, so he gratefully knelt at the edge, stripped shirtless and did his best to wash off, dousing his shirt as well.

He'd never gone toe to toe with a sorcerer before, and images of the fight flashed through his mind as he wrung out the blood. Those spells could have killed him, and the soldiers' bullets almost took his head off. He shuddered, realizing how close to death he'd been. He couldn't wait to get his things and get the hell out of there, back to the forest, where things made sense.

Collecting himself, he walked back to the two women. Arinya's head hung as she listened to the old witch, who held both her hands in comfort. The corner of Mali's lip twitched as Ex walked up, and when Arinya lifted her head, she quickly averted her gaze.

"Keeping in pretty good shape, Ex." The lecherous old witch's eyes roved over him, and in response, Ex turned up a lip and shook his head. She laughed. "Did you get some new charms?"

"Not since the last time I was back." Ex looked down at his torso, where sak yant tattoos covered most of his chest and arms. The masters gave them out as marks of protection, charms for luck, honors for passing rituals and killing certain types of phi. He inspected the blank spot where his true demon slayer badge would go, once he killed Shar-Ala.

Abruptly, Ex realized that the shameful brand on his ribs was in plain sight – a gift from the crown to any survivors from his rebellious village. He turned away from them and wrung out his shirt, though there was little water remaining.

"So," he called back, "Are you two sticking around for the next group of assholes?"

"I'm not going anywhere," Mali said, "but the two of you are. Ex, you're going to escort the crown prince's consort back to her kingdom before the queen's men decide to show up again."

"What? Who?" With his shirt only halfway on, Ex stared at Arinya, whose eyes were sheepishly fixed on the ground.

Mali wiggled her eyebrows at him, sitting back with a smug smirk.

"You." Ex pointed to Arinya. "You're the princess? We have a princess?"

"The *prince's consort*," Arinya said.

"That's a fancy word for concubine, right?"

Mali threw an agberry in his face. "You imbecile! The consort of the crown-prince is his most prized female companion, the most esteemed position in his personal court. She is chosen by him, rather than *for* him. Though he hasn't married his Loramese princess yet, correct?"

Arinya nodded, still sullen.

"Sorry, didn't mean to, uh, offend." He pulled his shirt fully on, then pretended to inspect a rip on his sleeve.

"You didn't. We perform some of the same duties as his concubines. He's branded me as his favorite – not literally," she blurted, and Ex felt his cheeks grow hot.

Another, more worrisome, thought hit him. Ex stared at the pendant around her neck with the soul trapped child. The child that *he* trapped.

Fuck.

"Yes, the child is his," Arinya said, reading his thoughts. "And once he's married, I fear the wrath of the new queen."

"There's a new queen, too? I thought you said she was a Loramese princess?"

"The king is ailing, so everyone suspects the crown-prince to inherit the throne soon. Officially, she is still a princess, but everyone refers to her as the new queen."

It still seemed strange to want to murder a child. "Aren't you court ladies all friends?"

"Ex!" Mali threw another agberry. "You may be from the mountains, but were you born under a rock?"

He held up his hands in surrender. "I don't know!"

"Disputes in lineage are what the royals are known for," Mali said. "Murdering all potential threats is common sense." Ex thought back to the bleary tavern song of the night before. He knew it was disparaging, but he didn't realize the whole "drinking his brother's blood" part might actually be based on reality.

"Well, the thing is..." Ex sighed, resting his hands on his hips. The women waited. He was already cringing before he said it. "I'm on a schedule. I have to get to Jinburi swamp in two days, and diverting all the way down to the Capital will take longer than that–"

Mali was on her feet and in his face before he could blink. Her nostrils flared like an angry ox ready to charge. "This woman and her child's soul are in danger, and all you care about is chasing some monster around a swamp?! You've never even *seen* the creature!"

"I've seen footprints! And it's going to be different this time." He sounded like he was trying to convince his mother to let him go out and play. "I made a deal..." With a pret? No, he couldn't say that. "You know how I keep to my schedule, I can't just go wherever I want, whenever I want."

Mali scoffed. "Of all the hunters I've known, I've never met one with such anally retentive qualities."

Leaning to speak over Mali's shoulder, Ex asked Arinya, "If you want to go home, why don't we just find those men? I'm sure they'd understand we were just being a little... defensive before."

"Those weren't the prince's men," Arinya said. "They were the future queen's."

"Wait." Ex pointed to the dead one. "They were wearing the crest of Suyoram."

"Boy! The men change their clothes as a gecko changes his hide! Obviously, after they killed me, they would trick the girl into going with them. Showing up in the Loram Kingdom's clothes would be a bit of a giveaway, wouldn't you think?"

Ex shrugged. All these ideas felt like a spider web – invisible, sticky, and something he didn't want to walk into.

"They won't kill me if they can avoid it," Arinya continued. "It would enrage the prince." She tapped her amulet. "But what if they find out *she's* in here?"

"The sorcerers don't know spirit magic." Ex glared at Mali for support, who couldn't disagree but rolled her eyes anyway. "You could just... hide her somewhere. For a while." For how long?

"Did you not hear the 'if they don't have to?' They could still kill her," Mali said, and to his relief, backed away from him to sit by Arinya. "Would the prince desire another child from you, my dear?"

Arinya nodded, though didn't meet her eyes.

"Then you *are* still in danger from the queen, are you not?"

"As long as I'm away from the palace, out of the prince's protection..." She closed her eyes, deflating with a sigh. "Yes."

"Ex," the old witch said, this time gentler, yet still great-grandmother stern. "Do not make me invoke your ancestor's wrath. Will you escort the prince's consort back to the Capital, or are you going to force her to hire some thugs from the village to protect her from the queen's assholes?"

"When you put it like that, you're making *me* sound like one. Look, I don't wanna *not* help." Ex stared into the woods, hesitating before his next admission. "But I didn't make enough money for my dues. Hunting down Shar-Ala is the only way I'm not laughed out of the Hunters Meet."

"You'd let this woman die so you won't be laughed at?"

"What? No. She's a better fighter than I am!"

"Not against the phi," Mali said. "The queensmen will be on the road. You have to take her through the wilderness."

Ex was about to make another excuse but wasn't sure how to counter that without sounding like a heartless bastard. She was right. That soul-trapped pendant was a beacon – it would smell like heaven to a Hungry Ghost. Even higher spirits like the Guardian wouldn't turn down a lure like that.

"What if we stopped in Jinburi before the Capital?" Arinya placed a hand on Mali's arm. "They won't search for me there. They'll think I'm still in the mountains."

Mali frowned, grunting in disapproval. "You would be wise to return to the safety of your prince as quickly as possible."

"I understand, but I am willing to compromise." Arinya stood and walked up to Ex. She took his hand in both of hers and squeezed. It surprised him so much that he almost snatched it back. "Hunter Ex. I have many riches and wealth apart from the prince. They're my own, and they are yours, if you will help me and my daughter return home safely."

Stunned, Ex opened his mouth, trying to form words. Yes, he had to hunt Shar-Ala. There was no escaping that. But if he couldn't kill him this time, Arinya's reward would provide what he needed. Maybe even more. The guild hall always needed repairs.

She held his eyes with a tender gaze that reminded him of the night before, how she held the amulet to her chest. She was desperate to get home. And Mali was right that any mercenaries in that little town weren't going to protect her from the phi. Even if they did manage to shield her from sorcerers and soldiers, he would never trust their manners. She could defend herself, of course, he'd seen it, but there were more of them than there were of her.

But if Ex could hunt Shar-Ala for a few days... *and* have some pleasant company? She smelled much nicer than the Hound, that was for sure. She'd have to stay in town while he went into the swamp, but it seemed she had the means to fetch a fancier room than he could ever afford.

His eyes drifted down to the amulet around her neck, and again, there was that feeling he couldn't explain. The soul-capture was his doing. It was a lie to say he didn't feel responsible for what happened to it next.

When Ex met Arinya's eyes again, she smiled, and he made some type of mumbled grunt.

Mali's chortling laugh jarred him out of his daze.

"Oh, I think that was a yes, my dear!"

Chapter Eight

On the Serene Way

The Long Road was the collective name for a string of government-sanctioned roads that ran like rivers from the northern borders of Suyoram to the deep south, ending with the Capital on the bay. Ex hated the high traffic, the roving bandits, and the nosy royal patrol. Above all, he despised the sheer audacity of cutting straight through nature regardless of what was there before.

That being said, it had benefited the country, as well as the guild. Historically, the Phi Hunter Guild's largest commission had been to kill the spirits that were disturbed by the enormous public work, the defining work of that old king's life. *All* spirits, not just phi. Violent and not.

The remaining spirits in the wilderness surrounding the Long Road still remembered the massacre by the hunters' hands. They *despised* them. What the kingdom had lauded as the guild's highest honor was also their greatest shame.

But there was no denying that the road was fast, relatively safe, and straightforward. Signs clearly marked traveler inns, friendly tax-paying towns, local landmarks, and every once in a while, some kind of monument. It was the fastest way to Jinburi.

Ex avoided it as much as he could. The hunters took the Serene Way, the network of unmarked passages that wound through the forests and the countryside like vines through a fence. These weren't like the back roads throughout the kingdom. These were paths embedded within the land, meandering with respect around sacred grounds, with access to areas of interest that human construction would have surely destroyed.

The Long Road would make the best time – three days, perhaps less so if Arinya could ride faster. And it was tempting, since Ex was behind schedule. But with the queen's men searching for her, it seemed an unwise course. As Mali suggested, they decided on a combination route.

They would take the Serene Way around the most populated regions of the Long Road, then only use the Long Road through certain parts of the empty countryside. Risky, but worth it.

Arinya didn't seem to be in any rush. Ex waited impatiently outside of Mali's as the witch loaded their bags with tinctures and snacks. The extra supplies came out of their trade agreement, of course, and Arinya's first payment offset some of it. Yet Ex couldn't shake the feeling that he'd somehow failed in his duties.

They left on a path south from the Bent Lake, through the Emerald Forest. Now that they were alone, Ex glanced at Arinya every so often, but for the rest of the morning they rode in silence. She didn't notice, eyes alight in awe of the naturally parted forest.

"How is this possible?" Arinya finally said. "The trees seem as if they simply moved out of the way. Did they grow like that?"

"The Venara grew these paths centuries ago. They had to make many bargains and tributes to the Guardians, but it was all very peaceful. They were far more attuned to the land than humans will ever be."

"The Monkey Kingdom people?" she said, amused. "Those are folktales."

"You've seen their ruins, haven't you?" Deep in the high mountain forest, the remnants of their cities were still embedded in the trees. The stone statues they built to the Deva Hanuman, the most well-known Venara, could be found hidden amongst the cliffside. Most people wouldn't wander that far if they weren't explorers or wandering thudong monks, but there were murals in the Capital depicting the grand tales of the very human-looking monkey race. There were bones, and pieces of their weapons and armors, their shrines...

"Yes, but it's been proved they were just an ancient empire." She sounded so sure of herself. "They were less evolved, but they were still human."

"You don't believe me." Ex muttered, slumping in his saddle. It was pointless to convince city people of these things. They had to see it to believe it, and most never would. "Well, if we see any sign of the tribe, we'll pay our respects. How about that?"

"Hmm. Not only do you say they were actual monkey people, but you claim they're still around?"

"Just because they haven't moved into the Capital, you think they aren't?" After seeing the face of the Emerald Guardian, he didn't think a meta-human kingdom would be so hard to believe.

"Have you ever met one?" she asked.

"I mean, not me specifically, but I know people who have." That didn't sound at all convincing. Some elder guildsmen claimed they had, but they'd also claimed they'd traded with the Crocodile King's tribe, too. If she didn't believe there were Venara still about, he couldn't see her believing an entire empire of crocodile people once thrived under the swamp either.

She laughed. "Oh, don't pout. I'm sorry, Ex. This is all very new to me. The phi, the spirits... magic, even. The king has taken many steps to reeducate the people on what's real and what's superstition."

"If magic is new to you, then how did you find out about the ritual through Somatra?"

"Oh." She sounded surprised. "You know of him?"

"Only his name." At her quizzical look he admitted, "Because you said it."

"Ah, I did, didn't I?" She smiled. "Somatra is one of the royal physicians. He's an elder from the Khrapong province who came to the Capital long before the rebellion." She eyed him, likely thinking about the brand on his ribs. "He had always been kind to me. After I confided my fears to him, he suggested this path to find the Bent Witch. Apparently, he knew her long ago and they had a..." She smirked. "In any case, there's no witchcraft allowed in the palace."

"It must seem strange," Ex said. "Life outside of the palace."

"I've only spent half of my life there," she said.

And she kept talking. With her big secret out, she had no resistance to sharing. She hadn't lied, she said – she was born in Sapphrachorn, her father was a fisherman who also worked the rice fields and supported her mother and two sisters in a humble cottage. But when the Grey Pox plague passed through, both her parents grew deathly ill, and it was up to her and her sisters to work. That put her at least eight years older than Ex.

She didn't elaborate on the type of work. They scraped by, though it'd been a hard life. Then, one day, the prince and his entourage stopped in her town on their way to a diplomatic mission. The townspeople put on a show for him, in which she performed. She caught his eye. That night, he sent for her, and they "talked" for hours. He asked her to come with him, and she never looked back.

"So, you were a dancer?"

She glared at him. "Do you think dancing is the only type of performance? I was a muay-boran fighter! That's how I earned money for my family."

"Oh." Now her perfect front kick to Girthy's jewels made more sense. "You were a buffalo girl."

"Yes," she said with an air of pride. "Not that I disrespect the work of my sisters. I just discovered I didn't have the temperament to please strangers and could earn more money in the ring than I did in the brothel."

"And you joined the prince's entourage as his champion, not as a consort?" Ex snuck a glance over, noting the toned muscles in her arms and legs with a new appreciation.

"At least at first. He intended for me to perform for his court at events, but..." She shrugged. "Love happened, I suppose."

Ex was about to ask what she meant by "suppose," but her face had fallen in a way that made him uncomfortable. He bit his tongue, and they rode in silence for a long while.

Around noon, they came upon a stream with a bridge created by two fallen tree trunks, secured to either bank with a web of vines. While Brownie and Ramble had a drink, Arinya sat in the shade, fanning herself in the savage heat. Ex took off his boots and wandered into the stream, enjoying the feel of the smooth rocks beneath his feet. Tiny silver fish pecked at his toes. He splashed water on his face, hoping it would wake him up. Normally, he'd be asleep during this time of day.

"So it is true," she called to him, waving a paper fan below her chin. "This heat doesn't bother you at all, does it?"

Ex wasn't suffering near as badly. After a certain stage of their training, hunters lost the ability to feel temperature. It wasn't by design, but rather a side effect of the Maijep Trial, one of the most important rites of passage.

After the ritual, if successful, a hunter no longer felt pain. Ex remembered standing in the kitchen of the guild hall with his hand on the stove, staring in wonder as his skin burned. Then Elder Nokai found him and beat him over the head. *Even if you don't feel,* he'd chided him, *the body remembers. You should too.* He marched Ex down to the Hall of Remembrance and made him memorize the names of every single hunter that had died after neglecting their injuries.

"I wouldn't mind it," Ex said. "Cold water on hot skin makes a dip in the stream far more refreshing. And it can be hard to tell when your body's had enough. I can't tell you how many times I've passed out without realizing I had heat stroke."

Arinya laughed. "I'll keep an eye on you then. How would I know?"

"When I start panting like a dog." Ex squatted down to inspect the rocks, pushing about pebbles for signs of the Venara tribe. You could find their arrowheads in the water sometimes, or even jewelry leftover from the tributes they'd paid to the water spirits. Water spirits loved shiny things.

If he'd been alone, he might jump into the Everpresent to see if there were any traces of useful spirits. There were some he always kept an eye out for, lesser creatures that were only game. But he wasn't wearing his coat, and felt acutely self-conscious about going in when Arinya could see. He glanced back at her, but she only stared across the stream to the other bank with mixture of awe and trepidation.

"Ex," she whispered, fan frozen mid-flutter.

Across the stream, a brown-furred fox half the size of a horse stared at them from the woods, eyes glowing a bright blue. Tufts of long fur sprouted from his ears, which curled back in aggression behind two razor-sharp horns. He took two steps out in a low crouch, head down, ready to spring. Ex's bow was stashed on Ramble, and all he carried was his skinning knife. Obviously, he had magic if it came down to it. But the spirit wouldn't attack unless he was defending his territory.

Or starving. And he looked a bit skinny.

Ex drifted into the Everpresent. Like animals, these spirits couldn't speak, but they could communicate to an extent. The two considered each other in silence, and an intrusive, external image came to Ex – a bestial, lurking version of himself with a sinister grin, fingers curled into blood-covered claws. But it flitted in his awareness with an inquisitive tone. Was he one of those human killers? A poacher, a monster who took pleasure in murder for sport?

Sometimes, but not for fun, Ex replied, while visualizing an angry phi attacking him in the dark, thirsty for his blood.

The fox spirit's flattened ears slowly raised.

Ex imagined the two of them standing peacefully together, side by side, both at the stream with their heads down for a drink. And then himself and Arinya climbing back on the horses and riding away.

The fox spirit lifted his head, showing off an old scar on the side of his neck. Scars on his feet from traps.

Ex reassured him again and tipped his head, taking a step back with open palms.

Finally, the fox glanced back to the woods, then walked down to the water.

A female sambar deer stepped out from the trees, a slender doe with a stripe of blue fur shadowing her gently glowing white eyes. She gazed at the two humans before joining her friend.

Another animal spirit followed them, this one much smaller. His horns curled upward, and his tail was long and fluffy like the fox, while his legs were longer and slender, like the deer. He looked at who Ex presumed was his mother, then his father, both drinking from the stream, then came up beside them.

"How is that possible?" Arinya whispered to herself, and from his half-awareness in the Everpresent, Ex could her as clear as if she were speaking loudly. He walked back to her slowly, then sat down and watched them.

He felt her fingers in his hair and froze, wondering what she was doing. Then, with a sharp tug, she plucked a tiny strand of his hair and held it in front of her face. It was silvery grey, reminding him he was still half away. He returned to the Blinds. The strand of his hair followed, even while detached from his head, back to the usual black.

"That's remarkable," she said, twirling it around. She flicked it away and stared at the spirits. "How is it possible? Two different animals breeding?"

"Probably the same way as usual."

She shot over a withering glance, and he bit back a smile.

"I figured that," she said, "but biologically, is it magic? You're going to say magic."

"I wouldn't call it that. It's their nature. Elder Nokai... He's one of the great guild masters, the most venerable, and the one who trained me in the Everpresent. He says spirits aren't limited by human imagination. Magic is just another word for things beyond that. Harnessing the natural energy that crosses beyond those limits."

"Human imagination," she murmured with a smile, and they watched the spirits disappear back into the untouched forest.

By the time the sun set, Ex could hardly keep his eyes open. Days had passed since he last slept, and in that time, he'd used more spells than usual. Especially the soul-capture – it was a shock he hadn't passed out and had a seizure right then.

Arinya looked equally as exhausted, and he caught her nodding off a few times.

They made a fire, and she rolled out a plush bedroll with a sewn-in pillow, large enough for two. Ex marveled at it, a little jealous, but hung his hammock on the nearby trees. She insisted on making dinner with some of the supplies Mali gave them. She steamed sticky rice in a sealed pot over the fire, then fried up a handful of heavenly beef-sauce-soaked jerky, which they ate with nam pik, a garlic and pepper infused fish sauce.

"No reason to eat badly on the trail," Arinya said, satisfied with his approving "this is delicious" groans.

"I'm kinda surprised," Ex admitted, leaning back on his elbows, full and happy. "I figured you'd have personal chefs at your beck and call."

"I do now. But after my parents grew ill, I cooked for my family. My sisters were helpless in the kitchen." She smiled, but it faded as quickly as it came.

"You miss them?"

"Terribly." She took a long drink from her cup and poured another. "When the prince took me into his service, his tribute to my family helped them survive, at least a little longer. After my parents passed, my sisters left for the border." Arinya sighed, looking away. "They didn't make it."

"I'm sorry," Ex said, willfully pushing the painful memories of his own family away.

"My mother would have loved a grandchild," Arinya said, and her hand crept to the pendant around her neck. She turned it about, her face softening. "Do you think she's scared in there?"

"She's probably..." He stopped himself just in time. Being soul-captured wasn't the most pleasant experience in the world, but he had no idea what the experience would be for something that hadn't been born yet, a being without full mental capacities. He doubted there'd be very much thought at all.

When soul-captured as an adult, one was fully aware of their surroundings, yet could do nothing about it. Conscious, ethereal, somewhat cognizant of the outside world, but not completely. That depended on how translucent the vessel was.

"She's probably very cozy," he said. "Gems are the most sought-after vessel. That's what kings in ancient times wished for. The more complex, the better, which is why you see diamonds all over living artifacts. Some poor souls might get trapped in rocks, or metal, or worse. Master Seua, he climbed to the peak of the mountain and put himself in a goddamn ice statue for a month, the crazy old coot."

"Incredible. He soul-captured himself? In an ice statue?"

"His master did the ritual, but yes, it's one of our rites of passage." Ex felt a swell of pride. So many of the phi hunter traditions weren't known to the public anymore. If more people still knew, maybe they'd be more impressed and less fearful of their ways. "We have to spend a month soul-captured in a vessel. Mental stability, oneness with the Everpresent. But once you settle in, it can be serene. Some people are really depressed when they come back to the Blinds, the normal world. Others hate it. Some even leave the guild afterwards."

"So, you have done it?" Arinya leaned forward, enraptured. "Tell me what it's like!"

The excitement in her eyes made him grin.

"Well, you know when you lay awake at night and your thoughts are turning about and you can't sleep no matter how hard you try? It feels like that at first. But you aren't tired because you don't have a body. You become part of the thing. You can see in between the lines, and it's…" He squinted at the stars. How could he describe how incredible and vast the space felt, no matter how small. He couldn't find the right words. It was an entire universe. "Anyway, once I settled in, it was over before I knew it. And that's how we learn the Hunter's Trance."

Arinya drew her hand to her mouth. "That sounds horrible. Isn't there an easier way to learn it?"

"Not that I know of," Ex said with a shrug. "All the rituals we do to gain our powers are uncomfortable. But they're necessary to go through if we want to practice this trade. But, if you want to know what I really think…"

"Yes, that's all I ask," she said. "Honesty."

To be soul-captured for an eternity? Sounded like hell to him. Ex didn't say that though.

"Ah, okay, okay. I think that, um, if it were me, I wouldn't want to hang around that long. I'd probably try to escape if I had the capacity to understand what was going on. I've never seen it myself, but I've heard it's possible."

Arinya went quiet, and when he looked up, she'd gone pale. He instantly regretted his words.

"Hey, don't worry too much. You're going to have her eventually, right? I don't think a baby would leave its mother, regardless of what form it takes."

She didn't look so convinced.

"Here, let me show you something." Ex reached over to his pack and retrieved a small scrap of yellow cloth from one of the pouches.

Laying it out on the ground before her, he revealed three idols, each about half the size of a finger – A kinaree angel, a wolf totem, and a kuman thong "golden child." He pointed to each one. "This is Sarai, Armaa, and Budin. They have all been soul-captured, but of their own will."

Supposedly. This type of magic dipped more into faith. Ex had no real evidence that there was anything in the idols but a soft glow when looking at them from the Everpresent. And many things glowed in the Everpresent. Flowers glowed too, sometimes even rocks.

"When kinaree, or other devas, decide to leave their realm, they often settle into these forms. You've probably seen the statues everywhere. Just like the ones of the Enlightened Lord. Humans put them up like empty houses, hoping a deva might manifest."

To his delight, she scooted to sit beside him and reached over to pick Sarai up. She studied the kinaree's bare-chested female form, a one-tiered crown on her head, bird wings and feet from the waist down.

"I've seen these statues in the old city shrines. They're beautiful," Arinya said.

Ex handed her the wolf next. "Armaa is a spirit who Master Exaran, one of the First Hunters, met in the Cloud Forest. He asked for Exaran's help to fight an invasion of demons. In exchange, Armaa offered to travel with her for protection. Master Seua gave me this charm after I killed my first phi."

"And that's why the Hound follows you?"

"Not at all," Ex said quickly, glancing around to make sure the Hound didn't hear that. If he was near, he didn't show himself. "He comes and goes, does what he wants. Sometimes I don't see him for weeks."

"How fascinating." She put Armaa down and picked up the last one, a lacquered gold idol in the shape of a strange little boy with an oversized head and a big, mischievous smile. "And who is this is cute little guy?"

"Budin. He's a kuman thong, which is similar to..." Ex eyed her necklace. "He's made by cutting a stillborn fetus out of his mother, which then goes through a graveyard ritual where they roast the bones over a pit and then cover with a lacquer–"

"Black magic!" Arinya gasped, dropping him. She shoved the group of idols back towards Ex and wiped her hand on her pants. "It's forbidden."

"Yes," he said slowly, afraid to spook her even more. "It's black magic, and the ritual is a little..." He waved his hand in a sideways motion. "Problematic. But–"

"You made it?!"

"No, no, no," he said quickly. "It's hundreds of years old, probably made by a necromancer way back. We don't practice that type of magic, and neither do most low magic users anymore. But we come across these artifacts sometimes. Especially in the old country."

She glanced from the kuman thong to her gemstone with mounting horror. Ex fought the urge to get defensive about it. Magic was hard to explain to people who didn't use it. Instead, he picked up a few leftover grains of rice and placed them in front of the golden child, flicking away the old cashews crumbs that had been in the pouch with him before.

"Budin's body was dead in the womb. He wouldn't have lived. Your girl was, *is*, very much alive. And what we did was a completely different ritual. A soul-capture is grey magic – spirit magic. Black magic is from dark rituals, drawn from the low realm. And it's not inherently evil. You saw what Mali did to that soldier to protect us, right? Great at the time, in another context, not so good."

Arinya relaxed a shade, but still considered Ex warily, as if he'd grown three new eyes. "I suppose she did do that in self-defense. Does that mean all sorcerers use black magic too?"

He wasn't sure about that. Sorcerers gained their power from certain rituals, which could be considered constructive or destructive. They could perform hexes and curses to varying degrees of success, but you couldn't actually *see* these things, unless you were in the Everpresent.

The stronger ones could use some spells, like the sorcerer they encountered. Ex never studied new magic, so he didn't know. Some of the Master Hunters would know, especially Master Rei, as she was the one that dealt with the public when needed. Ex just knew sorcerer magic was nothing like their own. The hunters borrowed power from the Everpresent and brought it within, to change themselves. And they gave back tributes of their own energy to maintain a balance, which high magic users did not.

He wasn't sure how to explain it, so he just said, "Maybe. Some of them. Probably."

Her eyes darted as if calculating sums. What was going through her mind? Was it about him? Or maybe someone she knew? Finally, she shook her head. "There's so much they teach us that isn't true, I guess. At least from what I've seen."

"How do you feel about it?" Avoiding Arinya's gaze while he folded up the idols, sure to give them equal space from one another, Ex held his breath. Everything he believed in, and the only thing he knew anything about and had stupidly bragged on... Did it disgust her?

"I'm not sure, but it's fascinating," she said. He let out a soft sigh of relief. "This is another world I never realized existed. Honestly, I had my doubts as to whether Mali would be able to help me at all."

She'd been truly desperate then, and he felt worse for being so uncooperative at first.

"What would you have done?" he ventured to ask.

Arinya stared at her amulet. "I'm not sure. Perhaps tried to find a family to take her in. I admit I hadn't thought it through completely." Her eyes grew distant, and she put a hand on her belly. "Somatra told me that I'd have to find someone to perform a ritual to return her to my womb again. And until then, I would have to protect this gem. He said that if it's destroyed, her soul would go along with it."

Ex nodded solemnly. Destroying a vessel would surely kill whatever being was trapped inside, which made Master Seua's legendary feat all the more insane.

She glanced at him. "I suppose I may be able to call on you when the time comes?"

He opened his mouth to protest, but realized he'd already gone too far by performing the ritual in the first place. It was his responsibility now, whether he liked it or not.

"Of course," he said, and smiled at her visible relief.

After some silence, only punctuated by insects and the crackling fire, she placed a hand on his arm. "Hey, Ex." When he met her eyes, her lips curled into a smile. "I never judge anyone for what they believe, or where they come from. You decided to help me when you didn't have to, and for that I'm grateful."

She left her hand on his arm, and he stared at the fire dancing over her face. Her smile widened, and he noticed a little scar under her bottom lip. Likely from her days in the ring. She was still staring at him, as if expecting him to do something. Hesitantly, he leaned his head closer, tilting it a little and hoped she'd meet him.

Nope.

She drew her neck back, scrunched like a turtle, and blinked rapidly in the awkward silence.

"Uh, um, oh, I thought there was something behind you," he stammered and leant in further to stare over her shoulder at the trees. "Ha-ha, nope, nothing."

Only a few good branches where he could hang himself.

"Oh, okay." She bit her lip, a blush blossoming on her cheeks, then averted her attention anywhere else. "Whew. I didn't think the forest would be this cold at night. The fire's nice. It's quite warm."

Feeling like a complete idiot, Ex forced a yawn, then jumped to his feet. "Well, I'm exhausted, we should get some rest. Long day tomorrow. Goodnight!" Without elaboration, he retreated to his hammock, cursing himself every step of the way.

"Goodnight, Ex," she called.

He could swear the last thing he heard before passing out was the Hound snickering from the trees.

Chapter Nine

On the Long Road

His body is small, and after he sees his hands, he knows he's dreaming. He's home again. His mother is in the garden, digging, but he doesn't want to go over, he doesn't want to see. But she calls him. He tries to go the other way, wants to turn this dream into something else, anything else. There's fire at the edge of the village, burning despite the rain, trapping him here. He stands next to her, and she tells him to reach into the hole. There are weapons, a pile of weapons. Take these to your father, she says. When he looks back from the road, there are knives in her belly, and demons standing over her. One of them points at him and a ball of fire erupts from its hand.

Ex woke up grinding his teeth. The sun hadn't come up yet, painting the forest in soft colors, a haze over the grass and the fresh smell of dew, a dove cooing. Arinya was still asleep by the smoldering fire, clutching the gem to her chest as if it were a stuffed animal. Though she looked perfectly peaceful, he sensed a readiness about her. Maybe there was an added maternal protectiveness now, or maybe she was always on alert. From what she told him of her past, he could imagine her sleeping with one eye open.

He walked into the trees to take a piss, trying his best not to replay the scene from his childhood. Every once in a while, he had a pleasant dream, but those were few and far between. Usually, he saw his home in various states of attack. Sometimes it was a fire, sometimes it was a flood, sometimes it was demons, or bandits, or even giant cobras...

But most of the time it was a reflection of reality. The King's army.

Mid-piss, Ex let his gaze drift up to the canopy. Five tiny monkeys sat in the trees, picking lice out of each other's fur. One of the small ones peeked down at him, its big eyes dark and pure. He waved, but the monkey didn't wave back. The big one stopped. After they stared each other down for a few seconds, the animal leapt back into the canopy. The rest of his tribe followed.

Phi hunters didn't have the same connection with animals that they had with spirits.

Then Ex noticed an old mark carved into the tree, stretched out from growth. Two lines of five claw marks, raked across one another. A mark of the Venara. Excited, he peered around for any other artifacts, something he could show Arinya. But no, nothing else. He could show her the marks, but then he deflated, already imaging her reaction. Probably a tiger, she might say, a tiger that would take offense to him pissing on his tree.

Arinya was awake when he returned, rubbing sleep from her face.

"Good morning," she said. "Sleep well?"

"Like a baby." Ex brought up the fire for the teapot. It was hard for him to make eye contact after his idiotic move last night. "You?"

"Perfectly well. For the first time in weeks," she said, brushing her hair. "It must be these woods. They feel quite different than the ones I traveled through."

"They are different," he said. The Venara had cleared at least this patch of the Serene ages ago, judging by their marks. Or that angry tiger could be lurking about.

She cleared her throat. "About last night."

"Sorry," he blurted, relieved for the opening. "I completely misread. It won't happen again."

"No, really, it's fine," she reassured him, casually. "Please don't hold anything back. I didn't mean to seem critical."

He stared at her, uncomprehending. Did he misread what he misread? She tilted her head with a cute squint of her eyes, as if amused he didn't remember.

"About the black magic?" she said.

Oh. Right. *That.*

"I admit it frightens me a bit. It feels like I've traveled through a door I can't return from. But from everything I've seen so far, I understand that it's not all evil. Meeting you and Mali proves there is much more to learn than what I've been taught."

"Oh." Again, feeling like an idiot, he took a long sip of tea. Master Seua would probably tell him that he'd dug a deep enough hole, and might as well lean in. "I get it. It's not your world. I'd probably feel the same way if I went to court, trying to talk to the king, I guess. Or the prince." He peered at her out of the side of his eye, "Or the prince's consort."

She rolled her eyes and laughed, to his relief. "It wouldn't be that easy."

"What would I have to do?"

"For starters, you'd need to impress my husband."

"Would guarding his runaway wife and potential heir from assassins and monsters be enough?"

"It would be for me," she smiled, which he slowly returned. "For my husband, I doubt he'd let me around a man like you." Ex liked the way she said it, even if sounded like an insult. "But," she shrugged, "I wouldn't blame him for trying."

They left it there and packed up. As he helped her onto Brownie, he thought he caught a small bit of sadness in her eyes.

It'd been a long time since Ex had someone to talk to, and someone so quick and playful, at that. In exchange for his lesson in magic, she told him about life in the palace. No, she didn't have to want for anything, but it was full of social climbers and intrigue – things Ex would never encounter out in the wild. He said as much, and she asked if the phi had any sort of social life. Maybe they did have a court? Maybe hunters just weren't invited.

Arinya's teasing was all good-humored, he soon realized. She must have thought he was an insolent child when they first met. But he could play along now.

By midday, they had turned from the Serene to take a back road. The loss of that surrounding in exchange for the human-made path doused him with unease. Arinya sagged in her saddle, and gazed back at the path to the Serene. The trees had already grown over to conceal the way.

As they approached the Long Road, the Emerald Forest faded away into dotted, nameless woods. Signs of logging and trapping could be seen from all around, eventually petering out into grasslands of the central plains. Mahout workers rode on the heads of elephants as they towed equally large wagons of logs behind them. Thankfully, the elephants seemed well treated, no signs of tears flowing from their eyes like some of the ones he'd seen in the city, forced to do tricks for the benefit of their owners.

They passed several villages, farmers pausing from their toil in the rice paddies to stare. Some of them recognized the crest on his coat and tipped their hats in respect. Others spat at their feet, making a circle gesture at their chests with their fingers – a sign of protection. They passed lines of thudong, strolling monks clad in saffron robes, wandering ascetics that were not part of the Sangha.

Arinya kept her hood down, especially when passing people on the road. She said she doubted they'd recognize her this far out in the country, but Ex knew she stuck out. If the queen's men came around asking if anyone had seen a beautiful woman traveling with a strange man, he doubted anyone would deny it, especially under threat of torture. (He'd actually said "overdressed aristocrat" instead of "beautiful woman," but he thought she caught his meaning.)

It was obvious where the country road ended and the Long Road began. It was five times as wide, the ground firmly beaten down. At some points, rock walls framed either side, with wooden markers every fifty miles. On the markers, alongside the symbol of the king, the public works had written the current province, and directions to any areas of interest.

At this particular juncture, a few merchant stalls dotted the corner, and the glorious smell of cooked meat filled Ex's mouth with saliva. An elder woman walked by, carrying a basket full of ant eggs, trailed by a flock of peacocks. She smiled at the two of them and offered her bounty for a low price, but Ex preferred whatever was making his mouth water at the provincial market.

It would be risky to stop, but a quick glance at Arinya confirmed that they both needed to eat whatever was making them drool, consequences be damned. They dropped off the horses next to the trough for travelers by two others, and he had to stop a boy from hitching them up. He allowed him to brush them down, though, and pick their hooves for pebbles.

After Arinya haggled at an old man's food stand, they carried their bowls of chicken and chili basil fried noodles to an empty seat. A serving girl not older than eight brought over cups of young coconut water, much needed to combat the heavily spiced dish. By the time she arrived, Ex had already finished his plate.

"You have an appetite," Arinya observed and politely swirled her fork around the noodles, as if searching for the perfect one.

He stared at her plate, then his empty one. "Magic makes you hungry." That wasn't really true, but wasn't a bad excuse for his lack of manners. "I don't get to eat much like this on the trail."

"Then what do you eat when you tromp around in the woods for three months?"

"Tromp? Hunters don't tromp. I have a very light step, actually."

"Oh, of course, I agree. You're quite graceful."

"Graceful?" He didn't know if he liked being called graceful.

"You know what I mean. You told me you don't hunt animals, only spirits, and that spirits taste terrible."

"Well, we forage. And only hunt animals if we have to. The wilderness is an eternal feast if you know where to look. And I fast a lot, too." Ex downed his coconut water in one long swig, hoping she'd change the subject. He didn't want her to think he was even more broke than she already did. Thankfully, the Hound hadn't left his scraps for him around the camp last night, a favor he usually anticipated.

"Hmm. Seeing as I cooked last night, I'm intrigued by this foraging."

Ex inwardly groaned and turned his attention towards the people hanging around. A handful of locals smelling of grass and old wood sat on fallen logs as they ate lunch, not giving Ex and Arinya a second glance. There were two other men apart from them, obviously travelers. One had an arquebus on a strap across his back and two daggers at his waist. The other was a much older man with long fingernails, probably never held a weapon in his life.

They wore floral patterned silk and sat smoking cigarettes. They appeared to be YinsengI – both had lighter skin and narrower eyes than the average Suyoram citizen.

From what Ex knew of Yinseng, they'd always been too

busy warring with the steppe tribes to bother Suyoram. After a failed invasion a hundred years ago, they'd left the country to fight amongst themselves. They weren't uncommon to see in the trading cities, and especially the Capital, but Ex hadn't encountered many on the road. Then again, he stayed mostly on the Serene, and it was uncommon to see any humans there at all.

"They can't be merchants," he said. Their horses weren't laden with goods.

"Likely messengers, judging by their colors."

Ex must have looked alarmed because she shook her head and waved dismissively.

"For business. A diplomat would not have stopped so casually."

"Why's that?"

"If their emperor found out that they'd stopped for a casual meal, he'd cut off their feet for dallying. He's not a man to defy. Even more of an egomaniac than our own king."

That was the first time he'd heard Arinya speak ill of the crown. "Do you feel that way about the prince too?"

She popped a piece of chicken in her mouth. After she was done chewing, she finished off her coconut water, then said, "He's still young. He has the capacity to change."

Ex wasn't convinced, but he kept that to himself.

Night fell quickly on the Long Road. Ex hadn't noticed any soldiers about as they journeyed. Only a few groups of travelers who wanted to be noticed even less than them, and a couple of trading caravans with bored guards who cast him an eye. He was used to getting those looks, but he still felt nervous. That damn sorcerer was still out there, and he probably thought Ex had sealed his magic away forever. It would come back soon, probably, but Ex wouldn't be surprised if he pursued the young hunter to the ends of the earth, just for the insult.

Normally, if the horses weren't tired, he would press on. But it was easier to ride faster on the Long Road, and the horses had been trotting for much of the trip. Ramble snorted every time Ex pushed him over a cantor, and by the end of it, he wanted to throw Ex off. Neither of them were used to traveling so fast. It would be nice to get far enough to find a better campground, but it was clear everyone had had enough.

"There's a tavern up ahead," Arinya said, pointing towards a signpost. "I remember the name. Cobra's Rest. I passed it on my way here."

"Cobra's Rest? Sounds *real* friendly." Ex glanced off the road, towards the countryside. It wasn't quite grasslands and it wasn't quite woods. More of a swampy thicket. "I think we'll be better off out there."

"You told me the spirits hated hunters around the Long Road." She fidgeted with her pendant, frowning as she gazed into the dark.

"I can deal with them," he said, though the thought wasn't appealing. "They'll probably just heckle and scream all night and try to keep us awake."

"You said they attacked all the time."

Dammit, he did say that. But it was mostly to impress her.

"It's only a problem if phi are around, and I'm sure the ground's been cleared recently." He actually had no idea, and searched the trees for marks.

She seemed worried, and when he thought about it, they had near enough the same chance of getting into trouble inside the tavern as outside. Maybe less so. A wandering, vengeful phi was one thing for a hunter, but if it went after Arinya, or the soul-captured child... That pendant probably smelled as delicious as the noodles they ate earlier.

Ex chewed on his lip, considering Arinya, then the lights from the tavern, then the woods, and back. Her eyes were so big and hopeful, her smile adorably sweet.

"Fine. Let's see what Cobra's Rest has to offer." He thought about his last bar experience, and was not sure if his ego could deal with Arinya acting as protector again. "We'll just keep our heads down."

Ex expected a provincial village hangout full of bigoted farmers, or a seedy watering hole for bandits and sellswords, sweaty men cursing at each other, itching for any reason to start a fight with a pale mountain boy. But as soon as they opened the door, it felt much stranger.

An ominous hum filled the room. Thick as a fog, the heady stink of sandalwood incense made him sneeze. The tables were arranged in a circle around a fighting pit. Rather than a muay-boran match or cock fight, seven Sangha monks in saffron robes sat in the pit facing outward, legs crossed, eyes shut, hands on their knees. The origin of the "ohm" came from them, and all the other patrons had their heads down. They held their hands in their laps, or in wais to their foreheads. It was a rougher crowd for sure. Most carried weapons in plain view, wearing varying types of clothes, some armored. They sat in packs that clearly indicated whether you belonged or not, but there were no uniforms, except for the monks.

Still, the guided meditation united everyone, even the middle-aged woman with face tattoos running the bar and her shirtless ox of a husband. It felt like they'd intruded on something private, like wandering into the privy during a meeting between forbidden lovers.

Arinya and Ex exchanged a nervous glance, then she quietly slid onto a bench at an empty table. He walked to the serving counter and waited for the prayer to end.

After a while, he wondered if it ever would.

Another few minutes passed as he tried to peer into the kitchen, where an enticing aroma of seasoned beef made his mouth water. Then one of the lead monks spoke in a chant-like monotone, in ancient devaskrit. Like most laymen, Ex had no idea what was said. But with the final three "satu," that everyone knew and mumbled along to, the room collectively returned to the present.

"Didn't see you there, son." The innkeeper spoke in a bouncing island accent, probably from the Kutsu Aisles. Her quick eyes hovered on his badge, then darted to Arinya at the table and back. "Room's twenty bits."

"Twenty?" His jaw dropped. "That's highway robbery, mam."

"Weren't you paying attention, hunter? The Sangha just blessed the whole place for the night. Prices go up."

"Bullshit. There's no phi lurking around here. Trust me, I checked."

"You calling my wife a liar?" the big ox enforcer boomed, arms crossed, with the hint of the west in his voice. There was a scar on his chest – a raised brand, dark and old, but deep. It was the mark of anyone who survived the Uprising of the Relentless Rains in the mountain province, and the purge of traitorous rebels afterwards. Surprising that he'd show the mark in public.

Most citizens would instantly distrust a man with such a mark, even though it was given by the crown as a sign of forgiveness. It marked those who hadn't themselves been rebels, but were unfortunate enough to have been guilty by association.

Just like Ex.

"Certainly not, cousin. Though we're closer to brothers," he responded. At the big man's sneer, Ex unbuckled the bottom of his coat, then pulled up his shirt to reveal the same brand on his ribs. Both the man and his wife raised their eyebrows, and the ox lifted his chin with a glare of disbelief. Ex told him the name of his village and the man's eyes softened. He glanced at his wife.

"I'll cover him for the night, sweetie. Would you get the cook to bring him and his woman a hot meal?"

Her face softened as well when she made the connection.

She smiled betel-nut-stained red teeth. "The good stuff then?" While she walked back into the kitchen, the man poured Ex a cup of ale.

"My name's Mu, and that's Ting. What's your name, kid?"

"Ex." He could tell Mu knew it wasn't his given name, but he nodded all the same.

"You're too young to have been part of it. Your parents, then?"

"My father was killed, and older brother. My mother," Ex stared into the drink. "I lost track of her. Sold into slavery, I think."

"Barbaric. Only monsters would mark an innocent child for his father's sins." Mu poured himself one. "I was a young man back then. We were just fruit farmers, mostly mangosteens, rumbatan, bananas, that sort of thing. I didn't like the new laws, but I minded my own business. My uncle had other plans for the harvest. Supplied the rebels." He took a quick drink, then said, "And yours?"

"My parents were hunters. I didn't know they were hunting more than game." Ex laughed humorlessly, swirling his ale around before taking a slow sip.

"It's not something to be ashamed of. At least not on this stretch of the Long Road. If anything, I get more respect."

"Well, I don't need respect for something I didn't do. I'd rather get respect for this." He tapped his badge.

Mu snorted. "Respected by who? Don't get me wrong, I'm from the mountains, I've seen phi hunters' work. But respect from the crown? Last I heard, they were trying to distance themselves from the old ways." Mu tipped his head towards the monks, who were now collecting donations of rice and coin.

Distancing themselves from the old ways looked a lot like profiteering. Ex couldn't really judge them though. The Sangha's wards and blessings *did* work to some extent, but they didn't last, and needed to be reapplied constantly. They didn't permanently solve the problem like phi hunters did.

"If you despise the crown so much, why do you welcome in the Sangha?"

"It's profitable," he said, "and I care less about the crown than I do the spirits."

"If you actually had a troublesome phi around here, I could make sure they didn't come back." Ex gave him a smirk. Mu returned it and rubbed his fingers together. He supposed there was no reason the innkeeper shouldn't profit off people's superstitions too.

"To profits," he said and raised his glass. They drank to that.

Ting returned with two steaming bowls of braised beef bo kho stew and a key to a room. Mu threw in an extra bottle of rice wine. Ex thanked them both and returned to Arinya, who, to his disappointment, was talking with one of the Sangha. Once Ex sat down next to the monk, it was clear she was moreso being talked *at*. The young monk was so enthralled in his own speech that he didn't notice Ex's arrival.

"…the complete severance of such earthly pleasures was found to have been the cause of neurosis, blocking us from the Enlightened Lord. Our Holy Abbot saw this, then decreed that all ordained men must partake on the second night of the full moon."

"I see," Arinya caught Ex's eye and winked, turning her ironic wonder back to the monk. "And every one of you 'partake'? For one night?"

"No, uh, not on the same night. My older brothers have ascended to practice on the new moon. I'm still in training." His smile curled into a toothless grin. "Those that join in the ritual are twice blessed."

"They're twice blessed for the night of the ritual, or from then on, for the month?"

"For the night, although if the ritual is especially, ah, taxing, it's possible the blessing will last longer." He held his hand out, on the table. "If you let me see your palm, I will check if your soul is attuned for a longer blessing."

Ex held back the urge to smack the man on the back of the head, where it was still raw from a fresh shave. Instead, he snorted, and took another chug of wine before starting on the stew. Arinya stifled a giggle and placed her open hand on the table.

"Oh, I see, I see." The lecherous monk ran his finger ever so lightly across the small lines of her palm. Even Ex knew the Sangha weren't allowed to touch women, and especially not a small, creepy gesture like that. "Your soul is very, *very* attuned."

"How much does this ritual cost?"

"For you, since this is the first one, free of charge."

"Should we seek permission from your master?"

"Oh, no, no. That won't be necessary." He was drooling now, and the stink of his arousal made Ex hold back a gag. The bench practically shifted from the weight of the creep's erection. "I have everything I need to perform it myself. We need only to retire to your room–"

"How about it, dear?" Arinya said to Ex with a smile. "Shall we take this penitent man up on his offer?"

Ex froze, noodles halfway slurped up. The monk glanced over for the first time and recoiled. Taking Arinya's cue, the hunter slung his arm heavily across the monk's shoulders. He gave the man's shaved head a slow rub while slowly sucking up the rest of his bite.

"That depends," Ex said, smacking his lips. "How does the ritual work? One at a time? Or all together?"

"I, uh, uh," the man stammered and wilted under his arm. "I'm sorry, but the blessing doesn't work on whisp..." he stopped just shy of calling him something rude. Rude for a monk, at least. "I mean to say, it only works on women."

"Why is that?" Arinya asked. The gleam in her eye telegraphed her amusement.

"I'm glad you asked. Women are born into samsara and cannot obtain enlightenment, and so their souls must be refilled with karma twice more than a man–"

"Why?"

"Well, you must be born again as man, first."

Ex gave him his best pout. "So why can't *I* be blessed? I was born a man."

"But you're not a, a..," The monk floundered, turning to Arinya for help, but she only beamed.

"Human?" Ex said, chewing rudely with his mouth open. "Whispers need rituals too. And you smell like you're very, very eager."

Arinya covered her mouth but laughed anyway. With a flustered face, the monk squirmed from Ex's grasp, rearranged his robes and stormed off. Ex wondered if he would try his luck on another woman, which turned his stomach. He slid Arinya her bowl of stew and shook his head.

"Enjoying yourself?"

"That was amusing, wasn't it?" she said, watching the monks make their rounds. "It always amazes me how much people reveal when given the opportunity. I've never had a member of the Sangha approach me so brazenly."

"It's probably just that one." Ex cast the abbot a wary glance, but saw in his kindly, wrinkled face nothing but devotion to his order. The elder brought his palms together in thanks after a bandit dropped a handful of coins in their basket, murmuring a prayer and flicking a dollop of holy water over the bandit's head. "I wouldn't be surprised if that guy offered these unsanctioned 'rituals' to every pretty girl traveling alone."

Shit, did he say that?

"Good thing I'm with a pretty boy," Arinya said with a snicker. "However would I have resisted his charms?"

Chapter Ten

The Target

They put their bags down in the one room they'd been given, a room with just one bed. Mu must have had the wrong idea. He'd assumed that Ex and Arinya were together, even though Ex had made it clear he'd been branded. He figured anyone would take one look at the two and determine there was nothing going on there. Ex was a phi hunter, and the lifestyle didn't lend itself to marriage. That's not to say they were ascetic like the Sangha (or like the Sangha were supposed to be). Some of his fellow guildsmen had their post-hunt habits and told him he should seek company more often. Even Master Seua said so, just one more thing to tease him about.

Ex lingered in the doorway while Arinya jumped on the mattress, hitting it with a resounding thump. "Oi. I think it's harder than the ground," she groaned, then peered up at him. "That should make you feel more at ease, right?"

"I doubt I'll be getting any sleep – I mean, because I don't need to yet." Ex already regretted the second bottle of wine. He was quite tired at this point.

She raised an eyebrow.

"I'll sleep on the floor," he said. The two remaining feet of floor between the bed and the wall.

"Oh, there's no need," she said with a smile in her eyes. She rolled to her side and propped her chin on her hand. "I trust you aren't planning any rituals."

Ex laughed, but inched towards the big, open-air window for escape. "We don't do those kinds of 'blessings.'" Her flirting was just one of those courtly habits, he told himself. It didn't mean anything. Suddenly, he wished he had taken that offer of the blacksmith's daughter's company.

"What kind of blessings do you do?"

"Um, none with any lasting effect. It's better not to get tied to any particular place," he said, then told himself to shut the fuck up, to no avail. "That kind of magic lasts, you know? You have to nurture it and feed it like the kuman thong. Blessings and wards need to be maintained, given tribute, fed... If not, that little bastard might twist around and haunt you."

In the silence that followed, he instantly regretted bringing up black magic. Running a hand over his eyes, he tried to wipe the drunk out of his head, then sat down on the edge of the bed. "Sorry to mention that again."

But she didn't seem bothered, only thoughtful. "I was wondering. Do you think I need to feed Isaree?" Arinya held her necklace up. It surprised him that she'd given it a name. *Her* a name.

"As long as the mother eats, I think it's similar a thing to if she were still... you know." Ex pointed to her belly, which hadn't receded fully yet. "That was a lot of stew you ate. *We* ate." He waved his hand dismissively. "I never got hungry when I was soul-captured. It's fine."

With a bright gleam in her eyes, she suddenly leaned forward. "Can you speak with her? In your Everpresent?"

That seemed like a horrible idea.

"Nah, it'd be like goggling at a sleeping baby." Probably. If it wasn't, that would be an awkward conversation he wasn't ready to have. Besides, he'd been in the Everpresent with the amulet nearby and didn't detect any kind of conscious presence emanating from it.

"Maybe it's pointless, but I don't know." She sounded as if she felt guilty. "I did the same thing when she was in my belly…" Her voice arrested, and she went quiet again.

That would have been a good time to say something. Anything. Words of comfort, for a start. Instead, he twiddled his thumbs, then laid back on the bed, at the most respectful distance.

She turned down the lantern, leaving them in the moonlight from the window. "Goodnight, Ex."

"Goodnight, Arinya." He said, and closed his eyes, pretending to sleep.

The full moon lit the edges of the world in a silver sheen. In the dark, it was as clear as day – grey-blue, sometimes violet. The room's wide window allowed the light to catch on Arinya's unbound hair, the curve of her hips under the light silk blanket. She had fallen asleep almost immediately, and minutes later, rolled over to the center of the bed. His breath caught when her hand eased onto his pillow, brushing the side of his head ever so slightly.

Slowly, he peered over, wondering if she was actually asleep. A content smile twitched the side of her lips and she sighed, her breathing slow and steady. As her floral scent filled the small space between them, Ex's imagination started to run wild. If she rolled over again, she'd be on top of him. And then came the intrusive, carnal image of her gazing down at him from above, strong legs astride his hips, that mischievous smile twisting into a cry of pleasure…

Ex bolted the door and took the window outside, desperate for some air. He carefully climbed down from the ledge and then leaned against the wall, taking slow, deep breaths. Even sharing a bed with the prince's consort likely carried a death penalty, never mind if she woke up and, for some crazy reason, wanted to sample a son of rebel scum. He knew he could escape from his racing, lewd thoughts by leaving the Blinds.

In the Everpresent, he gazed at the softly glowing heartbeats of sleeping patrons in their rooms. Some of them made love, hearts beating faster as they moved together. Where it may have been sensual in the Blinds, in here it was only nature. A few more people lingered in the common room, though their hearts beat slower. Too drunk to move, really. He might have been one of them if left to his own devices.

A translucent glisten of high magic coated the tavern, like fresh rain. The Sangha had done a decent job. No doubt a strong enough phi would be able to force itself through. But when Ex stared out into the sparse woodlands, a stone monolith set with the royal symbol bore the cleared mark of the hunters. Moss and vines crept up and around the pillar, giving it the aura of something old and forgotten, rather than something that should put people at ease.

During his walk about, the Hound finally appeared, and trotted to his side. Thrashing his tail, he growled in displeasure at the lack of prey around the Long Road. Mortal animals didn't satisfy his hunger. Ex told him to roam on ahead, to the Jinburi Swamp, where they might find Shar-Ala. He agreed, with the hopeful sentiment of ripping out the phi's throat. The mental image of a hulking, skull-faced demon shifted and wavered, a dark cloud of hissing misery. No one really knew how Shar-Ala appeared, if he were animal or human. But the Hound's conviction was comforting, and bonded the two hunters.

Ex told him about the gift from the pret, and the Hound grunted in approval. Without another word, he trotted off. Ex stared after him, wondering if he'd leave for good after they finally killed the demon.

After a few hours of wandering, harvesting any moonlight hungry herbs and trying to meditate, Ex made his way back to the tavern, hoping there was still room for him on the bed.

Something felt off right away. A wagon had pulled up to the front, two dark-coated, hot-blooded horses were lashed to the post next to the others. Travelers arriving in the middle of the night weren't a rare thing in these types of places, yet he couldn't shake his suspicion.

The front door was ajar, so Ex peered inside. A slender figure in dark clothes stood behind the counter, bent over. Two legs stuck out from behind them, kicking and thrashing.

Ting.

Ex leapt towards them, vaulted over the counter and smashed into the figure's chest, feet first. They crashed into the wall, knocking over knickknack decorations and jugs of wine, scattering piles of dirty dishes and papers. The figure's face was shrouded but for their eyes, wild and furrowed into angry slits. Ex wound up to punch them, but they caught his fist, and then slapped him in the chest with their other hand.

The strike didn't hurt but felt like a sharp gust of wind, lifting him right off his feet and sending him sailing. His back crashed against the far wall, and then his face hit the ground. He didn't feel a shred of magic, but the attacker's sheer power stunned him. When Ex lifted his head, they were gone.

He scrambled over to Ting, whose face was already purple and her neck bent at a bad angle. A dagger lay loose in her limp hand. Her eyes bulged open, veins broken. No pulse. Fuck.

He hopped over the counter and realized that the unlucky few who hadn't made it to their rooms wouldn't make it anywhere, ever again. Including Mu, who laid facedown near the stairwell. Blood pooled across the floor, dripping from many slit necks, weapons loose in limp hands. There wasn't anything Ex could do for them, but that wasn't his largest concern.

With dread, he bounded up the stairs to their rooms. Two of the doors were open, a muffled scream and struggle coming from the dark.

Before Ex made it to the end of the hall, someone slammed into him from behind. Two skinny legs wrapped around his torso, two skinny arms around his neck.

The other one walked by – how many were there?! Now that Ex could get a better look, it seemed to be a man, wrapped head to toe in dark cloth. The shrouded figure glanced at him impassively, then followed his line of sight to the door where Arinya slept. He carried a long, thin blade, more of a razor than a knife. When he took a step towards the room, Ex's anger surged.

These were not kidnappers. They were assassins, come to kill them both.

He slammed his back to the wall – once, twice. Harder. The bony figure on his back grunted and fell.

Ex drew his hunting knife and flung it, smacking into the man's forehead, handle first. Momentarily stunned, he didn't catch Ex's fist this time. A good crack and Ex thought he'd broken his hand for a second. Wasting no time, he shoved the key in the lock and tore open the door. The blade flashed in front of him as he stumbled in and slammed it shut.

A second later, blood coursed down his neck in a torrent.

"Ex? I heard noises! What's happening?"

With one hand pressed against his slit throat, Ex held the door shut and jabbed his finger at the window. Clearly reading the urgency in his gestures, she didn't ask questions. Grabbing their packs, she tossed them out of the window but hesitated before lifting herself out.

"It's far!" she exclaimed.

It wasn't *that* far. Ex left the door to shove her out and followed right after, tumbling half-sideways, without a shred of grace. Meanwhile, she'd landed on her feet, and tugged the bags towards the horses. He tried to yell at her to forget them and run, but all he managed was a choking gurgle. All he could do was follow after her.

Ramble and Brownie knew something was wrong and were

already sputtering as they came around. Ex's head swam and he could barely hold himself up, using the hitching rail for leverage. Arinya glanced back and froze in her tracks.

"You're hurt!"

She reached for him. His fingers were going numb, but he grabbed her hand and pushed her towards Brownie. No time to heal. These were professional killers, and he'd never dealt with anything like that before. Trying to fight them would be utterly ridiculous.

As his knees buckled and his hand slipped against the pulsing cut, he was forced to drop into the Everpresent and pull, as hard as he could, into his wound just to stay upright.

But they were on the Long Road. There was very little spirit magic here. And the few spirits around that might offer favors had no desire to help. He fell to the ground, streams of blood pattering in the dirt as he grasped for anything, even to slow the bleeding.

"Kill the hunter and the child, but try to keep the girl alive." The man's whisper, cold and calculated, would have been too quiet to hear in the Blinds. They were not far behind.

"We'll see." A woman answered, her voice even colder.

Their pursuers stalked towards them with silent steps, the ground crackling under their feet. Two of them. Both spindly skinny, wrapped in black like corpses ready to burn. Heartbeats slow and steady. Both armed with knives, heads down like predators, ready to lunge.

The one who'd jumped on his back was the woman. The two exchanged a glance, and the man pointed. The woman circled him at a distance, but her eyes were locked on Arinya. The man wiped his razor on his sleeve, then walked towards Ex.

"Careful, brother!" the woman hissed. "He's an undying!"

Currently, he was very much the opposite. Ex noticed a ripple around the killer's step as he approached, and a shimmer in the air behind him. At first, he didn't understand what it was, only that it was some kind of magic. Then the realization hit him.

It was the remnants of the Sangha blessing, drifting in the Blinds like a dust cloud, circling around the entire tavern. Maybe he could use it.

Ex couldn't smell anything but his own blood, so he concentrated on the frequency of the *ohm* that they used, visualized their saffron robes as texture, the noise sandalwood might make. He closed his eyes and reached...

And felt the whisper of hope. A stranger's touch, but a benevolent one. The cloud of high magic gave him just a sip of air, but that was enough for a drowning man.

With that, Ex had gathered just enough magic to cast the spell for the Quick Fox's web and covered his arms with a glancing static – he settled for just one hand – and it lit up in bursts of light tendrils, just as the killer descended. It surprised him enough that Ex only managed to move his head an inch aside. The razor grazed his temple as Ex stuck his hand in the killer's face.

It worked. His body seized up and the figure let out a high-pitched squeal, curling into a quivering ball. Usually, the spell only stunned a phi, sometimes blinded them. But humans were different. Ex could only sit there and stare as the man quivered, and wondered if it would kill him. With every bit of magic he could find to propel his voiceless words as deeply into the Everpresent as he could manage, Ex asked Shivah for another favor while holding his throat with both hands.

He couldn't stay under any longer, the Everpresent becoming discordant with the disruption. Ex fell back into the Blinds and prayed that the First Hunter's deva felt generous tonight.

He'd paid his tributes, he thought. He tried to be a good hunter, and the devas had looked kindly upon him. Holding that gratitude in mind, he crawled away from the still-twitching psychopath, towards the horses and the commotion next to them.

Arinya struggled with the other assassin, though it was one-sided. Ex couldn't follow the traded blows, as she moved as quick as a mongoose. After a flurry of punches and nasty elbow jabs, the other woman staggered and started to fall. Arinya knocked her legs out anyway, and with a grunt of exertion, added a rather unsportsmanlike kick to the face.

Amazing.

Thoughts of Shivah faded when Arinya ran to Ex's side. She said something that he didn't hear, grabbing him with ox-like strength. He hardly knew what was happening before she hauled him onto Ramble, then jumped up behind. She kicked the horse's side and he actually obeyed, Brownie following.

Ex slumped over, grasping Ramble's mane as he clung onto consciousness. He drifted in and out in flashes and felt himself fall. Arinya wrapped an arm around his waist to hold him against her.

"Please stay alive," she murmured.

Even with a slow heartbeat, it felt so comforting, and he was happier than he remembered being in a long time. He didn't know if he would make it, but at least his last few breaths wouldn't be so bad.

His mind wandered into a haze, and he hovered on the brink of the First Hunters trail, a path that would lead all good hunters to a higher plane. Was he in the Everpresent now? He wanted to be there, but couldn't find the strength. Still, it called to him. And he drifted, drifted ever so slowly towards a brightness that was both welcoming and terrifying.

Then, darkness.

Chapter Eleven

Narissa the Haunted

Narissa awoke screaming, clutching her neck as tears coursed down her cheeks. Her cats stared at her in alarm, and one scurried out of her bedroom window. Another nightmare, this one even more vivid than the last. Taking deep, slow breaths to calm herself, she checked each corner of her small room for the monstrous figure.

Shuddering, Narissa rose from bed, too scared to return to sleep. Instead, she tied her sarong, gathered her basket, and began her second-to-last cursed day by making her daily trek to the swamp in utter darkness. She wondered if the dreams would ever stop, even when she gained her humanity, or if they would continue to get worse.

She tried to steer her mind from the events of the previous day, and how reckless she'd been with the stranger who'd followed her home. Indrajit mocked her for these bad dreams, but he couldn't appreciate how her nightmares surged to a fever pitch.

Her heart didn't stop hammering until she ducked through the veil of vines to enter her wild arboretum. A narrow, ebbing stream trickled through the clearing, no more than two paces wide, guarded by bright eyed, azure toads feasting on the pre-dawn clouds of mosquitoes. The energy hummed here, undisturbed – a perfect sanctuary for Narissa to nurture the plants she needed for her practice.

He loved these flowers. Narissa's long, slender fingers brushed against cloud-white jasmines, blushing frangipanis, sun-bright sennas, sapphire orchids. In this patch of the swamp, the blossoms flourished year-round, surrounding her plots of medicinal herbs in quiet beauty.

She brought Kiet to a similar place once, decades ago, in a different forest. They'd only known each other a short time, but being with him made time lose all meaning. He held her gaze with a tenderness she had never experienced before, as if in awe of her, as if she were the definition of love itself. She'd fought so hard against her urges, determined to suffer any physical discomfort just to be with him.

But in the end, it wasn't enough.

Before Kiet, Narissa had never known love, even in her mortal life before being reborn as a krasue. The memories of that life were hazy with age, but she often reflected upon it, as Indrajit suggested, to examine why she may have received such punishment. Perhaps she hadn't done enough reflection lately.

In her last life, before being reborn as a phi, Narissa had lived in a wealthy town in the high northwest, near the border, where her father owned several mines and mills. War was rampant across the northern borders of Suyoram, in the disputed territories of Qinseng. Business was growing, as were her families riches, but soon the streets were choked with foreign refugees attempting to escape the conflict. The spoiled daughter of the chief walked by the poor beggars every day and spit upon their bowls in disgust. When one had dared to grab the edge of her gown, she had the woman executed, unmoved by the infant at her breast. Less mouths to feed, she'd laughed. She hadn't given a thought as to the young mother's loved ones, that she was also a daughter, a sister, a wife. More specifically, the favorite wife of an exiled warlord, who would soon hear of this cruelty and take exception.

"Accept what you are."

A sharp sting of pain jostled her back to the present. She hadn't been paying attention, and a small thorn lodged in her fingertip. She extracted it, then peered through the thick gnarls of trees beyond her rosebushes for the source of that unfamiliar voice. It sounded ancient, as if the swamp itself had spoken, but in a mocking tone that she didn't associate with it. She did not reach out to answer, but the awareness of the thing reached for her in a sudden flash of visions...

Kiet screaming as her fangs ripped through his neck. The warlord she'd widowed, raising his machete as three men held her face flush against the rough surface of a tree stump. The three-eyed hunter, whistling while he carved out her heart with a knife.

"No!" Narissa cried out and stumbled back, away from the nightmares. Her foot caught on a root, and she fell to her rear. Her basket rolled away, contents spilled. She must have been too exhausted and dozed off still standing.

Breathing heavily, she crawled to the stream and splashed water on her face, desperate to stay awake.

"Are you thirsty, my dear?"

A different voice, this one gentle. Narissa looked up to see a smiling woman standing on the other side of the stream, having just encroached the thicket of vines. She was incredibly thin and quite old, her white robes thrown over an age-wrinkled shoulder and cinched around her chest. Her prominent cheekbones and shaved head gave her a somewhat skeletal appearance. Propped over her shoulder was a klot, a netted umbrella, and Narissa realized this was a thudong nun, one of the wandering ascetics that made their way all throughout the country of Suyoram.

Narissa grasped at her throat, making sure she was still contained within her body. Sometimes when startled, her spine detached in instinctual self-defense if she did not consciously stop herself. And right now, her mind felt raw and vulnerable.

The nun stood in patient silence awaiting an answer, so Narissa bowed her head.

The nun approached the stream and knelt down to inspect the slow-moving water. "It is no good to drink," she said, then reached into her satchel and produced a clay jug. She uncorked it and offered the fresh water to Narissa.

"I'm not thirsty," Narissa said. Ironic that she was always thirsty, always starving, but nothing could quench the perpetual hunger of her curse. Nothing but receiving her amnesty. The kind gesture moved her, yet she remained wary of the stranger. "Thank you, mam."

As the nun drank from her jug, her gentle gaze drifted around the garden that Narissa had created over the last thirty years.

"How marvelous," the nun said. "It is clear that a great love was put into creating this place." When Narissa remained silent, the nun didn't seem to mind. "A pleasure to see you well. I am Puhsin from the Wat Song Kha, the Temple of Two Legs."

A memory stirred in her. Where had she heard that name before? It was nowhere around Jinburi. "Where is that temple?"

"My temple is wherever my two legs take me," Puhsin laughed. "I've been wandering the wilderness for forty years, and I know a special place when I see it. Would you mind if I rest here a while? It is almost time for my morning meditation."

Although she felt ownership over this place, Narissa didn't feel she held any authority to grant the nun permission, yet she nodded all the same. The nun sat down cross-legged on the bank, and Narissa studied her closer. She was bad with faces, but there was something familiar about the woman's movements, steady and rigid, yet relaxed at the same time. The woman's shaved head reminded her of the hunter that almost slew her, many years ago, but the two were as far apart as a flower was to a snake.

She wanted to ask if they'd met before, in another forest, far away. But if that were the case, Puhsin would know that Narissa should appear far older than she did. Still, she found it odd that the nun chose to wander here. It was very rare she would see any human alone in the swamp who wasn't quickly passing through, or desperately trying to escape.

Quelling her fear, Narissa said, "This swamp is full of dangerous creatures. Do you often make your rounds here?"

"I've traveled all throughout northern Suyoram, Loram, and Qinseng, but this is my first journey into the Jinburi province." Puhsin placed her weathered hands on her knees and met Narissa's eyes. "The entire world is full of danger. Physical danger is the least threatening to me, for this body is only temporary. Spiritual danger is what we must always guard our minds against. Such cuts take far longer to heal."

"Do you not prefer the temples of the Sangha?"

"My order is not part of the Sangha," Puhsin said. "I have great respect for my brothers who have accepted the designation. But my sisters and I were not willing to denounce some of our more controversial beliefs in order to be officially recognized, as the crown requires."

"I'm sorry," Narissa said.

"Don't be! We are content. The Enlightened Lord recognizes us all the same. Through right thought, right action, and right mindfulness, I live only to spread his teachings."

At any moment, this nun could start preaching, and Narissa began to feel uneasy again. She avoided monks and the temples, worried that somehow, they would recognize what she was. She stuck to the outskirts, the market, and her own property. But the Sangha were unavoidable during the time they made their almsrounds, which was about the time she was here, anyway.

"You seem uneasy, my dear."

Narissa realized she was staring. "Oh, I'm sorry, I have not had much sleep lately. Nightmares."

Narissa rose to collect the contents of her basket, then continued her work in the garden, pruning plants, gathering ripe seeds, pulling up weeds. Soon, the thudong nun's silent presence comforted her. This was the first time she had received company in this private space.

Puhsin was still deep in meditation when Narissa finished her tasks. She glanced at the nun, who hadn't moved an inch, the corners of her lips held in a gentle smile.

With every step, unease began to creep back in. The urge to feed surged in her stomach, but she pushed it away. Even when she first became a phi, she knew better than to attack a monk – one of the gravest sins that anyone, living or dead, could commit.

Something else was stirring, though, a dark vibration that seemed to be swallowing the swamp. And Narissa did not want to reach out to whatever it was. Just beyond the clearing, when she brushed past the curtain of vines, Narissa met the glowing red eyes of another phi.

It was a moopop, his noodle-like limbs curled around a thin tree trunk in several coils like a python. Below his bulging eyes and upturned nose, he had only the upper half of his sharp-toothed jaw. Scraggly, matted hair hung down his back, and a foot-long green tongue flopped against his distended belly.

Fear gripped Narissa's heart, until she remembered that there was nothing a krasue had to fear from another phi. They did not harm one another, for there was nothing of substance they could eat. They shared a mutual understanding of their acute suffering, yet they did not fraternize. There was no community, as every phi's existence was wrapped up in itself. And Narissa had to wonder if that was what doomed them. If that was what prevented any progress towards redemption.

The phi's pupilless gaze focused over Narissa's shoulder and settled on the meditating nun.

Must eat. Drool bled from his gums. *Must eat must eat must eat.* Tears coursed down its sallow cheeks, and it slithered to the ground, fan-like hands steepled in a wai. Despite the lack of community, this clearing was Narissa's, and had been for thirty years. She claimed it from the swamp, nurtured it, protected it. And the phi knew this. Still, it begged her to allow him to feed.

No, Narissa said, *there is another way. You can break free of this curse. Indrajit has offered an amnesty–*

Must eat, must eat! The phi cried again, his whole body shaking, and he scraped his fangs against the dirt. Hunger had driven him into an animalistic state with very little capacity to reason.

Please, try to resist. Killing a monk is the gravest of sins. Narissa knelt down and placed a hand on his shoulder. *If you find the Deva Indrajit–*

He lies he lies he lies! He jerked away, hissing. *No escape! Must eat!* His odd body twitched sideways, limbs flopping, and slithered into the dense thicket.

Wait, what do you mean, he lies? Narissa stared after him but saw nothing but the swamp. It sounded as if he knew something about Indrajit that she didn't. She turned back to the garden, worried. If she left, there was no telling if the phi would respect her territory. There were no laws that phi obeyed. The only authority were the devas, who never made themselves known, but for Indrajit. And he was notably absent.

She needed to warn the nun that she was no longer safe there.

"Ma'am, I am sorry to interrupt your meditation, but there is a dangerous creature lurking near."

Puhsin did not respond.

"Ma'am, please. You must leave immediately, or you may be killed." Narissa heard branches shake as the phi slunk through the trees, his cries soft and desperate. She reached across the stream to shake Puhsin to alertness, but before her hand connected, the nun spoke.

"If that is my fate, then it shall be," Puhsin said in an even tone. "If I am but flesh to sustain another living creature, then I have lived long enough. That is nature."

"But it is not nature." Narissa clutched her basket with white knuckles. She swallowed a lump in her throat, then said, "Nor is it living. It is a phi, trapped in his wicked ways. He will kill you, yet his hunger will persist. It will be a waste, and only prolong his suffering."

Surely that would move her.

"Then my flesh will return to the earth, and be consumed again by nature, and my soul will return to the devas." The nun's smile never wavered.

Narissa drew back, astounded. "You do not fear death?"

"To fear death is to fear life, and to hold such fear will cripple you, drive you to anger, madness, and desire. My soul is clean, and I have no attachment to this body."

Narissa stared in awe and was not sure whether the nun was foolish or brave. So unshakable in her faith, and completely unafraid of a violent end. Narissa's only faith was in Indrajit's promise, but perhaps he was tricking her after all.

"I've met you once before in the forests of Bim Dang," Puhsin said. "Twenty years ago. You were thirsty. You were hungry. You wanted to eat me, but instead, you moved on. You suffer greatly, but persist with your right actions, and you will be rewarded. Accept what you shall become."

Her words left Narissa stunned. It dawned on her that Puhsin had seen her – known she was a phI – yet did not react in horror. Rather, she accepted and spoke to her as any other human would treat another. Narissa's fear turned to gratitude. She made a wai and bowed to the meditating monk, then chose a particularly beautiful lotus blossom from her bounty. She bent across the stream to lay the flower before the nun and murmured her gratitude.

Resigned to what carnage might befall the woman, Narissa left the garden. She walked through the swamp as the sun rose, towards the sanctuary of her home. With every step, she prayed for the darkness to leave her mind, body, and soul.

Chapter Twelve

The Lost

A dreamless echo of sleep passed. Had he drunk himself stupid and wandered out into the woods? Wouldn't be the first time. But after rubbing the hangover from his eyes, Ex realized he was lain on Arinya's soft bedroll inside a tiny break between a grove of mangrove trees. It felt just as lovely as it had looked, so cozy that he started to drift off again.

Then came the sleepy thought of being on *her* bedroll, not remembering last night, which might mean... He dared to peek over.

She was next to him, but not in the way he'd hoped. With her eyes closed, she sat propped up by a fallen log. His chainblade laid loosely in her hand. Her posture was cramped and couldn't have been comfortable in any sense of the word.

To Ex's relief, the simmering tension of disgruntled spirits around the Long Road had gone. They must have been closer to Jinburi, on the edges of the swamp that crowned the western and northern border. Spirits flitted about at ease here, snapping up mosquitoes, slinking through the muddy ground.

It wasn't morning, Ex realized. Despite just waking up, it was closer to mid-afternoon.

When he moved, a crust of mud crackled on his clothes. Everything felt tight in his neck, and when he touched it, he found a wrapped cloth tied tightly around. With dread, he pushed a finger underneath and felt fresh scar tissue from one side of his neck to the other, still angry and raw, but surprisingly narrow. With that texture of broken skin, an unpleasant memory surfaced – a black-cloaked psychopath slitting his throat.

He shivered, feeling sick. His entire body from the neck down was covered in dried blood, as well as the side of his face where the killer had nicked his temple, proving a cut didn't need to be deep to be deadly if you knew where to strike.

With a grunt, Ex sat up, and Arinya immediately startled awake. After several wide-eyed blinks, she sighed and leaned her head back, closing her eyes.

"Sorry–" his voice came out in a rasp, and he started coughing. "For... waking you up." He turned away and hacked up blood clots, which pushed him further to the brink of vomiting.

"The Enlightened Lord favors," she said. "I was so afraid you'd slip away."

"Where–" he choked on a scab again. She offered him a cup of water, which helped.

"I rode fast for a while, then took us east, off the Long Road. It became very muddy, and I couldn't see, so I stopped." She peered through the trees with bleary eyes. "I pray we lost them."

This time, Ex spoke with a little more than a whisper. "That was smart."

"I don't know," she shuddered, and slapped a mosquito. "I think we're lost."

He hadn't thought about that, mind still lingering on how she knocked out that assassin with perfect form. How she held him as they ran, and for that fleeting moment where he'd felt so at ease, even on the brink of the First Hunters trail.

"You're amazing," he said before he could stop himself. "I knew you could fight, but that was... amazing." He couldn't find better words than that. The more he grew to know her, the more he admired her – her wit, her fire, her strength...

She smiled. "That's the second time I've saved your ass."

He managed a half-smile in return, but quickly looked away. He couldn't shake the chilling image of the killer cutting his throat, how the scrape of the blade hardly registered on his skin before a torrent of blood let out. Carefully, he unwrapped the makeshift bandage around his neck. It was a piece of cloth from her wrap pants, torn off. He folded it up and placed it aside.

"It's healed." She moved closer, staring in wonder at the wound. She'd seen the spell work before, outside the public house, so it shouldn't have been a surprise. This must have been different... Well, it certainly was for him. Hunters didn't typically sleep in the Everpresent, never mind holding a spell through the Blinds.

"They killed Mu and Ting," Ex said, still in disbelief. "They killed everyone who fought back." The amount of red blood on his clothes turned his stomach, stirring up a memory of his childhood village after the soldiers came. The carnage, the executions, the bodies.

"Hey, Ex. We're safe now," Arinya said, jarring him from the thought. Perhaps she recognized the numb expression of someone reliving their worst moments. His breath was quick and shallow, and she reached out to squeeze his shoulder.

It brought him back from those dark recollections, and he met her concerned gaze with relief. He sighed, letting the tension in his shoulders deflate. She didn't look away, and the kindness in her eyes filled him with comfort. Yet there was something in her expression he couldn't quite read, as if she knew something he didn't, and was waiting for him to understand.

"Right. Safe." he finally said, and peered around at the thick gnarls of greenery filling every possible outlet. They were deep in the swamp, but not anywhere he recognized. Stagnant, clear pools of water feed the weblike roots of the mangroves. Not the cleanest water in the world, but it would do well enough to get the blood off his clothes.

With a grunt of effort, he slowly began to unfasten his coat.

"Let me help," she said, and moved to his side.

"It's fine." He pulled away quickly. "I can do it."

"Oh, don't be a baby," she said, and her deft fingers unbuckled and unhooked all the fastenings as smooth as a seamstress, her lips pursed in concentration. Streaks of Ex's blood had dried on her sarong top, sticking to her body, and in her proximity, he couldn't avoid looking at it. When she helped him slide his coat off, he felt her breath hot on his neck...

And he almost passed out – any remaining blood immediately rushed to his loins.

Violently, he forced his mind to think of Shar-Ala. The demon could be here, somewhere. That meant they were in danger. Or the assassins. Or... he thought hard. Uh, that fatty big chunk of beef stew, which was kind of soft in his mouth when he recalled it... No, math. Math would do. How many more miles did they have to get to...

His hormones didn't buy it, and those thoughts of her from the night before came rushing back. Especially as she unfastened his trousers. Even with the mess that covered all his clothes, that was completely unnecessary. He put his hand on hers to stop her, embarrassed she'd see his obvious arousal.

"Relax," she said, gazing up at him with the hint of a smile.

"Arinya," he murmured, looking away. She touched his chin and pulled his face back to hers.

"Ex. I thought you were going to die. It really scared me." Her eyes mesmerized him – dark, warm pools he would have gladly drowned in. Soft fingers traced his jaw, running down to the fresh scar on his neck. "You protected me when you didn't have to. No one's ever done that before."

As much as he wanted to fall into her, he caught her wrist.

"You don't know me." He forced himself to say, shuddering under her touch. He wanted to say he would have done that for anyone.

But the truth was, he never had.

"I know enough to know what I want. That's why..." she hummed in an amused manner, bit her lip and gazed up from under her lashes. "I should repay you." Comprehension at a low, his grip loosened and she slipped away. When she touched him again, he very much understood. It felt like there wasn't enough air. She scarcely moved, her breath soft on his neck, and he closed his eyes as she worked some magic of her own.

"Relax," she whispered, tongue flicking his ear. Then she bent down, lips trailing his chest. As soon as her tongue curled around his cock, his toes curled too, and he made a noise he didn't think he'd ever made before.

A precious few glorious seconds passed before an intrusive thought forced itself into his stupid head. This didn't make sense. Just like all the events of last night, this was unbelievable, happening to someone else. Here was the crown prince's consort, and there was no reason she'd be interested in him. Part of why he'd grown to admire her must have been her charm, her arresting, spirited grace. Maybe she had grown fond of him too, but the word *repay*...

Not that he blamed her for those instincts. These were things she must have had to learn to survive in a harsh world. But Ex couldn't ignore his guilt.

"Arinya," he whispered. He gently ran his fingers through her hair, wanting nothing more than to let her have whatever she wanted. But with a heavy sigh, he lifted her back up. When she smiled and licked her lips, he almost took her like a savage, but forced himself to turn away again.

"I'm sorry. I can't."

"What?" Her voice came low and soft. "Why not? I want to."

Right then, it was the only fucking thing he wanted too. He

wanted her on her back, he wanted her writhing on his tongue, he wanted her in every possible way. Worse, he knew she wanted it as well, the scent of her desire beckoning like a fly to honey.

Through gritted teeth, he forced the biggest lie of his life thus far.

"I don't." He regretted the words the second they left his mouth. Her eyes grew so cold that the blood froze in every one of his veins.

He'd be full of shit if he blamed it all on gentlemanly qualities, even though he did consider himself something of one, sometimes. They were raised like that in the mountains. You didn't just lay with anyone unless you were prepared for a long life together.

In retrospect, he should have just shut the fuck up and taken the service like any good boy would do, but the larger point laid with what the Guardian of the Emerald Forest told him, and what Mali warned him about in confidence.

Arinya had been hexed with a chastity warding, one that he wasn't sure she knew about. It seemed rude to bring up. There was a very subtle scent of charred cedar he'd noticed from the Everpresent, if he focused on that particular part of her. It was a vengeful spell that sat dormant, waiting for the slightest betrayal. Ex wasn't sure what it would do, but it wouldn't be anything pleasant, especially for her. Of course, there were plenty of other things that they could do without going there, but the idea of causing her any pain filled him with anxiety, finally beating down his hormones.

"Sorry," he said, and quickly pulled up his pants. "I'm just... not interested."

"What?" she said in utter disbelief. Then pointed. "Your cock disagrees."

"It's base flesh," he said with a shrug, avoiding her hurt expression. "You cut me, I bleed. Nothing special about that."

She blinked a few times, and her face took on a thoughtful expression. "Are you gay?"

"Uh, not that I know of. Maybe?" Fuck, she gave him the perfect opening and he fumbled.

"Then why did you try to kiss me?"

"Animal instinct. Humans are just as..." He peered over and trailed off. Her glare put Mali's to shame, and she wasn't buying it. But what could be said to someone who had a hex up their intimates that would probably melt his own into a withered banana peel, and then do something worse to her. "Listen, hunters don't take wives–"

"Did I ask you to fucking marry me?!"

"No," he said slowly, a bit confused. It seemed like one of those questions you weren't supposed to answer.

"Then what's your problem?"

"I don't have a problem!" Finally, Ex started to get offended. "You think just because you're beautiful and amazing that I want to sleep with you?"

"Yes, actually, I do." She crossed her arms. "Do you?"

"Obviously... not. I don't, not at all."

"You're a shitty liar."

"Better than being a good one."

Her eyes widened. "You think I'm a liar?"

"Why else would you come on to me?" he snapped. "You're a tourist. And I'm a scary whisper who carries around black magic babies. Suddenly you want to repay me for getting cut open in your defense?"

"Hang on. You think I'm trying to manipulate you?" She squinted. "Even though I *paid* you."

"Yes. No. Maybe, I don't fucking know." He groaned and covered his face, wondering if he should cast the Blind Eagle Eye and make a run for it. He shot her his angriest expression, which, compared to hers, was about as intimidating as a wounded puppy. "Look, lady. Fucking's like shitting to us, we just have to do it every so often. You could be any two-bit whore from any shithole river town and I would–"

She slapped him so hard he pitched over.

"Fuck you, Ex." She stomped away, disappearing into the trees.

He laid on his side and watched her go, unsure of what just happened, but pretty confident he did all the wrong things. If he could feel pain, surely his balls would be killing him about now.

Then he heard the Hound guffawing. Judging by the rustle of bushes, he may have fallen over too.

"Shut the fuck up!" Ex tried to yell and threw a rock in his general direction. "Er, not you, Arinya! I was talking to the... Shit. Fuck it!"

He rolled over and crawled into the nearest basin of stagnant water without bothering to take off the rest of his clothes.

Chapter Thirteen

The Grey Walker

If Ex thought the previous day had been awkward, this one was on a higher plane of existence.

They hadn't spoken more than a few words to one another by the time they set off. He tried to keep his mind off what was said, which wasn't too hard, considering he couldn't remember most of it. He also tried not to think about what had happened just before all of that. But they needed to leave the swamp as soon as possible, no matter how uncomfortable it was.

They took a muddy offshoot of what Ex hoped was part of the Serene. It wasn't the same as the way through the highlands they'd traveled after the Emerald Forest. The Venara never established a strong foothold in the swamp. This had been the domain of the Crocodile Queen, and her servants had made their paths in and under the Namleng river.

The swamp was immense, and despite being the dry season, remained swampy year-round. Even though he returned every few months, he probably hadn't explored even a quarter of it. But he didn't need to know where they were to know every mile was chock full of hungry phi and dark spirits. Often when hunters were hunting phi in other parts of the country, the Hungry Ghosts fled here for refuge.

Master Seua brought Ex here when he was first learning to hunt, and as they wandered for months, he lulled him to sleep with countless stories. "Every landscape has its history," Master Seua had said, "and the wilds are as rich, if not richer, than human memory. Territories shift and change, empires rise and fall, be it the reign of ant queens, warring ape tribes, or pestilence that sweeps over countries, wiping entire civilizations from the earth. Imagine if, to you, the river was the size of an ocean, crashing ever downward over mountains, full of beasts that wanted nothing more than to consume you. There are more souls, more universe in a mile of this swamp than man will ever know.

"Man implores the devas and the Enlightened Lord for guidance. Why is it shocking that beasts do the same? We may never know the intricacies of their faith, but one thing is certain. There is a Guardian that watches their domain, a Guardian that even the Kings and Queens must respect... At least, they did at some point, before they lost their connection to the land."

Ex met the Guardian of the Emerald Forest several times, but he'd never found the Guardian of the Jinburi Swamp. Master Seua said it was better that way. From what he pieced together from the other hunters, she had an affinity for dark spirits and little tolerance for trespassers. There was a reason why men never tried to tame this place, a reason why necromancers took refuge here.

A reason why Shar-Ala always returned.

"Bastards!"

Ex startled and glanced over to Arinya, who had slapped her arm at a swarm of mosquitoes. When he caught her eye, she glared and pulled her cloak tighter.

"This is miserable," she growled. "Don't tell me mosquitoes don't bite you, either."

"They do, sometimes," his voice rasped, throat still tight. His blood might have looked as red as any other human, but it wasn't quite the same as a human's, not after training. There were traces of spirit magic in hunters' blood after they passed the ritual to learn to walk in the Everpresent. And, as he'd told her before, magic tasted like shit.

He reached back to grab his alchemy kit, which resembled a leather-bound ledger. "Hang on. I have something for that." Inside, small vials of various tinctures and poisons were neatly fastened in rows. They were unlabeled but for etched symbols in the glass. Even the illiterate hunters knew what each one was. Master Rei would have smacked him for his lack of organization. *Keep the natural stuff on the top row, the creature stuff in the middle, the spirit stuff on the bottom...* But Ex's were just everywhere.

As he searched for the citronella and lemongrass oil, his finger paused over a cloudy blue vial with a smaller, swirling stream of onyx-black specks.

Dreamless. Cloud toad poison, crushed scorpion tail and corpse oil. With just a tiny prick of a needle, you'd descend into a dreamless sleep, hidden from the Everpresent, as well as the types of hungry phi that fed off the fear caused by nightmares. They were a rarer type of phi, but Shar-Ala was even rarer still. He was said to attack in dreams and draw his victims in.

"What is that?" Arinya's curiosity got the better of her resentment. It took a moment for Ex to realize she expected an answer.

"It's for descending into a trance when I hunt Shar-Ala," he said. "He's a true demon."

"I know, you've said that. But how is that different from a phi?"

"He used to be one, a very long time ago. All phi were once human. Master Nokai says that after they paid their karmic debts, they're reborn more favorably. But some persist and lean so far into darkness that they'll never return. So they get named, and become known. And that's how you become a true demon."

"He must be strong, then."

"They say he can smell fear from miles away, especially in dreams. They say he'll creep right next to you while you sleep, then use the stinger in his fangs to inject you with nightmares in the purest form. He won't kill you there, even though he could. He stares at you with his unblinking third eye, then you are plagued with his nightmares. If you don't go mad right away, you'll sleepwalk deep into the wild, straight into his clutches."

Her face went pale. "Even during the day?"

"Some people still have nightmares during the day."

"I suppose I should take some now, then, because I hardly slept last night."

"Oh, no," Ex said, then pulled Ramble closer to hand her the mosquito repellent instead. "Sorry, this is for bugs, nothing fancy. I should have given it to you earlier. You can't take Dreamless. One drop would kill you. Unless your teachers made you stab yourself with twenty needles every morning for years."

"Unfortunately not," Arinya murmured, staring off into the thickets, her hand on her daughter's necklace. He might have laid it on a little thick with the ghost story, but at least the silence took on less of an awkward tone, more apprehensive.

After another hour or so of pushing the horses through the winding, muddy path, Ex grew more nervous about where they were. He couldn't recognize any of their surroundings, even when he checked the Everpresent. When he whistled for the Hound, he didn't answer. Arinya squinted up to the canopy, worried by the small spots of sun fading between the trees.

"Don't worry," he said, though he was worried too. "We'll be in Jinburi soon."

"The city? But isn't Shar-Ala here?"

"Oh." Ex shrunk in his saddle, feeling drowned by everything all at once. And here to witness his shame was a fiery woman from a scummy river town who, through sheer force of will, became one of the most important people in the country. A woman like that witnessing the failure of a broke, prudish escort and lousy excuse for a hunter with delusions of grandeur. What was the point of trying to pretend anymore?

"Mali's right, I've never seen him," he admitted. "I just found some madman's book in the swamp and convinced myself he was here. The entire guild thinks I'm an idiot for trying to hunt down a demon who hasn't been seen for years."

"Yet you persist. Why?"

"I don't know."

Mercifully, she left him alone, and they pushed on.

Boy, we walk a fading path. Master Seua stared down at him, doubt clouding his face as the young boy knelt on the stone steps of the guild hall, begging for entry. Unwashed, starving, and stuttering in a broken, mountain tribe dialect, fresh brand on his body. He didn't understand the city. Everyone despised him and he had nowhere to go.

When the young boy spotted the symbol on the entrance to the guildhall, he didn't need to be literate to understand what they were. Aside from his mother's cooking, one of his most vivid childhood memories was when a phi hunter passed through his village. All the kids stared in awe at the stoic hero in foreign armor as he sat at the edge of the woods, his flaxen candles dripping over a small altar, tendrils of incense smoke snaking into the night. And under the new moon, in the pitch dark, he painted his face, pulled on his solid black mask, and went into the moonless forest without a semblance of fear to slay the monster haunting their lands.

Who wouldn't want to be someone like that?

Boy, this is a lonely life. Master Seua shook his head as the young boy stumbled over his feet when a group of girls walked by the training yard. Some giggled at him, but most turned their noses. One of them, the prettiest, walked by every day, and he swore she smiled at him every time. But the day she let him walk her home, and her parents saw his tattoos, she never walked that way again.

Boy, if you survive this, you will never be the same. Master Seua said, then stabbed the young man through the heart and let him down into the drowning pool. When he finally emerged, the hunters gathered around and raised their mugs with a cheer. Despite the shuddering numbness in his veins, he'd never been so proud.

Ex clung to those memories like an orchid needing water and nurture before withering away. He saw it fade in the others over the years, and swore it would never happen to him.

With his head sticking out of the canopy from the highest branch of the highest tree he could find, he tried to summon that pride, because now he felt the complete opposite.

'Swamp as far as the eye could see, the heady odor of earth and animals decomposing into a miasma of viscous slush. Ex projected his plight towards any spirits who'd give him the time of day, but their distrust remained rooted deep in this place. Centuries ago, man hunted the Crocodile Kingdom to extinction, capturing their citizens only to breed them in leather farms, turning them to cattle, not creatures. He wouldn't trust them either. He had nothing to give them anyway.

Mud slopped under his feet as he landed.

"You've gone into the Everpresent quite a bit," Arinya said, her voice flat and glum. "We're lost, aren't we?"

His eyes were glowing like coals, but he met hers anyway. The tension seemed to have eased since admitting his failures at hunting down the true demon. "If we can find the Jinburi river, we can follow it into town." He wiped sweat from his forehead and glared at the wall of green that continued to mock them. "There's just so much shit covering it. And these paths are" – he kicked a rock across the mud, and it scattered a tribe of newts in its wake – "bullshit."

Ex stared after it, the insects scurrying around on every surface, the maze of vines and thorns. These paths were probably intended to turn men around, if not snake back on themselves on purpose. He'd sworn he smelled that exact combination of dirty parrot feathers with a stale hint of viper poison twenty yards into the thicket, where the bird died... two hours ago.

Suspiciously, he walked into the Everpresent again, and to the edge of the path. Crouching down, he stuck his finger in the mud and tasted it. He chewed on it, the grit crunching between his teeth. With the realization he'd been made a fool of, he leapt to his feet.

"Fucking bastard!" Ex stomped over to Ramble and snatched his machete off his pack. Arinya called after him, but he'd already gone into the mess of vines and hanging moss, hacking and slashing in a violent frenzy, as if the swamp had insulted his mother. He tore at it until breaking through the first layer, revealing another. He gritted his teeth and pushed through.

There *was* a part of the Serene hidden beyond, he could smell it and see it, and they'd walked by countless times now, all in different places. The swamp had shifted and coiled and masked it, but here it was again, and he wouldn't let it get away.

"Ex?" Arinya called, "Have you gone mad? What are you doing?"

"Come on, before it gets away!" As Ex carved a new trail, he gestured for Arinya and the others to follow.

"Before *what* gets away?"

The web-like mosaic of scarlet vines twitched after he slashed through, sticky drops of spirit blood leaking from its veins.

"You see that?" He hacked at it a few more times than necessary, satisfied with its tiny, high-pitched squeals, then turned his wrath to the next one.

"The plants?"

"Don't let these assholes fool you," he said, in between swings. "They might be plants, but they're still dark spirits."

She didn't say anything, but her feet shifted on the fallen vines with unease.

Now that their struggles had a possible end, Ex felt giddy. "I knew I wasn't going insane!" He laughed, sadistically stomping one of the roots that tried to inch away. One more layer to go. He slashed through a thick, black gate of snakelike branches. They tensed like stringy muscles as he descended on them, and in turn, they projected a sharp scent of fear, groveling like a cornered phi. "Too late for apologies," he growled and tore them apart.

They burst through the brush and onto the Serene Way, or the equivalent of it. It was far wider than the trails they'd been lost on, and now that he'd made an example of the others, the vines that made up the walls and domed ceiling of the natural tunnel didn't dare twitch a tendril. Under their feet, the black, packed mud had a uniformity to it, dense magic drifting along the surface, as slow and sure as the lazy river they hunted.

Huffing and puffing, Ex leaned on his knees, squinting around at the new scenery as he healed the scratches and scrapes all over his skin. His initial joy faded quickly. He still didn't know this part of the swamp, so despite being safer and more comfortable, they were no less lost.

Arinya led the horses out into the Way and gazed around, taking time to inspect the natural archways above.

After Ex returned to the Blinds, his neck started to itch, and he ran a finger over the cut. Something felt off about it. Maybe it was from using the Sangha charm to heal, as he'd never been the subject of that kind of magic before. Or maybe he was allergic. Irritated at the sensation, he hung up his machete and rummaged in his tincture bag for something that might help.

"Ex," Arinya called over. "Look."

After he wandered over and stared around, there was nothing more but the same. "Look at what?"

"The flowers," she said, pointing to something on the side of the passage. He still didn't see it. She walked to the edge and knelt before a group of dark violet blossoms.

"Um, sure. They're pretty."

"No, look at the shape of the petals, and how the leaves curl. These are the same ones that led to the Guardian in the forest, but they're purple rather than red."

Ex leaned down to peer closer, and sure enough, they were the same. He'd never thought to make that connection before and grinned. "You're a natural."

She smiled at him, a smile he hadn't seen since the disturbingly lustful one that morning. It cheered him at first, but then followed it with the memory of what happened next and he glanced away. His heart sank even further as he surveyed the path of flowers.

"Maybe they can help us," she said, a tinge of hope in her voice. "The Guardian?"

Ex took a deep breath as he leaned back, staring down the path in the opposite direction. He wasn't sure where it would lead, or how far, but he was sure they'd escape eventually, even if it took a few nights.

He glanced at Arinya's necklace. A few nights with a beacon like that wasn't the best idea. How might the Guardian react? He'd only heard worrisome stories, but it was possible the others were just trying to mess with him. Maybe the Guardian was perfectly mannered and benevolent. Maybe she'd even feed them.

"That's a great idea," he said, and hoped he sounded convincing.

Chapter Fourteen

And the Guardian

The sanctuary of the Swamp Guardian looked a little different than her brother's in the forest.

Ex and Arinya stood before a perfectly circular pond, its far bank surrounded by towering, moss-covered rocks that curled into sharp points, clawing the thick air. Swirling mist obscured the ground, which was just as well – glowing dots of color scurried and slithered, and he'd rather not see what they were. Swaymoss and mangroves choked the perimeter, branches clotted with squirming cocoons. The canopy loomed above as dark as the night but for scattered spots of pale sun, yet the light remained even and diffused.

Where the rest of the swamp screamed with mosquitos and biting flies, they were noticeably absent here, only voiceless creatures and a steady hiss, a vibration so low and heavy it felt flat, yet massive. By the expression on Arinya's face, she would probably have preferred the mosquitoes.

"Wait here." Steeling his nerves, Ex took a step towards the pond and into the Everpresent.

The centipedes and snakes stopped their meandering and turned their heads towards him. Even the caterpillars retreated, inching safely into the cracks of rotting bark. He took another step, and the mist parted around his feet. Even the *vapor* detested the touch of a human trespassing onto its sacred ground, even if he walked with the spirits.

The dirt twisted under his feet as slimy worms burrowed away, leaving a strangely pleasant smell of lime and shrimp. He focused on the pool, as dark and still as glass, yet reflecting nothing.

A great presence lurked just underneath. Watching. Waiting.

Ex crouched at the edge of the pond. With his carving knife, he cut the palm of his hand over the altar of bones, wilted flowers, and dark stones left by the creatures of her domain.

Forgive me for trespassing, oh venerable one. He made a wai against his forehead, channeling every ounce of respect he could muster.

When she didn't respond, he wondered how much flattery she desired. Couldn't hurt.

I am not worthy of your divine presence, goddess of the swamp and all souls within it, and I prostrate before you with my humble offering—

Silence! The Guardian snapped.

Ex flinched, but managed to keep his posture.

Your pathetic groveling disgusts me. A croaking rumble vibrated the still pond, and he nervously shifted his weight.

I apologize, great one. I mean not to offend—

The rumble silenced him again.

Your befouled breath is finite, hunter! Be wary with your words and announce the reason for your presence.

I seek only passage to the town of Jinburi.

For what purpose?

To leave you in peace.

The Guardian flexed, coiled, and the pond began to simmer. Then boil. As bubbles popped with flashes of violet, his nerves started to wither. Was that the wrong thing to say?

With a sudden splash, an enormous naga head erupted from the water. A tidal wave of pond scum soaked him from head to toe. Water streamed down over her keeled scales as her serpentine body rose, coiled to strike.

Her reptilian, diamond-shaped face loomed over his, jaws wide open to brandish fangs as long as his body. Narrow, glaring eyes with paper-thin slits for pupils dilated when she saw him, and the crest of armored plates crowning her head lifted in animalistic display of aggression. A screeching hiss lanced through the fog, and behind him, Arinya stifled a scream.

The Guardian's tongue whipped outward and curled around his torso twice, oily as an eel. He let out a surprised gasp at the sudden sensation of weightlessness as she hoisted him high into the air.

"Ex!" Arinya cried. He craned his neck to see tendrils of fog swirling upward, over Arinya's body. It became solid and held her in place. She tried to struggle, to no avail.

"It's just how she says hello! Don't worry!" He was so worried he near soiled his pants.

I know you. The ancient creature's tongue constricted, and his breath left him. His head snapped as she drew him closer, jaw widening into a vicious grin.

You are the one who returns every third moon to kill Shar-Ala.

A tiny pinch of excitement poked through his terror. *He's here?!*

Foolish creature. Are you so arrogant to believe you will succeed where my seekers cannot? I should end your futile quest.

More hope. If the Guardian had been hunting Shar-Ala too, then they might have a chance.

We're aligned, then. He stared into her eyes. *Perhaps if we work together—*

A hoarse, stuttering hiss erupted from her mouth, coating him with sticky venom. His skin sizzled where it landed.

Work with a feeble mortal? I should drink your blood for such an offensive suggestion! She laughed, strands of thick saliva vibrating in her throat. *Yet… your ignorance does amuse me.*

Her grip loosened slightly, which he took as progress.

If Shar-Ala is killing your children, allow me to hunt him for you, he said.

Every time I have allowed man into my swamp, they do nothing but take. They've butchered my children, they burn my lands. Why should I trust you?

You know my kind. We aren't like them. Ex pushed, but her grip tightened again.

Then why did one of yours kill the Pale Mother?

That stunned him. A phi hunter wouldn't dare hunt a legend like the Pale Mother. She was said to be one of the only living remnants of the Crocodile Kingdom – centuries old, a great, wise creature, revered by animals and spirits alike.

It couldn't have been. It would've been known. We would have seen the silver skins. No, the Guardian had to be mistaken. If a human killed the Pale Mother, it would have been poachers. A whole army of them.

Your kind infected her lair, drew her into the open and slaughtered her, just as they did to Lord Chalawan–

Lord Chalawan wasn't killed by a phi hunter! He was killed by man!

You dare interrupt me! The Guardian drew him close enough that if Ex leaned his head forward, he could have kissed her fangs. *Such arrogance! A Grey Walker may have merit with the spirits, but you will always be born of human filth.*

"Ex!" Arinya screamed again. "You're making her angry!" From the bank of the Guardian's lair, several black, glossy eyes blinked awake. Perfectly hidden in the mud, the enormous crocodiles had been sitting within the reeds, jaws open. All their heads turned to Arinya and they crept forward.

"It's okay!" he called back, panic breaking his voice.

"Clearly not!" The mist crept up her neck and circled around her mouth. She struggled anew and gasped for air in shallow breaths.

The crocodiles neared her, tensing their muscles to lunge, jaws first.

Please, ancient one. Let my passenger go. She's done nothing to disrespect your lands. I'm the one who has trespassed.

As if you have a choice! Your blood burns hot when you speak of her. She is more to you than just a passenger.

Yes. He wondered how sentimental this Guardian was. She obviously cared for all the creatures in the swamp. That might be the key. *She is. She's very special to me. I care about her, and I'm bound to her.*

Why? Do you want her for your mate?

It… doesn't matter. I made a promise to keep her safe.

How foolish of you to attach yourself, hunter. Have your masters taught you nothing? Let her watch as I rip you to shreds. Your blood is foul to my lands, yet sweet to me. And your passenger's even sweeter. The Guardian's lips curled upward in a sneer. *My children are hungry. They've not tasted the flesh of man for years.*

That gave him an idea.

Listen, spirit! Ex pulled the Smoking Palm of Anewan spell over his body like a blanket. Her nostrils flared at his irreverence. He had her attention. *There are no men in this swamp to feast on, like you said. And the Pale Mother would never have been drawn out by poachers. It must have been Shar-Ala with his nightmares. He has been bound here for only a short time. He must have killed her to keep a feast great enough to sustain him for years, and he wouldn't have to reveal himself.*

The Guardian's eyes narrowed, but she said nothing.

Let me hunt the demon for you, as vengeance for the Pale Mother. And from then on, I promise he'll leave your children alone. When she didn't respond, he let the spell heat his body hot as steel in the sun. The skin on her tongue sizzled, yet she made no reaction. If she killed him, he could at least make himself unpleasant to eat. *If I fail, take my life as tribute. I won't fight your judgment. You have nothing to lose.*

Her eyelids twitched. She was thinking about it. Actually thinking about it!

Or, go ahead, let the demon run rampant. Let him plague your lands and kill your "beloved" children. Eat me now and I'll burn your throat, and I'll feel even worse when you shit me out.

The Guardian shook then, trembling in rage. Wrong answer? He braced for her teeth. Then came the same noise she made before. A laugh, and this time less scornful.

Finally, you show some spirit. Then she whipped his body as if cracking a whip. He slammed to the ground. She snapped her jaws an inch from his face, and her children snapped theirs in unison – a sound that inspired deep, instinctual fear, a crack as loud as a volley of arquebus.

Very well, hunter. You have one night. And if you fail, you both will die, and I take the unborn soul as tribute.

In a blur of black and green scales, she disappeared into the pond as fast as she had emerged, sending a wave of water slashing over the ground. Arinya collapsed as the mist released, clutching her throat. The crocodiles sauntered back into her waters, leaving behind a loud and clear grumble of disappointment.

Wiping nervous sweat from his face, Ex steadied his breath and let the Everpresent drain away. After he was sure nothing was broken, he sprinted to Arinya and placed his hands on her shoulders.

"Are you hurt?"

She shook her head, then stared towards the pond and pointed. The mangrove roots rose from the earth and coiled into a tunnel, violet azaleas blossoming as the vines twisted the passage apart. Without another word, they climbed on the horses and hurried through.

As soon as they were out of sight from the sacred ground, every muscle in Ex's body relaxed and he had to cling to Ramble to keep from falling.

"Her temperament was much unlike the Emerald Guardian," Arinya said with a nervous titter. He made a pathetic attempt to laugh, but now that they were out of sight, all his false bravado was drained.

"I have to tell you something." He coughed and cleared his throat, searching for the best way to break the news. "We planned to go to Jinburi first, but we need to stay in the swamp tonight. Um, because–"

"We have to hunt Shar-Ala. Or she will kill us and take 'the unborn soul' as tribute. I heard."

Ex stared at her in disbelief. "Heard? You heard us talking?"

"Yes. Not at first, I could only hear her awful growling. But after I breathed in that strange fog, I felt Isaree grow warm." She patted her chest, where her amulet hung. She'd given her daughter a name, which made Ex even more nervous if things went terribly wrong. "Then everything grew brighter, and I could hear the Guardian. It was muffled at first, but when she drew you in, it was if I had emerged from a pool of water. Every word was clear."

Ex had never heard of someone going even partially into the Everpresent without training. It was impossible. Yet in a short time, she'd been in the presence of two powerful god-spirits, which was unusual even for a hunter. Clearly something happened when she breathed in the Guardian's mist. Maybe some kind of reaction with her soul-captured child?

"That's amazing. Can you hear them now? I mean, sense them? The little ones don't really talk the same way we do."

She closed her eyes and squinted. After some thought, she shook her head. "I can't tell. I could only hear the Guardian's words." She smirked. "And yours."

"You could hear the Guardian. Amazing…" Ex grinned, which quickly faded when he realized what she'd said. *And yours.* He rubbed his face to hide his expression of humiliation. So much for all that work this morning trying to deny wanting her.

"Don't worry on it," she said, nonchalant. "I was tired this morning and was not thinking clearly. I've thought about it. I'm accustomed to my husband dealing with stress by sex, and was trying to ensure that you could carry on. I'm the crown prince's consort, and anything between you and I would be impossible."

"I know, we're friends," Ex said. "And that's enough for me."

"No," she said, expression flat, "we can't be."

"Hang on." He didn't buy it. "You don't even want to be friends?"

"What's the point? In your words, I'm a tourist. You weren't wrong. Once you leave me in the Capital, you'll go on your way." Strange choice of words, *leaving her*, when she was the one going on to a charmed life, completely out of his reach. He wasn't sure how to address that and went for the obvious instead.

"You're not just a tourist. You just heard into the Everpresent without training. That doesn't happen to everyone. Or anyone that I know of."

She scoffed. "Are you saying I belong out here?"

"I just mean you aren't a stranger, that's all."

"We will have to be strangers," she said, side-eying him with complete detachment. "I've seen your brand. Obviously, in the Capital, I couldn't be seen with you. Even in passing."

That stung. Even though he already had his suspicions, some dumb part of him thought he might see her again after this was all over. He didn't realize it wasn't about him as a phi hunter, but him as a person, a remnant of the uprising. He set his jaw, kept his face neutral and nodded, focusing on the path ahead.

The only real positive was that it wouldn't matter anyway, since he was pretty sure they weren't going to leave the swamp alive.

Judging by the gaps in the tunnel and changing foliage, the Guardian was leading them straight to Ex's old hunting grounds. With a tiny bit of satisfaction, he realized he'd been correct in pinpointing Shar-Ala's territory. It wasn't much longer until the passage yawned open into thick-trunked forest. After they emerged, the path melted back into the ground, the roots rearranging as the trees slid back to their homes.

He recognized these surroundings. They were still in the thick of the swamp, but nothing like the choking heart from which they came. Here, the dry season was far more evident, as there was visible ground, though still spongy and gnarled. It would be misty in the dark, but here you could walk between the trees.

Two incomplete phi hunter's markings were carved onto the nearest trunks, marks Ex made himself despite no evidence that the demon was waiting beyond. Perhaps the villagers would have pushed their industry forward if he hadn't. Maybe that was a reason for the Guardian's mercy.

The Hound slunk from behind the trees and sat expectantly, his eyes glowing bright from the heavy magic surrounding them. His jaws dropped open in a canine grin, the flash of fangs accompanied with a low growl.

Late.

Ex didn't need to enter the Everpresent to know what he said. The Hound was a beast of precious few words and saved his breath only for critical thoughts. Ex held the impression that the Hound felt quite superior to humans and was honored he chose to speak to him at all.

"There were problems," Ex said, and told him what the Guardian said. He didn't seem as disturbed as Ex was, but didn't blame him, as his life wasn't at stake. With a huff, the Hound sniffed towards Arinya.

"Yes, she has to come too."

His eyes shot to Ex, narrowed, ears back. No, he didn't care about her presence. He cared if the hunter still carried their gift from the pret.

"I have it."

His tail wagged a few times, and he turned, leading them past the markings.

"Have what?" Arinya said.

"Something that might make this impossible thing possible."

Arinya stared at the Hound, and back to Ex. "How?"

He smiled in anticipation. "We're going to fight his nightmares with one of our own."

Chapter Fifteen

In the Trance

Even though Ex knew the land now, or at least better than he had, it would be futile to try and escape. The Guardian would know his failures, either through the whispers of the grass or her children of the sky, all ready to run, fly, or slither back to her sanctuary and guarantee their deaths. Arinya, bolstered by her new connection to the spirit realm, looked far more confident than he felt. Did she actually think he could do this? He'd already admitted his previous failures. Maybe it was an act.

Ex began his search on foot, the horses following quietly behind. Silently checking his traps, he contemplated how to approach the task at hand. A long hunt took meticulous preparation and unrestricted time. They had none of that now, and to start the real hunt, he needed to go into deep trance, the Hunter's Trace – a step below the Everpresent. Preparing for that ritual often took a full day, but they didn't have that much time.

With no obvious signs of Shar-Ala in this quadrant, Ex proceeded to one of his outposts. Over the last few months, he'd built these out in advantageous locations, areas strong with magic and brilliant with relatively cheerful spirits. Pushing aside the curtains of their chatter, he stepped past the thickets of bushes and into a small clearing. A half-domed shelter made of bamboo stood on the western side, hidden by layers of palm leaves and moss that rendered it almost invisible. There was a sleeping platform underneath, but he had never used it. Next to that, two locked boxes of supplies. He prayed he'd restocked this camp at some point, having lost half his bags back at the tavern running from assassins.

The sun waned. He needed to hurry. He rummaged through his badly organized box until he found a bag of coca leaves, the root of a jagbush, one fermented owl eye, and a few other base ingredients. Two black candles, red string, his mortar and pestle, and a fire pot. He swore he had a supply of readymade darts somewhere.

Two. He had two. Why did he only have two? Then he remembered chasing a minor phi three months before, needing its skin for something or another. He hadn't needed to use them for that ghost, but he'd been lazy that night.

"I'm making some tea," Arinya said, and sat on a log next to the stone-lined fire pit in the center of the campsite. She'd already struck a fire. Ex sat on the ground against the log, laying his supplies out on a clean, white cloth. The *glok glok* of his mortar and pestle was the only noise other than the insects until the teakettle whistled. After she poured two cups, she set one down next to him and said, "I figured we both need to stay awake tonight."

After their talk earlier, he didn't expect the sweet gesture.

"Thanks," he said. "I have something for you, too." He used a spoon to scrape the mixture of lejía ash and spices to coat the coca leaves. "After I leave, put one of these in your cheek every hour. It'll work a little better than tea."

She inspected them doubtfully but didn't argue. Ex cleaned the pestle off and started on his next task. Using ingredients from this swamp, he created a concoction that would pull him deeper into the Everpresent, specifically here. After he mashed the dry ingredients into a fine powder, he squeezed the owl eye, letting the sludge from inside drip into the mix. He chuckled as Arinya made a gagging noise.

He lit the candles while the mix simmered in a tin, melting wax onto the altar to stick them in place. Evidence of his earlier attempts were visible on the stone. Arinya watched in quiet fascination and didn't react when he laid out his idols between the candles. He didn't always bring them out before a hunt, but there was no downside to adding even a fraction of extra luck.

This time will be different, he told himself, and the idols. *We have a new plan. And unless you wanna rust here forever, I need any fortune you can spare.* He fed Budin with a sweet mushroom, Sarai a swanflower petal, and Lord Maaba a tiny shard of the pret's spine, still fresh.

While the mixture cooled, he checked the sharpness of his tools. He believed, with no real evidence, that Shar-Ala moved like a flickering shadow, so he would travel light, leaving the bulk of his processing tools behind. But he hesitated on the rest.

How tough was the demon's hide? Did he use poison? Ex had seen his footprints three times before, and they'd all been around the taul's lair. His feet were long and narrow, like a hare, with long strides and no visible claws. When he brought a mold back to show the other hunters, they laughed it off. They told him he was probably chasing a fat rabbit spirit.

Full armor, then. Chainblade, straight dagger, and two darts, coated with the strongest poison he had. He laid it all in a neat row. He placed the mixture next to him and threaded a long needle, coated with dreamless.

After all these preparations, the candles had dripped halfway down in rivers of black wax. From the Everpresent, Ex laid two fingers in a tin of black paint and swiped a streak across his eyes to symbolize the last slash when a hunter crossed off their mark.

Arinya continued to watch him as if observing an alien creature. The leaves from the wooden tray of coca plant sat untouched on her lap.

"Once I'm in the Trance, I won't be able to see you," he said.

She wrung her hands, a worried frown on her lips. "What if you don't come back before dawn?"

There was a strong chance of that, but that was true for every hunt. The demon might be deadlier than he planned. Another phi could lie in wait, one that he prepared no defense for. A skulking tiger could kill him. Too much magic from the wrong place could melt his insides. The list went on and on. The thought crossed his mind to make up some half-baked idea that she could take the horses and ride east as fast as she could and escape the swamp. Something reassuring and heroic and confident.

"The Guardian will kill us," he said, and his gaze drifted to her necklace. "And possibly worse."

"Ex, I need to tell you something," she started. Her heart beat faster, her mouth hanging on words that he prayed she'd leave unspoken.

"Save it for when I see you again," he said, and moved away.

"Promise you'll be back?"

Ex half-smiled, then pushed the needle deep into the sak yant tattoo of the Phi Hunter symbol in the crook of his arm. Spreading like a pale inkblot over his body, the color drained from everything, even his blood.

"Not this time," he told her, then turned away and began to recite the chanting, voiceless words that sunk deep into the soul of the earth.

The Hunter's Trance welcomed Ex with beckoning arms. He'd been away too long. It held him with an eternal warmth, the breath of devas.

The Trance existed in a vibration below the Everpresent. In the Trance, all mortal creatures went silent. Tiny sensations vibrated through the air, as subtle as the edges of leaves scraping together. Sometimes you heard the whispering thoughts of minor dark spirits as they went about their night. Rather than the bright, overpowering sensations of its shallows, there was a loss of stimulation on anything not in focus, and that focus narrowed to the finest point. All was iridescent here, the light gleamed glossy and packed deep between its layers.

Ex turned over his hands, flowing bright with the essence of the spirit blood hidden in his veins. In the light of the candles, he retrieved his armor and weapons, then stood and pulled down his mask, opaque in the world of men, transparent in this one. He moved through the dense foliage with practiced ease, and the grass moved with him in silence. He knew these paths.

The Hound waited in the shadows, wearing the sharpened stare of a warrior with his enemy in sight. The hunter nodded to him, and they stalked forward together, eyes and ears and noses focused for signs of the demon, all of them trespassers in this pure land.

There were others, of course. Minor phi, Hungry Ghosts, spirits who walked the line between low and black magic. None of those mattered. Ex and the Hound paid them no mind, and thanks to Ex's preparations, the creatures ignored them as well, if not outright fleeing the two hunters. Ex and the Hound focused solely on Shar-Ala, that was all.

The dead necromancer – the taul – had forced the trees to grow in a winding path many years ago that spiraled down into a murky pit. At the bottom laid the entrance to his underground hovel, skulls embedded into the mouth of the cavern where a pit of spiked punji sticks discouraged all trespassers. Ex and the Hound always made their rounds there, with no luck thus far.

Tonight would be different. It had to be.

The Hound growled in agreement.

The stars and moon had forsaken this place, hiding behind the canopy overhead, leaving them in utter darkness. As they descended into the pit, Ex laid small noise snares along the path, traps that would flare if stepped on, though he hadn't the time to prepare as many as he liked.

He tensed when he spotted a long, white-colored figure lurking in the darkness. Immediately, he struck his chainblade, but the figure made no reaction when it connected. He pulled, and found the thing was impossibly heavy. But when he managed to drag the creature out, he saw the glistening scales of a crocodile half eaten, its bones sticking up between its torn skin.

The Pale Mother. Last remaining god-spirit of the Crocodile Kingdom.

That's when he knew tonight would be different. Tonight, they expected a fight.

At the entrance to the lair, he knelt and opened the lead-lined drawstring bag he'd carried for days. Inside, his hand closed on a slimy, soft organ the size of his fist. It shuddered in his grip ever so slightly, and when he pulled it into the cold, gloomy air, the dim glimmer of its dying veins constricted into tiny, needle-thin lines.

This was the boon he had bargained the pret for, in exchange for mercy. Originally, he'd planned to set a trap, believing Shar-Ala would hear the miserable calls of his fellow phi and come to investigate. A long shot, but Ex's dwindling confidence in slaying the demon made any possible advantage look attractive.

Ready? Ex asked the Hound. He licked his chops with a low, eager growl in response.

Using only his fingers, Ex ripped the pret's heart into two chunks and dropped one on the ground for the Hound. Afterward, he lifted his mask and brought the other half to his mouth with both hands, drinking the spirit's blood like a bowl of soup. Then he took a bite.

Soft flesh squished between his teeth. It broke apart in ragged chunks, like a lychee. That's where all likeness ended. The best way to describe the taste of spirit blood was simple. Fucking horrible.

Ex didn't know if it was the unique way in which the pathetic creature died, but if he had to be poetic about it – it's hard not to be in the Trance – his heart tasted like a durian boiled in the sun for days, sautéed in a bucket of a diseased drunkard's stomach bile.

Consuming tonics and elixirs made with parts of spirits and magic-infused plants had always been a staple of a hunter's diet to boost their senses. Consuming unprocessed parts of a phi was considered bad karma by the elders, despite its benefits in tuning one's senses even more keen. But at this point, Ex didn't care about karma.

Shar-Ala needed to die tonight. If his awareness were anywhere else, he would have instantly vomited. Though he could taste its foulness, disgust didn't register in this state. The Hound munched and slurped at his portion while Ex chewed methodically, like a water buffalo on a piece of cud, swallowing every piece after grinding it down into paste. He subtly burped, then rocked off his knees into a crouch and peered around at the sway of bamboo surrounding the pit. How long would it take? Would it feel like the slow shift of dream mushrooms, or a sudden hit like a shot of rice wine?

The Hound licked any remnants of blood off the ground, then paced around in a slow circle, eyes bright enough to shine red light over his face. Ex was sure he looked the same. With his chainblade in one hand and blow dart in the other, he turned to match him with careful steps.

Come out, come out, we're ready to dance, he sang, and the Hound's lips twitched in a grin.

It wasn't clear how long they circled like that. It might have been minutes, it might have been hours. The only certainty was that Ex was facing east and the Hound was facing west when the waking nightmares hit.

Chapter Sixteen

The Demon Hunter

The boy's fingernails tear from his hands as he digs, digs, digs. Skin peels back into bones, opens the case and sees a stack of gleaming blades piled high as timber. The sounds of battle rumble with the thunder, a storm of black powder gunshots, the crackle and roar of flaming wood as houses burn. It's raining, but not hard enough to fight off the pitch splattered with careless disgust. He hears his mother's voice frantic and fast, but not what she says – only his name.

He wants to run to his hiding spot under the wagon and wait for it to end. But he pulls out the weapons and drags them. Drags them through mud and blood when the shadows start to melt upward, curling into creeping forms with long arms and legs and claws and teeth...

Ex wasn't prepared for this. He'd been confident that the dreamless poison would protect him. He wasn't prepared for an all-encompassing vision made not of nightmares, but memories. He tried to force himself awake, but like a well-rehearsed play, his child-self went on.

They aren't demons, they're men, but they growl all the same, arquebus rifles like pointed fingers that choose who must die. A fireball erupts, and he's too scared to flinch. They don't shoot at him, they shoot above and behind. Hot blood splatters on his bare back like dropped soup, but he doesn't look. He scrambles away as the men yell and he runs and hides under the wagon like he promised himself he wouldn't. He covers his face and sobs. If his father and brothers were here, they would sneer and call him a coward...

Ex's hand tightened around the hilt of his chainblade and something dripped on the forehead of his mask. This wasn't in the plan. He cursed the pret, praying it could hear his thoughts from hell. The bastard must have made a deal with Shar-Ala, transferred all its nightmares into him in order to truly die.

And this is why there are rules, boy, the masters would have said. *And the first rule is the most important one.*

You didn't protect her, slack lips moan through bloody mouths, sneering with repulsion as the soldiers drag them to their graves. You let your mother die. Their bodies churn in the blood and gore, then another eye peels open from each of their foreheads, a third eye, all sickly, feverish green. The corners crinkle upward, as it would when someone smiles. They grin and sneer, their arms outstretched, grasping to drag a condemned soul to hell.

No, no, no, Hunter Ex! Come here, quickly!

His mother's voice rings out from the darkness. A warmth fills his belly. He turns from the discarded bodies of his village and sprints towards her voice. She's bloody, but glorious, an angel of death, but now he sees that none of it is her blood.

Why couldn't he remember this before? He always saw her on the ground in these dreams, riddled with gunshots. But here she is, and she reaches out and snatches his small arm, drags him towards the familiar woods. His woods. A sanctuary where the Guardian will be. Her gaze is sapphire blue, her skin lacquered gold like an angel, and then she smiles–

* * *

Ex's back hit the ground and light burst into his vision. A hideous thing lurched above. A demon with a curled, arching neck like a cobra. Its jaws were peeled back in a horrid grin, stinking of thick, sour rot. Three rows of teeth where old bones were embedded in his dark, scabby gums. His face was far smaller than he thought it would be, humanoid, but with a tiny nose and wide, glowing green eyes, the third on his forehead.

Shar-Ala.

Hunter Ex. You're late.

Ex realized with a start that a long, black tongue had encircled his neck and fastened onto his mask, suckling and squirming like a leech. It couldn't break through, but was straining to peel it off. The demon's spindly arms ended in long, curled claws. At the bottom of his protruding spine, he sat on rabbit-like feet.

For a brief, stupid moment, Ex felt a pinch of validation. He *told* them it wasn't a fucking rabbit!

He jerked up his chainblade, but his arms were held fast. Shar-Ala's claws had pinned him down, unable to penetrate his armored coat but strong enough to render him still. The muscular tongue flexed, and all Ex's satisfaction instantly vanished.

You gutless pig. Ex pushed his head forward as far as it would go, which wasn't far. *If you were really a true demon, worthy of legend, you'd face me on my feet.*

A true demon does not fall for a child hunter's tricks. The fastenings on Ex's mask creaked under the pressure. *You've failed again and again. Your brethren gave up ages ago. Why do you persist?*

You've killed countless innocent people. In your mortal life and in this wretched existence now. You shouldn't go unpunished.

Innocent? There are no innocents. Only unfulfilled wishes, base desires, and dark secrets. Shar-Ala smiled wider. *Wretched thoughts of the sick and depraved are all I feast on. I beckon forth monsters from your so-called innocents. Must I tell you the sins my prey have committed?*

I know what you are. You don't discriminate.

Do you speak of women? Children? Why would I feast on the purity of children? Shar-Ala continued, and Ex wondered why he still spoke. Did he care what the hunter thought? *Purity does not taste good.*

Oh? What does purity taste like?

The sweetest honey, gilded in sunshine. His mocking smile deepened. *But how would I know?*

He was trying to scare him or enrage him. If Ex had not been in the Hunter's Trance, his heart would have burst from fright. But things were different here. This is what phi hunters trained for, what they sacrificed part of their humanity for. What they lived and died for.

He'd been wrong, for the demon didn't move as quickly as he expected, which now made sense if sleepwalkers blindly walked into his trap. Shar-Ala was strong and heavy, that couldn't be denied, but he didn't seem to be physically inclined for a fight. His powers were mental, his strength focused on fear and stunning his enemies. Perhaps that could be used to their advantage.

You're doing a terrible job of killing me.

I want to watch your face when I do. Shar-Ala's tongue flexed again. He wanted to taste his fear, but right then, it would be as bland as water. *You will scream. Even if I must tear off your tiny head and drown you in your nightmares, pathetic monkey.*

Ex's head swam, everything fading, fading. The vertebrae in his neck began to crack. He'd been so close, he thought. The true demon was right here. The Hunter's Trance blunted emotions, and so while being strangled, he felt only mild disappointment.

Then the Hound lunged and gnashed his teeth through Shar-Ala's arm, snarling with blood-curling rage. He shook his head back and forth, ripping flesh from bone.

Cut a snake in half, the Hound growled, *and it still bites.*

The pressure lifted from Ex's arm. His fist tightened around his blade and he swung in an outward arc. A shower of spirit blood burst forth and Shar-Ala's tongue was severed. The thing thrashed like a worm skewered by a hook. Ex peeled the other end off his neck and flung it aside.

The demon roared in pain and anger as his bones cracked between the Hound's fangs. He let go of the hunter to swipe at the Hound, who rewarded him with a yelp.

That was all Ex needed. He had him.

Whipping the chain around his neck once, twice, he grabbed the hilt of the blade as it swung down. Knees to his chest, Ex pushed and pulled as hard as he could. Shar-Ala screeched and reared to the side and the hunter rolled with him. Still choking him with the chain, Ex put his foot to his neck.

Shar-Ala swung his claws again, but Ex slipped aside and smashed his other foot down on his arm. The other arm, relieved of claws, thumped uselessly against his leg. The demon kicked his legs but couldn't reach. Finally, his face contorted, flinching in anguish.

Hunter! Stop! Shar-Ala strained against the chain. *You are making a mistake.*

And you're making jokes. Ex rolled his wrist, wrapped another loop around his hand and pulled tighter. The demon hissed and his mouth sagged open, skin turning darker as his blood collected. He should have been gone, but like most legends, he persisted.

Not for much longer.

I can give you what you want. I walk in dreams, plant thoughts like seeds in the minds of mortals. Imagine... your wishes fulfilled, all your desires. Everything, even her.

Go to hell.

All of his eyes rapidly twitched, out of sync from one another.

I'll take you both with me, I'll take–

A snap ricocheted up the chain and his neck turned to rubber. His body laid still, and a trickle of spirit blood ebbed down his mouth. Ex stayed there watching him, waiting, just to be sure. He could still be dangerous, some mindless reflex hidden deep within. With the chain taut, Ex stuck the blade end into the ground, through one of the links in order to hold the head still.

The claws hadn't hurt Ex, but they'd cut through the Hound, so, as retribution, Ex began to saw the demon's arm off from the elbow with the serrated part of his hunting knife.

The Trance was good for killing, but he needed vision and critical thinking for harvest. So, humming gratitude to the devas and the First Hunters, Ex emerged first into the Everpresent. All at once, the horror and fear filled him and overflowed, like a pitcher of water poured into a shot glass. He gasped and peeled off his mask with shaking hands. It would be even worse when he returned to the Blinds, so he stayed there a while, trying to still his pounding heart.

Everything – the nightmares, the demon's revolting face, and how he almost broke his neck – it all hit in retrospect, the shaking realization of how close he'd been to death. All of them.

In a sudden panic, Ex searched for the Hound. He laid on his belly a few feet away, panting hard, too angry and proud to whimper. Spirit blood pooled down his side. Ex took a step towards him, but he barked and trashed his tail.

Are you hurt?

He snarled, then struggled to rise. He took one limping step forwards. He was hurt, but there wasn't much Ex could do. It was up to the Hound to survive. The Hound crouched down again, then barked twice. Finally, Ex realized his eyes were focused behind him.

Stop her.

He whirled around to spot Arinya standing at the entrance of the cave, her shoulders slumped as she took slow, stunted steps towards the darkness. If she took two more, she'd fall into the pit of stakes in front of the cavern. One more step and she'd be skewered.

The dismembered end of Shar-Ala's tongue was wrapped around her neck, its lamprey mouth fastened over hers. Eyes wide open, her face was blank with the emptiness of a sleepwalker. With a yell, Ex sprinted towards her.

Just as her foot tipped over the edge, he grabbed her around the waist and yanked her back. She went limp in his arms, and he shoved his fingers between Shar-Ala's tongue and her face, trying to break the seal.

The tongue squirmed away from his hand. Afraid that it would hurt her if he tore it free, he grabbed the end and stabbed it with his carving knife, then slid the blade up and through to slice it in half longways. He continued with a gentle, even cut all the way to the end, and split it completely apart.

It shuddered and fell away, leaving a filmy residue on Arinya's mouth and a bruise on her neck, but no further wounds.

She looked asleep, and her chest still rose and fell, Isaree's gemstone still bright. Her heart still beat. At first, relieved, he sighed. Then Ex's anger quickly flared. How had Shar-Ala brought her here? He must have crept into the camp while he and the Hound were waiting in his lair.

With everyone now safe, the full realization of what had just happened hit him, and everything in his mind went quiet.

"I did it." Shaking with joyous laughter, Ex brought his hands to his face and wiped away tears of relief, residual terror still causing him to tremble. He killed a true demon, and not just any demon. A legend. This was all he ever wanted.

With glee, he rose back into the Blinds, where even the rotting stink of the taul's lair gave way to the smell of cleansing ash, as the blocked magic of the swamp reemerged to cauterize the wound. The grey mist of pre-dawn chased away the darkness. Ex laughed again, then his tongue slid over the remnants of the pret's flesh between his teeth and the foul blood coating his throat. With a choke, he turned away and spit out strands of arteries. Just as he leaned away to vomit, Arinya murmured, stirring awake.

Ex turned back to her and made sure his lips didn't part when he smiled. "You're okay," he said, and brushed some mud from her cheek. She sighed, eyelids lowering, and leaned her face against his hand. He wondered if she meant to do that or hadn't noticed at all.

"I don't know what happened," she murmured, and he helped her sit up. She blinked at him, as if trying to clear her mind. "The demon," she said with a sudden gasp, her fingernails digging into his arms.

"I killed him." It still sounded unreal.

She didn't smile. She stared beyond him and screamed.

Ex turned in time to see Shar-Ala's dismembered head bounce towards them at shocking speed, his lips peeled back in a deathly grin, eyes bright with hideous joy. Ex had time to push Arinya behind him before the demon's fangs sank in under his jaw. The skin split along the same still-healing wound where the assassin had cut him. A hoarse, high squeal of laughter grated from the head, even without a throat.

Ex grabbed Shar-Ala by the hanging spine and pulled. He didn't let go, and more of his flesh ripped apart. Blood poured from his neck, and Ex shoved both hands between the demon's mouth and his skin.

Fucking second rule! By the First Hunters, why did he keep doing this?

Shar-Ala's jaw twitched as he chewed, gnashing on his fingers. Stupid way to die.

But then it stopped. With that, the pressure from Ex's hands cracked open the bones in the demon's jaw and tore it apart like a rotted chicken carcass. The head flopped away, with one of Ex's poisoned darts stuck in Shar-Ala's third eye, and Arinya's fist clenched around the feathered end. The green glow of the demon's eyes faded to empty, white pupils. She dropped the dart and scooted away from the head.

The demon was finally dead.

In awe, Ex plucked out the dart. The eye slid out of its socket with no resistance. Even in death, Shar-Ala's gaze felt heavy upon him. Quickly, he dropped the eye into the lead-lined pouch previously carrying the pret's treacherous heart. He grinned and tried to say something about Arinya being a natural hunter but choked, nothing but blood in his throat.

Oh right, that.

Ex grabbed his wound to find broken skin, and wet, torn muscles. Even more blood than before, jumping out in bursts. Shar-Ala didn't have a jaw left to smile, but even from hell, Ex felt his mockery. Just what he deserved for failing to heed the rules of phi hunting, again.

He deserved to die for his stupidity, but here, in the thick of the swamp, almost suffocating with magic, he could dowse himself in the Everpresent for Shivah's Kiss. While he pulled the magic into his wound, Arinya crouched nearby, face flushed with concern. He tried to wave his hand to reassure her, then remembered her sensitivity to magic.

I'll be fine. Ex peered at her face for comprehension that she could hear him like before. She slowly nodded. *Are you?*

"I think so," she said out loud, and brought her hand to her mouth, shivering. "I was, I was awake, and it – he – came out of nowhere. I'd never seen something so awful. I must have fainted."

I'm sorry I left you there. The blood had coagulated around Ex's wounds, sinew and tendons snapping back into place. He still couldn't speak normally, but he could sit up. *You really saved my ass just now.*

"Again," she said with a small smile. He tried to return it. Then she clutched her chest, her entire body starting to shake. "It's so cold."

Alarmed, Ex focused on her, and saw a growing cloud of green energy creeping down her throat. It swirled into her lungs, crawling around in an attempt to find and poison her heart. She stared up at him in confusion, gasping for breath.

Shar-Ala's curse. One last act of malice.

Without another thought, Ex scooped her into his arms and ran up the path that led from the pit into the swamp. He knew the way to Jinburi from there, but had no idea how far away the horses were. He whistled for them, hoping the sound would carry but knowing they were likely too far. He couldn't wait for them to come.

He ran past the Hound, who'd limped over to Shar-Ala's corpse, and didn't look up during his well-deserved feast. Usually Ex would be there too, setting up his tools to harvest the demon's claws, his teeth, his hide, that disgusting tongue. Every piece of the cursed creature was priceless. But none of that mattered. If he couldn't find someone to stop the poison, Arinya would be dead by daylight.

Chapter Seventeen

Narissa meets the Butcher

After Narissa had fed her chicken and pigs, she retrieved her basket and was just about to set off for the market when a breathless man ran up the steps to her house. Tall and strong-bodied, he was dressed for violence. Stinking of fresh spirit blood, the density of his magic hit her like a gale of burning wind. Weapons dripping with death hung about his armor, and his eyes ebbed bright red when he met her gaze.

She knew what he was. A Grey butcher. A Hungry Ghost killer. A phi hunter.

Narissa reared back in terror, dropping her basket and holding her arms over her head.

"Hey! Hey, I'm not gonna hurt you," the hunter panted, leaning against the post of her porch. He held up his empty hands. "Are you the healer, Narissa?"

Narissa stared at him, silent. His black hair looked three months short of shaved, golden skin pale from skulking around in darkness. Despite his glowing eyes, he wasn't in the Grey. He couldn't *see* her. But he had been recently enough, so much that the magic lingered. And that didn't mean he didn't know what she was. Her hand crept behind her to the door handle.

A black smear of paint over his eyes confirmed he'd just

been on the hunt. There were fresh scars deep in his neck, and she thought she smelled elder poison. But more prevalent was the sweet, enticing waft of fresh blood. Then an even sharper, pure scent of something precious caught her nose, something divine...

"My friend's hurt." Panic laced his voice. Then she noticed the figure propped against her stairs – a young woman hovering on the brink of death. There it was. The elder poison swirled within her, as did the sweet smell, emanating from a point near her heart.

Narissa swallowed a lump in her throat. "There's a surgeon in town."

"Surgeons can't help her. They said you were a healer, of low magic. Are you?"

She nodded but offered nothing else.

"I have money, I can pay," the hunter stammered, then met her with soft, puppy-dog eyes. "Please, miss?"

Narissa supposed that look likely melted hearts, but she was immune to that type of power. To her, the man chilled her entire being, and she saw only the poisonous gaze of a blood-soaked murderer...

And then she saw the small lump in the woman's belly. She was pregnant, or had been recently. Through all her years healing, Narissa made sure never to act as a midwife, even though she had always wanted to be one. The blood of the unborn was too enticing, the temptation too great.

She shook her head vigorously. Yet something stirred within her chest. Not for the hunter himself, but for the softness in his eyes as he crouched down by the woman, hand gentle on her cheek as he ensured she still breathed. Then he held his face in his hands, shaking.

Narissa's breath slowed and felt his heartache, remembering the way Kiet smiled at her in the moonlight.

The boy's head shot up when she opened her door.

"Come in, hunter." She prayed she would not regret this.

After gesturing for him to set the woman on the cushion in her treatment room, Narissa walked to her kitchen and put on a kettle, then gathered supplies from her apothecary nook.

Her clients were always ordinary citizens who came in search of good fortune, charms of protection, cures for aching knees and lingering coughs. Never a phi hunter. Never a woman marked for death by an elder spirit.

When she returned to the room carrying a tray of supplies, the hunter sat on the floor next to the bed, a despondent expression on his face. Narissa froze again. She felt as if she were a mouse approaching a cat, treading on the pure faith that he'd already sated his hunger.

Without a word, Narissa knelt next to the bed, and dabbed the sweat off the woman's feverish brow with a cool rag. She lit a bundle of sandalwood, then wafted the smoke around the woman's nostrils. Just with her first breath, the elder's poison halted on its journey to her heart, alarmed by the presence. Narissa watched the hunter from the corner of her eye.

"This should halt the infection," she said. "But this poison is strong."

"So she'll live?"

"She will. But it will take time." Narissa could coax the poison out, right from the girl's mouth, but to do it would take more than a little smoke. If she used even one drop of her demon magic, the hunter would sense it as strong as if she split open a fresh durian. No. She had to work with what would be expected of alchemists, of low magic users. First, the woman needed cleansing tonics to break down the poison, then she would need to sweat it out slowly, as if coaxing down a fever.

"What's her name?" Narissa asked.

"Arinya."

"Is she your wife?"

"No, no," he said quickly, as if the thought disturbed him. "Just a friend. A good friend."

The hunter sighed, laying his head on his arms. Narissa left the bundle of sandalwood burning on an incense holder next to the bed and walked into the kitchen to fetch the tea.

"May I ask what happened?" Dread shook Narissa's hands when she returned with two cups. From Indrajit's words, she could already surmise. But she had to make sure. The hunter took it gratefully.

"I was working, and she happened to come across the hunt before my target was fully dead." Suddenly, his eyes brightened, and he smiled a youthful grin that showed his age. "Not just any ghost," he said, leaning forward. "A legendary demon. Have you heard of Shar-Ala?"

Narissa forced herself to drink slowly. She set down her tea and hid her trembling hands. Was this just a game? Was he playing with his prey before he crushed her between his jaws?

"The name is familiar."

"I've been after him for two years. No one believed me," he laughed, eerily gleeful despite the state of his friend. "It was hard, and I didn't have much time, but we still did it. You probably know this, but the swamp doesn't like humans in there."

If he spoke the truth, he was not a cat, but a tiger. And she was still a mouse. Unless… She considered him again, with the mind not of a healer, but her base, womanly form. A young man on the road for a long time always had need for company. As with most men, she caught a hint of subconscious appreciation when he noticed her feminine traits. If this woman, Arinya, wasn't his mate, then perhaps this tiger could be declawed before it inevitably discovered what she was.

No, it was too dangerous. It was a mistake to simply see a young man before her. It was a skin, a disguise, just as hers was. Underneath, he was the same as all of his kind. A powerful, merciless killer.

No, she promised Indrajit that she would not eat another human soul. Only one more night of hunger, he told her, and her curse would be lifted.

But what was the benefit of that if she died before it was

realized, condemned to be reborn again in an even more cursed form? Killing a man was not the same as eating him. Perhaps the devas would understand. Perhaps they wouldn't fault her for self-defense.

Just as the deva said, twenty-nine years was only a blink in time, as was twenty-nine more.

"Miss?" He'd asked her something, but she'd been lost in thought.

"I'm sorry, hunter," she forced a smile. "I didn't catch your name."

"Ex," he said. An alias, of course. Hunters never revealed their true names, even to the mortals closest to them.

"Ex," she repeated, then stood, brushing her hands over her skirts. "Would you mind helping me in the apothecary? It's much easier to make the next tincture if there are two more able hands."

He glanced at his sick friend, chewing on his lip. How much Narissa admired his concern, behind all his bravado of slaying the Elder Shar-Ala. The legendary phi had stayed quiet, just as she did, but he would still find his prey between the cracks of society, people that no one would miss. Obviously, he'd harbored no desire for redemption…

The hunter still seemed uneasy to leave the woman's side, and eyed Narissa with suspicion. "You really need my help?"

"No, but she is well and safe now. You, however, could use some calm."

He considered it, then to her relief, rose to his feet with a sigh.

At the apothecary table, Narissa pushed him over a mortar and pestle with a handful of herbs. Automatically, he began muddling them with an expert hand. Hands that knew how to make tinctures to strengthen his powers, and poisons to kill her kind. Meanwhile, she peeled fibrous strands off a wasari plant, gently placing them in a tin of water to soften. They worked in silence for a long time, Narissa expecting him to speak first. Mortals were uncomfortable with stillness, and silence. But when he said nothing and finished the task, she pushed him another handful.

"You look quite young for a hunter."

"I'm not *that* young."

"How old are you?"

"Twenty-four."

A blink in time. Fleeting.

"You're new to the work, then?"

"Well, no. I've been in twelve years. I joined young."

Far more experienced than she thought. He must have been to Jinburi before. It was a crossroads town, a river town. Anyone who traveled to the country and back had been here.

Nervous again, Narissa realized she'd done nothing to further her goal. She touched his hand, fighting the urge to recoil. He glanced at her from the corner of his horrid eyes, and she peeked into the mixture, fingers gentle on his.

"That's good," she said, and returned to her task. "Just a little more will do."

He grunted like a child who'd been asked to sweep the floor. "Sure." But his shoulders relaxed slightly. He seemed more at ease, a small progression, but progress, nonetheless.

"How long have you lived here?" he asked, finally inquisitive.

"About three years, but I learned this trade from my mother." Long ago, before she became what she was. He made no response, so she pressed on. "I fear it is a dying art. New medicines come from outside Suyoram, from Yinseng, and Pale East Nations. The new ways are not necessarily improved."

He murmured in agreement, then scratched a fresh scar on his neck. These hunters were numb to pain, but their bodies remembered, and those movements remained, deep within the animal brain.

She recalled the hunter who'd almost slain her. The cold, cruel sneer when the woman entered the Grey. Her steady, fearless movements, empty of humanity, as dead inside as a machine. And even after Narissa had slashed her to ribbons in desperate self-defense, the hunter lived somehow, and ran away. It happened a long time ago, a direct result of her mistake. Ever since then, Narissa lived in fear of the hunter's return. But they couldn't have tracked her through two countries and three decades, could they?

"Were your parents hunters?"

"Not like me." He stepped back from the table, then glanced around her house. "Could I use your washroom?"

"It's outside. There are clean towels in drawers next to the bed."

"Thanks."

Narissa watched him enter the treatment room, then walk out carrying his clothes, shirtless and with a cloth tied around his waist. She sucked in a breath when she saw the black sak yant tattoos along his arms, his back, his chest. They were neat and orderly – the marks of violent deeds were more akin to diagrams than the decorative skin art worn by laymen. Ancient mortal superstition. Most of those designs had long been perverted through the centuries and offered no real protection, yet they turned her blood to ice just the same.

She spotted the symbol for the krasue, and underneath, four black marks. He glanced at her as he passed, and she quickly averted her gaze.

"I'll be right back," he said, with a slight smile. "Thanks again for helping us."

Narissa watched him through the window as he proceeded past the animals. He slowed his step around the chickens, then walked behind the wooden screen where the buckets were set. She tried to recall if she'd cleaned them recently.

Even though she'd allowed a predator into her home, Narissa felt a strong urge to help the woman. There was no better merit than saving a life – no, two lives. Surely the devas would look upon this act kindly. When she saw the water flow from under the washroom screen, Narissa took the newly mixed medicine in a bowl and returned to the woman.

To her relief, the hunter had left behind his belt, laden with compartments, small pouches, weapons, and hooks for other bags. His knives were still crusty with spirit blood. Somewhere, here, the sweet nectar hid. What did he carry that produced such a scent?

Listening for his steps, and hearing nothing but the splash of water, she opened one of the pockets. Idols of a lesser deva, a spirit god king, and a golden child. She smiled kindly upon the child, but that was not the source of the smell. Her hands moved to the lead-laden purse, but she quickly withdrew. Only gruesome things were kept inside such bags.

Then her attention turned to the soft breaths of the woman. Narissa felt practically feverish as she gently dabbed the woman's sweaty forehead again, leaving the rag over her eyes. Then she untied the woman's sarong and slipped off her shoes and her pants, leaving her naked on the bed.

With the newly mixed exacting balm oily on her palms, Narissa gently massaged her, working the medicine into her skin. The woman had a strong physique hidden under her soft layer of flesh. Her back and shoulder muscles were especially taut, along with her calves and her thighs. Old, tiny fractures lay hidden in the bones of her hands, her forearms, her shins, even her skull. She must have been a fighter at some point. Her nose had been broken and set with new magic.

Narissa avoided touching the woman's belly until last, but it had to be done if she were to live. Her hands slowed as she worked in the medicine, then tightened into claws. The intoxicating scent made her dizzy. The memory of an unborn child's taste set Narissa's mouth watering anew. She bent down to inhale the sweet aroma gracing the center of the woman's chest, her mouth inadvertently slipping open to suckle at the skin. Tiny, invisible remnants remained, fragments of a pure energy that danced on the tongue like sugar. The woman's breasts were heavy and swollen with pregnancy, out of proportion to her frame.

Narissa's powers were far too weak after being a starving phi for so long, and this one meal would fill her with renewed strength. It could be done without harming her, yes, a miscarriage as a result of the poison. It was only a matter of time before the hunter found her out. And when he did, in her current form, she'd stand no chance.

It was the only way to survive.

Narissa's lips peeled back far over her gums, and her fangs began to grow. She reached inside the woman's entrance, searching, but there were no signs of a child.

It couldn't be, it didn't make sense. She smelled it somewhere inside, or was it some kind of strange magic? She removed her hand and sniffed, then took a tentative lick. A tart, stinging sensation glanced down her tongue.

Ah, there it was. A type of warding but turned inward. Could it be beyond? Was this the spell hiding the unborn soul?

The warding would have to be removed to know for sure. Drooling with hunger, Narissa floated up from her body, her spine elongating to bend her head between the woman's legs. With a grimace, her forked tongue slithered out of her jaws, the ends flickering across the flesh before it snaked inside.

The woman stirred. The taste was *wrong*. It was laced with pain. It made her stomach sick, but she fought through the discomfort and absorbed the warding. It melted away with a sour aftertaste. Now, the fetus could be consumed.

But where was it?

The woman stirred then, a soft groan, and then she murmured something in a feverish, hoarse whisper.

"Please… if I die… save her."

The hunger remained, lurking as it always did, but this time Narissa tilted her head curiously, then floated closer to the woman's head to hear her murmurs.

"Deserves… a chance."

A chirp from beside the bed stopped her. One of her cats stared up and meowed, then darted away. It jarred Narissa out of her trance, her awareness washing away to see herself from another's eyes.

What was she? A monster, a demon? As horrid and foul as she was when she hovered before the boy yesterday, ready to tear him apart. And here she was again, ready to devour an unborn, had it been there.

Throughout all her years as a healer, the hunger remained, always lurking, but Narissa always managed to fight it off. It was the only way to become closer to what she wanted to be. She didn't understand why the hunger had returned so recently, with so much force.

Narissa pulled back shaking, and she laid her head on the woman's belly to cry.

"I'm sorry," she whispered, tears warm as blood.

Then a shadow fell across them, and her demon heart froze.

It was too late.

Chapter Eighteen

And the Krasue

For such a clean-looking lady, perfume thick enough to water his eyes, she kept her bathwater rather stagnant. Ex dumped a bucket of water over his body, cringing at the musty smell, then scrubbed off with a rag. Then he doused his clothes in the wash bin, clouds of blood muddling the water. After drying off with the cloth, he wound it around his hips and legs into wrap pants. The rest of his clothes could dry out here under the oppressive sun.

Ex lingered in the yard, watching two of the chickens flap their feathers and peck at each other in some kind of dispute – likely over the lack of feed. They were slightly malnourished. It added to the feeling that there was something odd about this healer. She had no cooking utensils or food in her kitchen. But one of the busiest markets in all of Suyoram lay nearby, so that wasn't odd in itself.

Maybe it was the way the locals spoke about her, with a tremor in their voices. Also not unusual. Any type of old magic carried with it natural fear, and being what he was, it was a feeling he knew too well. And then of course, he was covered in blood and in a state of panic, which certainly put people off a little more.

Strange he hadn't heard of her. Narissa said she'd been living here for a few years, so someone in the guild must have known her. She should be on the ledgers like Mali was, alongside the countless other hedgewitches, healers, and shamans scattered throughout the countryside. But he noticed that her table didn't have much raw game harvested from phi and spirits, but instead foraged ingredients. That could be a reason she wasn't on the list.

Regardless, because of that nagging feeling, he brought Isaree with him while he washed.

Maybe he was being paranoid, trying to turn his mind away from the overwhelming fear of Arinya dying in his arms. It still twisted his guts. Taking deep breaths, he paced behind the house. She shouldn't have been on the hunt with him, she shouldn't have been in the swamp at all. It seemed as if she were stable now, but he still couldn't relax.

Two yellow eyes blinked out of the darkness from under the stilted house. The slivers of feline pupils reminded him of the Guardian of the Swamp. She hadn't appeared again after they killed Shar-Ala, but a passage had opened up by the taul's lair, which could only be by her favor. It brought him out of the swamp far quicker than the way he knew.

A fat yellow cat slunk from under the stilts, curling his tail around the post as he critically glared. "Hey little guy." Ex knelt down to pet him. The cat stretched out his neck to sniff his hand, then drew back with a hiss.

"Little jumpy, aren't we?" Ex smiled. The cat didn't. With a feline grumble, he crept back under the house, but curiously, a small metal handle peeked up from the ground from where he'd just been.

It was a trap door, recently opened, but hastily covered with a straw mat. That wasn't entirely strange. Uncommon, maybe. And he might have left it there if it weren't for the handful of other things that had him on edge.

It was probably nothing. And if it were nothing, no harm

done. Still, Ex hesitated, and glanced at the cat for advice. It might be a little awkward to explain to the lady why he was rooting around in her cellar. Awkward, but not an egregious offense. Maybe there was something useful, like a bottle of wine that he could ask to drink.

Giving in to his curiosity, Ex lifted the trap door for a peek. A few raggedy stone stairs led down into a dark, humid, underground hole. It didn't appear to be dug out with any kind of shovel. The walls were raked with scratch marks, the earth gouged into a tunnel as if a large animal had burrowed there. Maybe it was. Witches kept pets, like Mali's owl, and he knew another shaman who doted on his parrot. Mostly birds, though, if he thought about it. He knew one witch that kept a koi pond, with one spotted black and goldfish the size of a dog, and Ex didn't go near it. But whatever this lady's pet was seemed more... carnivorous. It certainly smelled like one. There had to be at least one rotting animal carcass somewhere in there.

A giant weasel? Rat colony? He didn't sense anything crawling around and was about to shrug it off to typical old whisper weirdness when something else caught his eye. Buried half under the dirt, laid a fine silver hair comb with pearl inlays.

The finery was not something he'd expect from a hedgewitch, but even if it was, it seemed an odd place to leave it. He picked it up, then peered into the darkness. The tunnel wasn't long, but the end was obscured by torn silk curtains. Maybe the family fortune, hidden away for a rainy day.

With a dead animal?

Ex hated being underground with a rare passion, even more than he hated being on boats. Still, his curiosity got the best of him, and he ducked his head to walk further in. When he pushed aside the curtains, all humidity dried from the air and the temperature dropped from a cliff. His breath fogged, something that only happened in the extreme altitude of the high mountains.

Cold dread flooded his chest.

A nest. A cocoon of reedy, twisting tendrils formed the end of the tunnel, a sinewy mass of interlaced vines that were less grown from the ground, and more invading it. Though the nightmarish growth formed a solid wall, there was an imprint, as if someone had laid on a bed of mud and waited until it was dry.

It was in the shape of a headless woman.

Ex burst into the house, ready to rip the demon to shreds with his bare hands. He halted in the entrance to the sick room, unable to comprehend what the fuck was going on. The foul krasue had unclothed Arinya, and laid her cheek to her belly. Her head had detached partially, entrails hanging like decorative ribbons between her skull and her neck. She shook softly, as if laughing.

Fucking demon!

The krasue gasped and started to recede into her body like a snail into its shell and Ex burst in. He snatched her by the hair and yanked her back out, the bloody lungs and intestines spilling forth like pig slop. Before she could bite, he crushed his hand over her mouth and shoved her head against the wall. A spell radiated from his palm. One word and her jaw would melt straight off. By the fear in her eyes, he trusted she could sense it.

He snarled into her face, which remained human, masking the disgusting thing coiling beneath. *What did you do to her?*

I did nothing, hunter! I swear! The krasue tried to shake her head, but he held her too firmly.

Liar.

Please! I wasn't going to hurt her.

Why did you undress her? Why are you out of your skin?

It was only to apply the balm – And I... I thought I smelled an unborn.

Her eyes darted to Arinya's pendant, hanging around his neck.

Looking for this, were you?

The krasue shuddered. *Yes. But she, she had a malicious warding... I only removed it.*

He assumed the creature was lying, but leaned his head towards Arinya anyway, averting his eyes from her intimate areas. She didn't appear injured, and he couldn't smell the warding's distinct cedar scent anymore. But that didn't mean it wasn't there. The krasue had proved herself a master of disguise, hiding the rotting stench of her lair, and her own aura. Who could say she couldn't do the same with others?

I'm no threat to you. I've lived peacefully for twenty-nine years without taking a soul.

Until today?

Tears streamed down her cheeks and over his hand. Despite her nature, it still alarmed him to see the face of a woman in pain. He eased his hand off her quivering mouth, but kept it close to her lips, spell threatening. Her glistening lungs expanded in rapid breaths between her pulsating heart. He could reach out and crush it in his hands so easily. Master Seua would have, without hesitation.

"I speak true, hunter," she said out loud, her voice barely above a whisper. "Yes, the thoughts came. I wanted to kill you before you discovered what I was. I wanted to devour the unborn child. But thought and action are not one and the same."

Why should I believe you, demon?

"I am becoming mortal again through the Blessing of Indrajit's Amnesty. If I pass thirty years without taking a human soul, the devas will grant me humanity."

Highly doubtful, that. From what he'd been told, the devas despised the phi, especially the dark ones. He snorted with disgust. "How creative."

"I don't expect you to believe me." She cast her eyes down. "Please, sir, allow me to help her. Shar-Ala's poison shall kill her without proper treatment. And after she recovers, judge me as you will. I will not fight my fate."

Ex wanted to believe her, for Arinya's sake. He couldn't save her on his own. Trying to find another old magic healer here might be a hopeless effort.

Who was your last meal? Twenty-nine years ago?

"Kiet," she said. "The only man I've ever loved."

She shut her eyes then, ready to die. Ex felt his jaws tighten, and his fingers twitched. The guild members killed these phi without question, without remorse. Everything in his body and mind screamed at him to kill her, and all he could do was imagine how he should.

But if he considered what she'd done...

She could have attacked him when he was distracted. She could have killed Arinya when he left the house. Instead, she treated her and removed the prince's malicious warding. If he considered what Narissa had done, apart from being a delusional phi...

Ex clenched his fist, and with a long exhale, dropped the spell.

He had no cause.

With a shuddering sigh, she stared at the hunter in relief, clearly not expecting this mercy. Slow as a slug, she receded back into her body, watching him the entire way as if he would change his mind.

He could still.

"Please don't make me regret this," Ex said as he emerged from the Everpresent.

"You won't," she said, palms pressed together in a thankful wai. "I promise with all of my soul."

Here he went again, breaking the first rule. It never seemed to work in his favor, yet he kept doing it. If the masters knew how reckless he'd been, they'd strip him of his symbols, ink out all his tattoos.

Maybe an argument could be made for following the third

rule – exploit their fear – but it was less of a rule and more of a tip. Or in this case, an excuse.

Ex sat sentinel against the wall as the demon worked on Arinya, now fully dressed in his armor, all his weapons securely fastened. He even put his boots on, because this demon's hovel deserved no respect. He idly stared at the marks on his right forearm, where hunters wore all symbols for the phi they'd slain. He had many different ones, all given by the masters once confirmed.

He'd killed krasue before. Mostly the male versions, who weren't as dangerous. Their hair, their lungs, and especially their spines were highly valuable. He could use that extra money. Under the symbol for the krasue, there were four marks. Three had been brothers, terrorizing a matrilineal tribe in the highlands. The fourth had been female, stalking an outskirt village near the Capital. It had been an easy, quick kill. They weren't fighters, they were tricksters and ambushers. Like all Hungry Ghosts, once they'd tired of livestock, they graduated to human flesh.

Narissa's deva "amnesty" sounded like complete bullshit, but it was possible the krasue hadn't killed anyone recently. Surely the guild would have heard of it, especially in a town like Jinburi. They left very distinguishing bite marks on their victims. Odd enough that she managed to live here without being discovered, but that would explain the livestock and nothing to cook with.

Ex twisted his wrists to show the underside of his left forearm – bare, reserved for true, named demons. It wouldn't be bare for much longer. Shar-Ala's eye felt heavy in his pouch, laden with all the pain and terror he'd caused. He couldn't wait to see everyone's faces when he plopped it in front of them.

Once he met back up with the Hound, they had to celebrate. Well, *if* he met back up with the Hound. This may have been their last hunt together, and it wasn't certain he'd survived. Despite his hunger, he'd suffered grave injuries. Any normal creature would be dead, but the Hound was still half-spirit. If Ex never saw him again, it was easier to believe he died gloriously in battle, the way warriors of his tribe respected.

"Is the child yours?" The krasue's voice was chillingly soft, yet still grated on his nerves. She'd redressed Arinya in clean clothes, and sat at her side, waiting for the balm to do something. With her delicate, very human hands, she braided Arinya's hair. Eerie, yet endearing. Ex sneered at the sentiment, annoyed at himself for even thinking it.

"How many people have you killed?" he shot back. His mercy was not akin to friendship.

"Hundreds," she said without a shred of emotion. "I would have continued."

"And no hunter ever found you?"

"A hunter almost killed me, but Indrajit saved me from her blade. Then he offered me salvation, on this condition. I took it."

"Her..." Ex murmured. There weren't many women in the guild, but the few that were earned twice their names. If it'd been thirty years ago, then it could only be one of three ladies. "What did her mask look like?"

The krasue's fingers ceased, yet her expression didn't change. "A snarling red cat."

Master Rei, the Blood Panther. She had plenty marks on her forearms, true demons included. Ex knew she had dozens of krasue as well, and it seemed unlikely that she would let a hunt go unfinished.

"She never found you?"

"No." The krasue continued the braid, then tied it off with a small, gold string, woven throughout the strands. "For luck," she said and tucked it behind Arinya's ear. She sat quietly, staring down at her work, though not quite at it. Her eyes always remained unfocused, as if lost in thought. "Might you entertain a question, hunter?" She took his silence as permission. "If you had one wish, for anything in the world, what would it be?"

Her words reminded him of Shar-Ala's as he begged for mercy. Empty promises designed to distract, to taunt and twist. Shar-Ala had peeled back the layers of his psyche to its raw flesh, and scraped at it with his claws.

"Maybe I want to be a demon," he said with a mocking smile. "But a wolf can't become a snake just by wishing for it."

"When the Enlightened One first laid eyes upon the Deva of Justice, she appeared as a swan–"

"You're religious, too?" Ex had to laugh then. "Come on."

"To be born a phi is divine punishment." Her head dipped, and Ex detected a hint of hurt. "What more evidence is needed but my mere existence?"

He shrugged and scratched the fresh scars on his neck, wondering if he'd been cursed. Maybe the sorcerer hexed him. Made a stabbing doll and looped a wire around his neck. When he finally received his true demon killer sak yant, he'd be sure to ask for a protective one on his throat.

He wondered if Arinya would want to come to the ceremony. Maybe she'd get an honorary mark. It was her who dealt the final blow, after all.

His smile faded as quick as it came. The prince would never let her mark her body like that. He made it clear with the warding that she was his. It was a stupid thought anyway. Obviously, she couldn't be seen with the spawn of a rebel. Not even as friends, she'd said. Once they returned to the Capital, she'd return to her life. She'd pay him as promised, and that would be that.

She'd remember all of this as a magical adventure through the woods with the awkward, branded hunter who kept getting his throat slit. An unbelievable tale to entertain the other aristocrat ladies. Given a few lavish meals and princely gifts, Ex was sure she'd forget he ever existed.

As for him, with the money he'd earn, he could survive without wasting time on these lesser phi. He'd go on and find another true demon to kill.

Just go on.

The krasue gathered the old rags, the ashen sticks of incense and empty bowls. From what she told him, Arinya would be awake by sunset. She dipped her head, then walked towards the door.

"Narissa."

She froze in the door frame and her back straightened, but she didn't turn.

"It's not mine," he said and removed Arinya's pendant, and fastened it back around her neck.

Chapter Nineteen

And the Consort

Into the evening, Jinburi blurred into a hive of lights, flickering like frozen fireflies across the land and the two rivers. People carried lanterns as they went about the streets, the crossroads town still bustling and active under the newly waning moon. Trade goods were hawked over in the night markets, flesh and favors in the brothels. Music played in the streets, punctuated by intermittent cheers from gambling houses and boxing matches.

Sitting on the roof of Narissa's house, Ex could just make out the center of town, crowned by the steepled roof of the famous Pearl Temple, the non-traditional designs and murals making it more of an art exhibit than a place of worship. Narissa lived closest to the Namleng River, where men sat in their boats smoking cigarettes, casting about nets for nocturnal fish without fear of the dark.

These rivers had once been the main passage for the Crocodile Kingdom, and a battleground between their disputing tribes before man moved in. Before man burned back the swamp and turned the rightful residents into boots and purses. Ex wondered what it might have looked like back then – their underground cities below the river, citizens laying about the banks to sunbathe with their families.

What would they say if they knew what they'd be reduced to? Mindless creatures in pens more plant than beast, piled on top of one another like stacks of raw goods, waiting for discarded meat or death... He thought their monarchs would have drowned their entire kingdoms before living that way.

What would they talk about, if the two types ever met? Would they despise each other? Feel pity? Would they become friends? It was hard to make friends when you were worlds apart, practically a different species.

The only friends Ex had growing up were the groundskeepers' sons, Piglet and Swan, nicknamed for their resemblance to the animals. He played with some of the hunters' children from time to time, but they didn't come to the grounds often enough to make any real connection. They stayed in town with their parents.

But Piglet and Swan lived on the compound too. They had a few years on him and didn't have to get up at the crack of dawn every day to train, so he didn't go with them on their excursions into the city very often. Once Ex grew a little older, they convinced him to go out. They liked to gamble on cockfights and visit opium dens, both of which made him more than a little ill. On his fifteenth birthday, they brought him along to the brothel. At first, he was eager, falling over himself as he ogled all the beautiful women. It amused them to buy him a room. He sat on the dingy, canopied bed, already hard and drooling, and in walked the biggest, brawniest lady he'd ever seen. He was terrified. Before he could back out, she threw him around like a rag doll, and after it was all over, he felt as if he'd just been beaten down for fumbling a spell.

Master Rei found him sniffling on the rooftop of the stables. It was a surprise to see her there, since it was where he went to be alone, a place he thought no one knew about. She wasn't known to be a warm woman, having to be hard enough to rise to her position in a trade full of surly men. But she'd always been kind to him, kinder than Master Seua, anyway.

What are you searching for? She asked.

Ex said he just wanted friends.

I know you want to be like them, she said, *but you don't belong to their world. You'll never belong to their world.*

But he was lonely, he told her. All the hunters were at least ten years older than him.

Seek comfort in the Everpresent, she told him. *And you'll never walk alone.*

"Ex."

Narissa stood in the yard, her disquieting eyes dark, even in the starlight.

"Time for bed?" Ex raised a brow towards her lair. She didn't react, much to his disappointment.

"She's awake."

Arinya sat in bed with a steaming cup in her hands, face somber and steady. She smiled when Ex walked in and set down her cup. Before she could say a word, before he could think about it, he closed the distance and wrapped his arms around her. He wasn't sure what to say, but her body relaxed, and she laid her head against his chest.

"Miss me?"

"Just a little bit," he said. She laughed and ruffled his hair, as you would do to a child. He drew back, sheepishly and avoided her gaze. "How do you feel?"

"Better." She picked up her tea and inhaled the warm mint and lavender steam. "Better than I have in a while, to be perfectly honest. How did you get to Jinburi so quickly?"

"The Guardian led me out."

"Narissa told me I was moments away from death."

In more ways than one. Ex glanced over his shoulder to the krasue standing in the doorway with her meek, unassuming smile.

"Did she tell you?" he asked Arinya. Why wasn't she

anxious to be in the company of a demon? After Shar-Ala, he wondered if anything could shake her.

"She did. I know you can be friends with spirits, but I didn't know you could be friends with phi."

"We're not friends. We made a deal."

"I see." She set down her cup and stretched.

Narissa crouched down and laid a hand on Arinya's forehead. She shied away from Ex, as if he would be the one to bite.

"Now that the fever has broken, these tonics should bring you strength. You're welcome to rest here tonight."

"No, thanks," Ex said. "We're not far from the Capital now. We should keep moving, and uh..." Both women stared at him. Arinya seemed especially cross. "What?"

"You want to travel? Now?"

"If we ride overnight, we could probably make it by tomorrow, or midnight, at least–"

"Ride?" Arinya said. "Ride what?"

Oh, right. He left Ramble and Brownie back at the camp. He had to go back and get them, which he could do on his own. Not to mention the harvest. Shit, it was going to be a long night.

"Okay, sure. It might be better if you get some sleep tonight. I just thought, you know, you've been sleeping all day, so..." He drummed his hands on his knees. "We should find somewhere else to stay in town."

"Don't be ridiculous. Narissa kindly offered her home, free of charge. It's only polite we accept."

"Of course she would," Ex muttered.

"Ex, didn't she tell you about her deal with the devas?"

"She did. It's an adorable story, but it's not, you know..." He waved his hands. When she didn't answer he finished, "Possible."

"How do you know?"

What was it with her? He wiped his eyes and squeezed his temples, at a loss. Maybe Arinya had a distorted view of magic due to the things she'd seen, but it wasn't anything goes. There was an order to it, there were rules, there was truth and falsehood. Perhaps he did a shitty job of explaining it all.

"Allow me to bring you fresh towels." Narissa took Arinya's empty teacup and left the two alone.

"You can never trust a phi," Ex said, and Arinya raised her eyebrows with an astounded look. A *she's standing right there* look. "I don't care if she hears me. She knows better than anyone."

"Do you see what she's done? She saved my life, Ex. Perhaps the life of Isaree. I… I think if I die, she would too." Arinya patted him on the arm. "I'm sure we can trust her."

"The last time I trusted a phi, he traded me death for a heart that almost got us all killed." She tilted her head in confusion, and Ex shook his head. "Never mind that. The question is, do you trust *me*?"

"Of course I trust you."

"Then, listen. A phi will say anything to get what they want. They lie, they beg, they appeal to your humanity. It's not real."

"In this, Ex, you are blinded by your trade. Narissa must be different." Arinya twirled the braided strand of her hair. "I can sense it."

He groaned, but knew it would be pointless to attempt to convince her. She'd made up her mind already, and the only thing he could do was stick around and kill the demon if she tried to kill them. The demon knew her life was in his hands. He didn't need the rest, but Arinya was right. She did.

"Fine." Ex glared at Narissa, who idled around the kitchen. "On one condition. We seal her in her creepy little lair for the night."

Arinya looked horrified. "What do you mean *seal* her?"

"Lock the door, put rocks over it, the usual." He shrugged. "It's not that hard, I've done it before. They can still starve to death."

"We're not doing that," Arinya snapped. "She told me she hasn't slept down there in years."

He sucked his teeth, fighting the urge to roll his eyes. "Really?" He called over to Narissa. "Smelled pretty used to me."

"I go down to water the veins," she answered. If she were offended, it didn't show. "But yes. I have a bed upstairs. I've grown quite fond of it."

"Then I lock you in the room," Ex said, avoiding Arinya's disapproving glare. "Don't worry. She won't let me leave town without letting you back out."

Narissa dipped her head. "If it will put your mind at ease, hunter, I will gladly do so."

After an uncomfortable silence, Arinya frowned. "I'm sorry," she said to the krasue. "Let me take you for a night out, I know of a likay theatre here that I've just been dying to return to."

"That sounds quite wonderful."

It was Ex's turn to stare at Arinya in horror. "You want to… go to a show? In town?"

"Is there in issue?"

"Did you forget about the queen's men after you? Or the assassins that slit my throat? You don't think they'll be searching for you there?"

"What can they do? Isaree's in no danger now. And the assassins won't kill me. Besides, how would they know where we are? We left them far behind."

This had to be the worst idea she'd ever had. He glanced at the krasue. "Are you sure the poison's all gone?"

"*You* don't have to go," Arinya snapped. "In fact, maybe it should be just us girls."

"I can't believe this." He flopped on the ground, on his back. "You aren't going to take no for an answer, are you?"

"I won't. What's one hour to relax? It'll be perfectly fine. You may be at home in the forest, *hunter*, but I know the city."

A longing in her voice told him she missed it. And something else, something she wasn't telling him. He peeked at her, and she smiled. "The question is, do you trust *me*, Ex?"

Chapter Twenty

The Tourist

In the center of town, people were already making preparations for Rom Laithong, a week-long holiday to celebrate the arrival of the rainy season. Residents and travelers alike would fill the rivers with tiny boats made of flowers and candles, and release tiny paper balloons into the night. In anticipation, they hung strings of beads and flower garlands over buildings, restocked their Spirit Houses, haggled over the best cuts of meat.

Ex felt like a monkey in a suit. It had been a long time since he wore civilian clothes. The two ladies had overdressed him in long sleeves to cover his tattoos and plopped a square cap on his head – who wore caps?! Arinya assured him he looked "somewhat normal." If the Hound could see him now...

All his bellyaching immediately ceased when Arinya emerged from Narissa's room in a borrowed sapphire silk dress with bronze details, her hair pinned in a braided bun. She'd draped a translucent silver shawl over her shoulders and turned in a circle.

"What do you think?"

He couldn't, really. Ex realized his jaw was hanging open and quickly shook his head. "Maybe you should wear something less, uh, you know..."

She propped her arms on her hips, pursing her lips. "Less what?"

As he stumbled over his words, both she and Narissa smiled at each other. It felt like they were conspiring against him. Then, at the last minute, Narissa said she was tired and would rather wait at home for them. Arinya didn't goad her into coming along and he wondered if that was their plan all along.

"It's the eve of Rom Laithong. Everyone wears their finest." Arinya assured him as they walked down Narissa's dirt road and into town. Once they entered the market district, he relaxed just a little. She was right, of course. Some women had full-on crowns, men wore silk or cotton suits and... caps. Fancier caps than his.

A festive atmosphere had turned Jinburi into something not quite as garish as a circus, but not quite refined enough to watch your manners. Being on the crossroads brought a certain segment of society out to celebrate – travelers either wide-eyed in wonder or looking for trouble before skipping town. The locals played to all audiences.

Ex had been staring at a paper statue of a dragon, currently being lacquered by artisans, when Arinya took his arm.

"Come on, mountain boy," she laughed, and led them through the crowd, stepping around a drunken juggler who couldn't manage more than two pins at once. He paused before a large, open-walled shrine devoted to the elephant-headed, pot-bellied Deva Phra-Phikanett, his brightly painted idol draped with lotus and jasmine garlands. His followers gathered around the steps, paying tribute with candles, incense, and golden bowls of fresh fruit and baked goods.

It brought back memories of his mountain village. Phra-Phikanett had been their patron deva, and his mother often took him to their humble shrine to lay bananas for favor. During his month of tribute, villagers would break coconuts and throw them in the nearby stream to cleanse them free of their karma.

Quickly, he turned his mind away from the bittersweet memory, eager to keep his spirits up.

Ex couldn't help but smirk when people watched them walk by, with a purely juvenile air of pride. That thought was followed by the nagging feeling that people might recognize Arinya, or worse, that there might be agents of the crown here. There had to be, and the stupidity of strutting around like a show horse hit him in full force.

"We should go back," he leaned down to whisper in her ear. "If someone recognizes you..."

"No one will," Arinya said. "I'm the prince's consort. I don't attend him in public. Act like we're just a normal, happy couple, and no one will bat an eye."

A normal, happy couple? The two of them together was far from normal, and the last time he checked, they weren't even friends. He managed to bite back that response. He was about to ask how thoroughly they should play along when she came to an abrupt stop under a solidly built, wooden building with a soaring roof and gaudy, carved panels down the pillars. "This is it."

"What is it?"

"A theatre."

"I've never seen a play before."

"Oh, it's not your typical theatre," she said, and when they entered the large double doors, a roar exploded from the crowd. After walking through an airy lobby packed with raucous people, they entered into a large arena. In the center was a square ring where two men circled each other. At least, Ex thought they were men. They both wore decorative khon masks and tight-fitting, colorful cloth costumes imitating armor. One of them spun a two ended spear, just like Charnchoi from the old tales.

At the threshold, a sallow-faced kid who looked sick with boredom accepted a few coins for their entry and pointed to some seats in the back row. Arinya slipped him a few more, and he brought them down near the front, then signaled a beermaid over. The woman handed them two cups of ale before moving onto the next customers.

"It's half theatre, half combat," she explained, as the man with the dragon mask launched into a series of spin kicks which seemed to take the spearman by surprise. The spearman flinched in an obviously practiced way before bashing the other guy in the head, knocking him down. He lifted his arms and the crowd hooted in response. Afterwards he pranced around the ring in a manner that would be frowned upon in any real muay-boran match.

"There's no way this is real," Ex said, half-heartedly clapping with everyone else.

"Oh, don't ruin it," she nudged him with her elbow. "The prince hates this, but I find it quite joyous. I don't need to see men break each other's noses for fun."

"What else does the prince hate that you find joyous?"

"Well... he has a very strict diet. No meat, no fish, only vegetables."

"I love meat *and* fish."

"He doesn't like to dance."

"I like to dance."

Arinya squinted at him in disbelief.

"What?" he said. "Hunters do all kinds of rituals. Some of them involve dancing."

"Really? I think you're going to have to prove that."

"Sure..." He narrowed his eyes. "Does that mean you want to go dancing after this?"

"Depends, hunter. Is it a *ritual* dance? Or just a dance?"

He hid a giant smile behind his cup. "Depends on the music, I guess."

"Hmm." She still seemed skeptical. "What does one of these dances sound like?"

"Mostly drums, sometimes a khlui."

"And what does the dance look like?"

"Slow, fast. There're no real rules." He glanced over and met her eyes. "Whatever you're in the mood for." For the first time, he saw some color on her cheeks, then a loud thump from one of the performers drew their attention.

Arinya cheered just as loud as the rest of the crowd when the dragon guy grabbed the spear guy by the ankle and yanked him flat on his face. Ex burst out laughing at how stupid he looked, waving his arms in exasperated surprise. Sometimes the audience jeered.

After they finished their performance, pretty dancers in traditional costumes paraded out for an intermission. A server walked by slinging ales, and they took two.

"To living through nightmares," Arinya said as they lifted their mugs. As she drank, there was a far-away look in her eyes. What had she seen when Shar-Ala invaded her mind? Maybe she wondered the same about him. That vision, one he'd seen a hundred times, had never held so much clarity as it did then, and he wondered what was true.

Had his mother brought him to the Guardian all those years ago?

No, it couldn't be. How else would he have ended up in the custody of the crown, brought to the Capital in chains, branded like an animal and dumped onto the street? He thought she'd died all those years ago, her body lost under the mud and ash. Yet she appeared so vivid and real, even called out to him... No, she didn't call his name. She called him–

"Ex?" Arinya squeezed his elbow, jarring him from his fog.

Ex took a quick drink and turned back to the stage. "Who's next? The one-eyed thug in the pig suit?"

As the show went on, the crowd grew rowdier. Ale thrown from the upper seats splashed down on them. A few fights broke out in the stands. After some of the disorderly men started to leer at Arinya and sneer at Ex, he took her arm and gestured towards the exit. Thankfully she didn't argue, ducking behind him as another flagon of ale smacked a man right in the bald spot and another sour shower rained down upon them.

"This way," she said, and pulled him in another direction. They went away from the arena, through a dank hallway behind the seats where workers scuttled with full trays, and a few shady people lingered, seeming to do nothing in particular. Ex stopped and asked Arinya where they were going, and she told him not to worry, taking his hand.

Finally, there was another door with a stadium guard standing next to it, smoking a roll up. He barely acknowledged them before he bid them a good evening and opened the door.

They were near the river now, the docks here more commercial than the ones nearer to Narissa's side of town. Couples strolled together, vendors hocked desserts and flowers, kids sat laughing with their friends. Arinya let go of Ex's hand and walked down to one of the piers and sat on the edge. Ex felt hopelessly lost without her leading him, even if she'd only walked a few feet away.

The paper lanterns strung overhead bathed her in a sheen of red and gold, reflecting off the peaceful waves. On the last day of the festival, people would bring lotus flower lanterns and float them into the water. The banks would fill with the murmur of prayers and appeals to the devas and Enlightened Lord for blessings. It was too bad they'd be in the Capital before then. It would have been fun.

Her fiery eyes settled into a slow burn as she stared over the water and sat down on a bench. "It reminds me of home," she said with a soft sigh. "The people, the river, the noise…"

The city gave Ex anxiety, even though he'd spent half his childhood in the choked streets of the bustling capital. Somehow, inside the walls of the guild compound, it felt as peaceful as the country. Rather than voicing all his thoughts, he took a seat beside her, leaning back on his elbows to observe the dark river, sparkling bright with colorful reflections from the city.

"I suppose you feel at home in the forest," she said. "The quiet."

"The forest isn't quiet. It's full of energy, and noise. It's just... just different."

"Hmm. You're right, come to think of it." With a deeper tenor of sadness in her voice, she rubbed her hand over Isaree's pendant. "Thank you, Ex."

"For what?"

"For coming with me tonight. It was reckless, I know. But I just wanted to remember what Suyoram was like. Before I chose this other life." Her lips parted to say something more, but she frowned and stared down at the water instead. He worried he had said something to upset her but had no idea what it would have been.

"Arinya..." he ventured, and she looked over. "What's bothering you?"

She took a sharp breath in and closed her eyes. "I can't stop thinking about those nightmares. They were so horrible."

"That's the phi, for you. They prey on our weaknesses." His explanation felt hollow. Too simple, too dismissive. "They were bad for me too."

She blinked in surprise. "The dreamless didn't work?"

"I'm sure it did." He considered playing it off, then decided she could handle it. "Me and the Hound ate a raw pret's heart to draw Shar-Ala out, and that brought on a waking dream."

She raised her eyebrows, mouth ajar.

Ex cringed. "Is that gross?"

"Pigs heart soup is the king's favorite. I doubt it's any less gross than that," she laughed then, and leaned into him. "Come on. What did you see?"

"The last time I saw my mother." His voice broke, and that was where he came to the end of his words. Somehow, he couldn't explain what he'd seen and what it meant to him. The visions were simple, but even thinking of them, thinking about his village and the last memories of his mother, stung his eyes.

"I'll tell you about mine," she said quickly, following him into his somber state. But her voice came out strong. "I dreamt that Prince Varunvirya comes to my room, wakes me up in the middle of the night. He leads me somewhere I've never been before, deep in the palace, past the catacombs. He brings me out to a passage that leads to the moat. A man stands there. A sorcerer. He gives me a tonic, and tells me to drink it at midnight, every night, for a week.

"Of course, I know what it will do. The prince doesn't want a usurper just as much as the new queen doesn't. I understood that, and I even accepted it… but he wanted something worse." Ex peered over in alarm, but she had gone distant. She was back there now, seeing it all again. "He wanted the sorcerer to take her tiny little body, his *own child*, and make her into a kuman thong for his own power… I couldn't let that happen. So I ran."

She stared down at the pendant, then let her hands drop into her lap. "That was it."

A wave of futile anger washed over him. First, this prince imposes his insecurities onto her through black magic, and *then* he tries to imprison a soul that wouldn't even have a chance to return to the higher realm. Ex's hands clenched into fists.

"I'm sorry." He didn't know what else to say. He wanted to take her into his arms, to take her sadness away, in any way he could, but didn't think she'd react well to that. There was nothing he could compare it to in his own experience. All he knew was that he didn't want her to be sad anymore.

"I can't stop thinking that I'm doing the same thing. That I'm keeping her trapped here, by my own selfishness. Keeping her from going somewhere else, wherever else, becoming someone else." Her voice shook and she sucked in a breath. "I keep telling myself that I'm going to wait for the right time, when it's safe, when there's a proper heir. But it's never going to be safe, Ex. Not in Suyoram."

"Then why are you going back?" Ex asked. "Is it the comfort? The money? It sure as hell can't be love, can it?" The bitterness in his own voice surprised him. "Ah, I'm sorry. It's not my business."

"No, you're right." Her tone brightened. "I thought I was stuck forever, to behave and be grateful for all that I was provided. But now I see that there's so much more. There's so many wonderful things hidden away from the 'new' world, like magic and spirits, and... you."

That took him aback. When he glanced over, she was smiling. Smiling at him. And then she slipped her hand into his.

"I admit I was scared at first. Of magic, of spirits, of hunters. Yet you still brought me into your world. You protected me and showed me that you're a good person." This was new territory. Ex couldn't remember a time anyone had said that type of thing to him, and again, was speechless.

"May I ask you something?" She drew closer, her fingers tightening around his.

He thought his heart stopped.

She peered up through her lashes in that manner that completely disarmed him, and he braced himself for her next words. He'd never felt so helpless in his life as he did right then. Forget the night before, pinned down, in the clutches of a true demon.

"Anything," he said in earnest. She could tear him to shreds if she wanted to. He hoped, with all his being, that she wouldn't.

"Will you help me get to Yinseng?"

Ex blinked a few times, thinking he might have heard her wrong. What? Was she serious? She raised her eyebrows, still smiling. He hadn't said anything out loud, thank the devas, and he wasn't in the Everpresent, even though it felt like he had been.

He withdrew his hand from hers in order to snatch the stupid cap off his stupid head and rub his temples. "Yinseng. You want to go to Yinseng?"

"We can disappear there," she said. "I could become someone else, and I could raise her there, where it's safe. No one will bother us."

"You can't just…" Ex waved his arm at her, trying to encapsulate her entire being. "Become someone else."

"I've done it before," she said, and her steely hardness returned. Her eyes darted to his chest and back, and his brand seemed to burn under her gaze. "Haven't you?"

"But what about me?" That came out wrong. "My reward, I mean. I promised to bring you back, and if I help you escape, I'm pretty sure that moves me over from escort into traitor."

"No one will know it was you," Arinya said. "I only need to get to the gates of the Jade Star, that's all. I can handle myself from there."

As tough as she was, Ex hated to imagine her trying to make her way through the wild border town. It was far more dangerous than the worst areas of Jinburi, or the Capital – hell, maybe even the swamp. At least the creatures there would only kill you and eat you.

"I'm sorry, Arinya. I can't help you with that. I'm sure there's a sell-sword around here who will get you to the Jade Star with more protection than I can."

"Not if we take the Serene Way, right?"

Technically, she was right. But he shuddered to think about the Long Road through the badlands. He knew very little about the land up there. Some of the other hunters would, no doubt, but it wasn't part of his rounds. It was an ugly, war-torn land, overrun with cultists. The phi there weren't just angry and dangerous as they were in the countryside. Up there, they were also lost. Desperate.

Master Seua took him there during training. They stalked the badlands for a few days, quietly observing the miserable, wandering phi in the skeletal, dry forests and fallow fields. These were not to be hunted. The ones they did hunt were mostly tai hong – cruel, vengeful phi that had met violent ends and indiscriminately focused their savagery on the laypeople, murdering them in the same fashion as their own demise.

A particular tai hong led them to a lair lined with the heads of his victims, and Ex could only stare at the display with numb horror. Master Seua had to intervene, dispatching the phi before it added Ex's head to the pile.

On the journey home, Master Seua decided Ex was too emotional to hunt there. He told him he needed to wait to pass the Trance ritual, and to "toughen up" before he would have any luck. That was the time he most reminded Ex of his real father. It was completely humiliating, since he knew he would have had to explain it to the other masters, and the other hunters would hear about it as well.

"The Serene Way goes there, but..." Ex sighed. "The Long Road is faster. Or better yet, a transport up the river. If you want to escape, someone else would serve you better."

"I understand," she said, her voice going soft again. "It's a lot to ask. I know you want to get back to your guild and get your badge."

He hadn't thought about that yet, but she was right. He had worked for it for so long. The guild would always be there, though, and Shar-Ala would still be dead. He'd still be a true demon killer whenever he returned.

Why did it feel so far away?

"You never planned to go back to the Capital, did you?" The bitterness stung his throat. Even though he made a promise, and it didn't matter if she cared for him or not, he didn't expect to be tricked into doing something that could potentially ruin his life. He glanced around for an escape route and considered swimming to the other side of the river to protect his flailing ego.

"Yes, I did, Ex. I meant it when I asked you to bring me home. I had every intention of going back to that life, with Isaree hidden away from both of them."

Both of them.

"Wait, you mentioned the sorcerer," Ex said, slowly. "The same one who attacked us at the Bent Lake?"

She bit her lip, caught.

A wave of anger coursed through him. "So... those weren't Loramese soldiers. They were the prince's, meant to bring you home."

She sighed. "Yes, I'm sorry I lied about them. I was desperate. I didn't think you'd help me if my life wasn't in danger. But it's also true that the queen might have her people after me as well. She would not miss the chance to get rid of us." Arinya tried to lay a hand on his shoulder, but he childishly moved away. "Ex, I meant it when I said these wonderful things made me realize how much more there could be. I meant what I said about you."

"Oh, sure. Long enough to convince me to take you to Yinseng," he scoffed.

Her eyes narrowed, and she leaned closer to him. "Do you think I'm just a whore that came onto you because I wanted something?"

"I didn't say that."

"You didn't have to."

"I didn't think that either!"

"Oh? Then what are you thinking?"

"When? Right now, or when you had my cock in your mouth?"

That was the wrong response. He braced for a slap.

Instead, she jabbed him in the chest with her nail. "What *do* you think of me, then? The prince's property or a manipulative bitch toying with you?"

A quiz with two wrong answers. Ex just shrugged. She glared and pressed her finger harder, hard enough to leave a bruise.

"I have to pick one?" He didn't mean it the way it came out. Fuck swimming, he should have just drowned himself. "I mean, I didn't mean, uh, how it sounded–"

"I thought I knew you, but maybe I was wrong. You see the world one way and that's as far as it goes. Have you ever stopped to think that if you took the chance to get to know people, you'd be more human?"

Damn.

Ex's throat went dry as he tried to think of something awful to say back. "If it means being like you, lying and playing with people, then no. I'd rather be... anything else." It didn't seem to sting as badly as he wanted it to. Her pitying glare said as much and she stood up, brushing off her dress in a violent manner.

"You're just scared," she said, her tone less insulting, more an epiphany, which felt worse.

"And you're just... impossible!" Ex avoided her eyes as he jumped to his feet, getting self-conscious as people started to notice their raised voices. "I'm going back to the demon's house."

She blocked his way, and despite her shorter stature, seemed to loom over him. "You'd really leave me here?"

"N-no, of course not," he said, at a complete loss. Then he remembered one of the hunters saying he'd rather face a true demon in his underwear than argue with an angry woman. Better to just agree and wait until the next day. Ex didn't understand back then, but now it seemed very wise indeed.

"Come on. We'll figure this out in the morning."

"Why wait? You said I should go find a sell-sword to help me. Maybe I'll go do that now."

"What?" Ex stammered, just as she turned her heel and stomped off towards the street. "Where are you going?"

"Where one finds them! The seediest taverns in town!"

"Arinya, wait!" Ex rushed to her. "You can't go by yourself." When she didn't stop, he grabbed her elbow.

That was a mistake.

She whirled on him, standing on her toes to glare into his face. "I *can't*? Why not? I've taken care of myself my entire life, Ex! And you don't have to say it. I know you were branded as a child. I know you watch out for yourself too. But do you want to know the difference between us? I've taken care of others. *Without* being paid for it."

Ex backed away then, hands up. "Fine. Pay someone else to care, because I sure as hell don't anymore."

She grit her teeth, but said nothing else, and stomped off.

He stood there like an idiot, left with a bunch of people snickering at his expense. If the Hound had been there, he'd be chortling along with them. The thought of the empty trees that awaited him wilted his resolve. He wished the Hound was laughing at him.

"Damn, she just fired that working boy."

"Can you blame her? He looks crazy. I wouldn't want crazy in my bed either."

"You kidding? Crazy's great for whores."

"I'm not a prostitute!" Ex yelled at the two ladies, whose rice cakes dropped out of their hands. He kind of did feel like a prostitute, to be honest. He realized he'd ripped his stupid cap in half and threw it down in frustration, then ran after Arinya.

Chapter Twenty-One

The Hunted

Maybe it was the drink and boxing theatre letting out, or Ex's foul mood, but the town had turned sour, with angry shouts rising between rapid conversation and obnoxious laughter. He wasn't sure how Arinya managed to disappear so quickly into the noise, and worse, he had no idea where she would go. He picked through the crowd, searching for a glimpse of her face, or her dress, even the hint of her jasmine perfume. Had she been serious about going to the seediest bar in town? At that point, he decided to stop trying to predict her and went towards the darker, rougher, and frankly, smellier part of town.

Next to a wasted street musician who missed every note on his three-stringed harp, Ex caught a whiff of opium off an old man passing by. He grabbed him by the shoulder.

"Where can I get a pinch?"

The man stared at him with glazed eyes, then pointed weakly towards a wide alleyway. Crude signs hung on unkempt awnings, with names like the Forgotten Prayer, the Happy Rooster, the Pissing Snake. The sounds and smells of liquor, drugs, and sex drifted from open windows. People hung about in clusters, just like they had down at the river, but here they were a shade different – harder and rawer, carrying weapons instead of flowers.

Ex hesitated at the entrance of the alley, feeling like a lamb in his upstanding citizen clothes. If he went into the Everpresent, it would be easier to find her. Maybe she'd even hear him yelling out, his internal voice more in a frenzy than he put on out here.

A group of young men, about his age, were sitting together on crates outside one of the bars and stopped talking as he approached.

One of them stood out, with dragon tattoos covering the shaved side of his head. "You lost, cutie pie?"

"Fairy house is one street over," another one said. Fairy house? Ex wondered what the demon woman had dressed him in. Was it the uniform of a male prostitute or something? Why did everyone think that?

"I'm looking for a girl, did you see one come by here…" He trailed off, as they were already laughing.

"You know how many girls come by here, cous?" a skinny one grinned. "Pick any door, you'll find one."

"Not just any girl," he said. "Gold ribbon in her hair, blue dress. She has a little mole right here." He tapped his cheekbone. They rolled their eyes, and his frustration kicked up a bit. "You would have noticed her if you had a sack."

They stopped laughing and Dragon Boy turned up a lip. "We woulda seen her, cous. We get first grabs on any girl comes through here."

"She probably gave you that broken nose, then."

They stared at him like he'd just dropped his pants and started dancing. Two of them burst out laughing, which riled Dragon Boy even more.

"Get the fuck out of here," he sneered, taking a menacing step forward.

"Gladly," Ex backed away, but couldn't hide his smirk. It had always been a problem whenever he dealt with these types of people. He opened his mouth for a parting shot, but bit his lip, glad he hadn't drunk too much at the show. There were more important things to do than brawl with a bunch of bullies.

Priding himself on his self-control, a sure step towards adulthood, Ex had only gone halfway down the alley when the skinny boy piped up again.

"Wait, cous, come back!"

Excited they may have changed their minds and had useful information, Ex walked back to see them huddled around a piece of paper. The boy held it up to him with a grin.

"This girl?"

His stomach dropped.

A perfect image of Arinya stared at him with a demure smile, drawn with the attention and care of a true artist. In this portrait, her eyes had been painted into sharp points on the edges, her hair pulled back and topped with a small crown. The mole on her cheek was drawn over into a tiny heart. Her petaled lips were slick with dark glaze. Ex lost his breath, but it wasn't only her face that stopped him.

Ex's own portrait was next to hers, but crudely drawn, as if someone bribed their brain-damaged ten-year-old to do it, for shitty candy. He looked mean, with angry, almost vertical eyebrows, and they chose to draw his hair white as if he were on his magic. He supposed the crown wanted everyone to know what he was.

More than outraged, Ex clenched his jaw. He wasn't a kidnapper! Or a pervert who planned to "sell the prince's prized consort into slavery." They didn't even bother with her name.

According to this bounty, Ex was an eighteen to thirty-year-old whisper about 5'10" to 6'2" and 12 to 15 stone. A pretty loose range. The doodle could probably pass for anyone if it weren't for that stupid scar across his face.

Still, not the worst thing. The worst thing was the prize money offered under their names. A lot, specifically for her alive, and a fine and prison sentence for her dead. Him, just dead.

"Fuck," he said out loud. They gave him one second of lead time before pouncing like a bunch of rabid rats for the last scrap of garbage. Ex managed to duck their wild swings, but one of them knew a bit more than drunken brawling.

The skinny kid grabbed him by the elbow and whirled him around before landing a knee to his gut. He followed with an uppercut that should have dropped him, but Dragon Boy grabbed him from behind and accidentally pulled him out of range.

Ex ran backward with him until he tripped, and then bit his arm as hard as he could. He yowled and let go, and Ex scrambled out of the alley. He tripped over the drunken musician, ruined his song, but managed to keep his feet. The yells followed close behind as he wove around pedestrians and ducked through market stalls. The skinny one cut him off somehow, so he grabbed a searing bowl of fried noodles off one of the vendors counters and hurled it at him.

Honestly, he regretted that as the boy crumbled in screaming agony, but mostly for the attention it drew from everyone around. The cook cursed at him, and but Ex didn't have time to stop and apologize. The other guys actually stopped to help their fallen friend. It gave him a few extra seconds to duck into a parade of paper puppets and slide under a stopped wagon.

Once he crawled out from underneath, someone seized his arm in a weird spot that made it go half limp. He tried to swing with the other but missed.

"Ex!" Arinya yelled in his face. She glanced back at the gang searching around, then pulled him down a different alley and ran. She leapt over a fence to someone's house, sprinting through a garden, then vaulted over the next into a residential street. Ex could hardly keep up, amazed she could move like that in her dress. She kept jogging until they were down the way, towards the quiet country houses. When she stopped to catch her breath, he leaned over, hands on his knees, very close to vomiting.

"What the hell were you doing down there?!" she yelled between gasping breaths.

"Looking for you!"

"Why?"

"Because you ran off to hire some assholes!"

"Wouldn't it make more sense to check the Long Road *escort* guild!?"

"…Yes!"

They glared at each other in icy silence. Then burst out laughing.

A woman screamed from a house nearby. "Will you kids shut the fuck up out there!?"

Arinya clamped her hand over her mouth, and they tiptoed away. She seemed to know where they were going, and the houses began to grow sparser, more fields and farms than cluttered townhouses pushing against one another.

"You idiot," Arinya said with a grin, and smacked him on the arm. "Why do you get in fights everywhere you go?"

"Not everywhere," he protested, covering up for the next one. "They started it."

"Without fail, everywhere I've been with you, you get your ass kicked."

"Spirits and Guardians don't count. And besides, there was a reason." His good humor faded away.

Hers followed. "I know." She pulled a crumpled piece of paper from a fold in her dress. "I found this on the town bulletin. It's freshly pressed, so… they must not be far behind."

"Shit." Ex's words turned bitter. "Now I'm a kidnapper and a slaver. How's that going to go? I might as well disappear into the badlands and live in burned down houses forever."

"I'll clear your name."

"From Yinseng?" He sucked his teeth. "I doubt the guy who gets you there will get a pat on the back from your prince."

She crumpled up the wanted flier and tossed it into the bushes. With a sigh, she craned her head back, regarding the stars. "I won't go."

"Won't go where?"

"I won't go to Yinseng. I'll go back to the palace and clear your name. Then I'll wait and find another way to get there, eventually."

Ex sighed, fighting an urge to plop down in the dirt. Somehow it felt like a failure, even though it was his promise in the first place.

"Or..." She stopped, then clasped her hands at her waist, wringing them. "You could come with us."

He stopped with her.

"What do you mean?" He edged back, suspicious. What was she saying? That he should jump the border with her, and disappear into a country he knew nothing about? He shook his head, mostly to himself. He wouldn't fall for this again. She couldn't trick him into doing something against his better judgment.

"There's demons up there, right?" she said.

"...Probably?"

She laughed, and when she peeked up, he flinched, ignoring her half-lidded gaze – she must have known that it got him every time. "I know I've been contradicting with my desires... and I purposely deceived you. But..."

"Hold on," he said. "You told me we couldn't even be friends, and now you want me to, what, exactly? Be your escort?"

She smirked. "You think I need an escort? Really, Ex?"

He frowned and did his best not to pout. "You said you couldn't even be seen with me."

"In the Capital. But it's different anywhere else," she said. "I meant everything I said about you."

"Even the mean stuff?" he said, nervous as she took a step towards him, so much so that he took a step back.

"Not all of it. But you are scared."

The little kid in him wanted to protest, *I'm not scared of anything! I fight demons for a living!* But for this, for her, he had no defense.

Especially when she laid a hand on his chest and drew closer. She tilted her head with a challenging smile, as if daring him to prove his bravery. Half of him wanted to bolt, but carefully, he reached up and held her wrist. Her pulse quickened.

It was real, it had to be.

Then for some odd reason, he laughed, and the stars seemed suddenly brighter. The entire world seemed brighter. Her smile widened, and he felt light, so light he could fly away.

"You know," he said, and wet his lips. "I think there *are* demons in Yinseng."

He wrapped his arms around her waist and pulled her close, savoring the feel of her body against his. They both laughed with relief and joy, and she buried her face in his neck. When she ran her fingers through his hair and pulled his head back to peer up at him, he leaned in to kiss her.

Her fingers tightened in his hair, and she jerked back with a gasp.

Ex kept his eyes shut, inwardly crumbling. He must have been going insane. How could he have misread that so badly? But when he forced himself to peer down at her, she was staring over his shoulder and into the distance, mouth hanging open in acute horror.

He smelled it before he saw it. Wood burning, heavy smoke.

How hadn't he noticed it before? It felt like the entire world had gone dark while they were talking. But the world came roaring back now. With ash and steel.

Without a word, Arinya sprinted towards the fire, which was the opposite of his first instinct. "Ex!" she yelled. "Hurry! It's Narissa's house!"

* * *

Arinya wasn't the only one standing in the yard, watching the flames. An entire squad of men blocked the road, three carriages and several horses. Ex slowed his step, and reached for the only weapon he brought along, a small sap that fit in his pocket. It might as well have been a flower, considering the handful of archers waiting for them – bows pointed down, but arrows notched and ready. A big bastard in real, steel armor and a thick black beard sat on top of a glossy brown horse. He carried a nasty curved sword and an arquebus slung across his back, confident enough to leave them sheathed.

"Arinya," Ex hissed. "Wait!"

"She's in there!"

He was sure the krasue had found her way out. She was a survivor, after all. Meanwhile, Arinya only thought of the human inside. What he formally thought was naivety, and if he were being blunt, ignorance, had transformed into something else in his eyes. It was true compassion, and with an intensity brighter than the fire.

Ex ran towards her until the thud of several arrows stopped him in his tracks, a barrier between them.

"Be still, whisper." A cold voice and colder hands jerked him backwards, off his feet. Someone else caught him around the arms, in a far more efficient way than Dragon Boy had in the alley. Something stung his neck, like a pinprick. Ex kicked at the shadows, and they easily danced around him. With a lump in his stomach, he recognized their slinking movements as the two killers that slit his throat at the Cobra's Rest.

They weren't hooded anymore, and their pale pink skin and short, golden hair stood out in the night. Foreigners from the far east, beyond even the Baghani Republic. These types were hardly seen, especially in the countryside. Ex started to curse, and one smashed the side of his head with something blunt, sending his vision into dizzying loops. He reached for the Everpresent, ready to burn them to ash.

But he missed.

The impossibility of that stunned him harder than the hit. He heard Arinya cry out, along with gruff male voices.

"You have one chance to get the fuck out of here, whisper," the big man on the horse bellowed. "I won't tell you again."

Through his blurry vision, Ex glimpsed a commotion in the street, a flash of sapphire silk in the light of the roaring flames. Arinya was still yelling, still struggling.

The man snapped at his subordinates. "Shut that whore up."

Her yells grew muffled, and through a stream of blood coursing down his forehead, Ex saw two soldiers struggling to hold her. She gave them hell, kicking and thrashing like a cat getting a bath. One yowled. She must have bit one of their hands, because her voice became audible again.

"Sidom Da!" she screamed at the big man. "How dare you touch me like this!"

Sidom Da, the Loramese war hero? Said to have fought off an entire regiment single-handedly, even after his general called for surrender? Sure enough, Ex spotted the black-bladed sword for which the man had been named. Despite the damage, it still looked deadly. He glared at his men. "I said shut her up, you idiots!"

When the soldiers exchanged nervous glances, he jumped off his horse and stomped up to her.

"When Varun finds out–"

He smacked her across the face with a fat hand and she went limp. Ex saw red. He landed an elbow to the assassin's nose and lunged forward. The archers stopped him again, and this time he took one in the shoulder. The sheer force knocked him back.

As he staggered, a leather strap looped around his neck and dragged him to his knees. He tried to work his fingers between it and his skin, but it was too tight. He swung at his captors, but the collar was attached to a wooden pole, and they stood out of reach.

"He's as rabid as a stray dog," said Sidom Da as he rumbled towards him, his footsteps as heavy as an elephant's. "Let's put him down and get on with it."

"Not yet." An odd voice floated out from one of the carriages, with a tenor that raised the hairs on Ex's skin. First came a leg, braced with a cast, then a crutch, and then a sorcerer, bundled like one of the paper parade puppets in his ridiculously flashy robes.

That fucking guy. The one at Bent Lake. Ex struggled anew, but they had him wrapped up now. The sorcerer tapped a finger to his lips, appraising him like he was an animal at the market. Without turning to Sidom Da, he said, "Remember our deal."

Sidom Da turned up his lip, scoffed, and shook his head. "Not much to look at. Sure this is the one?"

"I'm sure." The sorcerer must have done something, because the rope tightened in a coiled way that defied a normal noose. It shrunk. With a choking growl, Ex grabbed the end of the pole and snapped it in half. That stunned the soldier for all of a second, and he yanked it from his hands and cracked him in the jaw. He started towards Arinya again and met a boot straight to the face.

Sidom Da called him a rabid dog once more, and it was the last thing he heard before the rope tightened harder and stars flooded his eyes.

Chapter Twenty-Two

And the Minister

A steady rumble vibrated through Ex's body, which was slumped over, semi-upright. When he could see again, he was in a small room with curtains drawn over windows, and two benches facing one another. There were other people, two on either side of him, one across from him. It took him a minute to recognize the insides of a carriage – he hadn't been in many. It took him another minute to remember what happened.

The memories flopped by like turning the pages in a picture book. A fight in an alley. A dragon tattoo on a man's head. Arinya in the moonlight, no, the firelight…

The crack of a book slamming shut sounded. Everything came rushing back in a flood, and he recognized the man sitting in the seat across from him in disbelief. The sorcerer with the broken leg, draped in silk robes, ropes and ornamental sashes over his shoulders as if he were a general. He had finally removed his veil, revealing a pointy face with smirking lips. Scars upward on each corner of his mouth accentuated that smirk. Ex wanted to smack it off his face.

"Finally, the little dog awakes."

Ex tried to punch him, but his arms didn't budge, firmly tied behind him. He settled for a "Go fuck yourself," which dribbled out as a mess of vowels and drool. Something was wrong. He licked blood off the side of his lip. Whatever they had drugged him with, it didn't feel like any poison or tonic he'd ever used. It felt more in line with two or three bottles of unfiltered moonshine and a dash of the flu. The concussion didn't help, spots of his vision blotting out at random intervals.

The sorcerer laughed humorlessly, and the two on either side grabbed him by the shoulders and shoved him back against the seat. No, they grabbed him by the stub of a broken arrow still stuck in his shoulder. The man twisted it to the side, and the other one – the woman – said, "Don't bother. Undying feel nothing."

Undying, that was a new one. He supposed people from far away had their own words for everything. It was misleading, however. Hunters did die, and died often, but like a phi, could return under the right conditions. But at least once in their lives, they wouldn't come back. Ex had a sinking feeling he was heading towards that time.

"I'm so pleased we could meet under less boorish circumstances. I am the prince's own, the crown's minister of magic, Iyun of the Righteous Storm."

Righteous Storm? Ex laughed, but his next thought erased all amusement.

"Where is she?" His words were barely decipherable, as his tongue moved a second or two behind them.

"Safe. Do not worry yourself. No harm will befall her." Iyun raised his eyebrow and said, "Of that, I am certain."

"You…" Ex bristled, "you put the warding on her."

"And thank the Enlightened Lord I had. How does that cockrot feel?"

Ex glowered, a sneer on his lips. Did they really think he was such an animal? Of course they did. The collar was still around his neck, no longer blocking air, but still uncomfortably snug.

"I wouldn't know. How does that leg feel?"

His smirk wavered only a fraction. "I can make do with the leg. But if you had silenced me permanently, trust that I would not have allowed you another breath."

"If I knew how much of a cowardly blowhard you were, trust that I would have."

"Your insolence is quite baffling compared to others of your guild. Believe me, it was difficult to keep you alive. It was only my deal with Sir Sidom Da that kept you breathing, until we return to the Capital."

He parted his sleeves to reveal a tiny figurine in his hands. It was a little doll made of white cloth, and two tiny red dots for eyes, with strands of Ex's hair fastened to its head. He must have ripped them out during their brawl. A little wire looped around its neck. With a slow twist of the wire, the scars in Ex's throat itched, and the collar constricted enough to leave him breathless.

His first time hexed. That might explain some of his recent injuries. Ex wondered if there was a badge for that.

"It would take but a flick of the wrist to pop your silly little head off, but I'm certain the crown-prince would prefer to kill you himself. Saves money." He loosened the wire, and in effect, the collar, and his eyes crinkled in satisfaction.

Ex loathed being so helpless. If they wanted an animal, he could give them one. But every time he reached for the Everpresent, something blocked him. He rolled his head to stare out the window. Or at the window's curtains, moreso. The minister cleared his throat.

"Tell me what this is."

Ex refused to look at him. The assassin grabbed him by the hair and jerked his head forward. Ex couldn't think of this man as a storm, and certainly not righteous. More like the piss of the sky, a tiny, self-important dribble.

"I don't know, Piss Dribble. A bunch of assholes giving me a cart ride?"

Minister Iyun scoffed at the nickname. "How juvenile," he mumbled, but lifted his gloved hand closer to the cabin's small lantern. Ex was about to insult him again, but the curses froze on his tongue. With a chilling, reverent expression, the minister rolled Shar-Ala's eye between his fingers, his face wavering as the deep hum of power ebbed from within.

"Of all the useless baubles you carry, this one is different. This one is pure, perfect. Alive." The man was practically drooling. "It wants, it needs, it hungers. I feel its whispers. All this time, it was meant to be with me."

This wasn't a sorcerer. This was a necromancer.

No one but a magic user drawn to death magic would have a hard on for a dead demon's eye. But the Crown had outlawed black magic, the last Ex heard. Then again, it'd been three months since he'd been to the Capital. It had always been frowned upon, for decades before he was born. How much could have changed? Having a pet sorcerer was one thing, but a forbidden necromancer seemed beyond scandalous. Ex glanced at the other two for any kind of validation.

"What are you two ballsacks? This creep's left and right hand?" They should have been shitting their pants.

The woman snorted. "We're rich."

"Fucking gutless sell-swords." Ex wanted to add more, but the collar tightened again.

"Bark, little dog." The minister leered and held Shar-Ala's eye closer.

Ex winced and his hair stood on end. There was a reason he kept the damn thing encased in lead. There was a reason he wasn't going to sell it, a reason he had to bring it to the guild.

Shar-Ala's eye drew his gaze, despite his attempt to look away. He heard whispers of darkness, of screaming, of nightmares. He couldn't relate to the minister's reaction, but he couldn't deny the true demon's persistent power, lurking just inside the thin membrane between the ghost realm and his.

Ex jerked his head back and squeezed his eyes shut. The son of a bitch erupted in delighted laughter.

"I knew it. There is real power in this orb. And you will tell me what it is, and how to use it."

"You can't *use* it," Ex said, hiding in the darkness. His head pounded with unconscious pain, which made him dizzy and nauseous.

"Oh, I can. And I will. It's only a matter of time. I have ways." The minister let out a heavy breath, then put the eye away. Ex relaxed, but only until the minister squeezed the wire around his doll again, and the air seized in his throat. "And if you won't speak, she will."

This time, he didn't fight, and let darkness take him.

Chapter Twenty-Three

Astrama the Twice-Risen

The flesh of demons could not be described in any simple terms. Neither sweet nor sour, perhaps spicy? A little. If one did not have a refined palette, they would never appreciate the decadence of such succulent juices, the infusion of raw power and pure energy. A taste rich with blessings of the devas.

Astrama the Twice-Risen hadn't yet licked his wounds when Shar-Ala fell. He forewent such trivialities in the favor of a fresh kill.

Yes, spirit blood tasted all the same to the unrefined tongue. But this one, old, aged like fine wine...

Perhaps it's just my imagination, Astrama pondered, chewing on an especially gristly piece of meat. He and the young hunter had been after this beast for over a year, many full moons with nothing to show for it. For such an anticipated kill, the boy spent no time harvesting the corpse. Unusual. Things he usually valued were left behind, things inedible. The claws, the teeth, the bones. Perhaps he would return for them.

Astrama waited a respectful amount of time before he ate the organs. Only then did he lick his wounds until he could walk unhindered, the fresh meal infusing his body with strength. It was almost daybreak by then, and still, the young hunter hadn't returned. Perhaps he'd been too distracted with the female in heat. They'd been amusingly resistant to mating. Why? Astrama wasn't sure. Both were so heavily reeking of pheromones that it made him sneeze in their presence.

When morning came, Astrama picked up Shar-Ala's arms in his jaws, still heavy with claws. He returned to the young hunter's camp, where the campfire had long shriveled to ash. Only a few coca leaves remained scattered on the ground, where the girl had sat...

Her name is Arinya. Her aura had hints of precious gems, painted wood and jasmine, the sounds of silk, things only found in the company of man's royals. She was a sort of queen, or a princess, or someone in the vicinity of power. The hunter had begun to gaze upon her as one, his own reverence, his own precious queen in the wilds.

What a joy to see cubs playing in the den.

It'd been many years since Astrama left home. His kind were not often seen in these woods. Then again, a half-spirit was not often seen within his homelands, either.

Half-spirits do not play well with others. Astrama had not been cast out, but he was not the most respected. To many, his mere existence had been a constant reminder of King Maaba's infidelity to his pack.

The horses remained, both the haughty and the sweet one. They still wore their packs, laden with the hunter's things. He hadn't returned here since the hunt ended. Neither had his queen. After laying the demon's arms on top of the hunter's ashen campfire, Astrama laid down nearby and took a nap.

He dreamt of home. The fresh, whispering mists stirring over the lush moss. And the relentless flood that washed away everything, even the bones.

When he awoke, the young hunter had still not returned. After a long, languid stretch and a deep yawn, Astrama snapped at the black horse's heels.

Come, then. Let us find your master.

They'd marked the trees during previous visits, the hunter with his blade, Astrama with his scent. The paths were bright and clear, though he took care in picking them, for the horses could not move easily throughout all the swamp. No creatures paid them attention, and the dangerous ones that did sensed the fresh demon blood on his lips and shrunk away. The spirits took interest, but only with respect. However, the hunter's trail had been interrupted by the Guardian. With the trees reordered and path shortened, it took longer for Astrama to find it again.

The Twice-Risen left his mark on the last tree when they emerged onto clear land. He hated being seen in the open. Man didn't look kindly upon him – they feared him and sometimes hunted him, for no good reason. Out of fright, or for sport. Astrama did not enjoy the taste of their blood, nor the foul flesh of their mindless, complacent cattle. Though he ate them well enough. They were soft and easy to kill.

He steered clear of their villages, thick and churning with death and rot. This one, in particular, he found loathsome – a horror show covered with the skin of the Crocodile King's subjects. The relentless noise was as choked and dirty as the stench. No living creature could make sense of such a place, save the rats and the birds and roaches, who'd been born blind in the muck.

Astrama paused to sniff the sky. The rains were coming, and they wouldn't cease for the rest of the year. This swamp would become a river, inaccessible to him. Sometimes, other phi hunters traveled in boats to hunt the aquatic monsters, but the young hunter would not. The boy hated boats, which impeded his travels at times. Just as well for Astrama, who shared his distaste. They both preferred the Serene Way.

Finally, he caught the scent of the boy and girl both. The young hunter had been bloodied, as per usual. The boy was far too careless. But the girl, her aura faded with each step, a life trail growing weak. Astrama hadn't realized she'd been injured so, to the brink of death, even. She'd let out no blood though, only wore his.

To Astrama's relief, the hunter's trail wandered into the village, but quickly out and into the outskirts. Astrama lurked about the edges until he came upon the last place he could smell the hunter.

Nothing but the smoldering skeleton of a house. Onlookers had been there earlier to gawk, some sifted through the ashes for things of value, perhaps survivors, but the wreckage still burned hot. There were fewer people now, and once the drizzle started, they went back to their homes.

Yet, something remained.

Embers hissed in the rain as Astrama poked amongst the ashes in the night, his dark coat obscuring him in the dimness of the first storm. The scorched wood stunk, an opaque veil which hid any remnant scents of the boy. The horses flicked their tails as they lingered on the road, sensing something sinister, but unsure as to what. The creatures were more attuned to their master's mind, in that his often-torrid emotions shifted their own. This made Astrama believe that the fire had been a malicious act. Indeed, he sensed a great many people had been here before the villagers, ones that reeked of oiled leather and steel and death magic.

Once more, the Twice-Risen swept through the wreckage, tossing aside animal bones, ceramic things, a few weak magic items that somehow survived. There was something else here, something strong. Though the rain would let up soon, he persisted until finding a door in the ground, half burned. He pulled it free. A heady scent hit him like a fresh breeze, dark, yet free of man's stink.

A demon lived here.

Bristling, muscles tensed, Astrama descended into the tunnel, where a freshly dead human had crawled, blackened skin peeling from its bones.

She did not make it far.

Her body had been burned away, meat scorched, bones stark white in the black ashes. Any remnants of her skin were blistered, beyond repair. But her head was intact, and she still breathed. Her organs splayed forth, untouched by the fire but fused to the ground from her melted clothes.

Demon. Astrama snapped his jaws, growling. He licked his lips, but more in disgust rather than hunger. She would have made a grand meal if the fire hadn't ruined it.

Spirit. The demon's eyes strained to meet his but couldn't move without a neck. *Please. Have mercy.*

Why should I? Astrama sat back on his haunches. *The ashes leave me no appetite.*

No, I wish not for death. Bring me to Lord Indrajit. He will grant you favor if you return me to his shrine.

The gods of men have no compassion for your kind. You will find a more merciful end here, rotting beneath the earth. He turned to leave.

Wait. Spirit. Why have you come? Are you searching for Ex? The hunter?

Astrama barred his teeth, glancing back. Demons often lied, especially out of fear, but he smelled none from this one. He smelled only despair.

Yes. Where is he?

Men came calling for them both, warriors and killers from the girl's keepers. When I wouldn't speak, they locked me in here and burned my home.

So the hunter is hunted. Astrama laughed.

No, they returned, and the men took them both. A black witch took his things. He had hexed him days ago and followed his trail. I fear he will be killed by her people.

Why do you fear for him? A strange thing for a demon to say. *He gladly hunts your kind—*

But he didn't. He trusted me, and I saved her life. She trusted me too. Because of Indrajit's gift, I no longer take lives.

Astrama snapped his jaws in her face, fangs gnashing a hair from her head.

You disrespect me with your lies, foul creature. I should shred your remains only for that.

What need do I have to lie? If you refuse to save me, perhaps you could save him.

I have no reason to. We've completed our hunt. Our paths diverge.

Astrama backed away, his growl fading. Tears coursed down the demon's cheeks as her ruined lungs shuddered. She closed her eyes in defeat.

Astrama trotted out of the tunnel and gazed at the swamp, which he could take to the Serene Way, and back to the Forest of Clouds, the cold grass of the mountains he ached to tread. Yet before he entered the woods, a lingering doubt remained. He had no reason to seek the young hunter, but he had done so, out of professional courtesy. He knew Shar-Ala's claws were valuable to the boy, and he owed him as much for the kill. He'd eaten more than their agreed-upon share. The horses were dear to the boy, and the Twice-Risen had grown fond of them as well. They would have died had Astrama left them in the swamp. If the hunter had been alive and well, perhaps they would have continued working together. It was a mutually beneficial arrangement.

If the royals had captured him, he would die. Not quickly, for those men were known for their grand displays of cruelty. Whatever they believed the hunter had done, he would surely pay with every pound of flesh.

The thought disquieted him. The boy had turned into pack at some point, Astrama realized, with a shred of sorrow. The cub had grown into a fearless warrior, as free as he could be from his kind's corruption. To be paraded like a macabre trophy was an unfitting death for a warrior. Astrama shuddered, recalling his own family's skins turned to base blankets for man's amusement.

A warrior deserves a true death.

He returned to the demon's lair, and she smiled in gratitude when he took her skull between his jaws.

Chapter Twenty-Four

The Undying

Spirits will fight, especially when they're cornered. They kill to live, whether it's defending or feeding themselves. They were just like animals in that sense. Pragmatic, mindful of minimal injury to themselves, expending the least amount of energy. Phi were different. They could be sadistic, but only because they were once human. But no other animal, save for man, fights just to fight. No other animal revels in the pain of their enemies. Even tiger cubs playing with their half-alive prey are doing so for a natural reason. There is no sadism in their survival.

But men like these... That was why Ex despised them. Sadists that loved violence for violence's sake. Arinya was right, he was drawn to fights, maybe he was a violent man too. Perhaps without an outlet in the hunt, there was no place for his aggression. Perhaps he needed to find it somewhere else. It never seemed to go very well for him, especially once he realized his limitations. He'd fought many phi during his career, and came within a hair's breadth of death more than a few times, but he'd never been so injured before he came under mortal hands.

The necromancer was dead set on torture, despite Ex's

lack of feeling pain. Ex figured it was the public's willful ignorance to what phi hunters really were. Maybe they'd heard the rumors of their powers and chalked them up to boisterous lies. Iyun had peeled off his fingernails, poked him with hot needles, flayed his skin. But it only gave Ex shivers of disgust, and he gave them biting insults in return. He'd call this treatment inhumane, but that was an insult to all inhuman creatures.

What disturbed him the most was that the Everpresent eluded him whilst they doused him with their drugs, and so he lacked his usual ability to heal. But he could still talk shit and spit blood, and so he endured. He could insult their mothers, too.

Every time Iyun choked him to unconsciousness, they woke him up again. The ministers made full use of his hex doll, frequently spun threats and lies and stepped back to allow new volunteers to take a crack at physical encouragement.

Ex had heard plenty of attacks on his character from the mouths of phi before, but his rebel brand meant nothing to their kind. These men focused on that first, and were especially nasty, insulting his family's honor and what not. Nothing groundbreaking. These were all things he'd heard before as a child. Still, the memories stung, as they relentlessly peeled open the old wound, again and again. Ex grew sullen as it went on, preferring silence to save his energy.

The lack of sleep was where he started to fade. Days went by, and after being in the Hunter's Trance, he needed a drink, a bowl of noodles, and a nap like nothing else. Exhaustion soured his mood every time he was jarred into consciousness with a clash of a sword or a bucket of cold water.

It was this rude awakening that must have given them the idea to use water torture, which, really, they should have opened with. But the problem with that was they needed more room to do so. The men needed sleep too, as traveling with such a large escort slowed them down, and they weren't taking any chances with him or Arinya, guarding them constantly. At least they knew she didn't want to be there. Ex overheard some whispers from the guards that "the hunter had brainwashed her with magic." Only one gave him the benefit of the doubt, murmuring that he thought she'd likely run off with the young man on purpose. Apparently, Prince Varunvirya was a spoiled asshole behind his benevolent, public front – still a selfish, bratty child at the ripening age of forty-nine.

While Minister Iyun remained solely focused on what he'd dubbed the "orb of power," others had different questions. Sidom Da wanted to know what Ex had done with the child, as the war hero was a subject of the queen-in-waiting, Loranese. Truth was, it was one of their only reasons to keep Ex alive, so rather than play dumb, he leaned into it.

It might have been the wrong choice. The only thing Ex was certain of was that they couldn't know the child's soul was safely around Arinya's neck. Necromancers had no sense for living spirits, though he wasn't sure about Sangha monks. He supposed the ones with any leanings into low magic might sense *something* there, but he hoped they wouldn't make the connection. It would be scandalous indeed if any monks in the company of the crown shirked their vow of nonviolence. Though, it wouldn't entirely surprise him, considering the minister was a practitioner of black magic.

The Capital was another full day south. They threw him onto the mud, hands and feet cuffed with lead manacles. With the rainy season in effect, big Sidom Da carried around a parasol two times too small for his ox shoulders. Any snickers from the guards were quickly silenced, but Ex howled in laughter on their behalf. Until the big man kicked him in the face.

He peered around for Arinya, but they'd locked her in the other carriage. It stood nearby, close enough for her to hear his miserable gags and heaves as Sidom Da stuffed a rag in his mouth and poured water over his face. Ex played it up, begging them to stop with I don't know, she wasn't pregnant when we met, I was lying, please stop, blah blah blah...

The necromancer hovered close by, fretting that they'd kill him – worried, even. It was almost touching.

The problem with water torture and phi hunters was simple. The technique was remarkably similar to how they'd been trained to break into the Everpresent. To drown was a primal fear rooted deep within the animal brain, perfect to practice with before the final ceremony, in which they had to completely empty themselves of the fear of death and offer their souls to the mysterious judgement of the Everpresent.

In that moment of death, a hunter asked the devas for the gift given to the very first hunter. Ex didn't know if it was a question of "divine worthiness," as some called it, a judgment of their souls, but a fair number of hunters seemed to think it was a numbers game. Others were convinced it all depended on their physical conditioning, just as any of their combat tests.

It wasn't pleasant, by any means, but it didn't inspire the same amount of distress as one would expect. The point is, Ex wanted the men to push him to that point. If he could go to that place – to the origins of the Everpresent – then maybe he could do something, anything, to strike back.

In theory. It was a strong possibility he'd just die.

But of all the people he wanted to kill, it was only Minister Iyun that he *needed* to. Necromancy was one thing, and certain practices were not considered "evil," Mali being a good example. But this man was different. He had nothing but bad intentions. Even then, it wouldn't be Ex's business to judge. But that changed the minute Shar-Ala came into the picture. The masters would agree, and they'd chide him if he didn't at least try.

One of the pale assassins took Sidom Da aside after several hours of waterboarding. Thanks to the guards, he'd learned her nickname was Snow, due to her origins in a notoriously cold, faraway country. With her brother, Ice, together they were known as the Frozen Two. Not creative, but fitting. When they made their appearance, his heart sank. Of course they'd understand what real pain looked like. They seemed the type well practiced in it.

Sidom Da was enraged at Ex's deception, beating him half to hell the old-fashioned way. He screamed at his men to fetch the oil and bring up the fire. He was ready to burn him alive.

It would be decades until Ex went through the master's ritual that would allow him to walk through fire, so this would one hundred percent kill him. He watched the pyre build with heavy dread, the hazy memory of Master Seua emerging from a similar inferno inspired a sharp sting of nostalgia. He longed for home.

Still, Iyun convinced Sidom Da to let him have one more shot before the burning. After slipping him a heavy coin purse, the general and his guards took a slow stroll through the woods. Ex was alone with the necromancer and the twins.

Ice marched Ex, his so-called "undying" prisoner, over to a log by the fire and pushed him down. He held him up by the collar, while Snow stood beside the Minister, arms crossed, eyes blank but for mild distaste. Ex could barely move at that point, as all the fractures and blood loss and shock had added up. The only thing keeping his heart beating was every ounce of will he could summon. He needed to know that Arinya and Isaree would be safe. They probably would be. The necromancer might never find the trapped soul. Isaree's soul could find release… somehow. The crown-prince wouldn't harm his prized consort, although that became more and more uncertain. If the queen's men were willing to enact such violence, Ex doubted it would be hard for them to cover up an "accident."

The exhaustion would get him, eventually. He felt the call of the First Hunters. If he just let go…

"It's admirable." Iyun's smirk never ceased. "I admit, I hadn't expected you to do so well under torture."

Ex mustered a slow blink and half an eye roll, which probably wasn't visible under his swollen face.

"I think Sidom Da was having a little fun, wasn't he?" The minister caught Snow's eye, who made no expression. "But where you've hidden the child isn't my concern. You know what I want, and I want to give you one last chance."

This again?

"I know you will break and burn before you betray her. I'd even venture to say you're quite a masochist. But what I wish to know is if the same could be said about her?" He leered at Arinya's carriage.

He wouldn't.

"Of course, *I* am the prince's loyal subject, and therefore, avowed to her well-being. He loves her dearly, as she loves him. And as you may have guessed, she loves him as only a whore from the mudlands could. Repeatedly. Subserviently. On her back and her knees, with every hole and inch of skin."

The hate in Ex's face must have burned so bright that even Snow took notice, her eyes darting towards Iyun and back. Until then, the minister had left Arinya out of the violence. Too many ears. These guards had already proved they weren't immune to gossip.

"Do you know how he uses her? How his tastes vary? He loves to share. He likes to watch." Iyun leaned forward. "I'm sure you've seen the birthmark on her thigh, right next to her used-up cunt? I have. Many, many times."

"You're a piece of shit," Ex sneered, voice little more than a whisper, but he had just enough energy to raise his head and glare. "Don't fucking touch her."

The man laughed and shook his head. "Oh, I wouldn't. What I'm trying to get through that thick skull of yours is that the prince won't notice if every man in camp ravages her. He revels in her pain. I suppose you found a way around it, with your depraved whispers. But that warding is old, as old as she was when she first came into his service."

Ex wanted to tear his face off with his teeth, and the thought dazed him. Perhaps they were right – perhaps he was nothing but a rabid dog. Arinya must have convinced them he meant nothing to her. Even though it hurt to think about, he hoped she had. She was smart, and if she'd been so abused in the prince's service, why would she have thought of returning in the first place?

If it were true, she would have found a way out long before she'd met him. It was possible the minister was telling the truth, and she could have been completely helpless to their power. But if that really was true, Ex was almost sure she would have said so during her plea to help her escape. At least by the time she pressed her hand to his aching heart, her beauty surpassing all the stars above.

Ex closed his eyes, willed himself to be there again…

No, he must stay here, in the now. If that were true, and the prince would affect no consequences, these men might have already done disgusting things. With that in mind, he backed away from the thought and forced a choking laugh. "Fuck if I care. Ravage her all you want."

"Foolish child. Don't insult my intelligence. I know that look. How savagely you fought to save her when we first met. At first, I thought you were only protecting the bounty. The body may resist, but you can't hide the futile infatuation in your eyes."

"You wouldn't lay a finger on her," Ex sneered, with just enough energy to spit blood on his shoes. The minister didn't raise a brow, used to the hunter's spitting by now.

"I don't need to." Iyun nodded to Snow, and the woman casually walked to Arinya's carriage, slipping in and slamming the door behind her. With a flourish, Iyun removed a hex doll from his sleeve, this one with a feminine form. A lock of Arinya's shiny black hair was tied to it with a golden string.

"There are ways to hurt without even leaving a scratch." His long fingernails stroked the doll's body, slowly beginning to dig in. Ex's throat went dry, and Iyun half-smiled. "It would be a sin to bruise skin so delicate. It takes a deft hand..." A small, shiny needle glinted in the firelight. He dragged the needle gently over the doll's body, lingering on the midsection. "Boxers say the kidneys are quite sensitive. She was once a boxer, yes? Perhaps this will remind her."

He wouldn't. Could he make a hex doll so quickly? Ex wished he'd paid more attention during his lessons on low magic.

"Hmm... no, that might cause too much sickness." Iyun moved the pin to her face, where two black dots were crudely drawn on. "A whore has no use for her eyes, does she?"

"Wait..."

Slowly, he pushed the pin inside. A muffled cry came from the carriage, and the curtains rustled.

"Stop, stop!" Ex stammered, and fell forward to his knees at the minister's feet. This time, Ice didn't stop him. "Please don't. She doesn't deserve this."

"I do not see how that relates, hunter," he said, then moved the pin to the other eye, twirling it on the fabric. "Tell me. What is the orb?"

"I'll tell you," Ex said, head bowed. "Just stop."

It was quiet, then he grunted in satisfaction.

"Speak quickly, then. Sidom Da will return soon, and without my guidance, he will have no mercy."

"Promise me she won't be hurt." The necromancer's promises weren't worth shit, but Ex needed something.

"No harm will come to her, if you speak true."

He sighed, sitting back. Iyun waited with rapt attention, smirk twitching. Ex held his gaze best he could. "It's the third eye of the legendary Shar-Ala, a true demon, harbinger of nightmares, destroyer of dreams. I slew him two days ago in the Jinburi Swamp. That's my prize." The hunter waited for recognition of the remarkable feat, but the man made no expression. "You do know who that is, right?"

"Shar-Ala," Iyun tested the name, the words sounded wrong on his lips, a dark prayer. He frowned. "You expect me to believe an old wives' tale? No. It can't be."

"Stare into it long enough under the blood moon," Ex told him with a shrug. "You'll see."

"Stare into it. That's how I harness the power?" He rested his hand on his chin in thought. "What does it do?"

"Gives you paralyzing nightmares," Ex said. "Sleepwalk, mind control. Makes you believe things you fear the most."

"Why would I want that?" the minister said, and Ex only waited for his racing thoughts to catch up. "Oh, I see. It works on anyone I desire. And if I can control it…"

"You can't control it," Ex said bluntly.

"If I can control it," Iyun repeated, a sliver of a smile returning to his face. "How interesting. How delightful. How many possibilities there might be."

"I know you're not a stranger to black magic." Ex did his best to convey how serious he was, dropping all of his snark. "But this isn't something you mess about with. It's nothing you can control. This is a true demon's power, and it'll drag you to a deeper hell than even your asshole brain can imagine."

"Ha! And why should its custody rest with your kind? All you will do is fill your coffers. I would buy it from you, if I could not simply take it." He narrowed his eyes. "Unless, this is how you train your little monsters?"

"No. It's a remnant of a true demon. We don't sell those. We seal them away, out of reach of people like you."

The fire crackled in the silence. The minister looked lost in thought, staring at the pouch with a mixture of awe and fear. He made a thoughtful noise, but nothing else. Ex felt Ice shift, his hand tightening ever so slightly on the hunter's leash.

"I want to see her," Ex said. When Iyun didn't respond, he said it again, more forcefully.

Iyun blinked a few times, and glanced over as if seeing him for the first time.

"Yes, you do," he said, and rose to hobble away on his crutch, limping towards the carriage.

"You really want to be a part of this?" Ex said, straining his neck to glare at Ice. "Demon magic is a cloud that infects anyone near it, and you'll choke on it just the same. I know you've felt it already."

He didn't respond, but Ex thought he saw the man's eyes narrow.

"Is it worth whatever he's paying you to go insane? Become this asshole's mindless puppet? More than you are now, I mean." Self-preservation often trumped loyalty for these types. And perhaps sibling loyalty was strong in their culture. After all, they were strangers, surviving together in a faraway land.

"Shut the fuck up." Ice jerked the leash, but just a hint of uncertainty was all Ex wanted.

Iyun tapped on the side of the carriage.

Maybe another approach. "Wouldn't it be more profitable to kill them all and take the bounty for yourselves?" Ex said. Finally, the assassin's eyes flicked to Ex's and back. Interesting. The Frozen Two must have thought of this before. Perhaps his resolve was wavering. "Not only that. My guild will pay double for that evil thing he's been drooling over like a horny dickbat."

Ice sucked his teeth. "You're full of shit."

"You know I'm not," Ex said. "Hunters are just as mercenary as you. Think we hide in the woods and hunt monsters for fun? We have money, too."

The door to the carriage opened, and Snow slipped out. Ex waited anxiously for Arinya, but the assassin shut the door when the minister started speaking to her in a low voice.

"Your sister doesn't know. And he's going to test it out on her. Watch." Ex had no idea, but it seemed very possible. "He'll have two perfect killers at his beck and call, without the need to pay you a single coin."

"You're full of shit," Ice said again, though he sounded less convinced. "You said he couldn't control it. Twice."

"Of course I said that, why the fuck would I encourage him?" The truth was, Ex really had no idea what the man was capable of. It was possible to harness the power of demonic remnants, although the results were often fatal to the wielder. "You two are tough bastards, but you can't defend against this type of magic," Ex pressed him. "Think he can't make a hex doll of you too?"

Slowly, Ice met his eyes.

"I'll stop him from brainwashing you. We can end it all before that big lug gets back."

Ex held his breath, hoping with all his being that the assassin had a shred of humanity in his cold heart. Or a heart so black with greed that breaking his contract made logical sense.

Ice muttered something in another language, eyes darting between Ex and the minister.

Then he dropped the leash. He leaned down and fiddled with Ex's manacles. A pop and click followed. "Wait for my signal. And don't do anything fucking stupid." And he slipped the handle of a knife into his hand.

"Got it." It took all Ex's self-control not to jump to his feet and beat him to the necromancer.

But Ice stopped a few steps away, tilting his head towards the woods. Snow did the same, and at first, Ex wondered if they were already hearing nightmares.

Then he heard it too. A great many people crashing through the trees, angry shouting, terrified screams.

"What is that?" Iyun drew back, his back stiffening.

Ex peered into the trees. A flash of steel, then Sidom Da roared. A gunshot rang out. Another man's high-pitched squeal was quickly silenced. Then five of the ten guards broke through the edge of the campsite yowling, tripping over themselves, tearing towards their own horses.

"Run!" one of them screamed. "Demons!" He whirled around right in time to slam onto the ground, arms and legs flailing like a burning beetle. On top of him, a great, dark figure lurked, bestial and bristling.

The Hound's glaring red eyes narrowed into angry slits. With a vicious snarl, he ripped out the man's throat and snapped his head towards Ex with a deep bark. He didn't need the Everpresent to understand.

Get up and fight.

Chapter Twenty-Five

The Killer

His first real battle, and all he had was a knife. Not that it mattered, since he took one step towards Iyun and collapsed in the mud. The Hound made short work of the next man and tossed half his body clear across the camp. The remaining guards realized their horses had scattered, if they hadn't already died of fright. They tried to regroup, arrows and spears, a few guns, the best things to kill beasts with. But for a half-spirit? Only one got a shot off before the Hound barreled into them.

Ex limped over to the carriage, where Iyun and the twins were nowhere to be seen. Even though his fingers cramped and spasmed, he forced them around the handle and yanked it open.

Empty.

Nothing was inside except for supply trunks, bags, and assorted equipment for the caravan. No Arinya. Nothing. They must have sent outriders ahead to bring her to the Capital, but when?

One thing was certain. The necromancer made a complete fool of him.

Ex cursed and slammed the door shut, searching wildly for his trail. He couldn't have gone far with a busted leg.

The blast of a rifle jarred him back to the battle. Wood splintered next to his hand. Sidom Da staggered out from the brush, half his body covered in blood from the head down. He slung the arquebus onto his back and drew his sword.

"Where are you!?" he screamed, frothing at the mouth, one of his eyes reduced to a gory socket. Ex wasn't sure who he was screaming for. Him? The Hound? The necromancer? Whoever it was, he saw Ex first and charged forward. With the wagon keeping him upright, the most he could do was lift the knife halfway up with a wavering arm and brace for impact.

The Hound darted between them, but the general was just as quick. He slashed his sword in a wide arc and spun away, missing the beast by inches. The Hound slunk back to stand beside Ex, claws digging into the ground as they waited for the man's next move.

"You're behind this, you rabid whelp!" Sidom Da's mouth twisted with renewed fury. Even with the most ferocious beast in the land at his side, the sight of the battle-lusting general chilled Ex's blood, this impossible monster of a man who left men weeping in his wake. He stalked towards them with the rearing violence of a tidal wave.

The Hound pounced. The general was ready.

It felt like a nightmare, inevitable, with only one outcome, and Ex didn't have time to scream in protest. The Hound's jaws locked on the general's shoulder right as he'd already swung his sword. With an angry yelp, the Hound staggered back, then collapsed, sword stuck through his chest like a skewer.

Possessed by fury, Ex rushed the disarmed general. Sidom Da's mouth opened in surprise right before Ex slammed into him. Both on the ground, the man stared up at Ex in disbelief, then down at his chest, where Ex clutched the hilt of the dagger with both hands.

Right through the heart.

He managed to lift a hand to Ex's face and tried to push him off, war-weathered callouses scraping away fresh scabs. Ex gave the knife an extra shove. The man gasped, blood seeping from his mouth, then his head sagged back.

Left with sudden silence but for the rustle of rain and the soft, shallow breathing of the Hound, Ex crawled over to the fallen beast. Sidom Da's infamous weapon sprouted from the Hound's torso like the banner on a battlefield. Only fitting – a warrior falls in battle, and the Hound was nothing but. His proud glare found the hunter, and Ex placed his hand on his neck as he would a dying brother, his fur damp between his fingers.

"Thank you, old friend." Ex bowed his head in reverence, then uttered a voiceless mantra from the First Hunters. Afterwards, he met the Hound's fading eyes and said, "Run now in the eternal woods, and feast with your brothers and sisters."

The Hound's tail thumped once before his pupils dilated, and the grass brightened around him, welcoming his spirit home. Ex wavered in his wake, then collapsed onto the ground next to him.

As the Hound's heartbeat faded to nothing, Ex closed his eyes and felt their steps through the forest, moving together, in ready silence. He held no weapons, no prey in mind. And he felt true calm, his torrid heart at peace.

Then the Hound bounded past the hunter and disappeared into the bright mist of the Cloud Forest.

Your hunt has not ended yet, young one.

Bright, blue morning came. The rain had gone, but it left behind the brilliant sheen of the Everpresent. With his last ounce of strength, the Hound had dragged Ex back from the dead, and he'd never felt so at home. Next to his body, the shimmer of his pawprints led off into the woods. And next to them were another's, far larger, the same width of an elephant's.

From his prone position, Ex traced his finger along the print in awe. The King of Wolves, Maaba, come to personally escort the Hound into his pack of warriors in the eternal woods. Ex wondered if that had been his desire all along. They'd grown close in the last few years, in a reserved way. Much of Ex's life had been a mystery, and he often wondered, but didn't question. The Hound offered the same in return. Acceptance. Respect. For the most part. But those times he mocked the young man, he definitely deserved it.

Ex's bones were already cracking back together, blood under his bruises de-clotting, cuts and scrapes and broken skin reknitting. But it was a slow process. It would take longer than usual, especially the missing teeth, one of which had grown back only recently.

For a long time he laid there, unable to do anything else, content in the Everpresent to let the magic work itself through.

Eventually, his mind turned back to what had happened in the Blinds, and he realized the growing call of crows wasn't a coincidence.

Bodies lay all around the campsite. Not all of them bore the mark of the Hound's fangs. More than half had their throats slit, or were otherwise disposed of in a quick, efficient manner. Two people moved by the abandoned carriages, tossing trunks onto the ground as they rifled through them.

Two sets of eyes snapped over, their usual steady heartbeats thudding faster. Ex groaned as they approached, completely helpless.

Snow reached for her blade, but Ice held up his hand. He stared down at Ex warily, muscles coiled like a ready snake.

"Give me that necklace," Ex said, tilting his head towards her bag of choice treasure, where one spot softly glowed. "The purple one. You can have the rest."

"Why?" Ice said.

"It's important to me."

They considered, exchanging a few foreign words without taking their eyes off him. Then Ice grunted and lifted his chin. His sister reached into the bag, found the gemstone, turning it over in her hands. She must have felt something in it, for her heartbeat slowed, and she held it closer to her face.

"Hmm," she murmured, then shook her head. "No. This one is most valuable."

Her brother shrugged as she walked away. "No witnesses," she called back. Ex's heart sank. He reached for his knife, but Ice kicked it away and reached for his own.

"Nothing personal," he said. When Ex struggled to rise, the killer slammed him back to the ground with a boot to his chest.

Then Snow screamed. And sprouted another head.

No, it was a small, dark creature, with horridly long fangs that sunk deep into the woman's neck with a death grip. Snow flailed her arms in search of her assailant, but found nobody to grasp. Her feet left the ground, and her body shook back and forth savagely, blood spraying in the drifting mist.

Both Ex and Ice stared in abject horror as the krasue's exposed heart thudded with the effort. Her jaws opened lightning quick and snapped shut for another bite. Snow shuddered, limbs twitching as her body dangled by a string of flesh, then detached and thudded to the ground.

Without a word, her brother sprinted to the only remaining horse and leapt on, chancing not one glance back. Sibling loyalty did not trump the primordial instinct to survive.

Nothing personal.

Narissa dropped the severed head, bloody jaws hanging open, and her black snake tongue flicked across her lips. Satisfied, she floated down, curling her innards to slip into Snow's lifeless body. At that point, Ex had to avert his eyes, feeling as if he were trespassing on an intimate moment. But he also needed to vomit.

Mostly stomach bile, as he hadn't eaten in days.

He wiped the sour taste from his lips and spat, willing himself to erase the image from his mind. Hunters almost always arrived after a phi carried out its misdeeds. He was used to the gory aftermath, yes, but he couldn't recall a time he had witnessed the act itself.

A pale hand hovered before his eyes. He looked up at Narissa, her long black hair and darker skin contrasting with her new body. Snow had been leaner and taller than Narissa, but the krasue wore her skin easily, without so much as a seam to indicate where her neck ended and Narissa's head began.

The hunter's instinct took over momentarily and Ex reached for his absent chainblade. Yet Narissa didn't flinch, her calm eyes meeting his without shame.

He reached out to grasp her hand and rose to his feet.

"Thanks," Ex said, doing his best to pretend he'd only walked in on a woman getting dressed. No need to comment on her choice of clothing. With one glance over the battlefield, it wasn't hard to agree this was the most intact garment left.

Her placid gaze came to rest on the Hound with a small frown.

Oh no. She spoke in the Everpresent, her lip quivered. *I feared he might fall.* She walked past Ex to crouch by the Hound's body, stroking his head in a gentle, loving manner that Ex doubted he'd have tolerated.

Finally, Ex felt safe enough to emerge from the Everpresent. It would be wise to let the magic work and save his strength.

"Did you know who he was?" Narissa said. When Ex didn't respond, she said, "This was Astrama the Twice-Risen, the son of Maaba and the warrior princess of the Cloud Forest."

Ex stared down at the Hound's body in disbelief. "The Cloud Forest has been cleared longer than I've been alive."

"Yes. He was a legend. The last of his kind."

"Of course he was." Ex glanced between him and her. "What... happened to you?"

"My body was destroyed in the fire, and Indrajit did not find me in the wreckage. But the Twice-Risen did, and together we found you." She gave him a weak smile. "I gave these men quite a fright in the dark, then Astrama did the rest." Her smile faded, perhaps considering how her actions would affect her supposed amnesty. Then she reached into the bag attached to Snow – or rather, her new body – and pulled out Arinya's amulet. Her eyes gleamed, but she quickly handed it to him as if it were hot. "She's not here."

"No," Ex sighed, and spotted the horses at the tree line to the clearing. He made his way over to them and gave them a few good pats and scritches, even Ramble. After they were properly greeted, he checked the carriages for anything left behind.

The minister had kept what he'd left at Narissa's, thrown everything into a chest. He'd turned out all the pouches and bags and made a complete mess of things. At first, it seemed strange that he'd bring along his gear, but after finding Shar-Ala's eye, he probably thought there might be more to any of it. To his relief, his mask remained, one small token of good luck. It was broken in half somehow, but better than lost.

Some of Arinya's things were in there as well. Things Ex hadn't known she carried, like a small, folded up paper with a painting of a river village, which must have been her hometown. There was a hairbrush, a bar of soap, and a few other comfort items. Ex was drawn to a small, leather-bound book, the title of which he didn't recognize. Then again, he hadn't read very much aside from old tales and legends.

The story was handwritten, but as he flipped the pages in a blur, he noticed dates, and towards the end, maps. A diary? He spotted his name and thought about reading the last few entries for a glimpse into her mind. But that felt as wrong as if he were to sniff her undergarments, and he snapped it shut.

How long had she been gone? No doubt they'd ridden back

to the Capital by now, back to the prince's clutches. As much as it sickened him to think about, Ex hoped he'd welcome her back. He hoped she could blend right back into a comfortable life. Would she wonder about Isaree? They'd taken her from Arinya and thrown her carelessly into the bounty without knowing it was what they were sent to find. Idiots.

Ex helped Narissa drag the Hound's body into the brush, where it could return to the earth safely, away from the tainted bodies of the fallen men.

"I think she's finally gone," he said, staring over the bodies.

"Gone... where?" Narissa seemed genuinely confused. "She told me you two were going to Yinseng."

"She told you that? When?"

"When she woke up."

Ex searched her face for a lie but found none. Narissa drew back, surprised at his reaction. "She told me she planned to ask you during the festival."

"She did." Ex again felt a fool. "But she asked me to escort her there at first. When she asked me to stay with her, I thought it was her being impulsive again."

Narissa laughed, light behind her hand. "I suppose she lost her nerve."

Although he felt his spirits rise, none of it mattered now. The chance they had together was gone. He could still run, disappear into the forest and walk the Serene Way. Who knew how far word had spread of his "crimes." The Capital was the last place he wanted to be.

But what kind of life would that be? To live in the woods, hunt animals, and forage like some kind of hermit? Sneak into public houses to get drunk and hope they didn't recognize him? Ex wouldn't get any real work without the backing of the guild, that was for sure, especially not true demons. Hunting minor ghosts and peddling ingredients to hedge witches and shamans until the end of his days... He supposed he could run away to another country and start over. Maybe get a job as a butcher.

With a growl, he searched for something to throw, then plopped down on the ground, head in his hands.

"Are we leaving, then?" Narissa asked, quietly inspecting her new body.

Narissa already knew. There was no way Ex could leave it there. He had to bring Isaree back to Arinya, somehow, some way. If he didn't, she might worry forever that her daughter's soul would be trapped and lost in some bounty hunter's pocket.

And that wasn't all. He shuddered to think about such a heinous failure, but he had lost Shar-Ala's eye to a goddamn royal necromancer. The guild needed to know.

Think they'll still give me my badge? Out of habit, Ex looked to the trees. He could almost hear the Hound chuckling. Another empty spot in the world to add to his heartache.

Chapter Twenty-Six

The Returned

Riding fast down the Long Road to the Capital with a demon at his side, this fever dream of a reality didn't completely set in until Ex spied the far-reaching outskirts of the immense city, which had an absurdly long name.

The City of Devas, on the Wings of the Ascended, Magnificent Place of the Twelve Circles, Seat of the King, of all his Royal Splendor, Home of Gods Incarnate and the Enlightened Lord.

And so everyone just called it the Capital.

At near fifty miles wide, the jewel of the Suyoram Kingdom lorded between three rivers and the bay. It was an ancient place, exchanged throughout centuries by many powers come and gone. From the weathered stone roads of the outer city to the shiny royal interior, a mandala of walls, roads and canals ran throughout like lifeblood. Old shrines slunk in the shadows of new temples, schools, markets, theatres, whorehouses, bathhouses, factories, parks... anything human civilization had to offer, you could find there.

Even from this distance, you could see the scaffolding on the king's latest Enlightened Lord statue, welcoming travelers at the harbor – a signal of the encroaching new world, abandoning what was once pure and steady in order to move backwards and away from nature. Instead of forests, they had streets, filled with all manner of people. Tribes settled together, banded like mini villages.

Ex and Narissa approached via his usual route into town, but he didn't know many other ways. He figured they couldn't have posted his portrait on every single wanted wall, especially in the outer circles. Once they approached the old city, however, he'd have to be more cautious.

The rain continued to patter down, and he pulled his hood over his head. The auxiliary canals began to fill, along with reservoirs that laid dry half the year. They found a few conical rainhats from the soldiers' supplies, which provided some cover.

Before they had set out, Narissa chose some of Arinya's traveling clothes to wear. Arinya's body was larger than the body of Snow, but the rugged sabai blouse worked, and the chong kraben wrap pants by design could fit anyone.

"Are you sure you want to come with me?" Ex had asked as he waited while she dressed inside the carriage. "You can borrow Ramble if you'd like, he hates me anyway."

"I must find Indrajit to complete our deal," she'd said when she emerged, her mouth set in a determined line. "The Palace of Scales is in the old city, where his oldest shrine remains."

"He's a deva. Can't he find you?" Though Ex still wasn't convinced on the whole "demon becomes a human" idea, nothing seemed impossible anymore. He supposed even if it were a fantasy, if that kept a phi from their murderous ways, it was worth holding on to. It brought up questions about what that meant for hunters when faced with a Hungry Ghost that claimed to strive for this amnesty. But those debates were beyond him.

Doubt had clouded her eyes. "If he wanted to, yes, I suppose he could. I'm not sure that he will." She'd stared at the scene of carnage, as the crows cawed and picked at the soldiers' remains. "I just want the hunger to go away."

"You'll still have it," Ex had reminded her then. "Just cooked and seasoned better." He'd hesitated, trying to decide whether to say the next thing, but couldn't help himself. "Did you ever, you know, sprinkle something on one of your, uh, meals before you–"

"No."

"Not even salt?"

"Never."

"Wow. I can't wait to see you try spicy food."

"Oh, there *is* such a thing as spicy meat," she'd smiled. "Young phi hunter meat is the spiciest."

He must have gone pale because she tittered then. "Not that I'd know. I've just heard."

Throughout the outskirts, the locals acted in much the same way as they did anywhere else, either giving him a nod in recognition, or slinking away, making signs over their bodies. The locals in the Capital were used to him, though, and on this road, they knew him well. Some of the street kids ran up when they recognized Brownie and Ramble. They surrounded them, mercilessly pestering and teasing him as children did.

"Hunter Ex, Hunter Ex! What kinda monsters did you kill?"

"Show us the grossest thing!"

"Is that your girlfriend?!"

"Give us the sparklies!"

"Sparklies! Sparklies!"

They demanded sparklecrack buds, which burst with a bright fluff of pollen when squeezed. Ex usually had them in abundance, but they were all casualties of the minister's pillaging, lost somewhere in the mud. He dispersed the laughing kids by pulling out the top half of his hunter's mask and giving them his best "monster roar."

As they walked deeper into the neighborhood, an elderly lady sitting on a bucket next to a fruit stall whistled at the two.

"Is that Ex? Baby boy, come here!" She waved them over, gap-toothed grin stretching the wrinkles from her cheeks. "Where have you been? You never miss Rom Laithong!" She was right. Most of the hunters finished their rounds around this time and were probably already gathered at the guild hall for the festival.

"I got a bit sidetracked," he said, accepting the glazed mango and sweet coconut stick with a watering mouth and a wai of gratitude.

"Aren't you going to offer some to your lovely lady friend?" The grandma glared at him, and he quickly moved to check his pack for a bag of seeds to trade. "Oh, please, boy!" she called. "I've still not used up the last batch you brought back. This one's on the house."

Narissa took the fruit stick with a grateful wai and pretended to taste it.

"How's the festival going?"

"Not like the old days." She frowned towards the old city, where the gold-accented wall of the old city divided the haves and have-nots in no uncertain terms. "This king's done away with everything that made Rom Laithong any fun. No drunken Hanuman races, no paper parades, no animist orgies. All you hear is chanting, chanting, chanting!" She snorted. "The Sangha came through a week ago with a royal decree to teach all of us new prayers. New! I'm ninety years old, does he think I need to remember any more of that foolery? It's his son's damn new queen, I tell you."

It had been like this for decades, a shadow of what the elders said it used to be. They remembered Rom Laithong to be more of a hedonist, "release all your sins in three nights" kind of thing, whereas now, it was a softer affair, at least in the old city and inner districts. It grew wilder the further out you wandered.

"What about the fireworks?" Ex asked, with slight panic. "There's still fireworks, right?"

"Hmph. Ask old Nokai what fireworks were in *our* day."

He didn't have to. All he needed to do was imagine a wondrous spectacle of bright lights and color, but with magic.

It would be as close to glorious as you could get without the Everpresent.

"Thank you, Grandma." Ex already polished off the skewer and she snatched it before he could toss it into the trash bucket.

"You keep your head down in old town," she said. "My grandson says the kingsmen have been stopping boys your age and searching them with no cause or explanation."

The nervous pit in his stomach, temporarily suppressed by the mango, immediately returned. "No cause?"

"Something about the queen, I don't know. Just be careful and mind your manners."

As they came upon the gate to the old city, his uneasiness grew into full-on anxiety. There were always more guards during the festival every year, but something about the entrance put him on high alert. It wasn't just the kingsmen taking an extra minute to survey any young men. It was more the plain-clothed men lurking about, pretending to do idle things as they watched the crowd. One guy leaned against the wall, smoking, but there were a pile of rollup ends at his feet. Two sat at a table at the nearest tea shop, playing a game of checkers, but not making any real moves.

"They smell like those men," Narissa whispered. "Of bronze and roses. Of the Loram Kingdom."

"Queensmen." Ex wondered if the crown even knew they'd been posted here. Did they have his badly drawn portrait in their pockets? "Alright, we're going to need to find another way in."

"Is there one?"

"There's always one."

He had one more stop to make before trying to enter the old city. When his childhood friend, Piglet, got married a few years back, he took over one of the apothecary shops that sold a lot of the guild's public-friendly goods. Of course, if one knew the right thing to say, he'd send them over to his elder brother Swan's warehouse by the bay for special inventory. Ex's friends might have grown up around hunters and their stories, but they'd never done more than spar with him from time to time. They'd had higher ambitions than housekeeping though, and their stores kept their connections to home alive.

He certainly couldn't bring Narissa into the guild compound. Though she was so well-disguised, he could barely tell she was a demon even in the Everpresent, the masters had senses far beyond his. It would be safe in the store, at least. The masters hardly left the compound unless they were training hunters in the field. Hunters on return didn't casually go in to restock, preferring to send runner boys to do those errands.

The bell-laden door sent chimes ringing throughout the small shop. Narissa gazed in interest at the jars of various powders, seeds, and animal parts. Carved idols lined the shelves, along with taxidermied minor spirits, and potted medicinal plants.

Piglet did his best to keep the shop organized, but as his namesake, he'd left jars unfilled and mislabeled. Old food wrappers and his own empty bottles blended in with the real tonics. He was in the early stages of a solo card game when the two walked in.

"Welcome, sir or madam," he said boredly, without lifting his head. "If you need help finding anything, please ask."

"I'm looking for a few pounds, seems like you lost 'em."

His round head snapped up, and he squinted with his signature nose flare. "Ex?" His wide cheeks broke out into a grin. "Is that Little Ex!? I thought you skipped this season!"

"Nope, just wanted to make an entrance."

They clasped hands in greeting, and then he ruffled Ex's hair. "Oi! Don't let the big cat see how long your hair's grown. Come, let me fetch a razor."

"It's okay," Ex batted his hand away. "I don't think he'll beat me over half an inch of hair."

"During Lathong Hunters Meet? Ha, sure! It's your funeral."

He winked at Narissa. "So, *you* must like it this long? I don't know any other reason my little brother would brave the big cat. Who is this beautiful woman, cous?"

"My *friend* Narissa," Ex said. "She's visiting." Before he could dig further, Ex laid a hand on his shoulder. "Has there been anyone around the house calling for me?"

"The house? I haven't dropped by in a while, so I wouldn't know." He scratched the patchy hair on his chin. "Are you expecting someone?"

"No, not really. But I heard the kingsmen are stopping guys in old town."

"I've heard that, but I think they're just cracking down for the festival. First year the new queen's in the city, after all." Piglet started to put two and two together, yet couldn't get to the final sum. "What's wrong, cous? Are you in trouble?"

"No, nothing serious," he assured him. "I just want to get home without being harassed, that's all."

"Well, you could see Swan. Use the tunnels."

"Is he in?"

"As far as I know," he snorted. "Just mind yourself. There's new blood down there."

"Thanks, cous." Ex clasped his hand again. Then he tilted his head towards Narissa, who was preoccupied with one of the displays. "I need a favor. She needs to get to the Palace of Scales, in the devas district of old town. Think you could escort her?"

He glanced over her, this time less appreciatively. "I *could…*" He didn't have to ask why Ex didn't want her to go through the smuggling tunnels with him. It wasn't the best way to impress a lady. Though his curiosity over Ex's concern rose even more. "Sneaky doesn't suit you, cous. What's going on?"

Ex wasn't well practiced in lying, so he did the next best thing.

"I did it," he said, with a genuine grin. "I killed Shar-Ala. I'm gonna get my true demon slayer badge."

Piglet stared at Ex with wide eyes. His mouth dropped open... Then he burst out laughing, doubling over. Ex's smile wilted into a frown as he waited, crossing his arms as it went on and on.

Finally sensing Ex's ill-humored silence, Piglet peered up at him with a pitying expression, one Ex was very familiar with and did not miss.

"Oh, little bro, I'm sorry, I'm sorry. You got me, wow. You just said it so convincingly."

Ex lowered his head, glowering. "I'm serious. He's in bits now." He looked to Narissa for help. She'd been preoccupied with a taxidermied crane, and finally turned her head to them.

"It's true," she said, and went back to browsing.

"Some of the goods are really delicate," Ex said, "and I don't want those guards poking around with it."

"They wouldn't bother a whisper, but with how shady you're acting, I'm sure they'd make an exception." Piglet wiped the merriment from his eyes, shaking his head. "Devas, you're so sure of it! Let's see it, then."

"Here?" Ex hesitated, "I can't bring that stuff out here. His claws are about..." He held out his arms for effect.

"Pssh, claws, claws. They could be from any phi. Show me the eye."

"That's even worse! It's cursed." At least that was true.

"Right, right." Piglet laughed again. "You're so full of shit."

"Look, I'm not asking for much. Are you going to help me or not? I shouldn't have to beg family." That was a stretch. They may have called each other brother and cousin, but there had never been much real closeness.

To Ex's surprise, the word softened him. Piglet sighed, shooting him a smirk, then scoffed at his card game.

"Well, it's not like I was winning, anyway."

Chapter Twenty-Seven

Narissa and the Deva

For all Ex's terrifying powers, Narissa finally saw the hunter without his mask – a boy falling in love, pure and simple. And in a way, he was just that – pure and simple as any animal in the woods. Certainly he was unsettled here. As soon as they entered the city, his shoulders tensed, and his eyes darted at the angry shouts of arguing city folk. He often held a cloth pouch of heady champa incense to his nose to drown the smells.

Narissa, however, was used to the overwhelming stench of humanity. Once she became mortal, it would be much easier still. The trick was to focus on those glimpses of relief – soap flower garlands, a mangosteen stall, and the lotus flowers gracing every roof as the festival swelled to its conclusion. When she suggested this, Ex shut his eyes, refocused, and began to breathe a little steadier.

After speaking to his kin, they went outside, where he began to remove bags from one of the horses. He cast a wary glance back to Piglet as he closed up his shop.

"You don't trust him," Narissa observed.

"Not with the way he gossips." Ex scrunched up his nose. "Even if I explained that saying anything might get me killed, he'd find a way to brag about it."

"How odd."

"But with a favor like this, I trust him. He'll get you to the shrine, and no one will harass you with him around. Everyone knows him."

Narissa turned her gaze towards the big wall that separated old town from new, but grew distracted by the context of certain glances as people passed by. Perhaps it was her pale arms in contrast to her face. But that was the least of her concerns. "That's not what I'm worried about."

"It's Indrajit, isn't it?"

She was surprised the hunter remembered. It was clear he did not believe her, for the devas scarcely appeared before mortals, if at all.

"Yes. I broke my vow, after all."

"But, well, you only had one more night to go when I met you," Ex said. "Couldn't you just say you, uh, found a fresh, headless woman's corpse and didn't want to waste it?" Ex shook his head at his own words. "Sorry. I don't know." At this point, she was used to his manners. Amusing how some of his thoughts slipped from his tongue so easily, while others gave him so much trouble that he chose silence instead.

Finished, Ex handed Ramble's reins to her. She stared at the horse, then at the hunter.

"He likes you," he said, and laid a hand on her shoulder. Despite knowing he was a friend, the contact still sent a shiver of quiet panic through her heart. If he noticed, he didn't say so. "I feel like you're about to go on a journey. So if he starts being an asshole, you can gift him back the next time we meet."

Narissa's eyes watered. She'd never been given such a significant gift before. Ex placed the reins in her hand and closed her fingers around them.

"You saved my life, Arinya's, and Isaree's." He cleared his throat, voice faltering on the last name. Quickly, he chuckled, retreating from that pain. "I can't believe I'm saying this but... you have a good heart. And I wish you the best."

Narissa cheered at his kind words and laid her hand on the hunter's. She returned his smile. "You'll find her, Ex."

Even at the mention of Arinya, his face softened, as if his very soul lifted at the thought of their reunion. Narissa knew that someday, she would find that same brightness in her lover's eyes, and she would wear it herself.

Narissa could hardly believe that *this* was Indrajit's grand shrine. The deva's altar squeezed into only a pocket of land hardly larger than her house. This must have been the stone inner chamber, pockmarked with empty holes along the pillars where jewels had been pried free. The remnants of what used to be the outer shell of his temple had been reclaimed by the gates of a tannery on one side, and the empty land dug out and prepared for construction on the other.

To steal from the devas... That such sacrilege was no longer considered a grave sin baffled her.

Indrajit's affiliation with Ravana cast him unfavorably with the mortals, compared to some of the other celestials who were associated with Shivah and his high court. But Ravana was not a dark being. Just as any force needed a counterweight, he brought balance. The devas exchanged in their collaborative creation and destruction. It was written all over the walls if one looked, although due to the inattention to his shrine, the murals inside had become illegible. Judging by the sour stink, it had been used as a public latrine fairly recently.

From a hole in the roof, pale light flickered in from the intermittent sun. The stone below was still soggy from the previous rain, from the year before, and the year before that. It wouldn't be long until a few more rains claimed the rest of the floor, but Narissa had the feeling it would be gone before then.

At least Indrajit's idol remained unscathed – the scowling, six-armed warrior deva represented as faithfully as he would appear in his own realm, though not as he appeared when walking the realm of mankind. She noticed a few candle stumps had been burned at the steps below his feet, though it was questionable if it were in reverence, or meant for a vagrant's opium pipe.

And there on the steps below his idol, the deva lord himself sat in his regalia and khon mask, hand propping up his chin in a glum expression.

Narissa stood before him and bowed her head with a wai in greeting. Indrajit did not move to return it.

"Do you see how they have reduced me?" he rumbled.

"It saddens me."

"What will replace this place, I wonder. A bathhouse? A cobbler? You see them tread about town in foreign shoes – even their feet no longer connect to the earth," he scoffed.

"There are still many places where you are paid respect."

"Maybe so. But for how long? Perhaps this realm has no place for us anymore."

"You would abandon all those who still seek favor?" Narissa approached, careful not to slip on the uneven, broken stone. As she did, Indrajit finally raised his head.

"You wear another's body, taken by murder."

"I do."

She steeled herself for his swift judgement. But he only tilted his head.

"In self-defense?"

She closed her eyes. "No, on behalf of another."

"Another?" She could not see beyond his impassive khon mask, but the bafflement in his voice carried through loud and clear.

"Yes. One who I thought was the three-eyed horror haunting my dreams. He was a phi hunter," she said. "A friend."

"Then you have failed, Narissa," Indrajit said and shook his head with a sigh. "I have failed."

Narissa then bowed her head. She sank down to her knees and pressed her palms together. "I did not feast on the corpse, my lord, despite thirty years of unsatiated hunger. I did not devour the pure soul of an unborn when tempted. I've healed others with my work. I've saved several lives at risk to my own. If that does not prove my humanity, what would? I will not succumb to despair, my lord. I will not stop striving to break this curse, even if it takes a hundred more lifetimes."

The shrine was silent as Indrajit considered. She held her breath.

"You are ready to live as one of them," he finally said, a defeated statement rather than a question. "Toil in the dirt as you waste away to rotting flesh and bone. A short, painful life, with no guarantee of karmic salvation. No guarantee you will not be reborn again as krasue. Or worse."

"I understand, Lord Indrajit. I am ready."

He stood finally, regaining a semblance of his former grandeur.

Her heart thudded in anticipation.

The deva lord crossed his arms, and then finally chuckled, the deep rumble bringing warmth into the shrine. "I am impressed, Narissa. To starve for thirty years after the death of your mortal lover at your hands. To befriend a sworn enemy. Was it worth the wait?"

"It was."

"Do you even know where they are now? Who or what they have returned as?"

"No," she said, and smiled. "But I will find them."

Chapter Twenty-Eight

Comes Home

Ex hadn't been alone since meeting Arinya, and the loneliness struck him after Narissa disappeared down the road with Piglet. He was used to a quiet world, and it shouldn't have bothered him. That was the hunter's life. That's how he started off, at least, until the Hound showed up. But that had been different. The Hound wasn't always walking by his side and only shared his campfire sparingly. But it provided him comfort out on the trail, knowing he might always be nearby, watching his back.

Now those days were over.

The guild warehouse was in the Rachophon District by the port, nestled between a grain trading company storehouse and a basket weaving factory. Similar merchant warehouses lined the entire street, both legitimate and not. There were some things that the guild couldn't sell in the shop. It wasn't always a question of legality. A lot of their harvest, from the phi in particular, carried volatile spirit magic, power that lingered after their demise. If someone didn't know what they were doing, they could cause major damage to themselves and others.

Over the decades, the guild manicured their clientele, vetting every interested buyer, confirming that the intent was sound when filling special requests. People came from all over in search of some of these things, some from far beyond Suyoram, across the oceans. Ex didn't learn all that much about the details of where things went and who bought what. Those were front-of-house details, an entirely different division.

That being said, there were things they couldn't keep in the warehouse, either. It was well secured, and no one had ever pulled off a heist. Yet some things were too precious to keep anywhere but the compound, under the supervision of the masters.

Like Shar-Ala's third eye.

Which of course, he didn't have. Actually, he didn't have much of anything, not even the goods he'd collected before arriving at Mali's. But at least he had his mask, broken as it was. The length of his hair wouldn't compare to the amount of shit he'd catch if he had to tell the masters he'd lost it to a necromancer.

Ex marveled at the forest of sails that swayed in the harbor, even recognized a few of them. This district reminded him of Jinburi, but far grander, with all the rough edges polished to an impersonal sheen. Beyond, the sails of the royal navy guarded the entrance to the bay, watchful cannons always at the ready. These weren't river folk collecting goods from surrounding villages and countries. These were continents meeting. Empires. Qinseng trading companies, Kutzu pirates, and Baghani privateers, merchants from beyond, speaking mumbling languages, paying heavy coin to buy flavor for their awful, bland food.

There was no easy entrance into old town for foreigners without the proper papers. As cosmopolitan as the crown wanted to be, xenophobia hadn't yet been bred out of the population. Therefore, all the riffraff stayed portside, alongside rich middle merchants.

It felt like staring at a brand-new road that led into an endless, colorless land. The overwhelming urge to get away drove Ex to put his head down, shove his hands in his coat pockets, and hurry to the warehouse. Some of the porters hollered at him as he walked past the fence, hands on their weapons, alarmed at his haste. He pulled his hood back and waved.

"Oh, it's the kid," they said, with condescending scoffs and dismissive nods. They didn't stop him from going in.

Swan was where he'd expected, in his office, sweeping his already immaculate floor. All around the warehouse level, his charges performed the same pointless, tidying chores. Even though he was only a year older than Ex, he commanded a severe presence that granted him an air of unshakable authority. He hadn't always been this way. Ex wondered where and when Piglet and he had diverged.

"Ex." He raised a brow when he saw him, but continued to sweep. "I haven't seen you in quite some time."

"I stopped by a few months ago," Ex responded, and crossed his arms. Swan had been the one gone on some mysterious overseas trip. "Good to see you too, cous."

"Of course." Satisfied, Swan placed the broom in an ornate bronze holder, the likes of which Ex had never seen before. He noticed his admiring stare. "Isn't it perfect? I found it in a tiny shop in Yequeza. I should have ordered more."

"I killed Shar-Ala."

Swan's eyes narrowed. "When?"

"Two or three nights ago." Ex wasn't sure how long he'd been in Minister Iyun's clutches. Hopefully not too long. There were things he couldn't tell Piglet, but there were things he could tell Swan. They'd shared certain moments in the past that no one else had. Secret moments that were, well, part of growing up and discovering, he supposed. "I killed him. But I lost his eye."

Swan placed his hand on his chin, a mirror, albeit narrower, image of Piglet's gesture. "Define 'lost.'"

"Did you know the prince is deep into black magic? Am I the only one who didn't know this?"

"Hmm." He tilted his head. "On the contrary. It seems you're the only one who knows it. Where did you hear that?"

"His pet necromancer." Ex watched Swan closely, though he'd always been hard to read. He didn't seem to immediately dismiss the concept, but he didn't seem to buy it, either. "Do you believe me?"

"I believe that you believe so." The corner of his mouth twitched, and he smoothed back his long hair, then rested his hand on his hip. "And how did this necromancer steal a true demon's eye from you?"

"It's a long story," Ex said. "Short answer – captivity and torture." Swan's eyes widened, and Ex went on before he could say more. "I'm pretty sure they're looking for me, for... other reasons." Ex realized he'd protectively placed his hand over the amulet at his neck. "I'll buy you and Piglet a beer later and tell you all about it. But right now, I need to use the tunnels to get home."

Swan's eyes darkened. "It's that bad?"

Ex shifted his stance, then looked towards the back rooms, uncomfortable under his gaze. "Is it clear?"

"As far as I know. There's been no need to use it for a long while." He opened his desk and retrieved a key, gesturing for him to follow. Some of the workers peered over to them in interest. It wasn't often that a hunter came down here. They seemed bored as hell, tidying up things that needed no tidying. Swan must have read Ex's mind. "There's been little to do for quite some time. The hunters bring less and less every month, and with the king's new decrees moving forward, requests come in slow. I've been told to start moving goods that have almost nothing to do with our trade. Decorative items, historical artifacts, and that sort, only to keep jobs." His voice carried a thread of sorrow. Ex felt it too. The new world encroached little by little, and here he had a front row seat.

"Maybe we'll get some new recruits soon," Ex said. "People will miss the old ways, and come around, right? Nostalgia." The sentiment felt hollow.

"I hope you're right, Ex." Swan agreed. He didn't sound at all optimistic. Then he looked at Ex and said, "I hope you aren't the last hunter."

They walked into the back room, where some of the porters were taking their lunch, weapons neatly hung on racks, coats on hangers. Swan didn't let them get away with anything, it seemed.

"Help me with this, please," Swan said to one of the burly ones, and they moved aside two large bookcases to reveal the old smuggling door. After turning the lock, Swan hesitated. "Do you need a light?"

"No." Ex smirked, not bothering to hide his disdain. "I remember the way."

Swan averted his eyes with a sad smile. He handed Ex the key for the other side. "Good luck, Ex," he said, "and congratulations on Shar-Ala. I'll be at the ceremony." A glint of humor played in his eye, but Ex met his gaze evenly.

"See you there."

Underground tunnels once webbed beneath the entirety of old town, a favorite method for smugglers to move goods. They were more ancient than the city, originally made by a kingdom of water creatures that used to thrive on the shores. People used to find their massive shells in some corridors of the twisting maze, but no remnants of their culture like the Venara. Then the crown came in and renovated many of them to use in their water systems. They collapsed the twisting, turning pathways that didn't fit their design.

But they didn't find all of them. The path Ex walked would lead straight to the guild compound, where he would emerge at the bottom of the old, dry well, hidden behind a thicket of bamboo. There was a lock on the other side, but with the key it shouldn't be a problem.

He'd snuck down there as a child with Swan and Piglet.

Back then, the arched ceilings and smoothed ground looked massive, long grooves running constant in the walls, guideposts made by the ancient architects. The carvings seemed to soar far over his head back then. Now, they were only chest high. It was still spacious enough for a few people to walk side by side comfortably, but nothing near what he remembered.

They used to play down here, laughter echoing as they scurried around with paper lanterns, usually until Piglet and Swan's mother caught them. To be honest, he had been scared to death, and just wanted to prove he wasn't. It never fooled the other kids, and he distinctly remembered a game of hide and seek during one of the first festivals, probably twelve years ago to this day. It wasn't just Swan and Piglet. The other hunters' kids were around. They had put out all their lanterns and gone back up, giggling. Practical joke.

Though the other kids participated in traumatizing Ex for life, Piglet and Swan had been the masterminds. That was one of the only times the masters were so angry that they almost threw the whole family out on the street. Their defense had been that Ex was a hunter and could see in the dark, so they were just making the game fair. Of course, Ex was still years away from any trials and they knew that, but Master Seua shrugged and said boys would be boys. Once Ex stopped crying, Master Rei told him that they were jealous, which didn't make sense at the time. If they wanted to be hunters, there was nothing stopping them from training with him. He only started to understand it when he grew older. *Child, this is a lonely life.*

The porters who used to work these tunnels used the grooves on the wall if their torches went out. Hunters had the Everpresent. Though spirit energy in general was low in the cities, there was a great hum of it underground. These old tunnels were made by reverent spirits, and the walls came to life with their ancient markings. Life flowed in the soil. Tree roots reached down this far, insects and worms and other crawly creatures.

None of it awed Ex, and he rushed through. This was his least favorite environment. He loathed any phi that took him below ground, so much so that there had been times he'd sit in a hunting blind for hours outside a hole, just to avoid the internal terror within. Only in the Hunter's Trance, where all emotion became a distant memory, was he able to enter without fear. But he preferred to promise the Hound extra meat if he'd burrow inside and run them out.

Small passages led off from the main, most of them boarded up. There were a few auxiliary rooms once used for storage as he neared the compound, and he began to recognize the layout. Once, they'd been stocked full of things needed to move down to portside, or from portside to the compound for rituals. From what Ex understood, it would have been possible for them to use the main roads, but there was drama and politics and economics involved that were far above his level of interest or understanding.

At the end of the tunnel, a staircase wound upward in a spiral. By then, he'd left the Everpresent, as there was enough light from the surface leaking down as a guide. His stomach grew tighter with each step. Two opposing images fought for purchase in his mind – the guild fawning over his accomplishment as he received his true demon slayer badge, and their horror at the fact that he let an artifact fall into the hands of a necromancer. Not just any necromancer, to boot. A necromancer operating under protection of the crown.

There were some hunters who, on rare occasions, tracked men. They'd picked up those skills in a former life, of course. It was one thing to hunt down a rogue necromancer who'd stolen from them, it was quite another to assassinate the crown prince's personal pet sorcerer. But now, Ex suspected Minister Iyun wanted to make the prince – if not the king – his pet, and make a shadow play for the entire country. Ex wondered what grand designs he had in mind.

The lock clicked open, and he slid aside the door. A rush of fresh air shot through his lungs like an icy dagger. He hadn't realized how stale it'd been down there, and drank in the familiar scent of home. Chalk from the stone training grounds, diagramming the principles of movement. The sweat-worn cedar obstacle course, whose balance beams he'd fallen from so many times. Straw-stuffed monster-shaped dummies, stuck with arrows in all the weak points. The cold stone of the guild hall, alive with vivid, spirit-soaked flowers and incense, proud banners and trophies hanging about the walls. Tight, oiled leather and sharp steel from the armory, acrid coal burning in the communal hearth, surrounded by long tables laden with beer and food.

Despite his sweating palms, the brush of the bamboo thicket against his face almost brought him to tears. He swallowed a lump in his throat and wiped nervous sweat off his brow. He pushed aside the trees, recalling the days playing here as a child, the nights he practiced silent movement, at the ready to dodge arrows. Nostalgia and dread made strange bedfellows.

He'd been home every three months for the last few years, and though every return was a comfort, it felt different this time. It felt like he'd been lost at sea, able to swim, yet drowning just the same. With land in sight, he stumbled towards it, gasping for breath.

Memories and dreams were useless distractions, the masters taught him. *Even when out of the Everpresent, in the Blinds, walk with the Now.* Ex had done a shitty job of following the doctrine lately, and that's probably why he almost walked right into the trap.

"Cub."

Ex's heart soared at the old man's voice that whispered through the bamboo thicket. He quickened his step, but right before exiting into the courtyard, a strong hand seized him by the collar and threw him flat on his back. Even the corporal discipline brought him a smile.

"Master Seua!" Ex brought his hands in a wai to his forehead in respect, practically weeping with relief. "You'll never believe what–"

"Shh!" He crouched down and clamped his weathered hand over Ex's mouth. In his late fifties, his lean, broad-shouldered figure was just as fit as any other hunter. He usually wore dark, wide-legged cotton pants and a long tunic more common with martial art teachers, but now he'd dressed in the ceremonious black robes of the masters, the white sash wound about the torso in the shape of the Phi Hunters Guild symbol.

His short white beard could not hide his deep frown, and he appeared as fierce as ever. Tattoos across his shaved head ran down from his temple to the jaw, one decorative curling tiger heavy across his blind eye. He never wore a pleased expression, except when drinking, but he always had a good-humored accent in his manners. That being said, he'd never looked as serious as he did now. Sensing that, Ex immediately tensed up.

"*Whisper,*" he said, at a subvocal level in which they barely moved their lips. It was a technique all hunters learned when training to use the voiceless words of spirit magic – undetectable to normal people, but as clear as speaking to other hunters. It was part of the reason people called them whispers.

Ex found his breath short even after Master Seua removed his hand. The old hunter's yellow eye narrowed as he peered between the trees. He hadn't gone into the Everpresent, however, so Ex followed his lead.

"*What's wrong?*"

"*What, young cub, could you have possibly got yourself into?*"

Ex rolled over, and crawled forward to follow his line of sight.

"Oh, shit," he said out loud, then clamped both hands over his mouth.

A squad of armed men stood in the wide courtyard of the guild hall, their boots shiny with drizzle on the weathered stone. These men who wore the colors of the crown, the four-tusked elephant emblem on the chest and shoulders of their armor, red capes clasped over their necks. They were the king's best soldiers, unlike the guards stationed about town to keep the peace.

They were in an animated conversation with Master Rei, her brows furrowed over her eyes, her hands calmly within her sleeves. Their voices were muffled by their masks, and Ex couldn't quite make out what they were saying. Four of the other hunters sat on the steps to the hall and lingered in the wide doorway, keeping a wary eye on the soldiers. They were in their civilian clothes, yet still carried their weapons, sak yant tattoos, scars, shaved heads, and maroon-red eyes casting them as wild as unearthly pirates.

Behind the officers, another line of soldiers stood at attention, wearing chrome masks with small eyeholes. They surrounded four court servants, who held something Ex had only seen at a great distance during royal parades.

A gold palanquin, laden with an obscene number of jewels that glistened in the rain, each corner and the roof adorned with a three-tiered crown. After a sharp voice rung out from inside the palanquin, the servants rushed to roll a dark red carpet along the ground in front of it. They bowed their heads and moved the silk curtains aside, while another servant opened up a five-tiered umbrella, straining to cover the man who emerged.

The crown-prince himself.

Chapter Twenty-Nine

And the Prince

"Enough with this charade." Crown-Prince Varunvirya's voice curled around his words in a lazy manner, as if he were in the middle of a condescending yawn. So, all those unflattering ballads they sang out in the countryside had a ring of truth to them. His royal attire fit his form well – a brocaded tunic dotted with symbols of his father's regime. His body looked fit, as if he spent a lot of time working out. His age showed in his handsome face, with lines around his scowl and grey about his temples. His portraits did not lie, Ex had to admit, he cut an impressive figure.

Immediately, Master Rei and the other hunters prostrated themselves, though they took their time. Despite the claim of divine right, many of them had seen too many princes come and go in the last few decades to hold more than sub-average reverence. Master Rei especially, as she gingerly lowered herself to the ground, pretending to be far frailer than she was.

After they spent a satisfactory amount of time face down on the ground, Prince Varunvirya lifted his chin. "You may rise," he said. As Master Rei brushed off her robes, she kept her shaved head respectfully bowed. The prince then said, "I know the boy is here."

"I would not lie, my prince," Master Rei said. "He has not been back since he left on his route three months past, sir."

"I will not argue with you, Master Hunter." Prince Varunvirya flicked his head, and some of the men brought a hooded man forward and threw him to his knees. They yanked off the hood, and Piglet's bright red face swung around in shock, a gag in his mouth. Sweat coated his brow, and he had a black eye. "This man from your guild said he saw the hunter 'Ex' here in the city. Did he lie to me?"

Master Rei frowned, puzzled at Piglet's presence. "I know nothing of this, my prince. I've known this man since he was a child, and he is not a liar, sir. Yet hunter Ex is not here."

"Then... someone must be lying to me." Prince Varunvirya placed his hand on his chin, squinting in confusion. It wasn't clear if he was being facetious. "Could my trusted servant, the crown's minister of magic, the venerable Righteous Storm have *lied* to me? Come, Minister Iyun. Explain yourself."

The blood rushed in Ex's head as the necromancer emerged from the ranks of the servants. He'd been washed and groomed, dressed in an even more ridiculously stylish outfit, and had traded his plain crutch for one adorned with jewels.

"My prince, perhaps we all speak true." Despite the veil obscuring most of his face, Ex could hear his smirk from across the yard. "Perhaps this man saw the young hunter and knows he is here. Perhaps his masters have not yet seen him. From my knowledge of the boy, my prince, he is quite sneaky, and very insolent. The spawn of rebels, sir. It's likely he paid no respect to his elders and is indeed in the city, unbeknownst to them. If there is nothing to hide, I suggest we search the grounds of this place–"

"You cannot," Master Rei said, and from her glare, it was clear she had no respect for the man. "By the law of the Sacred Stone Decree, our grounds are a sacred trust and cannot be violated at the heresy of a court magician."

"Sacred ground?" Iyun scoffed. "This is a crumbling museum, Rei. You are relics. Con artists wrapped in obscure rituals that prey on the superstitions of ignorant peasants."

"The only ignorance is yours, Iyun. Your kind steals from the spirits without reverence and claims their power for your own personal glory. Trust there will be judgment for you."

Prince Varunvirya raised a manicured brow, eyes flicking between Rei and Iyun as they descended into heated bickering, clearly fueled by deep, personal history.

"That's him," Ex said, and Master Seua squinted at the minister with a doubtful frown. *"That's the necromancer who stole Shar-Ala's eye from me."*

Without the chance to give context, Ex's words didn't move him. He could have been saying there was a dragon attacking the harbor and he would have given the same expression. Master Seua laid his hand on his shoulder and gestured to the well, the passage to the harbor beyond. *"Whatever it is you've done, boy, if you stay, I fear they will kill you."*

Ex was baffled. *"You want me to run away?"* It went against everything the master ever taught him. *"But I didn't do anything wrong."*

Master Seua sighed, a slight sneer to his scarred lip as he surveyed the scene. *"Wrong and right have no purchase in the jaws of power. These are fights you can't win."*

Ex knew that his word against the prince's pet wouldn't hold any weight, yet he still clung to the belief that everything would be okay if only he returned home and told the truth. The masters would surely get him out of it, somehow. They'd straighten it out. But now the man he trusted most in the world was telling him to run? To leave home and never return? Abandon it all? Everything he wanted his entire life?

A shriek erupted from the yard, choked and tortured. Prince Varunvirya had grown weary of their bickering. He stood next to Piglet, who had the bloody hilt of a golden knife in his belly. Being gagged, Piglet's screams were muffled and indistinct, and all he could do was stare down at the wound in gasping horror.

"I do not wish to be in this rain any longer," Prince Varunvirya said, and held out his arm. One of his servants produced a clean cloth and wiped a speck of blood from his sleeve. "Master Hunter, I will respect the Sacred Stone Decree until my father repeals it. But my minister makes an undeniable point. You clearly have no idea if the hunter Ex is here. This man is half lying, and therefore, receives half a sentence."

Master Rei brought her hands to her mouth, and then hung her head. "I beg you, my prince, please have mercy on the boy."

The prince narrowed his eyes, then flicked his head. "Take him."

Piglet sobbed softly as two of the hunters descended the steps and tended to him. Ex's anger boiled over, and he tore Arinya's amulet off his neck, shoving it into Master Seua's hands.

"Keep her safe," he said. Before Master Seua could stop him, Ex marched out of the bamboo thicket and straight towards the scene. When he crossed the yard, every hunters' attention shot towards him. The royal entourage followed seconds later.

"I'm here," Ex said as loud as he could, and hoped no one could see his hands shaking. "He's not a liar. A good-hearted gossip maybe, but not a liar."

The veins around Minister Iyun's eyes constricted. "See, my prince! They were hiding the traitor!"

"No, you were right the first time, Piss Dribble. I didn't pay my respects. Master Rei, please, I beg forgiveness." Ex went down to one knee and brought a wai to his forehead. He snuck a side eye to Piglet, who whimpered in a silent apology.

When he peered up, exhaustion weighed Master Rei's face. She let out a heavy sigh, her lips pursed into a thin line. Ex knew the same thing was going through her head as Master Seua's, and when she spoke, he felt another wave of shame.

"You should know better, child," she said loudly, and afterward, *"What the fuck did you get yourself into, boy?"*

"*It's a long story, just please, trust me.*"

"Is *this* the hunter Ex?" Prince Varunvirya stared at the new arrival with an upturned lip, his brows furrowed. "This is the boy you spoke of, Righteous Storm?"

"This is the rebel boy who defied your judgment, yes." By the glee in his eyes, Minister Iyun had been waiting for this moment. He addressed the entire compound, swinging his arms theatrically. "He kidnapped your esteemed lady in hopes of ransom. Murdered or hid your child, as well as murdering the war hero Sidom Da – your queen's personal champion–"

"Sir... I mean, my prince." Ex cleared his throat, trying to emulate the way Master Rei formally addressed royalty. He hadn't been commanded to rise, so he stayed on his knees. "It was never my intention to kidnap your wife, sir. She paid me for escort back to the Capital." Ex turned his soft gaze to glare at the minister. "And we were on our way until this asshole–"

"*Ex!*" Master Rei cleared her throat.

"Until this *sorcerer* captured us." The word was filth on his tongue, even with a low opinion of high magic, giving this necromancer the title of sorcerer felt far too generous. "I told him the truth, and he stole my wares. He stole from the guild. As for Sidom Da, ah..." Might as well come out with it all. "He killed my best friend and tried to kill me. I only acted in self-defense, sir."

"Don't believe the lies of this boy." The minister walked towards him. Ex grit his teeth and imagined wringing the man's neck. "His parents were traitors of the Highland Uprising, and so his blood is tainted. Furthermore –" he turned to address the hunters, "– perhaps you will appreciate this. He worked with a demon wolf to escape his bonds."

It wasn't quite the trump card he'd anticipated. In the silence, the other hunters only exchanged puzzled looks.

"*Is he talking about the Hound?*" one of them murmured to another.

Meanwhile, the prince, to his surprise, seemed to consider Ex's words. His expression had changed from shock to wary wonder, moving swiftly towards judgment. He glanced towards Master Rei for a response.

"I've known this boy since he was waist high, and have never known him to be a liar," she said, then folded her hands, pinning the boy in question with her one-eyed, omnipotent gaze. "What did the minister steal?" she asked.

"The third eye of the true demon, Shar-Ala," Ex said, and despite it all, grinned in triumph.

From the steps, the hunters chortled. They glanced at each other with incredulous expressions, and one of them said, "*That was your best excuse?*"

"*Should have run, kid.*"

The prince, like the guild, wasn't as impressed as Ex had hoped, but he didn't share their amusement. He crossed his arms and tapped his finger on his lips, thinking. In the silence, the rain grew heavier, pattering on the metal armor of the soldiers, making puddles in the uneven stone of the courtyard. With a wave of panic, Ex realized that he shouldn't have made eye contact with the prince at all, and quickly cast his gaze to the ground.

Finally, the prince spoke.

"I have but one concern," he said, then strode towards Ex so quickly that his umbrella holders allowed the rain to touch his crown. Ex braced for his other knife. Instead, the prince leaned down and snatched his chin between his fingers, yanking his head upward to stare into his eyes. His voice dropped so low that Ex doubted his men could hear him. "Where is my son?"

That was the one lie Ex was prepared to meet the devas with. Gone, he wanted to say. Died in childbirth. Killed by Sidom Da. Killed by a demon. Killed by him. But before any of those lies could leave his tongue, the curtains of the palanquin slowly drew aside. His breath caught.

Arinya. Reborn into the painted woman he'd seen on their wanted poster – hair perfect, swept tightly into her crown, throat and arms and wrists cuffed with gold and jewels, her body wrapped in a traditional chakkri and sabai, made of finer silks than even the prince's. It was hard to read her expression from where he was, especially with the prince breathing in his face. But behind her mask of makeup, Ex thought he saw a semblance of fear.

The prince squeezed his chin. "Do not *dare* look upon her," he said. "Answer me. Where is my son?"

If Arinya hadn't told him, neither would he.

"Safe."

The prince's lips twitched, but he still wore his calm, menacing expression. The rain dripped off his chin and onto Ex's face. "I will give you one more chance, young hunter. Where. Is. He?"

"She," Ex responded, meeting the prince's appalled glare at the suggestion his only heir might not be male. "I won't tell you." With that, Ex signed his death warrant. "She's hers, not yours."

And he waited for the knife. The prince continued to hold his face in his fingers, quivering with anger. Blowing a sharp stream of air through his nose, he maintained his composure, then released Ex's face with a jerk.

He turned his back and addressed his soldiers. "Cut off his head, and his limbs, burn the body and grind his bones to dust. Make sure he does not come back."

Ex's mouth dropped open. A knife to the heart would have worked just fine.

Of course, he didn't want to die like this, on his knees in the mud, shamed with dismemberment in front of all the people he respected, and cared about.

With finality, he shut his eyes and drifted into the Everpresent. Even if his guild didn't believe him, the First Hunters would know, and they'd surely accept a true demon slayer into their hall. If they called him, he would go. So he listened.

And he heard the fast approach of footsteps and relaxed, letting the peace of the spirit realm into his soul as best he could. His heart thumped as heavy as a goblet drum in an endless cave, and he bid it to slow... slow...

"No!"

Someone fell against him, so hard he almost fell onto his back. He snapped back to the world, still in one piece, and a figure in blue silk held him tight, her gold crown beaded with rain.

Arinya. Her scent of jasmine and sweet perfume. With her hands clutching the sides of his face, she pulled him close. And she kissed him.

Lost in her embrace, what felt like an eternity passed before Ex realized this was not a post-death vision. Her lips pressed hard against his, but remarkably soft, urgent, reaching for him to run with her, away from all this garbled noise. Whatever they'd said before, none of it mattered. With this act, she cast her lot with his, and it dawned on him as bright as the sun – she chose him.

He let his hands rest on her waist and felt his heart run with hers. If only they could disappear into the Everpresent together. The music of the spirits danced bright in the air around them, drawn in by her courage and passion.

I won't let you go. Her words dug deep into his heart. Whether she thought to say it, or only thought it, that didn't matter. It only mattered that she felt it. And he knew then that he couldn't let her go either. She pulled him back into the Blinds, into her world, ushering him away from the brink of the First Hunter's halls. If he had her heart, he'd gladly go, and he thought it, and he felt it, and he said it...

Tell me you love me, and you'll never have to.

But then she was ripped away, and the world went cold again.

The prince's fingers dug into her arm as he yanked her against him. Rather than struggle, she reached down to the hilt of his knife. The blade flashed as she jerked it upward to hold it against her own neck. The onlookers gaped at her action, some murmured, but it seemed everyone collectively held their breath.

Arinya said nothing, only glared at her prince with seething defiance. His face told another story, lips pressed in a line, eyes bright and stormy. Ex despaired, dreading how he would punish her. She'd not spoken of his cruelty in definite words, but the necromancer had painted a picture, and the queen's soldiers on the road held a very low opinion of him.

"My dear tigress." His cold, calm voice had melted around the edges. "You've always had such a wild heart. And for that I love you endlessly. I will always love you, no matter how you torture me." In response, her lipstick-smeared mouth turned into a sneer, and she pressed the knife harder against her neck. A small droplet of blood trickled out.

"Arinya, don't!" Ex rose to his feet, and the soldiers whirled on him, spear points instantly surrounding him on all sides. One of the soldiers shoved him back to his knees.

"Let him go," she said through clenched teeth. "He only did as I asked."

"My word is law, my love, and he is guilty of treason." His hand ventured up her arm, towards her face. "It is only his magic that twists your mind. We will heal you. Trust me."

"For once, my mind is my own," she said, leaning even closer to him. "Send him to his death, and I promise I will follow."

Their standoff continued, with only the rain hissing down. Ex could hardly breathe. Everyone stood silent as all the soldiers waited for his judgment.

"If I may, sir?" Minister Iyun's voice intruded on their duel of wills, woefully out of place. "A death sentence cannot be undone."

Master Rei hissed, "By the Sacred Stone Decree, my prince, if the crime is committed upon sacred ground, the punishment falls upon the guild to execute."

"His crimes occurred all throughout Suyoram!"

"And yet judgment was passed here." Master Rei bowed to the prince, and at the same time, all the hunters did as well. "My prince, sir, please honor the law of your elders. Hunter Ex is one of our own, my prince. Allow us to execute your judgment by our own laws. Trust it will be done, on my word."

Prince Varunvirya tore his eyes away from Arinya to consider the guild, his ego swelling by the sudden display of respect. Master Iyun bristled and made a noise, but the prince held up his hand to silence him. When he considered Ex again, it was without the sharp chill of hate. Dismissive, a lion staring down an insect, as if he wasn't worth another thought.

"Very well," he said, and let go of Arinya's arm. Breath heaving, she took a step back from him, and slowly lowered the knife from her neck. He didn't bother to retrieve it. The prince watched her face as he addressed the others. "I leave it to the guild to carry out his execution, Master Hunter. I expect proof of his death by tomorrow night, before the end of Rom Laithong. His body, to be officially discarded of by my will." He cast an eye to Minister Iyun, then said to Master Rei, "Defy my judgement, and the decree will not stop me from tearing this place down, brick by brick."

"You are most generous and merciful, my prince. You have my word, sir," Master Rei said, her voice heavy with relief.

Arinya's lips parted, as if to protest, but the prince's servants took her arms and gently but forcefully escorted her back into the palanquin. She cast one long look over her shoulder, and Ex wanted to run to her, straight through all the soldiers. Her voice rung out, but it was soon muffled. Prince Varunvirya didn't grace them with any more words and followed her.

The soldiers swung their spears to marching position, turning heel in perfect form. But before the entourage left the grounds, Minister Iyun leaned down to address him.

"Don't worry on her, little dog," he said, his voice slimy, feverish. "By your gift, she won't mourn you. She'll only remember what I let her remember, and will welcome your death as vengeance for the crimes you committed against her."

Ex lost composure and lunged for him, but was quickly spun around and tossed backward. Master Seua stood in his place. The master hunter lowered his fierce brow, arms crossed, challenging the minister to do more than sneer threats. Face to face with the Raging Tiger himself, Iyun reared back like a scared pony. Without another word, he limped back into the safety of the royal entourage.

In silence, the guild watched the men leave their grounds. The minute the gates shut, Ex felt Master Rei's soft, strong hand on his soldier.

"Welcome home, child," she said, and drew him into a hug. The pitying kindness in her voice brought tears to his eyes. He didn't care if all the other hunters were watching. He buried his face in her shoulder and held on.

Home never felt so far away.

Chapter Thirty

And the Hunters

By standard procedure, Ex awaited his sentence in a stone
cell in a rarely used wing of the guild hall. Latticed with lead
throughout the walls and a ritual ward, the ten-by-ten cube
blocked entry to the Everpresent. It wasn't the same as the
unnatural drugs Iyun fed him that clouded his mind. From
here, he could see the Everpresent, he could sense it, but it
danced just out of reach.

Though it had happened before, Ex had personally never
seen any hunter punished by the guild. There were instances
with the tradesmen at times, but at worst, they'd been stripped
of membership and kicked out. As far as he knew, in the entire
history of the Suyoram guild, carrying out a death sentence
decreed by the crown had never happened.

Because of this, Master Rei and Master Seua were in Elder
Nokai's chambers. Being the eldest, Nokai spent most of his
time up there, resting his old bones. Ex was sure they were
deep in discussion, shaking their heads at the boy's foolishness.
Tomorrow morning, they'd have to decide how to kill him. At
least it wouldn't be as torturous as anything the crown could
imagine. For that, he was grateful.

They left the cell door unlocked, and the housekeepers

brought him a piping hot bowl of shrimp bami, with a side of egg rolls, and fried fish... Some of his favorites. The soup, however, tasted like nothing. He gave up after a few bites and laid on the stone floor, staring at the ceiling in misery. A few of the other hunters stopped by, mostly curious about how he managed to fall in love with the prince's consort, trying to raise his spirits. Ex couldn't muster much humor though. Some of the more reverent ones expressed that the First Hunters would be honored to have him at the table. Ex hoped they would ask about how he managed to kill Shar-Ala, but no one mentioned him at all.

Ex knew Piglet was too gravely injured to leave the infirmary, but he thought Swan might come to see him before his execution. He didn't, probably resentful that Ex had inadvertently got his brother stabbed.

No one thought Ex would try to escape, and the thought didn't cross his mind as any real option. He had nowhere to go, except into the wilds as a disgraced exile. Even if he could scrape out a life out there, the prince would still take his vengeance upon the guild.

The only place he wanted to be was by Arinya's side, and that was impossible.

At some point, before the sun went down, he fell asleep. Thankfully, the devas took pity on him and brought no nightmares. There was a brief vision of fire, of running with the Hound through a fantastic, burning field. But even in that violently glorious setting, it filled him with bittersweet happiness to see his friend once more.

A metal hammer tapped. With it, a tapping pressure on his arm. Still in a dream, Ex flexed his fingers, staring down at a tiny, baby Shar-Ala, gnawing at him with a grotesque, yet oddly cute grin. With a muffled cry he jerked away and startled awake.

The tapping continued, and Ex rolled his head to see Master Seua sitting cross-legged at his side. He'd pulled Ex's left arm to lay flat on a red cloth. With a bowl of ink nearby, he dipped the tattoo needle into it, then continued to lightly hammer the design. Ex didn't need to look to know it was the badge for the condemned.

"Master," he said, his voice miserable and pathetic. "I'm sorry."

He acknowledged him with only a grunt. He wiped some blood away from his arm before continuing, and then said, "What do you have to be sorry for?"

"For bringing disgrace upon the guild. The ire of the prince. What if he gets the king to repeal the decree? It's all my fault."

"His father has threatened to repeal the decree for ages, yet backs down again and again. Do not waste your last thoughts on such trivialities."

Ex swallowed a lump in his throat, Master Seua's words leaving with him with a profound sense of finality.

"How am I going to die?"

"By the will of the First Hunter, you will follow."

"Will it be quick?"

"That depends on you."

Maybe it was better he didn't know.

His master sighed. "This child you spoke of, why is she soul-captured?"

"It's what Arinya wanted. The prince tried to give her stillborn drugs, so he could make a kuman thong. She sought Mali for the ritual, but I had to do it instead. And then she asked me to help her escape." Ex could see Arinya in the moonlight, in the flames, in the palanquin covered in jewels. "Master, was I a fool to believe we had a chance?"

Master Seua cast him a thoughtful eye. "I think you know the answer to that."

Ex groaned. "But that wasn't why I did it. I was keeping a promise. I didn't expect to… to…"

"Fall in love?" He scoffed. "It's a force of nature, boy. Sometimes it swells like a tsunami, and drowns you. Sometimes it grows as slow as a tree, and blossoms like a flower. Sometimes it strikes like lightning. Which was it?"

Ex exhaled as his will faded into slush. "How the sun rises. And the stars come out."

Master Seua chuckled in a fond manner that finally made him smile.

The tap-tap-tap of his tools blended into a hypnotic rhythm, and Ex's eyelids wavered. Finally, Master Seua stopped and wiped his arm with a cloth.

"I hope you will wear this with pride."

"The mark of the condemned?" Ex squinted at him. "I supposed I'm used to it. Already have one mark of shame."

Mast Seua wiped his arm again, and then sat back, cracking his neck. "Well? What do you think?"

Ex didn't know his meaning until he tipped his head down. He sat up and looked at his arm, and the new badge right below his elbow.

The sak yant badge of a true demon slayer.

And underneath, the name. Shar-Ala.

Ex could hardly breathe as he stared at it, running his finger across the crisp black lines, his skin raised and red around it. Was it some kind of cruel joke? The corners of Master Seua's lips turned up in a satisfied smile.

"I know you wanted a ceremony, but it will have to wait."

"Wait for what?"

"Hah, boy, you think treason is a more serious crime than losing an artifact of a true demon?" He placed a hand on Ex's head. "You have more hunting to do."

True Demon Slayer Ex. He ran the name over and over in his head, unable to stop smiling. It sounded good, it sounded strong, stronger and better than Hunter Ex, he thought. He doubted anyone would call him anything but hunter, which was fine. But now he had the badge to prove his worth.

Of course, none of it would mean anything if he failed the next test.

After giving him the badge, Master Seua brought him into Elder Nokai's chambers, where they spent hours discussing his fate. Empty teapots and polished plates laid around the table, as well as ancient books opened to dusty pages, and yellowed scrolls rolled flat. Elder Nokai was rather spritely for a man of almost two centuries. He didn't go outside in the rain, but he'd witnessed the entire exchange from the Everpresent.

Even though Shar-Ala's eye was kept hidden in the lead-lined pouch, Nokai recognized the spidery film of black magic swirling inside the minister's heart. It was recent enough to be clearly detectable for someone of Elder Nokai's level, and with the help of some of his books, he confirmed that it was indeed ancient demon magic.

"You must not fail," he told Ex in his raspy voice. He placed his thin hands on both the young hunter's shoulders, and held his gaze evenly, his one red eye milky with age. "At any cost, the remnant must be recovered."

"And how am I supposed to do that?" Ex asked nervously. They all looked at one of the scrolls, a wall of old devaskrit script and sacred geometry. To Ex, the orderly, mathematical yantra diagrams presented an aura of both authority and obscurity.

"There is another type of trance. Much older." Master Rei ran her finger along the script, resting at a hexagram shape with a dizzying number of intersecting lines. "It's deeper than what we practice. Very dangerous. But once you enter into it, your body will, in a sense, die."

"Uh, in a sense?" Ex stared at the diagram as if he could actually read it. "What kind of sense?"

"The Venara hunters used this ancient method to enter the higher realm and walk softly amongst the devas," said Elder Nokai. "To return, you must traverse their realm."

"Can't I just take some scarpoison seeds and lay very still?"

"Under inspection, they'll be able to tell," Master Rei said. "Besides, waking from that poison will turn you sloppy drunk, and I expect resistance from Iyun. You need your wits about you, young one. Emerging from this deva trance will be as if waking from a dream."

"But how will I even find him?" Ex trailed off, his stomach turning in knots.

Master Seua crossed his arms. "Once your body is presented to the prince, and then given to Minister Iyun for dissection–"

"Dis – what?!"

"He's a necromancer," Master Rei said with no humor, eyebrows lowered. "The heretic would not pass the opportunity to harvest a hunter's body."

Ex felt his spirits sink. Their faces were all very serious. It must have showed, because Master Seua patted him lightly on the shoulder.

"Once you recover the artifact, you will have to find your way outside of the palace," he said. He tapped on another pad of paper, which Ex realized was a map. "There will be a celebration going on for the festival. Swan will be in the outer courtyards with the other vendors. If all goes well, you'll be able to ride right out of the compound."

"You will be dead, on all records," Master Rei said, satisfied in a way that made it seem like she was very proud of coming up with that particular detail. "We will suffer no ire from the crown."

"Hang on," Ex jabbed his finger at the map. "Can we go back to the 'find your way outside of the palace' part?"

"There are many exits," Master Seua shrugged. "And if you can't find one..." He glanced at the elder.

Elder Nokai fixed him with his one-eyed stare. "You will have to empty the remnant yourself. You will have to infuse Shar-Ala's soul into your own and drag him into the ghost realm with you."

This was starting to look far less appealing than a quick

death. If he couldn't find a way out, he'd have to... *eat* a demon soul, kill himself, and potentially be stuck in the ghost realm for devas knew how long. A ghost realm full of pissed off demons that hated hunters with the very core of their being.

"Ex?"

He made a noise, half a grunt, half a whimper.

Master Rei walked to the window. "We don't have much time. If the texts are correct, the ritual for the deva trance will take hours to perform. He hasn't been through the master's trial, so it may even take longer."

May?

"Wait, wait, wait," Ex stammered, "you've never done this before?"

They were silent. Master Seua gave him a guilty half smile with an apologetic shrug. Ex slunk to the ground and held his head in his hands.

"Worry not, child," said Elder Nokai. "I have seen my own elder achieve this state and return. He stayed buried for ten days and ten nights. It is possible."

Ex wanted more than just possible, but it was the only thing on the table. Another thought occurred to him then. Arinya would be there, somewhere in the palace. If he could get to her, he could bring her Isaree, and maybe, just maybe... they could find a way out. Together.

He couldn't say that out loud, of course. Adding an obstacle with an even smaller rate of success seemed unnecessary conversation. Ex took a deep breath, rose to his feet, and looked at the plans again. In the mysteries of the deva trance diagrams, it revealed his path forward in very simple terms.

Do the impossible, or die an unspeakably horrible death.

As Ex prepared himself for the ritual, soaking in a warm bath sprinkled with pale yellow frangipani petals, he wondered how many other secrets the guild held. This was only one page out of countless books. He was told that a lot of those spells were irrelevant. Newer, better methods existed, or the items needed were unavailable. Some were unattainable, lost to history. It seemed they lost more and more every year. What did their future hold? Would the guild survive the king's new decrees, as he continued to pass bans against old magic?

Ex mused over the uncertain future to keep his mind off the immediate, which sounded more and more impossible with every passing minute. There were so many ways it could go wrong.

If he was caught in the palace after being "executed," the prince would know he'd been betrayed. His wrath was undeniable. If he wanted to tear the guild down, he would, and beg his father for forgiveness later. The king would likely welcome the act, relieved that he didn't have to shoulder the responsibility himself.

Ex's mind kept returning to those points – trying to plan how to get through the palace, how to find Arinya. The complex was sprawling, heavily guarded. The only thing that might help was that it was the last night of the festival. Swan said the courtyard would be full of people getting in their last big holiday celebration before the heavy rains came. If the new queen was now in the city, she'd be on the prince's arm, at least in public. It was clear to Ex that the prince cared deeply for Arinya, and though he wondered how much she cared for him, all he needed to do was think back to the way she kissed him...

Even worrying over those possibilities was jumping too far ahead. The most terrifying reality was what came next, this deva ritual, which sounded almost completely hypothetical. It would apparently send him into a realm where mortals were not allowed – a realm that many doubted existed at all. The only instructions given to him were "walk softly and return," which meant try not to get sent to hell for trespassing.

Elder Nokai also gave him the extremely helpful advice that he should try not to die there, in his "mortal state." Why? He said it would upset the balance of karma. If Ex then returned at all, it might be in an "undesirable form."

Sounded like there were better odds of escaping the palace.

He asked Master Seua what they planned to do if he failed, to which he only said, "Don't." He may have been saying that to motivate him. But with the amount of noise coming from the main hall, Ex had a growing suspicion that the guild was already preparing for a quick exit.

Ex's trepidation rose even more when he entered the ritual hall, where they'd already started the preparations. In addition to the three masters, a few of the scribes were present to assist with all the grunt work. They gathered the ingredients in order and prepared his body for delivery. The hall was closed off to everyone else.

Elder Nokai sat directly in front of the hearth, in the Everpresent, his body white, rendering his already frail form completely ghostly, a stark contrast to his black robes. With his eye unfocused, he summoned vast waves of spirit magic to the room, flowing seamlessly into Master Rei's preparations.

She bid Ex to sit on the white cloth spread over the floor, then handed him incense. She instructed him to recite the Ten Precepts while Master Seua burned twenty candles. She started mixing the ingredients, barking to the scribes if something was not currently in front of her. With the book laid open to her right, she used a reed to draw the guild symbol over his heart with a bright red mush of kaffa lime leaves, blood ginger, and seven different poisons.

"First we will go into the Everpresent," she said. "Then, you will go into the Hunter's Trance."

"And then?"

"And then, we will send you deeper. You must fight the urge to escape. It will feel like a sinking death, like the KunNam

Trial, and your animal instinct will react. Gaze beyond. Inside. But beyond." She drew a length of white saisin thread from a spool, and wrapped it three times around his wrist. "This is your timing bracelet. We will light it here, and it will guide you there. Make sure you leave before it burns down." Then she drew another, smaller pattern on his forehead. "Transcend. Transcend. Transcend."

Master Seua was less inclined towards this aspect of spirit magic – he specialized in the martial skills of the hunt – but they were all proficient. Soon, he joined Elder Nokai by the hearth and slipped into the Everpresent.

Master Rei set a needle in front of Ex, already coated with the ingredients that would send him into the trance. Next to that, a bowl full of something new. Both reciting voiceless words, Ex paid homage to the First Hunter, and savored this moment – the fear, the uncertainty, the grief, and the glimmer of hope. All things that would fade from his mind in the trance. With a slow exhale, he slid the needle into his vein and descended.

He hadn't been in this state inside city walls since training. The screeching noise, the chaos of motion, millions and millions of specks of souls knocked the breath out of him, and he fought the urge to clutch his ears and scream. Spirit energy whispered around them, ebbing from plants, the other hunters, and their bounties. Beyond the compound walls were far fewer. Every so often a spirit would linger, though most were of diluted blood. There were minor, harmless phi that lurked about, light and dark spirits that lived around shrines, but both grew fewer and fewer every year. There were no demons in the visible radius – not with the guild here.

The spells chanted by Elder Nokai and Master Seua filled the air with a sheen of pale violet, veined with streaks of silver. Though mortals, like the scribes, were unseen, the masters burned bright, like beacons in a starless night. Master Rei especially, almost blinding.

Recite the words with me. Her words felt limitless in the Trance. Voiceless, they repeated the new mantra, one he'd memorized an hour prior. It was far easier with her guidance. Where he faltered, she drew him back to the light.

There was no way to know how much time had passed. The masters remained steadfast, the ritual chamber, unwavering. Eventually, the chant took on a vibration with no empty space, one steady hum of a tenor he'd never heard before.

It was time. He brought the bowl to his lips and drank deep. The fluid had a weight and a texture, as if made of steel. It slid down his throat, pulling his essence along with it. He felt the sinking that she'd spoken of, and, for one brief second, his body startled as if every blood cell wanted to burst from his skin. He held on, and a numb, distant feeling radiated from his belly. It ascended upward, throughout, shimmering around his head and chest and he joined hands with the chant, the eternal sound.

Then it seized his heart, and he dropped dead.

Chapter Thirty-One

The Visitor

The trance ceased. The chant ceased. The Everpresent ceased. His soul ceased.

There was no sense of self here. Yet his consciousness persisted.

First came a point of light in an eternal void. It twitched, then expanded into a line. Ex had the sense he could wait there, a story stopped mid-sentence, while the book remained, unwritten, with enough pages and ink to fill it.

A sucking sensation pulled him towards the light, and then the line moved upward. It left behind a swath of bright light, like a paint brush across the void. Afterward, a distinct sound cut through – *rrriiiiip*! Like tearing an ancient scroll. The light ripped away in streaks, and then color and shape exploded into view.

Sudden, warm air entered his lungs. Startled, Ex moved his arms and saw both where they should be in front of him, attached to his body. Shirtless and barefoot, he was dressed the same as he'd been for the ritual, with a cloth version of the hunter's trousers. Although Elder Nokai didn't think he needed it, Master Seua insisted he carry a ritual knife and short sword as well, and there it was, strapped to his back. He was in the same position as he had been in the last act of the ritual, pitched over on his side, dead as a stone.

And now here he was, breathing, surrounded by a world that felt as real as the one he left.

Had it worked?

Ex couldn't yet comprehend the shapes of the objects around him. They were alien, formed into things that he couldn't understand. A bell struck, followed by another, discordant music playing about the air. In Master Rei's place, a being stood. As Ex's breathing steadied and relaxed, his surroundings faded into something he recognized.

Before, there had been spiraling lattices woven with streams of sound, rushing webs of sensation. Now, the strange visions had settled into a literal blanket, with rusty red and cold blue cotton, embroidered with threads of gold that reminded him of devaskrit. A wicker basket lay open, its contents spread on the blanket. Ex couldn't believe it. It was the bowls of food that they'd set around the ritual hall, though here they had blossomed into larger dishes. Basil fried beef and rice noodles, cooked with tomatoes, chili peppers and onions – a dish that worked wonders for hangovers. Two empty bottles of rice wine lay on their side. Grass surrounded the blanket, and beyond were bushes full of blossoms, dotted with flowering trees.

"What... in the five realms?" A voice as clear as day grabbed his attention, and his eyes snapped to the figure sitting in front of him, which at first he thought was part of the picnic.

A picnic. In a meadow. With a... a...

A Venara.

He was taller by at least a head and a half. He had a monkey head with a snout, dark blue fur surrounding the shorter, lighter blue on his face. Webs of scars drew maps over his arms. He wore bulkier armor than human hunters, pieces that Ex recognized from the carvings found in their ruins. Underneath, he wore a sleeveless tunic shirt and wrap pants, both rust-red like his blanket. With his monkey mouth hanging open, he clutched an eggroll in one hand, and a crumpled piece of paper in another. Next to him lay a quiver of arrows and a bow as tall as Ex was.

Ex sat up slowly, rubbing his face, and red paint came away on his fingers. Then he peered back at the Venara and did what people normally did when they met each other.

"Hello," he said.

The Venara tilted his head back, unsure whether the bug could bite. "Hello?" His voice sounded as human as any other.

"Sorry," Ex gave a wai and tipped his head. "I've never met a Venara before."

The Venara raised an eyebrow but didn't return the gesture. "I've never met a human before."

That seemed odd. Humans were around when their kingdom existed.

"Never?" Ex asked. "Aren't you from the Emerald Mountains?"

"My ancestors were," he said, then slowly took a bite of his eggroll, chewing with his mouth open. "I was born here. Wait, how did you get to the deva realm? There hasn't been a human here in... I don't even know."

"We did a new ritual. Or maybe a really old one. Anyway, I'm a phi hunter. Well, true demon slayer now."

"True demon slayer!?" He stopped chewing, and a piece of cabbage tumbled out. "Which one?"

"Shar-Ala," Ex grinned. "True demon of–"

"Nightmares!" The Venara coughed, then swallowed quickly. "I know the name. That's impressive."

"You've heard of him?"

"Yes! His name's on the wall of the unslain in the guild hall! Wait." He pointed at Ex's weapons. "You're actually a hunter?"

"Yes! Are you?"

"Yes!" They both grinned at each other, then the Venara grabbed another eggroll and offered it to him. It was much larger than any eggroll Ex had ever seen, but he took a bite. It tasted the same as the ones the guild hall cooks made.

"It makes so much sense now," the Venara continued. "Why you appeared, I mean. Perfectly wrapped in a package along with the offering from the mortal realm. I thought it was dessert at first." He chuckled. "I was going to save it for last, but I couldn't wait."

"You're one of the First Hunters," Ex said, astounded. "From the original tribe. Are there demons here?"

"There are. But I'm sure they're different from yours." Without putting down his snack, he lifted a leg and held out his foot. "My name's Macchanu."

"Ex." He took his foot and shook it.

"You should come back to the guild and meet my masters. They'll be so interested." Macchanu picked up the noodles and started to eat them at record speed. "Want some?"

"I'm pretty full, thanks." Ex had eaten about three bites of the eggroll, and looked closer at the foliage. The trees resembled some in the mortal realm, but blossomed with flowers he'd never seen before – they looked to be made of glass. He noticed the lack of minor spirits or creatures, no call of insects or birds. "You don't have animals here?"

"Not really. That's why we get our meat from these offerings." Macchanu gestured to a plant next to the picnic blanket that Ex originally thought was a flattened fern. He noticed another about twenty meters away, though smaller, but in the shape of a pod. "I haven't seen an offering plant this big out here before. How funny, the deva realm accepted a human." He polished off the noodles and started on the rice, finishing it in about three bites. He burped, then put the empty plates into the basket. After he closed it, he inspected his visitor with furrowed brows. "Why are you here, anyway?"

Ex had been so distracted by the new land that he completely forgot about his mission. It seemed so far away now. He didn't know if time worked the same here, but if

Macchanu was descended from several generations of the original Venara, it seemed to work similar to theirs.

"I had to die temporarily in order to sneak into the royal palace to give the prince's consort her soul-captured child." In this strange place, it didn't even sound that crazy. "And stop a necromancer from brainwashing the crown with the eye of Shar-Ala. So... I need to return to the mortal realm, as soon as possible." Ex scratched his head, glancing at his saisin thread bracelet. "Not sure how to do that."

"Really?" Macchanu mirrored him and scratched his head, using his foot in an impressive show of flexibility. "That's the stuff ballads are made of." He hopped up and stretched his arms. "How long are you going to be visiting?"

Ex stood and stretched too. "If time works the same here, I can only stay for a few hours. Or that necromancer's going to harvest me for parts."

"Oh. From what I know, it's a little slower here, but not *that* much slower." He tapped his foot and pursed his lips in a very human gesture of contemplation. "I don't know if we have time to make it back to the guild then, it's at least two days away. But we could go to the outpost."

"You have outposts?" Ex stepped off the blanket so the Venara could fold it up.

"You don't?"

"Not anymore," he frowned. "There's not enough of us left in Suyoram."

"That's depressing."

Macchanu put the basket in the middle of the blanket, then scooped it up by the ends, making a bag. Then he twirled it around and the whole thing shrunk, and kept shrinking until it was the size of his hand. He put it in one of the pouches on his belt, then noticed the human's awe. "What? You don't have service magic either?"

Ex shook his head, envious. That would make traveling with all his gear so much more pleasant.

"Interesting. I figured humans were more advanced since they came after." Macchanu started walking along and Ex had to jog to keep up.

"You've never met a human, or there's no humans in the realm?" Ex grew concerned that none of his fellow fallen hunters would have made it to the hall.

"I don't know, the deva realm is a pretty big place, much larger than the mortal realm. As far as I know, technically, if a human is here, they are no longer a human. The elders would know. But there's no humans in the guild, if that's what you mean." He stopped in his tracks, then cocked his head. "Do you hear that?"

"Hear what?"

"It's the demon I've been hunting! Come on!" He bounded away and Ex broke into a sprint to keep up. The trees grew denser, and he had to slow down to move around them. Macchanu ran so far ahead that his blue fur and shiny armor started to disappear into the woods.

"Wait!" Ex yelled.

His voice echoed from beyond his sight. "Are you all this slow?"

"Yes!"

"...Just find..." His voice faded. "...Everpresent!"

A low hanging branch slapped Ex in the face. He yelped in pain and clutched his eye, doubling over.

Pain? He hadn't felt pain for so long that it completely stunned him. He blinked rapidly as his eye watered, then stared incredulously at the branch. With a hesitant finger he poked it, expecting it to bite, or sting. Just a regular branch.

Curious, he drew his hunter's knife and pressed the point into his skin, rewarded by a sharp sting. A tiny droplet of blood surfaced. Strange, though as he thought about it, it made some sense. He hadn't done the Maijep Trial in this realm. Could he even go into the Everpresent?

He reached for it, and though he felt a hum of familiar energy, he couldn't find it. It didn't feel like it did when Iyun poisoned him. There wasn't a block as there was in the guild prison cell. It was like staring at the horizon of a beautiful island across the ocean, and not knowing how to swim. So that meant he couldn't use magic here. And everything would hurt. A lot. Wonderful.

By the time he recovered from these new realizations, Macchanu was long gone. With no idea of where to go, Ex walked in the general direction Macchanu went, doing his best not to stop and gawk at every detail of the alien landscape.

Ex spotted a saffron-barked tree with branches spaced evenly throughout, unlike the pines and alatus trees, which were mostly straight until reaching the canopy. Carefully, he climbed up, hoping to get a view of his surroundings at the top.

The tree kept going, further and further and further. About halfway up, he peeked down and gasped. He was twice as high as the top of the guildhall. The height made him dizzy, and he clung onto the trunk, trying to still his racing heart. He'd made it that far. No reason to turn back.

Taking extra care with his hand holds, Ex eventually made it to the top, where the branches grew much thinner, swaying in a cool breeze. When he peeked out of the canopy, the sight took his breath away.

An incredibly large, silvery bayon tree stood in the far distance – the beating heart of the forest. With massive roots spilling forth and twisting upward to support its smooth trunk, its branches curled towards the bright blue sky, disappearing into misty golden clouds. All the surrounding trees reached towards it, stormy jade leaves that began to gradually grow blue and red and purple as they neared.

After staring for a while, he noticed smoke drifting up between the roots, then twinkling, multicolored lights in the shadows they created. He thought they were glowflies at first, then made out pointed shapes – a city, nestled around the foot of the tree.

He tore his eyes from the glorious sight, and carefully looked behind him. The forest grew sparser and sparser until it went rolling into grasslands. What looked like constructed roads curled about the hills, along with a sapphire blue river. Other giant trees sprouted up like the first one, though they weren't nearly as large. Crystal castles floated in the clouds, with bridges between them like spiderwebs. Nestled between the far mountains were towers of jade and onyx and bronze.

Did this realm appear as he saw it or had his mind translated it into something he could understand? If he managed to get back and see the masters again, he wondered if they'd believe him.

Despite how impressive everything was, Ex had a mission. He hoped Macchanu might come back, but he couldn't count on it. There must be someone in the city under the giant tree that could help him. But it looked farther away than he had time to walk. Macchanu said there was an outpost nearby. Finding that might be his best bet.

The saisin string wrapped around his wrist was already growing shorter, the end burning away like incense. Elder Nokai hypothesized that once it burned off, his body would be dead for good. He wondered what would become of his mind if that happened. But if there weren't other human hunters around, he doubted he'd remain either.

It gnawed at him, the uncertainty of it all. He descended slowly and, strangely enough, the distance seemed much shorter. With a start, he realized the tree had actually stretched, as if it knew he needed help. When his feet hit the ground, he peered closer at it. It was different from the others, and not only in appearance.

"Thank you," Ex said, and placed his palm upon it. He concentrated, listening for any kind of response. Did he feel a nudge of acknowledgment? Maybe it was wishful thinking, but he continued, just as he would to any Guardian. "Spirit of the forest, if you are a spirit, I beg for your favor. I'm a visitor to this realm, and must return to my own. If there is any wisdom you might grant me, I will be forever in your debt." He waited, then pressed his cheek against the tree.

Then he heard it. A slow heartbeat, one thud every thirty seconds.

"You're alive!" he gasped, which was dumb, since all trees were alive. "I mean, *alive* alive. Please. Could you point me in the right direction?"

It seemed that good manners were recognized in the deva realm as well.

Chapter Thirty-Two

And the Devas

Why would a tree lie? It had pointed in a direction, so Ex jogged that way.

Things began to change around him. The trunks grew larger, paler, and further apart, but the foliage thickened overhead, dimming the sunlight. Orange fireflies flickered quickly in a dense blanket on the highest branches. Dark blue moss began to replace grass, and patches of wild orchids grew next to some of the trees. He listened for creatures of any sort, but the woods were eerily quiet except for the hum of magic, the soft thud of ancient hearts.

He came across a shallow stream and knelt for a drink. The water tasted just like water, but shockingly cold. Gauging temperature in food and drink was something he did miss, especially when it came to spice. It wasn't the same just to sense the heat. He really regretted turning down those hangover noodles now.

In the reflection of the water, he inspected his forehead to see where the tree smacked him, which he was beginning to suspect had been on purpose. There was a little red mark but not much else. The red paint on his forehead and the black paint on his eyes had smeared a little, but Master Rei said he needed to leave it on in order to "remember himself." He was a little surprised Master Seua hadn't insisted on shaving his head before the ritual, as his hair was almost long enough to grab. In general, he looked pretty much the same, maybe a little raw around the edges, with a wildness where he liked to think he usually appeared serene.

Then his eyes flared red, his skin and hair drained of color, and he smiled.

No, *he* didn't. His reflection had.

Ex brought his hand to his face, which did not mirror in the water. Instead, his reflection raised its eyebrows in a bratty expression that gave him new insight as to why he got punched in the face so often. He smacked the water to disperse the phantom image, and a stream smacked him back. Not a little pissing stream, more like a wet rag being slapped across his face.

Ex coughed and sputtered, blood rising at the sheer disrespect. With his fist raised, he glared back at his reflection. It laughed at him, holding up its hands in mock surrender.

"Asshole," Ex said.

It stuck its tongue out, then mouthed back, *No, you're an asshole.*

"Fine. We're both assholes."

Then it gasped and disappeared, leaving behind his actual image, which was that of an idiot trying to punch his own reflection. He was surprised a few choice words would chase it away, until he realized it was only a reaction to something standing behind him, its mirror image lurking in the flickering water.

Something very large loomed over him.

He half jumped, half tripped trying to whirl around to face it and tumbled into the stream.

A spider-like creature twisted its head, a mass of pupil-less orange eyes blinking out of sync. Its skin was the same pale blue color of the tree trunks, blending into them seamlessly.

Its body was relatively small compared to the size of its legs, which were covered in spines. Ex's throat constricted, feeling faint and small as he stared at its slimy, quivering fangs about the size of his forearm.

With horror, he realized what he'd previously thought were fireflies flickering in the trees were eyes, more than he could count. None of them moved. Yet.

Drawing his short sword, he rose to his feet, taking care to make no sudden movements. He half expected it to eat him, while the other half anticipated a friendly conversation. They watched each other warily for a for seconds, until Ex tried a tentative, "Hello."

It hissed in response, its entire body shaking with the effort. At first, Ex thought that might be its way of greeting... until it pounced, fangs first.

Ex swung his knife, rearing back. It bobbed its head to dodge, but the blade caught the tiniest tip of its fangs. It slunk back and rubbed its face with its two front legs. Before it recovered, Ex scrambled up the other bank and ran. The skittering sounds let him know it was right on his heels. Throughout all his hunts, Ex never fought anything with that many limbs. Did you go for the legs? Or the head? The eyes? Which one? Something with that many eyes and hairs must rely on movement, but standing still was not an option.

Against his better judgment, he glanced over his shoulder. He wished he hadn't.

He was hopeful that it was just one spider chasing him. It was not.

Not far behind his original friend, a mass of the creatures skittered forward, more legs and fangs than he could count. Several spells would have been useful, blinding the most obvious. But without the Everpresent, he was a useless, fleshy meal full of blood and pain, running for his miserable life.

Maybe it would get tired. Ex was getting tired. Did spiders

get tired? If he made himself annoying enough, it might pick something else – what else?! He hadn't seen signs of any other creatures. He might be their first meal in centuries.

He hurtled over a rock and the ground dipped, transitioning into a downward slope. His speed increased faster than his feet could keep up with, and he stumbled, barely able to remain upright.

The slope flattened out, the blue moss replaced by crabgrass and dirt. Across the clearing, the ground rose again, but this time sheer, into a rock wall face that blocked the way forward. Dull black boulders jutted out of the ground on either side. They'd led him into a trap.

No choice. He had to fight.

Ex turned back to the horde and started swinging, with both his knife and his sword, in an attempt to create a shield of steel that would slice off anything that came near. He caught nothing. The spiders had drawn back, moving to cut off any escape through the boulders. His only way out was up, but even if he had feet like a gecko, he was sure they could climb much faster. Their pale bodies swayed, a field of blinking eyes that was almost mesmerizing. How would one of him feed them all?

The largest spider crept in front of the others, head bowed and legs rearing up to pounce. Ex held the tip of his blades level with its head. Behind it, the other ones hissed and shook, as if egging their friend on.

It was waiting to surprise him. So he surprised it first.

With a soft thud, his knife sunk into one of its eyes. It recoiled and shook, clawing at its face. Ex took the opportunity to hack at its limbs. Whichever one moved towards him, he struck back. It must not have been prepared for its prey to bite. With three of its eight legs now six feet shorter, it teetered on its feet, wobbling as it tried to make sense of the world.

Screaming curses, Ex continued to stab and slice, finding openings on its legs and abdomen. Desperate, it swung its head down to bite, but Ex hacked at its mandibles with his sword again and grabbed the hilt of his knife, still stuck in its face. With a twisting yank, his knife broke free and several of its eyes popped out, along with a spurt of dark fluid. Ex threw himself back, partially to dodge one of its flailing limbs, but mostly to avoid getting drenched by bug juice.

One long leg smashed into his side and flung him back against the rock wall. The impact sent a shock through his spine, and he groaned at the pain in his arm after the awkward landing. Real pain. His skin was torn where it had struck, leaving a nasty scratch in its wake.

The first spider was curled up into the dead bug position, body twitching. The second, who'd hit him, was now staring him down. Three more had slunk out from the crowd, seized the first one, and started to eat it. All the others were still watching, but now they were creeping forward, together.

"Fine. I'll kill you one at a time." Ex leaned against the rock wall to push himself up. He raised his sword, but it clattered from his fingers. One arm had gone completely numb. All he could do was ready his already bloody knife and wait for the next thing to stab. By the looks of it, he wouldn't have to wait very long.

"Stop!"

A woman's voice rung out from above. All the spiders froze, their attention caught upward. A shadow flickered in the corner of his eye, and then a form reflected in theirs.

An animal about the size of a horse landed in the clearing, footfalls practically silent. Thrashing about a fluffy tail, it snarled at the nearest spider with a wolf-like maw, and drove it back with a snap of its jaws.

Then Ex realized there was a woman riding the creature, wearing all white but for a black cloak. She leapt off the animal's back and leveled a long scythe at the horde. Collectively, they shook and hissed again, then lunged at her all at once.

Her scythe flashed in a wide arc, as wide as the entire clearing. Limbs and eyes and bodies flung back from her range, and a wall of black blood sprayed across the rest. All parties stared each other down – her, the giant wolf, and the spiders.

As for Ex, he couldn't stare anywhere else but at her. The gold-skinned woman twirled through the air, black cloak billowing as she cut down the giant spiders with a scythe as long as a canoe. Even the giant wolf seemed less grand in comparison, though his head was at the same level as Ex's and adorned with a necklace of jewels fit for a king.

After an impressive display of carnage, the spiders backed away, hissing.

"You overstep!" She wagged a finger at them as if they were naughty dogs. The spiders shook again, this time vibrating at an unnatural intensity. The edges of their bodies blurred, and they began to melt.

Was it some kind of spell? Their forms turned black to match their blood, then began to fold in on each other into one singular mass, including the dead spiders and the ones eating them.

The mass molded into a human shape and started to glow. When the glow faded, it left behind a short, jaundiced boy with orange pupils and a fat, pouting mouth. His bald head seemed disproportionately larger than his skinny body. He couldn't have been older than six. The boy clutched one hand with his other, blood oozing from where there may have been more fingers. "Boy" probably wasn't the right word. Both beings were decidedly not human and perhaps some type of deva.

"Overstep?" the boy growled, his low voice a rasping whine. "He was in *my* woods!" He turned his ire towards Ex, and although his puny body was much less threatening than his previous forms, his gaze was just as chilling. "It was my turn to play!"

With that, he shifted into a fruit bat and fluttered away. Spider? Boy? Bat? The woman watched him go and said nothing.

"Old friend." The big head of the silver-furred wolf bumped into Ex, then nuzzled his neck. "It hasn't been long. Have you perished already?"

His aura was unmistakable. Fierce and noble, without an ounce of uncertainty.

The Hound!

His fur was silver and laden with jewels, like Ex imagined the Wolf King Maaba might appear. Still, he held the same strong, sharp regard.

"You made it here!" Ex cried, and grabbed his face, ruffling his ears.

His tail wagged once, and then he scoffed and shook his head, like an old, hard uncle batting away an annoying nephew's token of affection. Then Ex remembered his name.

"Astrama the Twice-Risen," he said, with fondness and reverence.

If that was the Hound, then who was the woman? She hadn't turned to him yet, her cloak and hood still obscuring her body as she watched the trickster deva disappear into the woods. She twirled her scythe, which shrunk down to hand-size and hung it onto her belt.

"Thank you, fierce warrior," Ex ventured, offering a wai. "As a phi hunter, I've had many deaths, but being eaten by a horde of demon spiders would have been my least favorite."

"Hunter." Her voice was deep and resonant, but she spoke as gently as a feather. A lullaby.

She turned her head to the side, and a curtain of black hair fell from her hood, obscuring half her face. Still, a soft ebb of light lit her cheeks. Ex's heart started to race as a nervous pit grew in his stomach, though he wasn't sure why.

The woman drew her hood back, meeting his stunned gaze with startling ruby red eyes, pupilless, faceted and gleaming like cut gemstones. She wiped a spot of black demon blood off her cheek. Her traditional clothes were in a man's cut, a sleeveless tunic over wrap pants with interwoven patterns of diamonds and gold, her figure slender and androgynous. With a jeweled ring in her septum, and a curl to the edges of her bowed lips, she seemed so familiar, yet Ex was sure he'd never seen anyone like her before.

"Who are you?" His voice came out in a whisper.

"My boy," she said, then pinned him with her serene, opaque gaze. "Why have you brought us here?"

Chapter Thirty-Three

And the Pure Being

Images flashed through Ex's mind at once. Digging in the dirt. The blood, the burning village... her hand reaching towards him to save him from the fire.

It took him a few shaking breaths before he was able to form the word. "Ma?"

The woman smiled and rested her hands on her hips. "In some lives. I could call you the same in others."

Before Ex realized it, he'd closed the distance and crushed her in a hug. He buried his face in her shoulders, breathing in her scent, one he'd known, one that comforted him deeply. A torrent of emotions raged through him. Relief, joy, despair, comfort, anger...

"Where did you go?" Ex said, and heard the whimper of a lost child.

"Resting. Waiting." Her fingers threaded through his hair, and with her touch, the warmth of maternal comfort and safety flowed through him. He drew in her familiar scent again. The hearth of the kitchen fire, fresh tinder, herbs, coals. Home.

"Why? Why did you leave me?"

She pulled him to arm's length, a thoughtful eye regarding him. "I had to, to protect you. But we never truly leave, little one. We always return." And the scent dissipated as quickly as it came. She let go and walked away, leaving him stunned and cold.

"What do you mean 'return'?" he finally said, following after her. "Return to the deva realm? I thought there were no humans here."

"A human is just another vessel. The deva realm is only another plane. There are countless more, ones even higher than this." Her voice carried back in echoes. "We are pure beings."

Ex faltered in his step, head swimming. "You aren't my ma, are you?"

"Would it comfort you?" She kept walking. "If I spoke of our village, and how you loved to play with Gingerball in the garden? How you would sneak her your vegetables at the table? I helped you bury her in the forest. You didn't want your brothers to see you crying."

No one except for his mother could have known that.

"Or might I speak of our short lives in the trenches of the Grongtua Empire, as brothers in arms. Do you remember taking a spear through the heart for me? A loving, useless gesture, as I followed you moments after."

"The Grongtua Empire? That's…" Thousands of miles away, hundreds of years ago. A churn of blurry violence flashed before his eyes. The flash of steel, the smell of blood, fire, and death. A tearing thud against his chest, a cold hand on his face. He gasped and drew back, but the vision was gone again.

"I could tell you about the others we love – both of us. Other beings to which we're bound across space and time, over and under the relentless wheel of karma. We are all things to one another. Sometimes, even as enemies." She hummed, and the echoes seemed to harmonize with her voice.

Bound together. Pure beings. With the realization of what she was, what *they* were, the evidence of eternal souls driven towards one other throughout lives, beyond time, Ex leaned against the wall to stop himself from collapsing. Sure, he was raised to believe in the devas, reincarnation, and some imperceptible higher order. But to see it and feel it, that was another level.

The cavern wall gave slightly. It wasn't quite a wall. This wasn't quite a cavern. The rock felt mutable, it felt alive. It moved with her, spoke to her, showed her the way.

He followed her, and she walked to the edge of the rock wall, disappearing into a hidden, cavernous opening.

Ex hesitated. The thought occurred to him that he might have been dreaming this entire time. But it didn't ring true. Everything about this place felt just as real as his own world. Still, something didn't add up, but he followed her into the darkness regardless.

The path quickly brightened with glowing crystals growing on the walls, forming twinkling mandalas. Though the passage was so narrow he had to walk sideways, the ceiling seemed to soar high above, and the smooth, cool floor felt good on his feet.

The Serene Way existed in the deva realm, too? The masters would never believe this.

"Wait," Ex pushed forward and reached out, trying to catch her. "You asked me why I brought us here. What did you mean by that?"

As he drew near her, the cavern wavered, crystals clinking together as the walls shifted to accommodate them. Her soft smile melted away, and she lifted her face towards the roof of the cave, where gemstones bloomed like constellations. Or perhaps they were stars. "I did say that, didn't I?" Then she tapped his chest, the spot under his neck. "The wheel calls to me. Instead I am here, waiting, caught between realms. Remember me, or let me go."

His skin felt cold and empty where she'd poked, and he knew there was something missing. How had he not noticed it before?

"Isaree."

Upon hearing the name, the pure being blinked both eyes slowly, like a cat in the sun. "In some lives," she said.

"You said 'remember me,'" Ex said, grasping to understand. "What does that mean?"

"If I am not to be born, release me to be here in full."

"But you'll die." His words felt flat. It was painfully obvious that death was insignificant here, at least in the realm of devas.

"If that is my fate, so be it," she said, and moved away, disappearing down a bend in the cave.

"Wait!" When he rounded the corner, Isaree stood in front of an end to the passageway, a blank wall. But Ex was surprised to see a large carving of the Deva Phra-Phikanett above, his pot-bellied, elephant-headed figure just as he appeared in the realm of mortals. The likeness of the deva's serene eyes blinked to sight, a blue sparkle within, and fixed Ex with a knowing gaze.

The opener of roads, the breaker of karma.

Indeed, Isaree bowed upon one knee and murmured. Ex strained to hear her words, but they seemed to be between only her and Phra-Phikanett. In response to whatever she said, a streak of light cut through the darkness, and below the cross-legged statue, the cave split apart to create an entrance, and Isaree walked through.

Ex peered curiously at the statue, but the deva's eyes had returned to stone. He made a wai in thanks anyway and hurried after her.

Above, the sky burned dark, bleak orange with billowing clouds of black smoke. A great fiery sun flickered through the clouds, sputtering with bursts of lava as if being struck by a blacksmith's iron. Beyond, the ground was barren and charred. Lightning struck at intervals, with a startling crack and boom despite the lack of rain.

Ex peered over Isaree's shoulder. Sudden gusts of wind lashed banners on their poles, symbols and flags he didn't recognize. Alien skeletons littered the landscape, some quite larger than human, some as large as temples, their armor rusted and weathered beyond any distinguishing marks. Not that he'd know what they might be – these relics were from the history of a world unseen.

The landscape stretched as far as the eye could see, but every so often, giant, curling, white pillars sprouted from the ground and stretched upward towards the sky, disappearing into the clouds. Then it dawned on him that they were the roots of an immense bodhi tree.

Ex took a step out into the melting sun and his foot fell soft in ashes and charcoal as if they were the sands of time itself. Or perhaps the illusion of it.

"What is this place?" He turned back to Isaree, who stood at the exit of the cave.

"This is the Field of the Fallen," she said, gazing out over what looked like an eternal battleground. "This is where ascended warriors prove their worthiness against the asura. Where dark and light celestials settle their differences. Where legends and civilizations come to die."

"That's incredible," he said, then looked at his wrist, where the saisin string had one rotation left. "But... I'm afraid I don't have time for a grand tour of the deva realm. If this burns out, your mother – in this life, anyway – will suffer at the hands of a madman. Can you help me find a way out, or not?"

"If there is a way out for a mortal, it's through here." She hadn't moved, and sensed his hesitation. "Sorry, my child. I can't go with you."

"But I don't know the way."

"I do." Next to her, Astrama stepped forth. He thrashed his tail, sniffing the ground a few times before he stepped out onto the devastated earth. He grunted at Ex, then crouched down. Obediently, the human climbed on and leaned far forward, almost onto his belly in order to grab the scruff of his neck.

"Until we meet again," Isaree said, then smiled. Ex felt a wave of love, a pure kind that enveloped him in an embrace so achingly familiar that all he wanted to do was stay at her side and soak it in. He understood the depths of their connection. Over untold amounts of time, they'd loved one another in all forms, they'd hated and wounded each other so deeply, in the way only family of blood or bond could reach.

There were so many more questions he wanted to ask. So many more things he wanted to say. But he knew that it was not the place or time. He couldn't stay. He was only a visitor here. He gazed towards the endless horizon, and knew that somewhere, a soul they both loved just as fiercely would suffer far more than they deserved if he didn't leave.

"Until we all meet again."

The things Ex saw were real and true, he would later swear on his life, and not the fever dream of seven different poisons and the deeper trance of death.

As Astrama ran, and the skeletons flashed by in a blur, they passed pockets of frenzied motion, of other beings large and small, locked in conflict. He leapt over and around them, rippling through waves of warfare that surged around them like a monsoon.

Giants grasped for one another's throats, wrestling in fire and smoke, their growls and heavy footfalls thundering across the land. Six-armed, ten-armed, multi-eyed celestials hurled bolts of lightning and molten lava back and forth, efforts erupting with explosions and scorched earth. Overhead, winged apsara wielded swords and spears and arquebus, and below, Venara clashed while riding seven-tusked elephants of war.

Though Ex knew he and Astrama had no place in it, the war filled him with awestruck terror. His mind couldn't comprehend some of the things he saw and heard filtered through his mortal frame of reference. There were vessels, smooth and shiny as glass, dancing throughout the sky in battle. There were walking, screeching machines with snakelike heads.

There were crashing symbols and drums and screaming bells, a terrible kind of apocalyptic hymn.

Every so often, a spark flew from a clash of steel and burned his skin, or a shard of bone glanced across his back, and he grit his teeth in pain. Without Astrama, he'd have been crushed like the insect he was in this place. The Twice-Risen slowed his stride in the shadow of a mountainous reptilian creature, wolf-eyes gleaming sharp as he waited for a break in a parade of skull-faced warriors.

"If we're soul bound," Ex asked him, "why aren't you human too?"

Astrama laughed, a bit scornfully. "What makes you think I would want to be human?"

"The Sangha says we start as low as worms and work our way up to, you know…"

"On the path of Mabaa's children, perhaps humans are the worms that work their way up into wolves." He snorted, then his teeth bared in a grin at Ex's unease. "Does a carriage roll on one wheel? Karma is the force that drives it, the vessels are carved in many ways."

With that, he tore off again, darting between the feet of the mountain lizard. Ex realized they weren't heading into the heart of the endless fray, but towards one of the upward roots of the great tree. Just as they approached, a towering, green-skinned deva with six-arms and weapons in each blocked their path. Blood of every color covered his scale armor, swords, axes and clubs. The deva reached up and removed his full-face helmet, glaring mostly from the third eye on his forehead. With another arm he threw a spear, which missed Ex's head only by inches.

Astrama skidded to a stop, and Ex's fingers lost purchase. He tumbled onto the ground in a puff of ash.

"What is this creature that disgraces the Twice-Risen?" the deva said, striding to Ex in one step, and snatching him off the ground by the top of his head. His grip was so powerful, Ex thought his skull would shatter. He feebly clutched the deva's tree-trunk wrist to relieve some of the pressure as he held him suspended before his face.

"This is a true demon slayer," Astrama growled. "Leave him be, Indrajit."

"He trespasses upon the Field of Fallen, unearned!" Indrajit's acidic breath burned Ex's sinuses. Two serrated blades pushed against his back and two against his chest, their points burning hot on his skin. He tried not to panic.

Ex strained to lift his arm and show the fresh badge.

"You are no more than a killer for hire," the deva snarled, his teeth sharpened to deadly points. "A common thug that destroys for something as base as pointless coin. There are many demons that would pay in blood for your soul."

"I might be for hire, but I'm not a killer," Ex said. "I protect my people from harm. How is it wrong to stop demons from killing us?"

"Right or wrong is not my concern." Indrajit's snarl twisted into a smile. He pulled the puny human closer, and the blades cut into his flesh. "If you act as an executioner for souls that you deem unclean, by the law of karma, shall I inflict that same judgment?"

"What are you?" Ex spat back. "A celestial warrior who only knows slaughter?"

Indrajit's eyes flashed, nostrils flared. Wrong answer.

"Ignorant creature. I am the voice for the dark ones, I am the great balancer, a god of salvation!" The blades sunk another thread deeper and Ex screamed. Blood ran down his chest and dripped off his toes. "I bring the lost ones into the light. I am a savior. I am the answer and the reason." His eyes narrowed into slits. "I know you, Hunter Ex."

Below them, Astrama barked and snapped his jaws, but he didn't need to speak for Ex to understand him.

Ex let go of the deva's arm and drew his knife. With both hands, he jerked the blade up and shoved it through a small chink in his armor, through the wrist. A spray of cold blood rewarded him, and even though the deva made no sound of pain, his brows furrowed in disbelief. His grip faltered and Ex dropped, the tips of the deva's swords slicing lines in his flesh. He hit the ground on his feet and staggered back.

Before he fell, Astrama bounded forward and Ex reached out, catching hold of his fur. He hauled himself onto the Twice-Risen's back and hung on.

Astrama darted around Indrajit, who swung with another arm. The great club sent a spray of rock and dirt into the air, missing by inches. When Astrama's paws landed on the white root of the tree, the entire land tilted. Upward became straight ahead. Ex craned his neck to gaze at the battle still raging behind them, now a bird's eye view. Indrajit stared up with bulging eyes and an open maw. Before he became just a dot in a sea of violence, Ex thought he saw him smile.

Now the white root stretched before them like a great road that disappeared into a deep fog, growing brighter by the step. The eternal war faded away. It was only the two of them. With a sigh, Ex leaned forward, weak with exhaustion and relief. Astrama didn't slow down, but his gait felt less hurried.

The light grew brighter, and Ex thought he saw forms in the distant fog.

"Thank you, Astrama, Twice-Risen," he said, and glanced at the string on his wrist, now burned to only a millimeter of thread.

"Soon thrice," he grumbled. "I was not planning to return so soon."

From the fallen, into the bright light of oblivion, they ran together. With a numbness creeping up his arms and towards his chest – a feeling he knew all too well – Ex surrendered, and murmured, "Until we meet again, old friend."

Chapter Thirty-Four

The Ghost

Ex resurfaced from the depths of the deva trance, gasping for breath with lungs that hadn't flexed in hell knew how long. His muscles were about to snap, so constricted from rigor mortis he could hardly move. A shroud covered his face and body. Without another thought, he dived into the Everpresent and sunk as deep as he could, grasping for magic with fingers full of cotton.

He was cold, so unbearably cold. Though he couldn't feel the temperature, his body shuddered, numb and acutely desperate for warmth.

Clotted blood began to stir and unravel as his heart beat backward. Fighting the residual panic, he forced his body to relax and let life creep back through his veins. His eyes felt like putty, and he waited until they were strong enough to open.

It was dark and quiet. Surprisingly, he didn't feel as exhausted as he did when he emerged from the Hunter's Trance – he felt energized, even.

While his body healed from the trauma of death, he reflected on all the things he'd seen, but it was as if he were trying to clutch falling sand. Almost the instant he remembered them, the images disappeared between his fingers. There had been a great battle – or was it a forest? Or a feast? There had been fantastic beings and places either real or imagined. He had felt pain and fear, but also joy, and of all things… love.

Perhaps it would come back to him.

The last injuries that healed were two deep cuts on his chest, and one on his back. They were strangely fresh, which probably meant someone had started to prepare him for dissection…. But then they dressed him again? The masters had adorned him properly for a hunter's burial, in his coat and the guild's dark, ceremonial uniform.

Something felt wrong. His hand grasped at his neck, and he breathed a huge sigh of relief to find Arinya's pendant still there. Despite the necromancer's sacrilegious practices, laymen were still superstitious and kept their hands off his things.

Ex pulled off the shroud and peered around. The plain stone room had no windows, just a door, and the only light ebbed from a wide pillar candle burned down to the very ends. He'd been there for some time. A table with bins of autopsy tools stood next to the wall with a few jars of chemicals. He pocketed a scalpel, the only thing slightly resembling a weapon.

Two other carts were next to his. The bodies beneath the shrouds were very fresh too, and he wondered why they'd stored them there. One man wore the clothes of a soldier, and another was a Sangha monk. Both had gruesome, violent injuries, stab wounds all over the ribs and belly, and the monk had his throat slit. By the nature of their deaths – murder – it was possible they would eventually become phi. Ex felt spirit energy brewing down here, heavy on the ground like simmering soup.

He pulled up his sleeve where the masters had drawn a small map of the palace using the same black sepia color as their tattoos, with single lines to represent the passages. The inner compound of the palace was similar to a temple, with symmetrical, interlocking squares to represent buildings and rooms within the buildings. With the orderly design, it might as well have been another protective charm.

Ex nudged open the door and found himself in a long, cold hallway with more doors, lined with half-burned candles on wall sconces. Still no windows, so he picked up a tiny stub of a candle still alight. The walls were plain, the room as uniform as the one he'd awoken in. How many corpses were in here? Most black magic involved digging up bodies, but Ex wondered if Minister Iyun was harvesting them before burial.

There were steps leading up at the end of the passage. The temperature rose with each step. He had been in a crypt, then. He found another door at the top of the stairs, but it was locked.

Muffled voices came from the other side of the door. Ex pressed his ear against it. Two men were talking from a few feet away, outdoors, judging by the night call of insects. Further beyond that, the din of conversation flitted about, but it sounded like a small get together rather than a festival gathering.

"Did you see the roast? I hope there'll be leftovers."

"Shit. Anyone who's anyone in the Jade district was here. You think those rich gluttons left anything for us grunts?"

"Ahaha… damn." The crackle of a pipe and skunky stink of kajeleaf came through. One man coughed, and a weapon clinked. Guards. "This place creeps me out."

"Relax. Better than standing at the wall, waiting for nothing."

"When's the sorcerer coming back?"

"I don't know. He's doing something with the prince and his ladies."

"Some depraved shit, no doubt." They snorted in laughter and lit the pipe again.

Judging by the slur of their words and stink of the smoke, they were high and ripe for a scare. They continued to gossip and grumble about their lot. Ex withheld a snicker and knocked softly. Their conversation immediately stopped.

"Did you hear that?"

"Where'd it come from?"

Silence.

"It's probably nothing."

The younger one didn't sound convinced. "Maybe we should go. The festival's over anyway."

"And get chewed out by the captain? Nope."

"There's guys at the wall who'll see down here."

"Those idiots? Hah! Bet you they're already drunk."

Ex knocked again, louder this time. By the slink of steel, one of them had drawn his sword.

"It came from there!" His voice raised a few octaves.

"Shh! Keep it down!" The old one hissed, then chuckled, a bit nervously. "Kaje's getting to you, kid. Nothing but corpses down there. Come on. I'll open the door."

"No, no, no."

"Oh, calm down, you little coward. It's probably an animal burrowed its way in. You wouldn't believe how big the rats are in here." He walked closer while the other one hissed at him.

Ex would be waiting all night for these two idiots to let him out, and so he tried to think of a spell that could help. He supposed he could burn the door down, but that might alert other guards. Maybe... Maybe... He entered the Everpresent, and murmured the voiceless chant for the Hand of Khun Phaen.

The last time he used this spell, he'd extinguished a spell from Iyun's throat. His hand turned incorporeal and passed through the door, but his fingers were unable to get a hold on the latch. Borrowing a trick he learned from another hunter with a more colorful past, Ex let the mist drain from only his fingers, and flicked open the latch.

He slammed his shoulder into the door. It smashed into the first guard's face, sprawling him flat on his back. He didn't stir.

The young one dropped his sword and opened his mouth to scream. Ex tackled him and clamped his hand to his mouth, nose to nose, the flare of his eyes reflecting in his. He whimpered, too scared to cry. The sharp scent of urine stung Ex's nose as the man lost his bladder.

The young guard's heart hammered so quickly that Ex feared it would stop. He almost said relax, that he wouldn't hurt him. But appearing like this, likely demonic, only worked to the hunter's advantage.

Ex made his voice as low and raspy as possible. "Do you want to die?"

The guard vigorously shook his head.

"Do you want your family to be cursed for generations?"

He shook his head again.

Ex glanced around. He was on the outskirts of the royal grounds, surrounded by flowers and small monuments. A cemetery. In the center laid a pagoda full of fresh flowers, food and drink, offerings to passed souls and Hungry Ghosts alike. A couple of empty bottles laid around the guards. It seemed like these two had found the quietest corner to escape their duties.

He couldn't consult his map, but the soft conversation and hint of lanterns towards the east was likely the remnants of the festival, which was to take place in the courtyard in front of the palace. If the music had ended and the food was gone, that meant Swan was probably gone too. So much for that escape plan.

The guard underneath him softly cried.

"Listen." Ex stared into his eyes. "I must know some things. Will you answer me?"

He nodded. Ex slowly removed his hand from his blubbering mouth.

"Please, please, venerable ghost, I meant no disrespect, I've always paid tributes to the devas, every day, and, and, and–" He started to cry again.

Ex snapped his fingers in front of his face, and when that didn't work, smacked him lightly. That shut him up. "Where is Minister Iyun?"

At first, the guard didn't comprehend.

"The grand sorcerer? The..." Ex rolled his eyes. "Righteous Storm?"

The guard's mouth opened in an *oh*. "Minister... Minister Iyun told us to wait here."

"What was he planning to do the prince and... his ladies?"

"I swear on my life, I don't know."

"Where are they?"

"His personal dwelling! Outside of the palace in the, the, the eastern square." He sniffled, then his brows furrowed. "May I ask, sir, why do you seek him?"

"He's committed grave sins, and I've come to deliver his judgment." Ex fixed the man with the most threatening stare he could manage. "As well as all those who have assisted him."

"Please, please, sir, please let me live." He started to sob anew. "I know the sorcerer is doing wrong things, but I just needed a job to feed my family. I've always tried to be a good man. And I promise, I promise, from now on, I'll be a good man."

Just then, Ex had the oddest sense of deja vu. Usually in this state, it would be a phi staring up at him, begging for his life, not a man who looked younger than himself.

He smiled. "Let's start now, then."

Chapter Thirty-Five

And the Nightmare

For the young guard's divine punishment, Ex tied him up and locked him inside the crypt, along with his friend. He heard the murmurings of thankful prayers as he crept away.

As he left the cemetery, he paused in front of the largest pagoda. In the center, a man-sized bronze idol of the Enlightened Lord sat in the lotus position. With his eyelids shut, he wore a content smile, peacefully surrounded by candles, wood statues of apsara, and other protective creatures.

Of all the spirits Ex knew, this one remained silent. The Sangha claimed they found their power from his realm, a higher place than even the deva realm. Ex wondered on the truth to that, but still, it felt right to pay tribute. He needed all the luck he could get for the next part of his mission. He found an unlit stick of incense and lit it with one of the candles. As he held it between his palms and bowed, he murmured a prayer he had learned from his mother.

Could the presence of the Enlightened Lord have been the reason there were no phi lurking about? Once Ex crossed the stones that marked the end of the cemetery grounds, he saw the thin shimmer of wards, keeping whatever might be stirring safely contained. Minister Iyun couldn't perform his rituals there, but the guard had told him that his dwelling wasn't far.

The Blind Eagle's Eye spell had never been intended for use in a city, but it camouflaged him well enough. If someone were wandering about the palace grounds well past midnight, and decided to go on a tour of the grand pagodas and stupas with their golden steeples, they might see a glimpse across the wooden panels and disappear into the shadows. When there were no bushes and trees to hide in, Ex darted along the structures like the largest gecko in existence. He passed only one patrol, but they were similarly not paying much attention, chatting amongst themselves as they strolled.

Finally, in the eastern square, where some of the higher officials kept their homes, Ex spotted the old naga statue that the guard had told him about. It stood at the front of a tall fence, which blocked Minister Iyun's land from the other houses. He took a running start in order to grab the ledge and haul himself over.

When he landed, he immediately flattened himself against the fence.

Dark spirit energy, heavy like a soup of fog, seeped from the windows of the house. Condensed in bunches yet still churning together, they curdled like blood clots, like vines clawing outward, desperate to escape.

Hunter. They whispered in many voices, many pitches. Tiny, worm-like tendrils crawled on his boots, attempting to hold him in place with a residue as sticky and pungent as spoiled egg yolk. Their presence was everywhere, littered around the yard like discarded rags. None of this was corporeal in the sense of any phi he'd stalked through the woods. It seemed the minister hadn't graduated to the level of summoning demons into flesh and blood.

Not yet, at least.

Ex felt bad for them, and fought the urge to… what? Release them back into the Ghost Realm? These dark spirits were separated from their souls, unable to grasp onto anything, or have the chance to become something else, as Narissa had.

Hunter, hunter… With every step he took towards the house, the voices grew louder. The smell thickened, masking all else. He'd never felt that amount of black magic before. Sure, Mali's house was rich with it, but hers had a different vibration – old, but not rotten. Shamans and hedgewitches used the natural departure of life, decomposition, and the slow energy grown from that. This felt like the aftermath of ripping someone's heart out, a body suspended in the death throes of a violent end.

Even though Ex would rather stay in the Everpresent, he couldn't remain if he wanted to stay his unease. As he resurfaced, every muscle unwound. For once, he was relieved to return to the Blinds. Normally it was the opposite feeling. The stink and despairing whispers faded away, but the air still felt wrong. A chill remained over his skin, but at least he wouldn't be overwhelmed by the spirits' cries.

Walking in through the front door seemed unwise. There were gated windows on the ground floor, but none on the second. A small amount of light escaped. He listened intently and heard nothing.

Most of the dark spirits had poured from the same segment of the wall, the path of least resistance. It was soggy with rot, and Ex yanked at the edges, easily flaking away the wood as it crumbled into dirt in his hands. He used the sword he'd lifted from the guard to cut away the stubborn bits, and it sloughed off like an unhealed wound.

Once that was away, Ex pushed through into a narrow hallway, with a sliding paper wall made popular by foreign imports. A thick wave of sandalwood incense hit him in the face, but it was a relieving cleanse from the smell outside. At one end of the hall there was a set of stairs that probably led up to where the minister kept his ugly robes. But that way was darkened, with nothing but roaches scurrying this way and that. The light was flickering from behind the paper screens, towards the center of the house.

Ex took care to move with soft steps, and the heat began to swell. A sticky quality punctuated the air. This didn't look or feel like a house. More like the inner chamber of a temple, big and open, soft cushions to prostrate upon. Incense burned in several censors around the chamber room, itching his nose. They were only halfway burned down, which must have meant someone had been there recently.

Candles surrounded a pedestal draped with sacred cloth. Upon that sat a statue of the gold-painted Enlightened Lord, posture and expression similar to the one he'd seen in the cemetery. As with the shrine, he was surrounded by idols of Guardian devas. The sight of the revered captive in the home of a necromancer seemed grossly sacrilegious.

Something drew Ex to the idol, just the tiniest smell of rot, and he peered closer. All the food at his feet was already spoiled, flies crawling all over the prematurely wilted fruit. He took a deep breath and stepped away.

Focus, he needed to focus.

Passages around the atrium led off to other areas of the large house. He quickly surveyed the other rooms on the first floor and found a library, dining area, washroom, and a sitting room hardly used. No one. Nothing out of the ordinary.

Returning to the atrium, Ex checked the shrine again, this time meticulously. There must be something he missed. Then he spotted a segment on the back of the Enlightened Lord, where the gold paint had peeled away from his back. It wasn't made of copper or stone or precious gems.

It was made of bone, fused together by some unholy method and molded into a macabre imitation before being obscured by paint.

And there it was again. Some low vibrations. He crouched down to the base of the statue and listened. Were there voices? Maybe he could go into the Everpresent for a second and listen.

Like a tidal wave, the spirits screamed in his ears, raging and incoherent, panicked and grasping at him. He clamped his hands over his head and reared back, falling to the floor.

No choice but to stay in the Blinds.

Shuddering, Ex groaned as he pushed himself up. Wait. The rug around the back of the statue seemed disturbed, with fresh wax drippings from a candle. Something glinted. A hairpin crested with a diamond, fit for a queen. He peeled back the rug, and found a hidden door, secured only by a latch, which laid open.

A winding stone staircase descended into a damp, sweltering underground lair. This had to be it. Greenish amber light ebbed from the bottom of the staircase, enough to allow him stable footing on the slick stones. Just like the hunt, Ex held his sword ready, even though the blade was curved and awkward, far heavier than what he was used to.

The voices grew louder until it became one steady chant. At the bottom of the staircase, thin, silk curtains obscured the room beyond. Bracing himself for what lay beyond, he nudged them aside with the tip of his sword.

Another large idol sat upon a shrine, identical in size to the distortion of the Enlightened Lord above. That had been an unsettling discovery, but this… This thing was unlike anything he'd ever seen.

The statue was encased in a stitched web of leather segments that he prayed belonged to pigs. Judging by the different skin tones and blemishes, Ex had tanned enough hides to doubt it.

On its face, the idol's eyes bulged open, inset with onyx that shimmered in the sickly green candlelight. Its mouth stretched wide in a skeletal grin, fangs bared, tongue descending past its chin.

In its palms, which should have been empty, it held the

heads of pigs, dogs, and horses, freshly killed, clotted blood running in grooves down its arms to collect by its feet. Bowls of tribute laid before it, some of it twitching and squirming with maggots and leeches. Candles burned all around the room, wax shaped into uneven lumps, the stink of corpse fat wafting from their flames.

Ex's first instinct was to vomit, but he settled for clamping his hand over his mouth and swallowed the bile creeping up his throat. He tore his eyes from the horrid idol of a god he had no desire to know or name, and focused instead on the living and breathing people in the room.

Minister Iyun led the chant. He held incense sticks as he droned on, swaying back and forth, prostrating at regular intervals. The prince sat next to him, reciting the chant as well, though delayed by a split second.

Then Ex saw her.

Arinya sat to the side, her knees facing towards the idol, her head hanging down as she swayed, as if held upright by an invisible string. She was dressed just as beautifully as the last time he'd seen her, with even more jewelry. However, her clothes were damp with sweat, pulled partially from their tight folds. She wore no crown, and her hair had fallen out of its pins. He could tell she'd struggled against her captors before they brought her here.

She wasn't alone. Two other ladies sat next to her in the same position, dressed similarly, eyes half lidded and vacant. They must have been the prince's other consorts.

Across from them were another three. A woman older than Arinya, her features slightly apart from what was typical of Suyoram – wider eyes, smaller lips, and a reddish tint to her hair. The Princess of Loram, the queen-in-waiting. Next to her, a young boy who couldn't have been older than fifteen, dressed similarly to Prince Varunvirya – his younger brother. And next to the younger prince was an elderly, wizened man that Ex immediately recognized from paintings and tapestries.

The king himself.

Ex took a slow step into the chamber, afraid his thudding heart would alert them to his presence. It was a struggle to keep his eyes from drifting up towards the unholy idol. How he wished he were in the Trance, devoid of fear, devoid of hesitation. He wished he could take comfort in the Everpresent, where his magic gave him confidence, where the whispers of the spirits calmed his nerves. But his brief visit upstairs proved the Everpresent would have twisted into something beyond a nightmare in this place, with dark spirits that would make his ears bleed with their screams, or worse. There was nothing but darkness here, darkness beyond what he'd felt fighting any demon.

Then their chanting stopped. Ex froze, searching for a place to hide, but it was too late. He stood in the center of the chamber, as if he were a worshipper come to participate in the evil ritual before him.

"It's time," the minister said, his voice eerily calm.

Prince Varunvirya rose and turned around, staring straight at Ex. Ex flinched, his sword ready. But the prince's eyes were glazed over, unseeing. His face wore a resting expression with the same blankness as all the others, stuck in some kind of trance caused by Iyun's black magic. He walked towards one of the consorts, seized her by the arm and yanked her forward. In his other hand, he held a curved ritual knife with a bone handle.

She didn't struggle, and he ushered her to lay down on a stone slab between the minister and the idol. He raised the knife above her swollen belly, and Ex realized what was about to happen.

"Stop!" Ex shouted.

Prince Varunvirya didn't react. He couldn't hear from wherever his mind had gone.

"Hunter Ex. I did wonder if you might cheat death again." Minister Iyun didn't bother to turn around. "To be perfectly candid, I hoped you would. Prince Varunvirya, if you would declaw our guest?"

At the minister's command, Varunvirya leapt to his feet, abandoning the ritual knife for his own sword – a golden-hilted beauty of a weapon. The prince strode towards Ex in long, confident steps. Ex began to panic. He was no soldier. He didn't know how to duel another human with a sword, and Varunvirya held his own blade like he had trained every day since he could walk. Ex only knew how to kill, swiftly and humanely. If the prince were a demon, Ex would have already thrown his blade through his heart and broken his neck with the chain.

The prince's sword flashed. Ex blocked, but hesitated to swing back. How could he kill a member of the royal family? With that, Varunvirya's blade found the hilt and easily flicked Ex's sword away. It clattered on the floor, and his hopes dashed with it. It had to be the most pathetic sword fight in the history of sword fights. Prince Varunvirya leveled the razor-sharp tip at Ex's neck, yet stayed his hand.

"Disappointing," Iyun said. "I thought you'd put up more of a fight."

"What are you doing?" Ex demanded, and though he meant to sound forceful, his voice sounded choked and full of horror.

"Is it not obvious?" Iyun scoffed. "Harnessing the power of Shar-Ala, just as you suggested."

"I didn't suggest anything! I was warning you!" Ex threw his arms up in exasperation. The prince's sword twitched in response, so he kept his hands forward, palms spread.

"It is easier than I expected. These sacred words came to me in dreams, as if only a long-forgotten memory. Shar-Ala deemed me worthy of inheriting his power. He speaks to me."

"Speaking to the demon is one thing," Ex said. "But whatever you're doing here, this is *wrong*. If I don't kill you, trust that the guild will."

Iyun sighed. "Oh, calm yourself, whelp. I'm only doing as my prince asked of me, and this ritual will accomplish his wishes."

"As much of an asshole as he is, I doubt he wanted this," Ex said. "Release him from this trance and let him speak for himself."

"He cares only for the results, not the method. His willful ignorance is a mercy. I protect him and his conscience. I am benevolent." Iyun placed his hand on the consort's stomach. "He desired a kuman thong. I only provide what he wants."

Ex started forward, but the prince pressed him with a warning poke.

"Why is the king here, then? And the queen? You're going to tell me his little brother is pregnant too?"

"No," the minister sneered. "Don't debase my work. My prince has waited long enough for his throne. The old man lingers. This is what he wanted."

Ex laughed, despite it all. "So you're going to kill the king? And the young prince too?"

"Predictable that your own stupidity leads to such inane assumptions. Tonight we harvest, and plant the seeds for our designs. The king will speed the process of his own accord. We shall merely suggest."

Ex shook his head, lost for words. The only ones he found were directed at the devas, so he looked skyward. "What the fuck is wrong with humanity?"

The minister's voice dripped with scorn. "You and your whispers should show gratitude. The longer the king lasts, the longer he succumbs to the impotent promises of the foreigners he's so desperate to impress. Of the Sangha demanding our ways outlawed and reformed. Real magic will fade away. You and your kind will be nothing, of no use to anyone."

"Better we fade to nothing than have you pulling the strings."

"Pulling the strings?" It was the minister's turn to laugh. "My dear boy, we can both have what we want. With Shar-Ala's influence, I will ensure real magic continues to flourish. Rebuild it, even, perhaps disband the useless Sangha. Even wither their pointless ideals away to superstition."

"You're crazy, old man. You might be able to brainwash the people in this room, but the whole country?"

"Oh, you poor ignorant thing. People are terribly easy to control. Don't strain your little head over politics. This is not your world." He made a shooing gesture with his hand. "Take your whore and go. I'll ensure that no one will hunt you. One less mind to bother with, two fewer stupid children to worry on. I already have what we need, and now there's no use for either of you. *Especially* you."

Ex's gaze drifted to Arinya, and the bruises on her arm where the prince tore her away from him. They could disappear together, with no royal dogs chasing their every step. He could perform the soul release, letting Isaree's little body return to Arinya, to take her first breath and be reborn. It was a tempting offer, and after speaking to Swan, he hated to admit that he feared for the future of the guild.

No, Ex shook the thought away. Iyun was trying to distract him with an impossible dream. This couldn't be left unfinished.

"You might as well kill me," Ex said. "I'm not leaving until I have what you stole."

Iyun sighed. "Very well. I gave you every chance. It seems there is no reasoning with a simple beast."

Finally, Iyun stood, without his brace, and turned around. He stared Ex down much like the prince had, as if inspecting an insect he planned to crush under his heel. With a grin, he pulled back his hood, and Ex could not comprehend what the fuck he was seeing.

The pulsing green eye of Shar-Ala glared down at him. Minister Iyun had sewn the demon's eye into his forehead. The stitches were clumsy, likely done by himself and a mirror in the dark. The stitching poked thin through the membrane of the eye and fastened to his own skin in countless loops. Small droplets of the demon's blood leaked from the edges like black tears, tainting his forehead.

Ex's breath left him. He could hardly believe it. This man had the capacity to torture a true demon. In all his lives, he'd never imagine feeling sympathy for Shar-Ala. Had this darkness always been inside the man? Or had Shar-Ala twisted his greatest fears into a noose?

The candles flickered and began to grow into the fire of Ex's village. Iyun chanted a rising incantation – black magic, aggressive, cutting at him through his mind – and rather than words, he heard the clash of swords, the screams, the gunshots.

Not *now*. Ex tried to squeeze his eyes shut and resist the nightmare sure to come if he did nothing. But they wouldn't close, drawn to the demonic artifact. Fighting it felt the same as pushing against the winds of a monsoon. Iyun's face began to melt into the faceless soldiers who killed his family. With all his effort, Ex tore his gaze away, and clutched his neck, grasping onto Isaree's amulet.

Remember me, or let me go.

Then it occurred to him, a flash of inspiration, as sudden as a bolt of lightning. Why must this fire be his village burning, and nothing else? Why couldn't he transform this memory into something hopeful, something good?

He'd seen fire a thousand more times throughout his life, and far more often in comfort. The flicker of countless camps on the Serene Way, the gentle burn of the kitchen stove as his mother cooked his favorite shrimp bami soup, the candlelight in Arinya's eyes as she held a lotus float out to him and whispered *make a wish*…

That never happened. That was a dream, one of his rare, good ones. But just maybe a dream still possible.

Ex sprung forward, towards the nightmare.

Chapter Thirty-Six

The Slayer

From the day he wandered off the trail and into the world of men, Ex had been beat up, hexed, stabbed, shot, tortured, poisoned to death... and made into a killer. He stabbed the war hero Sidom Da through the heart. The look in the man's eyes the moment his soul departed would never leave him.

Maybe it was only karma.

Ex punched the prince right in the jaw and he toppled over without his sword. The only way for Ex to get close enough to hit him was to run straight through the blade. And he didn't stop there.

The nightmare of flames and death dissolved, melting into the soft flicker of light in the eyes of his loved ones. As Ex stepped over the prince, the minister drew the hex doll from his pocket, and yanked the string, squeezing its neck into a tiny strand.

On his next stride, Ex snatched the ritual knife off the ground. He shook the scalpel from his sleeve. Iyun's eyes widened, and he squeezed the doll even harder, shaking it in panic.

"No, hunter, wait–"

A knife went through Iyun's heart, a scalpel through the Shar-ala's eye.

Ex grabbed the Minister by the collar before he fell and pulled him close.

"How?" Iyun's eyes flicked to the hex doll as it dropped from his trembling hands.

Ex yanked his own collar and tilted his head to present the fresh sak yant tattoo on the side of his neck. Still deep black from Master Seua's needle, the clean lines and tiny script wasn't a typical protective hunter's tattoo.

Master Seua knew this charm from his former life, before he came to the guild. It was a common one for gangsters and criminals who desired protection in their violent, murderous lives. It didn't prevent them from getting murdered, of course. A tattoo can only do so much against a blade or a bullet. But hexes? Black magic? Yes, of course. What spirit magic took, it gave back.

Iyun's eyes met Ex's as Shar-Ala's eye deflated, demon blood draining down his forehead in thick, tar-like streaks. His mouth sagged and sputtered, a voiceless *how?*

"I was raised to kill demons," Ex told him, and let go.

When Iyun fell, so did the others under his control, leaving Ex in sudden silence but for his own ragged breathing. He may have been foolish at times, but he wasn't dumb enough to skewer himself anywhere too important. Certainly not through the heart.

At least, he thought so.

In a haze, he worried about shedding blood here in the eyes of this horrible idol. He wished he could say his first concern was for the hostages laying around, but in all honesty, he thought about how much he wanted a hot bath, to scrub himself clean of all this blood and black magic.

Quickly, Ex pulled the scalpel from Iyun's forehead and slashed through the stitches. Shar-Ala's eye slipped out like a peeled grape. He shoved it into a lead-lined pocket on his shirt, sewn in by the masters for exactly this purpose.

The prince didn't move, staring vacantly at nothing. He still breathed, but it was highly likely that his dabbling in black magic had rendered his mind to mush.

Ex staggered over to Arinya. She was breathing evenly, heart still beating as strong as he remembered. She groaned and slowly came around, her body trembling.

"Hey, come on." Ex placed his hand on her cheek, patting her lightly but urgently. He didn't want to be the one to explain to the king why the minister was dead, the prince was in a coma, and the royal family was sitting in a necromancer's lair that – surprise! – had been right under their feet for devas knew how long. Starting to panic, which didn't help his blood loss, Ex smacked her a little harder.

She grimaced, then peered up at him as if staring into the sun.

"Ex?"

With a huge sigh, he doubled over in relief, resting his forehead against hers. She reached up and pointed at the hilt of the prince's blade, flush against his collarbone. "You have a sword sticking through you."

"Ah, it's fine."

"Should we... remove it?"

"Better to leave it there for now."

She shook her head, then pushed him away to glare. "You better stop that."

"Stop what?"

"Getting hurt all the time."

"I don't, usually." He helped her sit up. "Only since I met you."

"Oh, I see. You're going to blame it all on me?"

"That's not what I meant, and you know it." Then he laughed, feeling his head swim.

She smirked, then grew serious. "Why aren't you in the Everpresent, healing yourself?"

"I can't get there from here."

"Wait, you have to..." Then her gaze drifted over his shoulder, to their surroundings. She paled as she took in the stirring royals, and all the other terrible, twisted things around them. She clutched onto Ex like a lifeline, shaking. "What is, what, where—"

"It's okay. He's gone now. Shar-Ala, too." Then he took her hand, and placed Isaree's amulet in it. "This is yours."

She stared down at it, and her fingertips grazed the stone gently, as if caressing an infant.

"Oh, Ex," Arinya sniffled, and her voice grew soft. "Listen. I had a dream last night, clear as daylight." Her fingers tightened around the jewel. "I saw her."

Something stirred in his chest, warm. An image in his mind. A flash of gold, a glow of twin red rubies. He grasped at it, desperate to remember something important, but it faded when Arinya placed her cheek on his hand. He met her gaze, and her eyes glistened with tears.

"Let her go."

He searched her expression for doubt, but there was none. "Are you sure?"

"Yes." Arinya pressed the amulet back into his hands.

And even in that godless place, in the eyes of a nightmare idol, they held each other.

Of all the fires he'd seen, this was by far the most satisfying. This was something he would hold onto for the rest of his life. A thick cloud of smoke choked the air as Minister Iyun's house went up in flames, guards standing sentinel with torches and spears ready for any dark thing that might escape. With the destruction of the idol, the fog of trapped spirits dissolved with a hiss of gratitude.

After carefully removing the prince's sword from his chest, Ex sat on the ground and stayed in the Everpresent only as long as he needed to stop his bleeding and begin to heal the wound. Everyone was already eying him with various expressions of suspicion and fear, especially the guards.

Nearby, Arinya comforted the young prince and the two other consorts, who were near hysterics. The queen-in-waiting prostrated before the prince's body, sobbing hysterically with crocodile tears. From the knowing looks exchanged between her servants, it seemed they were used to her melodramatic displays.

The king impassively watched the inferno, light and shadow rendering him as grand as the statues of his likeness. He was smaller and much older than the artists had made, yet still seemed healthy. But while in the Everpresent, Ex had noticed the distinct sour-rot stink of a wasting sickness. He was no doctor, but if he had to guess, the monarch was close to the end of his reign. He wore the same even stare the prince had in the courtyard – an airy posture, as if these matters bored him, were beneath his divine attention. Surrounded by a flock of retainers fussing over him, he stared down at his eldest son, then grunted and shooed most of them away.

"Hunter."

Ex met his gaze, hoping it was humble enough to sit rather than grovel on his belly. The king's mind had shifted, however. With deep pain hidden beneath his stoic expression, he gazed upon his son, and the bloody sword nearby.

"My king."

"Will he awaken?"

Prince Varunvirya's eyes remained open, blinking at intervals but dilated, his breath slow but steady.

Ex told the truth. "I'm afraid I'm not sure, sir."

The king stroked his grey wisp of a beard, then barked with sudden force, "Orai! Enough!"

The queen-in-waiting's head snapped up, her mouth sagging open with quivering lips.

The king addressed his servants. "Please escort my son and the ladies to the physician."

Arinya started towards him, eyebrows raised in concern, but the servants created a wall to usher them away. Ex's nerves rose considerably more with her gone, as she'd been the one to explain to the king what had happened after they woke up in Iyun's den.

After a long spell of silence, the king said, "How is this possible? My son… a necromancer?"

"I don't think he was. Just a patron, and that may be why he's in a coma, sir."

"How was it possible that this unholy filth remained hidden from the Sangha? They bless these grounds constantly."

Ex hesitated, searching his mind for the least offensive way to put it. "I think the monks contained it from infecting the rest of your palace. The Sangha pay tribute and give to spirits, but they don't take. The minister was a necromancer in secret, and those of their kind, they only take, and from a place of darkness."

The king studied the hunter as if he were an interesting yet dangerous creature, not to be approached. "And what do you hunters do?"

"We walk in the grey, my king. We speak to spirits both dark and light. We give back what we take."

"I see." He stared back at the fire, a thoughtful expression. A long silence hung between them, in which Ex's entire world swayed in the balance. The king raised his chin, then finally spoke. "I've spoken to the men, eager to distance themselves from the minister. You've been mistreated at his hands, and protected my son's consort during her travel. At the same time, you dispatched many of them, including a war hero. You were sentenced to death, and your guild defied the word of the crown. Yes, it was for an honorable reason, I see that now. But even if my son was…" He gestured at the fire, "…*involved* in this black magic, his word was still law."

Ex didn't know what to say. Defending himself seemed pointless, as the king summed it up pretty well. Except for the fact that it was the Hound who tore apart the guards, with the help of a reformed phi. But that seemed a good detail to leave out. The last thing he wanted was to appear as an insolent child trying to talk himself out of trouble.

"Though you and your guild acted in unforgivable defiance, you saved my life, as well as the life of what may be the new crown prince." The king raised his head as he delivered the verdict. "In exchange, I will grant you yours."

Ex let out a huge breath. "Thank you, sir."

"The Hunters Guild may remain intact under the Sacred Stone Decree, but as punishment for their disobedience, they must forfeit their lands in the old city and establish themselves elsewhere."

Ex's heart sank. He opened his mouth to protest but thought better of it, instead hanging his head. Master Seua's words came back to him – there are some fights you couldn't win, and considering the king's mistrust towards low magic, it might have been a lot worse. "I understand, sir. Thank you."

He dismissed him then, calling over some guards to escort Ex from the palace grounds. Servants had arrived with a palanquin to carry the king back to the palace, and he straightened his royal sash before walking away.

"Wait," Ex dared to call back to the king, straining to see over the guard's shoulders. "What about Arinya?"

The man furrowed his brows in a silent question. Ex wasn't sure what he was trying to ask. Reassigned to the child prince? Granted freedom?

Come to him?

At the young hunter's hesitation, the king gave him a bemused smile, and let his servants lift him into the palanquin. "Goodbye, Hunter Ex."

Chapter Thirty-Seven

In the End

"Not many wear this one," Master Seua said as he tapped the needle into Ex's arm. "Except Rei. But that was a long time ago."

They sat on a stone bench in front of the hearth in the great hall. Sounds of merriment echoed around the warm chamber, as the hunters held the last feast at their ancestral home. Of course, not all were happy to leave, especially the scribes and teamsters who'd spent their entire lives in the Capital. Many of them weren't moving to the guild's new home up north. But the truth was, they didn't have all that much to do anymore, thanks to their dwindling business.

But the hunters seemed quite content to be closer to the lands where they made the bulk of their living. Less time spent traveling was appealing for the ones with family. Jinburi was a crossroads town, after all, and nestled in the true heart of northern Suyoram. They did enough trading there already, and it was far closer to the wilderness than the fading magic of the Capital.

When Ex returned to the guild early that morning, everyone was shocked he was alive. He wondered if all the theatrics of the deva ritual had been for his benefit. But when Master Seua smiled knowingly, there was no uncertainty. His master had believed he could do it, and Ex made him proud.

Retrieving Shar-Ala's eye and escaping the palace impressed them, but the masters were even more interested in all that happened before that, in the deva realm. Ex wished he could have told them more, but he had only the hazy remnants of a dream, already long escaped. One vision did remain, and would remain for the rest of his life. A golden figure, startingly vivid, arms open as if beckoning him into an embrace. More vivid than that resplendent image was the feeling that filled his entire being when it flashed across his mind.

Pure love, whole and unrestrained.

"To Hunter Ex," Master Rei said, from her seat at the table next to Elder Nokai and the other hunters. "Dead and back." They raised their mugs and drank, already deep in their cups.

Master Seua wiped Ex's arm with a wet cloth, and he stared down at the new badge, next to the true demon slayer tattoo.

Necromancer Slayer.

It felt uncomfortable to have a badge celebrating the death of another person, no matter how twisted they had been. As Ex studied it in the firelight, he thought of Sidom Da, too, how the life faded from his eyes as Ex sank his knife into his heart. Maybe it was better to always have the reminder.

They sat in comfortable silence on the bench. The old man smoked his pipe as Ex sipped his wine. "Why are you so quiet?" Master Seua finally said, mildly irritated. "After all the shit we gave you, I was looking forward to your insufferable boasting."

"I don't know." Ex traced the fresh tattoo with his finger. "A lot happened."

He fantasized about Arinya showing up for the ceremony, somehow, which was closer to a party than anything else. But it had already been two days with no sign of her, no message, nothing. Ex even thought about going to court, but the king made it clear that if he showed up on the palace grounds again, he'd be executed on the spot. Perhaps it was for the best. Perhaps seeing him again would be too painful a reminder.

The last thing she asked of him was to release Isaree's soul, which he did that morning, with the help of Elder Nokai.

"Hey, Ex," one of the hunters called from the entrance to the hall. "Are you expecting visitors?"

Ex was at the doorway in seconds. The big hunter stepped aside to reveal a woman in a plain brown tube dress and red sabai draping her shoulders. Underneath, she wore a tight-fitting, high collared blouse that was of a foreign style, along with delicate white gloves.

"Narissa." Ex hid his disappointment with an awkward smile. And then panic hit as he realized a krasue had casually walked into a den of krasue killers. He peeked at the big hunter who let her in, but he had already walked away, eager to get back to drinking. Likewise, the others only glanced over with slight interest, but returned to their conversations. He noticed Piglet shoot him a grin with two thumbs up. Next to him, his brother Swan sat with a quiet, amused smile. Piglet should have still been in bed for his injuries, but he was never one to turn down a feast.

"Hello, hunter," Narissa said. "Or is it slayer, now?"

"Are you…?" Insane? Suicidal? Ex squinted at her, and her smile deepened. Something *was* different about her smell. Her perfume was far more subtle than he remembered, and beneath that, the very human hint of sweat. Astounded, he dipped into the Everpresent, knowing her spirit blood would light up, and the demonic aura would cloud his senses with the stench of death.

But she was mortal. Red blood and warm skin. Human through and through.

Narissa blinked in her languid way, and her smile deepened. She was proud, rightfully so. She must have done the impossible, and freed herself from her curse within the same lifetime.

You actually broke the curse? You're human?!

"Am I what?" Narissa said. "I'm sorry, you'll have to speak louder, I can't hear you from the Grey."

"I mean," Ex said out loud, and returned to the Blinds. "Are you hungry?" He grinned at her, and she nodded.

"I ate rice this morning, but I'd love something spicy."

He took her arm and led her to the table.

Three days passed, and still no word from Arinya.

A shadow had fallen over the city during that time, and quickly rippled throughout the kingdom, echoing through the rest of the world thereafter. The Crown-Prince Varunvirya had died in his sleep. A tragic and unexpected death, reported by the crown, for the prince was by all accounts healthy and strong, in his prime, expected to someday inherit the throne. Instead, his teenage brother would be coronated with the new title. The young prince would also be betrothed to his brother's widow, despite her being twice his age.

Of course, there were plenty of rumors milling about. The most popular being that Varun had fallen off his horse and a head injury rendered him a vegetable, therefore his father had mercifully euthanized him. Some of the hunters, knowing more of the story, said he had probably started to decay into something twisted by black magic, and the crown couldn't let that be known. However, no one seemed to know what would become of the late prince's consort-wives and concubines.

Ex couldn't care less about any of it. The politics, especially. He watched in slight distaste as crowds flooded the streets of the old city, dressed mourning-white, eager to pay respects to the merumat being constructed on the palace grounds. The Sangha's chants permeated the air as the grand funeral pyre went up, a sendoff fit for a deva. But in Ex's opinion, the prince should have burned alongside Minister Iyun in his debased lair for all that he'd done.

By then, most of the guild had already left. The halls were empty, all the grand decor, and the old texts, the workshops and storerooms and apothecaries, all gone. Piglet and Swan were staying behind to oversee their branch in the Capital – they were still allowed to operate trade, though the unspoken question remained – for how long?

Ex's room was only slightly larger than a stable, with not much in it, but it felt surreal to pack up. This place had always felt like his real home, a family to return to. He turned his training mask around in his hands, just a plain, curved dome with the guild's symbol painted over it. He packed some books. He learned to read here. The only other things he owned could fit into a single bag.

He was the last one to leave.

He gazed at the symbol of the Phi Hunters carved into the stone, the soft patter of the tail end of a downpour glancing off his rain hat. The symbol once filled him with hope, an oasis to a displaced war orphan, starving and desperate, prostrated on the steps. Now, a profound sense of sadness gripped his chest. Their glorious history had been severed from society. He wondered when they would be forgotten.

As he turned away from his home for the last time, he mused about what they would build here instead. Another temple for the Sangha? An aristocrat's mansion? A park? A public bathhouse?

With a last glance behind him, he took Brownie's reins and walked to the gates and pushed them shut. Afterwards, he pulled the old mare forward, but she snorted and didn't move.

"Hey." He gave her a pull, and stared into her doe eyes. "Don't you start getting Ramble's attitude." With another tug, then a yank, she shook her mane and remained still. Ex felt betrayed, but that softened as he realized this had been her home too. "Alright, alright." He patted her neck, brushed down her damp mane. "I know."

After she calmed, he tried to lead her away again, but she still didn't move. She scoffed, and this time, turned away, knocking off his hat with her snout.

"Oh, come on now." Ex glanced over his shoulder and followed her line of sight.

There was another horse standing idle in the street, a svelte, well-groomed stallion with a glossy white coat. A magnificent creature, bred from the finest of the fine, a common sight in the old city with the richest of citizens.

"What, are you in love?" Ex chuckled. "Trust me, sweet girl. That boy's out of your league. I would know." Still, he paused to admire the horse and his silky, brushed black mane. Then his gaze rose to his cloaked rider.

His heart caught in his throat.

"Hello, hunter," Arinya said, her lips curling into a playful smile. The last time he'd seen her, she'd been dressed as royalty, with jewels adorning her arms, her fingers and lashes painted, hair carefully pinned by the hands of countless servants. Now, she was dressed as she was when they first met, on a dirt path outside of that deep country tavern, what seemed like a lifetime ago. In wrapped pants and riding shoes, her hair pulled back in a loose ponytail, she met his eyes with a challenging gaze. His mouth hung open as he stammered for words. He glanced around for some kind of royal escort, but she was alone. Then he noticed the bags on the back of her horse.

"I heard that you were heading out of town," Arinya said. "And I'm fresh out of a job."

Despite the overcast day, it felt as if the sun had come out, shining between all the other stars in the soothing night. His spirits soared, and he laughed, shaking his head in disbelief. She rode up to his side, a satisfied grin on her face, and he didn't know if he'd ever smiled that hard in his life. He wanted to jump up onto her horse and embrace her, but she beat him to it, and slid off her saddle to stand before him.

They met in each other's arms. Ex reveled in the warmth gracing his racing heart, which he knew she felt too because he could feel hers beneath his chest. After he caught his breath, Ex pulled back to tenderly brush the hair from her face, drinking in the soft joy of her eyes. She held on to him and pressed her lips against his.

He knew then. But he had to ask her one more time.

"Arinya," he murmured between kisses. "Are you sure you want to come with me?" She playfully nipped his lip, then held his face in her hands, refusing to let him pull away. He gazed into her eyes, searching for any semblance of doubt.

She met him with none.

"As sure as the rain."

Epilogue

Ex had been tromping about the swamp for almost a week, searching for a sign of this lesser phi bastard. It had a rat face and bat wings but couldn't fly very high. The thing he hated most was using a bow and arrow. He always had been a less-than-average shot and his failings stuck in the trees, letting him know the phi had been taking him in circles. On top of that, every time he missed, it let out a mocking giggle that filled him with impotent rage.

During the rainy season, the swamp was a hellscape of twisted roots and jutting rocks, too wet to go on with boots, and miserable going barefoot with thorns all over the ground. Ex wondered if the bounty was really worth it, but the nearby villagers were getting the plague from the phi's midnight feasting. Mali wanted those wings, and Narissa insisted she needed his gall bladder for some kind of tonic. This would have been a good first hunt for some of the new recruits, fresh-eyed and eager, but it was still deadly, and they hadn't gone through the trials yet.

It would be another month until he saw home. Sitting around the small fire back at his miserable camp, all he could think about was his warm bed, but mostly Arinya in that warm bed. Just when he picked the last thorn from his foot, a rustle in the brush made him jump. He snatched his bow and nocked an arrow, waiting for whatever it was to show itself.

More rustling, then the reeds brushed aside to reveal a huge, black crocodile. Another head poked out nearby, then another. They'd surrounded his entire camp.

Man and beast watched one another in silence, but for the rain. Then he sighed and put down his bow.

"Alright," he said, snatching his coat. "Tell her I'm coming."

Ex had visited the Guardian a few times since killing Shar-Ala. True to her word, she appreciated his feat, and allowed the hunters to pass through her lands. Now that the guild was much closer, they had to keep up good relations. To his chagrin, Ex had become the official go-between.

When he arrived at the Guardian's sanctuary, she'd already emerged from her pool, but remained mostly under the water with relaxed, half-lidded eyes. The crocodiles napped, fog drifting lazily around their snouts. Quite a departure from when they'd first met.

Good to see you again, Guardian. Ex sat down cross-legged in front of her and pricked his finger to shake a drop of blood on her altar. He knew better than to flatter and grovel as some of the Guardians demanded. She demanded candor and brevity, as he learned the first time he met her, the first time Arinya heard voices from the Everpresent.

Hunter. You must leave immediately.

An odd thing to say. This was a very minor ghost, a pest, not something he'd think she'd take note of.

Why? Does this hunt bother you?

It is not the hunt. She blinked her big snake eyes at him. *It is her, your passenger.*

Arinya? Ex glanced around. She'd come along on hunts with him before, but never in the rainy season. It was the start of the qualifying rounds for the Suyoram Muay Boran championship, and though she wasn't competing, she helped train the others on her team this year due to her condition. *What are you talking about?*

You must return home now. The great naga let out a croaking rumble, and sunk back into her pool. *If you wish to see your daughter born.*

Ex thought she'd misspoken. *What? She's not, I mean, she can't! It's too early, isn't it?*

The Guardian said nothing, but the trees parted, twisting into a passage that would lead him home.

Though the Guardian had granted him a path far shorter than it was by foot, Ex was on the far side of the swamp, and it still took him all night to ride back. Once he broke through the tree line, he pushed Brownie into a run, hurrying to their house by the rushing river. Dread churned in his gut, his chest growing tighter with every breath.

Narissa opened the door before he could, and Ex breathlessly held out his arms for an explanation.

"Is she..." He swallowed the lump his throat, too scared to ask.

"Shh," Narissa took his arm and led him inside. "Everything went fine. She's resting."

Arinya laid back on the bed, sweaty with exhaustion. She looked up at him, a tired, happy smile brightening her eyes.

"She's so small," his wife said as he crouched by her side. "But she's perfect."

And when Ex held their first child in his arms, love swelled in his chest, a love that he'd never imagined. Familiar, all encompassing, as if he recognized her very soul.

His daughter blinked up at him in the light, and he could swear she recognized him too. She had Arinya's chin, and his nose, but the strangest thing, the most striking...

Isaree was born with red eyes.

Acknowledgements

This one goes out to Desola Coker, who plucked Ex from the slush pile, believed in it, and helped me write a better novel. Gemma Creffield, who made it shine, and for all your ending support. To my publicist Caroline Lambe, Amy Portsmouth, and the rest of the staff at Angry Robot. My agent Sam Farkas, who read this story in record time and always has my back.

To my DC Speculative Fiction Writers crew – Patricia, Daniel, Pepper, Andrew, J.D, Diana, and countless others, I've learned so much from all of you, and your support means the world to me. Ilya Nazarov who illustrated the amazing cover, and Alice Coleman for bringing it home. Beta readers Derek Salisbury, Curt Schmelz, Catherine Verdier for reading this wild little novel when it was rough and ragged. Highseas crewmate Lorena Loaiza. Christine Sanquist and Will Shen for giving me advice when I needed it.

To my dad, and the countless hours you read to me, your bookshelf full of fantastical worlds that filled me with wonder. For your tireless work ethic that shaped me into the stubborn, relentless bastard I am.

To my mom, whose heritage inspired me to write this novel. For cooking all the delicious food, for the sagely advice I so often ignored, for being so strong and brave in a country foreign to you, which taught me that I should never be afraid of anything strange and new.

To my son Sheamus, for whom I do everything. To my brother Teddie, for teaching me to think beyond the status quo. To my boo Houstie, and the rest of my friends and family who believed in me.

And last but first in my heart, Brandi Shaddick, my ride-or-die bestie from kindergarten and on. For the millions of words we wrote together (which we later realized would be shelved as self-insert portal fanfic power fantasy.) For reading every garbage thing I've ever written, and always inspiring and pushing me to be better. We did it bitch, boobly fuckin bee!

About the Author

SALINEE GOLDENBERG is a speculative fiction writer and multimedia artist who lives in Washington DC, and is drawn to outsider perspectives. A biracial, bisexual, diaspora writer, Sal often explores themes of identity, obsession and alienation in her work. A gaming industry veteran, Sal has created narrative trailers for titles such as Skyrim, Fallout 4, Dishonored, and Minecraft. When not writing, she likes to paint, listen to records, and play in punk bands.

1.

The touch for /*Donkey*/ is infuriatingly close to the touch for /*Mother*/ in fingerspeak.

For /*Donkey*/, the forefinger and thumb squeeze the middle band, and then the little finger taps the lower band twice, whereas /*Mother*/ uses the middle finger.

This is just a small example of why whoever came up with this bastard language should be thrown from Traitors' Rock into the Southern Sea.

Unlike the handful of other known languages, fingerspeak also has no permanence. You can repeat a foreign word in your head, and then mull it over until you can winkle out its meaning, but you can't repeat someone's touch to yourself, or replicate a sensation. If you had to dream up the most inconvenient language for us to learn, you would be hard pressed to improve on fingerspeak.

Which is bugger all use complaining about in my current position. I say 'current' as though it's a choice, like I'm weighing up a range of exciting career opportunities. The truth is that the elders will never let me leave; there's too few of us who can interpret fingerspeak. That fact used to make me think I was a cut above the other kids from the quarter – you could see their limited lives mapped out for them in the wrinkles of their fathers' leathery skin – but who turned out to be the fool in the end?

I stand in the High Chamber and wait my turn, watching the councillors in conversation. They all wear hooded cowls and their crimson robes denote the highest rank of the Keda. They are in pairs, each with their right hand on the other's bare left arm, fingers dancing between the three silver bands worn there.

There is one advantage of fingerspeak: it's virtually impossible for anyone to eavesdrop on your conversation. Even now, ten paces away – I'm not stupid or vulgar enough to stare at the Keda – I can see Double's fingers moving, but I don't have a clue what xe might be saying.

For over a century the Keda have ruled Val Kedić, and yet there's still so much we don't know about them. The language barrier keeps us apart, with us translating to maintain a purely functional relationship. The majority of Keda, in their blue robes, have next to no contact with citizens; it's only the councillors and Justices who matter. And the less we know of them, the greater power they have over us. Gender, for example, is a closed book. Someone introduced the pronoun "xe" to describe them a century ago, and there's been no advance ever since. Their mouths are another example: hidden by their cowls, but thanks to servants' gossip, we know they do have them – twisted and grotesque, but mouths for eating, all the same. Just not speaking.

There's only a handful of the Council I know by name – Double, because xe's the main contact for my quarter. Xe is the one who summons me to pass on instructions and information. Xer name is, by its nature, untranslatable to our tongue – being a mixture of taps and squeezes and no spoken words – but I know xer as Double because it's a repeated sequence of taps.

Then there's Giant, who I've never fingerspoken with, but xe is unusually tall for the Keda. Xe is the same height as me so xe always stands out.

The most senior member of the Council, though – they have no leader, but it is clear that xe is the top dog among them – is known to us as Eleven, because of the complicated series of eleven taps that make up xer name. At a rough guess, it means something like "xe-who-lives-by-the-eastern-something-something-tranquil-grove". But who knows. The taps all blur into one.

Then there's Chicken. Now xe, I can't stand. I mean, obviously, I hate all the Keda – they stole my son, they squeeze us dry, they've sucked the life out of our city. They are our captors. But Chicken? Xe is a real pain in the arse.

It pleases us to call xer Chicken because xer given name is not far away from the touch for /Chicken/. It also reduces xer somehow, takes away some of xer power over us. But no matter what we call xer, I can't forget the way xe looks at me.

You don't see much of a Keda beyond the bare left arm – their cowls cover most of their heads, so you can only see their flat noses and threatening eyes in the gloom of the hood. But I'll never forget that one time when we were fingerspeaking, I had to ask xer about the quotas due from our quarter. I essayed a phrase, something like:

(Question) / Number / Barrel /.

It was a simple squeeze and trill of the fingers. But the look of disgust xe gave at my clumsy accent took my breath away. The contempt blazing from xer flared nostrils and eyes felt like hard chips of marble cutting my skin. I wanted to scream at xer, "Don't blame me for not being touch-perfect in your stupid language!"

Needless to say, I sucked it up, received xer answer, and bowed before withdrawing.

Anyway. What I'm trying to say is, there are Keda and there are *Keda*. Most are anonymous; you see their robes, their piggy little eyes, you hear the occasional snuffly exhalations they make to express shock, pleasure or humour. While they're all scum, the ones I can't stand are those like Chicken, who treat us with open contempt.

I catch Ira's eye. She's standing by a column twenty paces away, waiting, as I am, for the Keda to summon her services. I raise my eyebrows a fraction, trying to convey "how boring is this?" But she studiously ignores me.

I used to do that with Borzu all the time, trying to read each other's minds and having a whole conversation with eyebrow twitches, side-eyes and grimaces. Afterwards, we'd compare notes, see how much of each other's part of the conversation we had understood. Very little, was the usual answer. But Borzu... well, it doesn't do to dwell too much on what happened to him. He is a salutary lesson as to why the best thing to do is keep your head down among the Keda and be as dull and obedient as possible, as Ira has clearly set out to be.

Astonishingly, some people act like it's a cushy number being an interpreter for the Keda. Some resent the occasional perks given to us: our interpreter's residence, and the fact that we skipped our seven-year service in Riona. It was only so that we could learn fingerspeak. But people ignore those years of study and the fact we're now on the front line, dealing with the Keda and their banal whims every day. Trained monkeys that appear at the snap of a finger. Our lives are not our own, not in the way most citizens can say, and I sometimes wonder why anyone would choose this path on purpose.

As if on cue, Double inclines xer head towards me and beckons with xer forefinger. Xe stands a foot shorter than me, but xe stands imperiously as if towering above me. I approach, bow, and xe places xer long, cadaverous fingers on my left arm. Like all the Keda, xer right-hand nails curve round like vicious scimitars, the better for fingerspeaking. Although I've been doing this a while, I can't help but swallow a grimace when I feel the nails' prickly caress on my skin.

In preparation, the rest of my body zones out and my whole attention focuses on the three bands that enclose my arm. Murky bronze, of course, unlike the delicately engraved silver ones that the Keda earn the right to wear on their thirteenth birthdays. It pays to keep ours unpolished – these small status signifiers mean a lot to the Keda, especially anything to do with fingerspeak.

I close my eyes and shut out the distant whisper of the sea, and the buzz of Val Kedić outside. I switch off everything that I don't need right now, and I feel.

Visitor / (Future) / Day /, Double says without preamble, *From / (Unclear) /.*

It's some distant land; I don't know the touch and don't need to know.

Pulse / Fish / Vegetable / Nut / Date / – xe breaks off to make a gesture with xer left hand, like "etcetera, you get the idea".

(Positive) /, I say. *Prepare / Many / Good / Food / Council /.*

Double does not react. There is no word for "thankyou" in their language. Or perhaps there is, and we've just never heard it. Then xe frowns, and grasps my upper band: *(Past) / Fish / Small / (Disgust) / Many / Bone / (Question) / Reason /.*

I ache to make a sarcastic retort, to say, "A million apologies, Excellency, our lazy fishermen must have guzzled all the plump mackerel themselves, I'll have them whipped." But I stifle my irritation and take xer bare arm to respond. It tenses, like it always does.

(Regret) / Councillor /, I say, *(Negative) / Many / Fish / Now / (Question) / More / Vegetable /.*

Double listens to me, then replies with a curt series of touches.

More / Fish /. Then, as an afterthought, xe spreads xer fingers and taps, *Girl / Send / Many / Girl /.*

It was my old teacher I have to blame. Myriam, I think her name was. I adored her, and her classroom. It was down by the beach, next to the wharf where most of us lived, where our fathers fished. The rest of Val Kedić called our quarter The Stain – a fetid blot that festered outside the city walls – but we didn't care. The shacks sprouted from each other like a fungal growth, staggering off in all directions, creating twisted alleys, and eaves that jabbed into other buildings. A reek of fish clung to the walls and our clothes. It was a dirty slum, but it was *our* dirty slum, and most of us stayed happy there, insulated from the rest of the world.

We knew little of what was going on in the city proper, still less of the Keda who rarely troubled to come out to such a distant fringe of Val Kedić. Occasionally, you might see a green-robed Justice striding down the alleys, but we were warned to keep clear of them, and they were the bogeymen in our bedtime stories.

By the time I was seven, I was helping my father unload his fish in the market each morning, and in the afternoon I would go down to the school by the beach. There we learned our numbers and letters, and, if the heat was tolerable, Myriam would take us outside to the famous black sands, and we would practise counting with shells and pebbles.

I found it all easy – couldn't understand the trouble numbers and letters caused the others – and I soon found Myriam was taking a special interest in me. At first, I noticed the lessons were increasingly directed towards me as the sole audience, while the others were allowed to play and bicker. Then, around the time of my eighth birthday, I took the first steps towards becoming an interpreter.

Myriam had sent the other children home, and sat down by me, unrolling a piece of parchment. She spread it across the table, displaying two lists of words in scratchy calligraphy.

"What's this?" I asked her.

"This is a different language," she said. "It might look funny, but just think of it as a secret code."

"Like the one they use in the market?" I said, thinking of the argot they all used to describe fish and customers – gillies for sunfish, stump for the massive lobsters that were considered a Val Kedić delicacy, dryden for outsiders who were ripe to be exploited, and so on.

"Exactly," she said. "I want you to take a look at the code, and see if you can learn it."

So I sat there, greedily drinking it up. I started to understand that I was good at this, and that not everyone could do it. Sometimes I asked her about a word from the list, checking how it sounded, but mostly I absorbed it alone. Years later, I realised she'd given me a glossary of Gerami, a creole from Mura – our nearest neighbours over the Southern Sea and a major trading partner. At the time, all I saw was the magic of language, and the realisation that the concept of bread was no longer just "bread" but had doubled in size to both "bread" and "deenah".

I learned it as best I could, allotting two names to every one of the concepts. Then she quizzed me: *"Three lemons?"* she would say in Gerami, and I, with the parchment in front of me, would have a go at understanding the message, and coming up with a suitable response. I loved it. It was a game, a good one, and my brain started creaking into life after years of fiddling around with numbers and letters.

We did that for a while, gradually getting harder, Myriam taking away the parchment, and giving me more complex constructions to decipher. I found it a challenge, and struggled to remember everything, but she didn't seem to mind.

Then, one afternoon, she took me to the beach, and told me to sit on a boulder. "There's someone who wants to meet you," she said. "He'd like to have a chat with you about what you've learned. Could you do that for me, Razvan?"

I nodded, a wary eye on the man who had emerged from behind the limestone steps that led up to the wharf. He was small, Mecunio, clean-shaven back then, a young man but already wearing the black sash of the city elders. He approached me with a bland smile on his lips, and Myriam turned away, leaving us to go back to her classroom.

"Your teacher's told me all about you, Razvan," he said in a deep, raspy voice that didn't sound right for such a small man. "She says you're a bright boy. That right?"

I didn't know what to say, so stayed silent.

"Show me," he said. "Show me what you can do." Then, in rough Gerami, *"Where do you live?"*

I recognised the words, and pointed towards the slum beyond the wharf. "The Stain," I said.

"Describe it for me. In the words you learned."

"*Small house*," I said in Gerami, "*near... fish shop*."

It was a long way from perfect, but he seemed impressed. We did a few more exercises like that, with him probing to see the extent of my knowledge, trying to trick me with some words that could easily be confused. Then he took out a baat pipe, tapped the stem, and lit it. It was an odd habit for someone his age, but I was to learn he had always been a septuagenarian, trapped in a younger man's body.

"Have you ever thought, Razvan," he said, "that languages don't just have to use sound?"

I didn't answer, so he went on. "What's that smell?" he asked, sniffing.

"The sea."

"The sea. Right. But go a hundred paces to the east, and you'll receive a different message to your nose – the stink of The Stain. The fish market."

"I suppose."

"Same with taste. I could blindfold you, give you a variety of foods, and each one would be sending you a different message. You'd be able to work out what food I was giving you, even though you couldn't see it. And touch is no different. Close your eyes."

I shut them, and he grabbed my hand and shook it twice. "What message is that?"

"What?"

"What am I saying to you with this touch, this movement? Translate it for me, just like you did with the words."

"Pleased to meet you?"

"Good. What about this?" He delivered a stinging slap to the back of my head, and I opened my eyes, and glared at him.

"Ow!"

"Translate." He raised his hand, palm open.

"I'm cross with you?"

"Right. But what if we could make it more complex than that, base the whole language on touch alone…?"

And that was how it began. Mecunio came to my father's stall with me that afternoon, and I sat by the fountain while the two of them had a long conversation in the shade of the tattered awning. At one point, my father turned to look at me, as if seeing me for the first time. Finally, they shook hands and Mecunio walked out of The Stain without another glance at me. When it was time to pack away, the two of us worked side by side, lifting the wicker baskets and putting the leftover stock in crushed ice.

"So," he said, "the man says you're clever. Says you could learn another language."

"The touch language?"

"That's it. Spidertouch, they call it. The one the Crawlers use." Nobody would risk calling the Keda "Crawlers" in public, but the market was nearly deserted, and we knew everyone who was in hearing distance.

We'd never talked about the Keda – I'd never heard of fingerspeak before Mecunio mentioned it – but I was beginning to realise my father knew more than he let on.

"Not sure I like the idea of you mixing with Crawlers," he said. "But it's a way out of your service in the mines. A way out of The Stain. What do you think?"

I had the arrogance of youth, the belief that I was destined for better things. "I like it," I said. "I could do it."

"You're sure you want to do this?"

I nodded. I wish now I could remember his face, but all I can see are his clothes, frayed at the edges and covered in oily streaks.

I didn't see Mecunio again for a few years. But a fingerspeak interpreter came to see me once a week, an old woman with knotted grey hair and a white armband on her right arm, and she began my training. Most families had to pay for private lessons like this, but I later learned that Mecunio had arranged it all – he took an interest in finding new interpreters.

The woman gave me three copper bands and we started by learning the different positions and signals – the taps, the squeezes, the finger trills. She didn't say a lot – she wasn't the mothering type, and we didn't have much else to talk about – but she was a good teacher. We would sit on the rocks, facing each other, holding each other's left arm. She loved the sun, and when we took breaks she would unravel her shawl and munch on dates, while I retreated to the shade. Once I had learned the positions and signals, she began teaching me the touches, and it started to get difficult. When I disappointed her or was too slow, she would show her displeasure with a tsk or a rap with a birch cane that she carried.

When I turned eleven, I left the black sands and The Stain for good. They moved me to a compound in the centre of Val Kedić to become an apprentice in the guild of interpreters. There were nearly thirty of us there, ages ranging from eleven to eighteen, and they expected more than half of us to fail.

On my first day, I realised how massive the city was. I saw Keda strolling up the broad avenues, and the alchemical plumes of silver smoke that hung high in the air. I met Borzu and all the other savvy apprentices, and for the first time I was ashamed of The Stain. I can draw a clear line between my life before that day and my life after.

My father left the city a year later. The Stain never really forgave him, I think, for keeping his son from the mines, for avoiding what they had all endured. The guilt became too much, and they say he sailed across the Southern Sea. I never saw him again.

I walk back from the High Chamber with Ira, along Victory Avenue, lined with palm trees. Until we reach the Bridge of Peace, we are on proper Keda territory – Val Firuz is an island-citadel at the heart of Val Kedić, and the only place in the city where they outnumber us. Some elders and high-ranking citizens are permitted to live here, but I'm not sure why you would want to. Ordinary, blue-robed Keda are all around us, though it's noticeable that they veer away from us as we cross paths, as though a bubble surrounds us.

"They seemed jumpy today," says Ira in a low voice.

"Who?"

"Council, of course. These visitors that are coming. They're nervous."

"How could you tell? Double was just ordering food for a feast. Yours?"

"Same, but xe was quite stressed by it. Got me to repeat back to xer what xe had said. And they were going in and out all morning, all these hurried conversations – Crawlers everywhere."

I glance at her in surprise. Most elders, interpreters and influential citizens don't use that word, not if they want to get ahead. But she's young, no children – she doesn't have the fear yet.

"Well," I say, "if it makes them jumpy, can't be a bad thing."

"Perhaps. It depends. An unhappy Crawler can be a dangerous one."

We pass the statue of Kedira, an enormous stone monstrosity that celebrates the victories of their ancestors. Keda are milling around in groups here, and we walk in silence. Nearby is the alchemical institute, and we both keep our eyes on the silver smoke billowing into the sky. Round the corner, and we come to the Bridge of Peace. A pair of iron gates frame either end of the bridge, with a Justice barring entry. Even if some foolhardy citizens managed to rush the first gates, the second pair would be long closed and bolted by the time they had crossed the bridge. Underneath, you can see the Little Firu, a horseshoe-shaped moat that winds its way around the island of Val Firuz, until either end meets the Firu River. This bisects the city in the east and rushes down to the Southern Sea. Between them, they lock the Keda in. Or us, out.

We approach the gates and come to a halt in front of the green-robed Keda. If the councillors are the Keda's brains, the Justices are the fists. Their job is to enforce discipline, exact punishments, and generally inspire fear in the populace. Like the councillors, I can't distinguish many Justices by sight – they all look the same to me. I know Scorpion, of course. Xe is one of the Justices who manage my quarter. Supposedly, xer name comes from how xe administers punishment – whipping with a studded belt, leaving the victim covered in xer "stings". But honestly, I wonder if they come up with these names themselves, and make sure they spread to build up their reputation. Any of the Keda who are particularly brutish or sadistic get put in line to be a Justice, that's for sure. The exemplar of this is Beast, a legendary Justice, known throughout Val Kedić for xer viciousness and rhino-like build.

The one here, however, looks like a run-of-the-mill Justice – xe takes xer time, checking our pass, despite the fact xe must remember us from earlier in the day when we entered Val Firuz. Eventually, xe lowers xer poleaxe, and allows us to pass through to the bridge.

The Little Firu is twenty paces wide here. We stop and watch the surface of the water, looking for the eels that swim there. I exhale noisily, and Ira smiles.

"How long you been doing this?" she says.

"Twenty-two years now."

"It get any easier?"

"Nope," I reply. A pause. I look at her curiously. "They say you quit, after you finished your apprenticeship. And travelled, before you came back here."

"They're right. I thought there had to be a better world than this out there. I went out to find it."

"And?"

"Turned out I was wrong."

I snort. "Didn't have you down as a cynic."

"Ah, I'm no cynic. Just a good old-fashioned disillusioned optimist."

"Right. What's the difference?"

"Don't know. Put it into fingerspeak, that'll get rid of the nuance for you."

"Was that a… *joke* about fingerspeak?"

"Don't sound so disgusted." She smiles. "I remember you, you know. When I was fifteen, you gave us classes for a year. We had you every few days."

"Really? I haven't had to teach for a while now. How was I? Was I terrible?"

"Not bad. Better than some, who were deathly boring. Mind you, you never looked like you enjoyed it much."

"No, I don't think I did. Imagine what it's like telling a group of hormonal teenagers how to touch and squeeze each other in the right way, *and* keep them all focussed."

She laughs, and we fall silent for a moment. I feel a wave of relief that working with Ira is going to be all right. She may play it prim and proper with the Council, but outside, she's a real human being.

I could stand here watching the Little Firu until dusk – the thought of having to see the elders bores me beyond words. But Ira jabs me in the ribs, nods at the Justice on the other gate, who is glaring at us for daring to dilly-dally on xer bridge.

"Come on," Ira says. "We'd better go before xe comes over for a frank exchange of views. Even your fingerspeaking skills won't get us out of that one."